KISMET

KISMET

WATTS MARTIN

Argyll Productions
Dallas, Texas

Published by Argyll Productions
Dallas, Texas
http://argyllproductions.com/

First Printing, January 2017

ISBN: 978-1-61450-586-0

Typeset in Arno Pro and Myriad Pro

To mom

Chapter 1

THE CALL THAT SHATTERS GAIL'S LIFE comes disguised as a gift from her past. It starts the way all of them have for the last fourteen years: a *beedle boop* and her ship's voice, a pleasant female contralto, sounding directly in her left ear. "You have an incoming call."

She's walking outside, or at least what she thinks of as "outside" here, heading for inside. Kingston's temperature stays at thirty-one degrees during its day cycle to make it more like its equatorial Earth namesake, but couldn't they have improved on the climate instead of slavishly emulating it? If she were cisform it might be tolerable, but as a totemic, it's crazy-making hot.

Kis should have said who it was, but it's got to be Dan again, with something else she can do while she's still on Kingston. *Hey, it'll be quick and you'll only need to buy a couple parts and you know I'll pay you back as soon as I get back on my feet.*

Right. Dan owes her twenty-four thousand three hundred and counting, and she doesn't have to pull that number up on her HUD to verify it. It's burned into her memory right now. So's another number: the payment she got just this morning from Smith and Sons Salvage, undervaluing her last haul by ninety percent. They'll drag her appeal out for months, and her budget is already on fumes.

She sighs. "Kis, tell Dan I can't—no. Tell him he can go fuck himself with—"

"The call is over an encrypted line, locked against recording, and there is no identification data."

Okay. Not Dan. She could ask Kis to try and override the lock, but they'd disconnect if they noticed. And hell, at this point she doesn't have much to lose by being a trusting idiot. "Connect it."

Another beep sounds, and a hesitant male voice speaks a second later. "Gail Simmons?"

"Yeah. Who's this?"

"My name's Randall Corbett. You probably don't remember me, but we grew up together in New Coyoacán."

Her ears lift. "No, yeah, I remember you." She does, a skinny cisform kid she'd been in first stage school with, who lived a few blocks away. They weren't great friends but they got along; his mother volunteered with hers at the River Totemic Equality Association's office. That's not why she remembers him, though. She remembers him because they'd both lost their mothers on the same day.

"Great. Uh. I know we haven't spoken in … it must be two decades. But I found your name when I was looking for a salvage operator. I pilot a yacht charter, see, and I think we might have found a wreck this morning."

"You think?" She cuts across the central greenway between the canal and the business district, dodging an errant fertilizer drone. On some visits, Gail stops to appreciate the steeply slanting roofs painted in searingly bright colors, the way the curve of the station's floor tilts them into a pointillist mosaic. This is not one of those visits. Her destination lies dead ahead: the third-best bar on all of the River. "You didn't stop?"

"I couldn't." He sounds regretful. "The client wouldn't give us permission."

If he's based on Panorica or one of the half-dozen platforms that have a compact with them, he could lose his license for that. Or worse. But a lot of the private yachts berth at places where space law is more space suggestion. "Who else have you called?"

"Just you. I'm pretty sure the ship's completely dead. The crew either got out already or didn't make it."

"Jesus, Randall." She runs a hand through her hair, stopping outside the bar. Could *she* lose her license for following up on this? "If it's dead, how'd you find it?"

"I picked up an emergency beacon. It stopped before we made visual contact."

"What kind of ship is it?"

"The beacon data was for a Horizon class freighter."

"A Horizon went missing and nobody noticed? When was this?"

"Yesterday. Maybe fifteen hours ago. I'll send you the telemetry data?"

This is insane. But if the ship exists, and she gets there first, and she can find the owners, and it doesn't get tied up by fighting judiciaries, it wouldn't just cover her lost payment. It'd cover it six or seven times over. It'd turn her worst month in two years into her best month in a decade. If if if if. "Go ahead."

"Okay." There's a brief pause; Kis chimes a couple times in acknowledgement of a secondary data stream. "So you're still involved with what your mother was doing, aren't you? You and Sky."

"Huh? No. Sky's with the Ring Judicial Cooperative, not out leading protests. And I've been a salvor for over a decade. How about you?"

"No." His response is comet quick and unexpectedly sharp. "Uh. Sorry. Kind of a touchy subject."

Maybe you shouldn't have brought it up. "I get it."

"I'd chat more, but I'm still on assignment. We have to be ready to ship out in a half-hour."

"Understood. I'll let you go. Maybe we can catch up sometime."

"Maybe. Good luck." Another *beedle boop* signals the disconnect.

She lets out a long breath and steps inside. This is the first time she's walked into the dim light of Ice & Spirit with outside still set at at full daylight; even her eyes need a second to adjust.

Robaire's poured a glass of something for her before she drops onto a bar stool. "What, am I enough of a regular for you to know what I like?"

"You're in here often enough." Rob's about forty, completely bald, completely cisform. His grin shows very white teeth against very dark skin. "And you look like you could use something strong. Isadore rum, twelve years."

"I could." She takes a small sip. A burn, but not much. Sweet, then a little spicy, then a little leathery. "That's pretty good."

"I know." He grins again.

She snorts. "How's Emma doing?"

"Emma left." He taps on a few panels behind the bar. "She wanted more stable hours now that she's a mother, and she said she wanted her son to grow up with other totemics. So she's moved to the Ring to manage a restaurant."

"Wow." Emma's a vixen, full transform like Gail. "So she decided to do a post-birth transform instead of waiting?"

He nods, keeping his expression neutral. That's what she is; she grew up as a totemic, rather than making a choice when she got older. She doesn't

3

think of it as too radical, but a lot of other people—both transform and cisform—do. She gets the feeling Rob doesn't approve.

"The Ring's your home port, isn't it?" He waves a hand at her. "Even if you dress like a Kingston native."

Her shirt's colorful, pink and blue patterns dyed on the inside, but compared to Rob's riotous rainbow-blotch pullover it might as well be as monochrome as her fur. "Just a birthplace. I don't have a home port."

"Everyone has a home port." Two other early drinkers ease in, both cisform, taking seats at the other end of the bar. Rob leaves Gail alone with her rum.

She shakes her head, then takes another sip. "Kis, how long will it take to get to the wreck Randall found?" The woman at the end of the bar gives her sidelong glances. What, she's never seen someone with cochlea and larynx implants?

"It will take eight hours and twenty minutes to get to the search area and six to twelve hours to search probable drift paths based on the data."

Gail groans. Well, dammit, she's going to enjoy her drink. She forces herself to sip slowly, watching a news scroll on a display behind the bar and listening to jazzy music playing on the bar's sound system.

When she finishes, Rob's still busy with the other customers. She throws him a wave. The cisform couple turns when he waves back, and the guy says, "Rats aren't a health problem in here, are they?"

Gail tenses, but she can tell from his expression he's trying to be funny. You're a rat, get it? Never mind that her body shape is still just as human as his, that she's one-point-six meters tall and dresses way better than he does. Never mind that that joke had to be tired in her grandmother's time. Not that anyone in her blood family other than her and her mother had ever been transform. "I'm pretty clean, I promise." That gets a laugh. She smiles stiffly and heads out.

Just like on her way to the bar, most of the people she passes on the greenway are cisform. She sees one totemic couple, wolf and fox, both in matching green polytees; when she waves, the fox waves back. The wolf smiles and tightens his arm around his husband's waist, and then gives her a double take, like he's wondering if he should recognize her. She picks up her pace before he asks.

It's another minute to the docking area, and less than a minute to get through the exit gates. As she approaches, the gangway doors slide open.

Kismet's inner and outer doors do the same, each sealing before the next unlocks.

The entranceway's at the front of the cabin, right behind the cockpit, only a few steps to swing herself into her seat and strap up the harness. An array of displays fades in across the nearly blank wall she's facing, followed by a forward view of space—and space station—outside. "Okay, Kis, let's see if this wreck even exists." The engines kick into life with a deep bass whine.

"Casting off," *Kismet* announces. As they fall away from the station, gravity falls away, too. After all these years the sensation still makes her stomach flutter.

She calls up the planned course as an overlay in front of her, but lets the ship fly herself. Half the control panels around her fade, and *Kismet* expands the display projection. The walls disappear around Gail's seat, as if she's floating in space. She turns to watch the station recede, until it catches the reflection of the distant sun just so, blinding her momentarily with a flash of perfect brilliant light.

"What's a seven-letter word for 'remove impurities?'"

The ship startles Gail by responding. "Are you thinking out loud or would you like a list of possible matches?"

"You know I'm usually just thinking out loud when I say things like that."

"Your voice was four decibels louder than your average volume when you are talking to yourself."

As co-pilot and research assistant *Kismet* does better than a human, but sometimes she's an awkward best friend. Gail sighs, letting go of the crossword and studying the last leg of the search course, sipping her coffee. It takes them close—under a megameter—to Alexandria's last reported coordinates. For as long as she's been a pilot she's heard rumors about that long-abandoned platform. Taken over by pirates. Or militant inner system unification nuts. Radical totemics. Radical purists. Just the ghosts of its many dead. Without anything running the attitude jets, though, nobody's clear on exactly where the arcology's remains might be now.

Wait. Clear. She grabs the smartpaper before it drifts out of reach and fills in the answer: *clarify.*

She's gotten through another five words when the ship speaks again, starting to decelerate. "A possible target has been acquired."

"What? Where?" Gail looks around the star field; *Kismet* flashes the red circle she's added to the view.

She pushes her coffee into a locking drink holder, raises a hand and motions toward her, zooming the display in far enough to lose a little optical resolution. It's clearly a ship, bigger than her tug-slash-houseboat. A lot bigger. In a relative sense, it's adrift, like the comets and asteroids sharing space with the River.

The red circle should be labeled with the other craft's name and registry. Gail should be able to call up records on its ownership, history, crew. It should be damned near impossible for an accident to disable a ship's ID beacon, to stop it from broadcasting a sliver of standard data all the governments across the solar system had agreed on—even the ones that didn't agree to call themselves governments.

But it isn't labeled. It's just a big blank circle.

"No transmission from the emergency beacon, either? When's the last transmission of anything from it on record?"

"No records of transmissions can be connected to the target."

Gail frowns. "Get closer." She leans forward as her spaceship glides ahead at a careful pace.

Parts of the holographic star field fade back into instrumentation panels, and information displays start popping up around the unknown ship. Holy hell, it *is* Horizon class. But not the cargo variant. It's an SC71, a passenger ship. What? How? If a liner didn't make port, the news would be everywhere. She'd have been beaten here by rescue ships.

They get close enough for her to do a visual ID, but there's no registration marks. Someone's gone to a lot of trouble to make this ship hard to identify. The fur on the back of Gail's neck prickles. "Any energy signatures you can pick up?"

"No. The target's temperature matches ambient space. The hull has been breached."

As *Kismet* glides slowly along one side of the Horizon, the bow of the ship comes into view. There's a hole, over a meter across, punched into the hull.

"Any other ships out here right now?"

"Two, both on standard courses. Unless they deviate they will not come closer to this point than one thousand three hundred fifty-eight kilometers."

She unstraps and pushes herself out of the cockpit, then pulls herself down—relatively speaking—to the airlock. "Synchronize velocity with our ghost ship here and I'll go check it out. Let me know if either of those ships change trajectories. This whole thing is weirdly... weird."

"Yes, Gail."

Pressure suits tailored to totemics cost more, but she's always been able to fit in cisform suits—her muzzle is short and her tail's thin enough to just slide down along one leg, and keeping her ears flat for short periods doesn't hurt too much.

There's an asteroid fragment a few kilometers away. That's unusually close, but it can't have been a collision; smacking into it at cruising speed would have left a debris cloud, not a hull with a hole in it. A miraculously light glancing blow? No, that would be a rip or a gash. Besides, navigating out here is a long-solved problem, and space rocks aren't known for making sudden unexpected moves.

She attaches her cable line to the hook outside *Kismet*'s airlock and ratchets up her visual sensitivity before she kicks off, unspooling the tether behind her. The hole in the bow is big enough to go through, but it'd risk cutting her tether, or worse, her suit, so she aims for the entrance hatch.

When a ship's stranded without power there has to be a manual way for a rescue team to get in. On this class of ship it's meant to be a two-person job; fortunately, she can fake that in brief bursts. The closed environment of the suit echoes the faint whine of her biomods engaging as she pulls down on the lever and back on the huge oval hatch. Latching her tether to a hook by the airlock, she floats in, switching on her headlamp before pulling the outer door shut and releasing the inner one.

Rapid decompression means—among other things—that everything inside the ship that could fit through the hole and wasn't otherwise restrained blew out at close to sonic speed. For a few meters past the breach the cabin looks like the site of a bomb blast: mangled brackets on walls, shreds of carpet, exposed conduit. Mara's Blood, maybe it *was* a bomb blast.

The rest of the cabin remains eerily intact. The seat arrangement— center aisle, two seats to either side, rows alternating facing, sixty-four seats total—cinches the sc71 identification she made. But there aren't any bodies buckled into seats; this definitely wasn't a passenger run.

Moving to the cabin's center, she gives the whole scene a once-over to record the images, then kicks off toward the ship's fore. The cockpit door's unlocked, but jammed shut. It takes her a good ten seconds to gingerly work it open, pull herself in, and smack right into one of the two floating bodies.

She jerks back, breath catching. Neither wears an identifying uniform. Of course. Both cisform. They look incongruously serene, in the way victims of slow oxygen starvation often do. The inner hatch had held, but sc71s only have one air circulation system. Once the cabin pressure had been lost, the vents in here sucked the air out.

She focuses on the faces of the two corpses and triggers a scan. After a couple seconds ID panels come up in her eye display. Finally, something—pilot licenses on file with multiple ports. But neither panel shows current employment, and no record trail runs between the two and a ship like this.

Her groan echoes in the suit helmet. Who do you take a salvage claim on a dark courier to? "It's probably too late to just leave this ship and pretend I was never here," she mutters aloud.

"We are not on a schedule, Gail."

She laughs. "Just wishful thinking, Kis. Somebody needs to get these bodies home, and I guess it's gonna be me. Sometimes it's a choice between the easy thing and the right thing, you know?"

"I will remember that."

Okay. Either she's the first on the scene and the cabin didn't have much in it to start with, or the wreck was cleaned out silently before she got here. Only one last place to look. Backing down into the cabin, she swings back to the airlock and performs the exit dance. Reconnecting her tether, she pulls herself via handhold along the hull toward the cargo hold.

Predictably, it's empty. It's the hole next to it she hadn't expected. The escape pod's gone.

She looks back toward the ship's bow, toward the hole, and tries to piece the story together in her head. An unregistered ship with an unknown—but very low—number of passengers suffered an explosion, more than likely sabotage. At least one passenger survived decompression and vacuum exposure and got to the escape pod, which strongly suggests they were prepared for it.

"Kis, we're closer to Molinar than Kingston now, right?"

"Yes."

"Let them know we're coming in with this damn thing, and fire the tow clamps off to me."

The clamps are big metal blocks, each one nearly Gail's size, lined with magnets on one side and attitude thrusters on the other. She consults the ship's specs as she places them: they have to be on the strongest parts of the Horizon's structure, where pulling on the cables not only moves the ship in the right direction but won't let it twist around farther than the jets can compensate for. Then she has to clamp the deceleration engine on the ship's stern. All told, it's nearly two hours of work before everything's set and *Kismet* can reel her in.

The work's not quite finished when the ship sounds a soft alert chime over the suit radio and speaks again. "The port operator at Molinar indicates a representative of Keces Industries wishes to meet with you about the wreck when it is towed back."

"Why?"

"The cooperation request does not list a specific reason."

Mara's Wounds. A cooperation request has no legal binding—no judiciary would back an attempt to enforce it, so she could just tell them to go blow themselves. But no judiciary would compel a company to do business with someone they find "uncooperative," either, and Keces is one of those old corporate beasts with their tentacles everywhere. They run the port on Molinar and a half-dozen other platforms. They own shops and repair facilities and for all she knows the Magnolia Café chain. Also, they're heavily involved with transforms. Every totemic knows their name, and probably two-thirds owe Keces in part or whole for the biotech that makes them what they are.

Back at the bar she caught something about Keces on the news. Shit. What was it? A series of explosions at some of their labs? This ship couldn't be connected, could it? That's a hell of a leap, but she's been a salvor for well over a decade and never had a request like this. "Fine. Accept."

Once she gets back inside *Kismet* she peels off the suit, pushing herself back into the sofa and breathing deeply, taking in the scents of the air circulation's cleaner—something only a totemic with a sensitive nose would pick up—and of coffee, a faint odor that's become part of the ship after all this time. "Lock in the tow cables."

"Locked."

"Okay." Her acceleration rate is reduced by two-thirds when towing and deceleration is even worse; the anemic little engine clamped onto the wreck is all that keeps it from merrily smashing into *Kismet* if the tug's speed is even a fraction slower. So she's not going to get in until mid-morning. She rubs her face, then snags the crossword from where it's floating. "Onward."

Chapter 2

BEEDLE BOOP

"Ms. Simmons?"

Gail's ear twitches at the voice on the radio. She's prying a beer out of a rack in the cabin's compact refrigerator. The beverage station does coffee well enough, but its "porter" tastes like cold strained oatmeal.

"Yeah."

"This is Phil with Molinar Port Operations. Keces Industries requests you let us redirect the ship you're towing to bay fifteen."

"Aren't *you* Keces Industries?"

"We're an independent subsidiary. Do we have your consent for the redirect?"

She twists the cap off the bottle and snaps on a zero-g lid to keep the beer from merrily floating out. *Consent* is a Secret Code Word from the same family as *cooperate*. Docking creates an implicit contract, but anything nonstandard requires explicit permission so nobody can come back later and claim to have been coerced. "Is this kinda unusual, Phil?"

"What?"

"Your parent company making you less independent."

The voice hesitates. "Someone towing in a wreck is unusual. They'll have inspectors in bay fifteen."

"So it's Keces' ship?" Gail climbs into the pilot's seat with her beer, strapping in.

Phil hesitates again. "I'm just the dispatcher, Ms. Simmons. I don't have that information."

"Right. Okay, do it."

"Acknowledged. Stand by."

Kismet disengages the tow cables and banks slightly to the right. Gail pivots the holo display around to see a school of guppies—tiny unmanned drones, little more than low-power engines coated in silicone—bumping up against the wreck and guiding it away. The wreck, and her still-attached deceleration engine.

"I'm gonna want that engine back, you know." Phil doesn't answer. Another ship—manned, not a drone—paces her now; it's painted in blue, with Keces Industries' interlocking triangle logo in white on its aft nacelles. A security escort. Lovely.

Molinar uses a stick-and-wheel construction style: a cylinder at the center remains stationary, docks running along it in both directions, and the wheel spins to hit point-nine G at the rim. She doesn't like to tie up at facilities like this longer than she has to; if she's going to be docked, she'd rather be at a place whose design extends the courtesy of gravity to *Kismet*, too.

Most of the view of space projected around her shifts to video feeds from her docking hatch and new instrumentation readouts. She gives them the once-over, then clears *Kismet* to perform the hatch coupling and to power down the propulsion systems.

She's switched shirts—this vivid green floral print shirt makes yesterday's look subdued. Combined with her favorite faux-denim plasticel shorts, it won't look like she's taking this meeting seriously at all. Perfect. She slips her furred feet into sandals and floats out.

Two cisform men in brown business suits wait in the access tube. They're big, burly, and armed. Their names don't come up on her HUD, and when she does a deeper scan, one shows the signatures of a set of biomods she's dubbed the cop package. These guys may be from Keces, but they're not corporate execs. The other one's giving her a weird look, like he's never seen a totemic before. Maybe just never a rat totemic. Foxes and cats are cute. Wolves are intimidating. Rats get weird looks.

As the hatch slides shut behind her, the first guy says, "Permission to come aboard," making it less question than statement despite the bad attempt at a smile.

What the hell? "Sorry, not open to the public."

"Excuse me?"

"Permission refused. And you're excused."

"Fine." His tone says it isn't fine at all. "Let's go meet Mr. Nakimura."

Gail flashes her best big-toothed rodent smile. "Yeah, we wouldn't want to delay the conversation he's requesting with me, right?"

They scowl in unison, and the second guy motions her forward.

The tube opens onto an industrial space entirely shaded in gray, with status displays for a handful of scheduled flights and for the rail car lines that run between the docking arms and the rim. Still no gravity, so travelers stick close to the handrails and well-marked floatways. Or bounce around bumping into things. The only splashes of color are the rail cars themselves, painted in primary colors, and a smattering of badly animated "Welcome to Molinar" banners. They might as well have subtitles reading *but not really.*

As they approach the rail car loading point, Unsmiling Security Guy One holds up a hand. "Wait here." The cars have a standard design— rounded boxes suspended between two rails, seats mounted on the sides. They slow down here, but never come to a stop. A car trundles past, then another.

Guy Two, the one with the cop package, points at a red car seventh in line from the one that just passed. Guy One nods. Gail stifles a sigh.

When the car gets there they pull themselves in. Someone else is already inside, as she expected—another cisform. Black business jacket, pale blue shirt, a bolo tie with the Keces logo on the clasp. He's of Asian descent, only a nose taller than she is.

There are six seats in the tram, three on each side. Gail leaps to take a seat next to Nakimura rather than one of the ones facing him, just beating Guy One to it. Both Unsmiling Guys smile even less as she straps in.

"Ms. Simmons," he says. "I'm Jason Nakimura with Keces. Tell me about the ship you've towed in."

Her HUD confirms he matches a Jason Nakimura with Keces, a VP of Special Projects. So he's important, and has an ominously nebulous title. "It's a Horizon SC71. No flight plans on file, completely unflagged, running dark. There's a big hole in the bow and pretty much nothing inside."

"An accident?"

"Doesn't look like it."

His face tightens for a second, but he doesn't react otherwise. "How did you come across it?"

A two-tone chime sounds and the car's doors slide shut as it picks up speed. "A yacht pilot on a run between here and Kingston tipped me off. Said he'd picked up signs of what might be a wreck."

"He didn't stop and go help?" Guy Two looks suspicious.

"He said the ship didn't have any signs of life, and people who charter yachts get pretty paranoid. Even the communication with me was encrypted."

Nakimura makes a thoughtful noise. "Do you know why he shared this tip with you?"

"There's only a dozen salvors operating around the River, and I guess I'm pretty well known." Not for being a salvor, but either Keces knows that already or they don't need to. They sure don't need to know the pilot was someone she knows. Knew. Sort of.

The Unsmiling Guys give one another a skeptical glance. Nakimura's tone remains mild, though. "I see. Would you share your telemetry data?"

"Sure." She reaches into her vest pocket; immediately Guy One drops his hand to his sidearm. Idiot. She holds a level stare, slowly pulling out a smartpad and pen. Formal contracts have a ritual that involves the physical, even when only the resulting data gets tracked. She scribbles a command on the paper to have *Kismet* prepare and transmit a report on the wreck. A signature line appears; she hands it and the pen to Nakimura.

He makes a quick slash of a signature across the pad, rips off the top sheet, and hands the pad and pen back to Gail. After a quick glance at the copy the notepad has kept, she tucks it and the pen away. At the same time he pulls a small notebook out of his jacket, opening its fancy cover—likely real leather—and presses the receipt into it, holding it for a moment until it seals.

A second chime signals the rail car is turning down a spoke, rotating so they'll be facing the right way as *down* starts to have meaning. Nakimura folds the cover back and studies the display on the other side, frowning, then speaks again. "You went aboard."

"Of course." Her right ear twitches in irritation. "The ship was basically empty. It didn't look to me like it even had more than one or two passengers."

"Assuming you were recording, I'd like a copy of all the video from entry to exit."

She clears her throat. "So I take it this mystery ship belongs to Keces."

"I can't discuss details about our interest."

Gravity's about as strong as it's going to get; they must be near the disembarking zone. "Jason, job zero for me is establishing vessel ownership. If I can't do that, I make a claim for pure salvage, and since we're talking about a mostly intact SC71 the finder fee alone is going to be pretty high.

If you want to discuss your 'interest,' you're going to have to be a little less coy."

The car's downward motion becomes down and forward, then just forward. The door opens with another chime and they get out.

"Understood." He leads Gail and his entourage across a short polished concrete floor to the exit doors, and they head outside to the station proper. The Unsmiling Duo stay a little closer to her than she's comfortable with.

Some arcology platforms go wild with greenery, like the Ceres Ring. Some go for a quirky theme, like Kingston. Molinar, though, chose to instantiate the platonic ideal of bland. Other than the eternal upward arc of the half-kilometer wide landscape, there's not a single curve anywhere. A vehicle corridor runs straight down the center; they've exited onto a pedestrian bridge over that avenue. Other bridges cross over at regular intervals. It's so free of style it feels malicious. Yes, it used to be a company platform, a mining venture that fizzled before she was born like most of them had by then. But they could do *something*. Paint the roof blue. Make a few buildings fake brick. Put up a single sad lonely plastic tree.

Nakimura gestures ahead to a point on the left half of the bisected station. "The office is a three-minute walk."

Gail nods.

"I have a simple proposal, then. If the appraisal team looking at the ship now reports back satisfactorily, you transfer the salvage claim to Keces. Finding the owners becomes our responsibility, not yours."

"Do you have a number in mind?"

"Three percent of the ship's current fair market value."

She runs a hand through her chopped blond hair. Given its current condition, fair market value is going to be maybe half of what it'd be worth used, which would be about two-thirds list. Making his offer roughly one percent of list. Making it roughly twice as much money as she's earned in her entire life.

Nakimura lifts a brow at her hesitation, the most emotion he's shown so far. "Is that acceptable?"

"I think it's workable," she says, tone studiously neutral. Way too workable. She's waiting for the hammer drop.

Some of the buildings they walk past have wooden trim, at least, but they're all metal, all anodized. The temperature of the diffuse light from the ceiling a hundred meters above has started to lower in a simulated sunset. Unlike the system on Kingston, Molinar's color temp never drops below 1900°K; "nighttime" here is a dim orange.

The building they're heading to stands out only by being larger—three stories—and having more wooden trim. Inside the lobby, there's another cisform waiting. Dirty blond hair, stubbly shave, ill-fitting tan overcoat. His blue tie, complete with little gold lantern tie tack, completes the fashion crime. If the Unsmiling Duo radiate security thugs, the new guy radiates Suspicious Detective. Christ, for a company with a major business line in transformations, you'd think they'd employ a few totemics.

Nakimura addresses him without bothering to make introductions. "Have you gotten the report yet?"

"Yeah." He glances at Gail, lip curling. "It's not there."

Nakimura frowns deeply.

"What's not there?"

"Let's have a talk, Ms. Simmons." He motions at a door just off the lobby. Suspicious Detective opens it, and they all file in.

It's an office, but looks like one nobody's ever worked in. Big desk, big chair behind it, a few chairs in front of it, nothing else. Grey walls, grey ceiling, even grey floor. Not carpeted, polished concrete.

Gail starts sending the feed from her right eye sensors back to *Kismet*. No telling what's about to happen, but from the turn things just took she's pretty sure she wants it all on record.

Nakimura sits down behind the desk and points at a seat in front of it. When she sits down the Unsmiling Duo take up standing positions behind her and to either side. "I'd like you to go over what happened again." As he speaks he pulls out his notebook, reading the screen as if he's going to be checking her answers.

"I got a tip, I followed it to the wreck, I towed it back."

Suspicious Detective crosses his arms. "A ship with no ID, no beacons, and not on a normal course. That's a hell of a good tip."

"Yeah, it was. They happen." Her tail flicks reflexively, sending a jolt of pain up her spine. These chairs aren't meant for totemics. Maybe they did that on purpose.

Detective snorts. "From what I was just told it looks less like a wreck than a bomb."

"I told you I didn't think it was an accident."

Nakimura sighs. "The ship was empty, Ms. Simmons."

She grits her teeth. "Remember the part about the big hole? It made stuff *inside* become stuff *outside*. If whatever you're looking for wasn't taken before I got there, it's probably floating in space."

"Taken before you got there?" Nakimura tilts his head.

"Your crew noticed the missing escape pod, right? It looks to me like a passenger on the ship either set off the bomb or knew it was coming."

"And it looks to *me* like you're part of their cover story. You knew right where to find the ship, you know just what to tell us." Suspicious Detective leans forward. "And you know a lot about bombs, rat, don't you?"

She flinches back, ears going flat.

"Come on, we know your history. Brought up as a totemic supremacist as a kid, decided to be a con artist instead. Maybe you're finally getting around to taking up where Mom left off, huh?"

"That's an offensively bullshit way to describe my mother, and what the hell does this have to do with her?"

"You tell me."

Don't yell. Deep breath. "Look, I've told you exactly what happened. Do you seriously think I went out there running dark, stole something, and blew the escape pod all without leaving any trace, then came back here to tow the ship in? I'd have just left the damn ship there!"

"Criminals are stupid."

"Clearly some investigators aren't brain trusts, either."

He curls his lip, raising a fist.

"Do it and I *will* hit you back."

Nakimura looks up at the ceiling as if praying for patience. At length he stares across the desk toward her. "Your story is plausible, Ms. Simmons, but finding you, specifically, involved after multiple attacks and major property crimes committed against Keces, all around this particular project…"

"Mara's Wounds, I don't even know what the hell this 'project' is!" She wants to throw her hands in the air and just walk out, or to leap up and pound the desk, maybe just pace. She gets as far as starting to stand. The Unsmiling Duo shove her back in the chair and keep their hands on her shoulders. "Hey." She can hear the nerves jangling in her voice.

Nakimura leans back. "You have no history of involvement with your mother's politics, her 'Totemic Equality Association,' as an adult. But you have no history of involvement with…" He shrugs fractionally. "With anything."

"I don't like entanglements." She squirms; they press down harder on her shoulders. "Come on. Do I have the 'history' of someone who'd arrange to wreck a ship and kill people just to steal something off it? Look. Maybe I can help you find whatever's gone missing."

Suspicious Detective snorts. "You seriously think you're going to scam a job out of this?"

She gives him a glare, then looks back to Nakimura. "You hired this ship to transport something, and you didn't want any records." She closes her eyes, concentrating. The puzzle's sliding together. "Until you took possession of the wreck, it couldn't be connected to you at all, and since you own the port operations here that'll be easy to make look normal." Her eyes open. "Now, though, somebody's stolen whatever was on that ship, and you don't want to let this crime get to a judicial market. So you're going to need someone who's good at finding things and keeping it all quiet."

"It's pretty easy to find something if you've taken it, and he's already got someone who's good at finding things. Me." Suspicious Detective jabs a thumb at himself.

Nakimura's voice shows edges of exasperation. "This is ludicrous, Ms. Simmons. Just return the databox."

"What's a databox?"

The detective leans down, his eyes as cold as New Coyoacán's sky. "Tell us where it is."

"I don't know what the hell—"

He straightens up and slams his fist into Gail's stomach.

She's still in the chair, still held by the other two, so she can't even double over. Her vision goes black for a moment as she gasps, unable to draw in enough air.

"Where's the databox?"

She can't get enough breath to speak. He raises his fist and she puts up her hands, hoping he'll wait. She could power up her biomods, but Guy Two might pick it up if she does. Fortunately, he waits.

She wipes spittle off her muzzle. Okay, if this is how she has to play it, she'll play. "Three things. Please."

Nakimura motions with a hand in a *go on* gesture.

"Okay." She takes another ragged breath, steadying herself. "One. I'm betting these three are unofficial contractors, too, just like that ship, right? Mister Detective here apparently missed the part about me being able to record anything I see. I've been doing that since before I followed you in here." She subvocalizes Kis's name so she takes the next sentence as a command. "Let me share a few seconds of video with you featuring you sitting there watching your thugs beat me up."

Nakimura looks at his notepad display, frowning, then pales visibly.

"We can either leave this between me and you, or make it between me, you and my judiciary. Do we understand each other?"

He nods stiffly.

"Good." Since she stopped paying their retainer she doesn't have a judiciary, but Keces might not know that. She moves to stand up; this time the Unsmiling Guys let her. "Two, biomods are a big thing to miss. So think long and hard about what that says about the guys you've hired. I don't think they're as good as I am, and I can work with people who are better than me."

The detective tightens his fists. "I told you we ran into security walls searching her background."

"The fact remains that your work has put us in an unexpectedly precarious position, Mr. Nelson." He nods to Gail. "And three?"

"I told this guy if he hits me I'd hit him back." She engages her biomods and slugs Suspicious Detective's jaw hard enough to spin him to the side, knocking him right into Guy Two.

Guy One's going for his gun, but she's darting behind Guy Two fast enough to be a blur, knowing he'll engage his own biomechanics when he recovers. So she doesn't give him the chance, grabbing his arm and twisting it behind him. "Power down or I'll break it." The detective slides to the floor, blood leaking out of his mouth. She probably fractured his jaw, but he's lucky she pulled the punch.

"Let go, bitch!"

"Power down." She glances at Guy One. "And put that gun away now." Guy One swallows audibly, and does as ordered.

Suspicious Detective—Nelson, evidently—touches his jaw, wincing, and shoots her another glare. "Animal senses don't make you better enough than us prims? You gotta add biomods, too?"

"I don't use the 'p' word."

"Enough." Nakimura rubs his face with both hands. "You've made your point, Ms. Simmons. Let him go."

"When I do, you and I talk alone for a bit."

Guy Two protests. "We can't protect you if—"

Gail twists his arm again and he yelps.

"You're not protecting me now," Nakimura says.

She waits until she senses him disengaging his biomods, then lets go. He storms out of the room. Guy One helps Suspicious Detective on out.

After Gail closes the door, Nakimura says, "Turn off your recording."

"No." She powers down her biomods, though, before they start to hurt. "What do I do to clear this up and go on my way?"

He drums his fingers on the desk. "You are, at this point, not just a person of interest in the theft, but the only person of interest. Why didn't you let my men onto your ship when you docked?"

"Because it's my home and you didn't have any business asking."

"Will you let us on board now?"

"Will that prove I don't have this..."

"Databox."

"This databox, or will you just think I've hidden it really well?"

He purses his lips, turning away and falling silent. When he speaks again, he's still looking at the wall. "The only way to 'clear this up,' Ms. Simmons, is to return our property. If you do that, I won't ask further questions about its provenance. If our analysts determine the data has not been compromised, we'll honor our previously proposed payment agreement for the wreck."

Her ears raise. He's going to go for it, isn't he? "Deal."

"Finish signing over your salvage claim to Keces. The contract will explicitly stipulate that any property belonging to Keces must be returned within seventy-two hours of the transfer. If you have taken the databox, consider this a grace period to return it. Otherwise consider that your deadline for playing finder."

What? Seventy-two...? "Look, I can't promise—"

"If the databox is not returned, your fee will be forfeit, and you will be reported to our judiciary as *socius indignus* and be sued for damages."

Her eyes widen. If the judiciary accepts the designation of Gail as an "untrustworthy partner," then all of their other clients might stop doing business with her. As a major company, Keces would use a major judiciary. That would mean she'd almost certainly lose the lawsuit. And lose about half the places she does business with now.

And, more than likely, lose *Kismet*.

"That won't hold up." Her voice shakes.

"Given that any counter-argument will be backed up by evidence that only you can provide and no one else can authenticate, I have confidence it will."

"I can't do this in three days!"

"If you or an associate of yours is the thief, you can do it in far less. If you are not, three days may frankly be too generous." He sets his notebook on the table in front of her, a signature line ready for her, and holds out the pen.

"You'd better at least tell me what this thing is."

"The keys to heaven and hell."

She stares at him blankly.

"Sharing details would put both of us at even greater risk. Just understand that Keces Industries is not the most dangerous party with an interest in recovering the databox."

"Yeah, you sure look like the good guys so far." Gail yanks the pen from his hand.

"When a complex situation appears black and white, Ms. Simmons, it's almost always an illusion."

She closes her eyes, feeling like she's volunteered to climb into a sealed airlock with walls slowly sliding together. After taking a deep, steadying breath, she opens her eyes and signs.

"I'll transfer serial information to your ship that will make identifying and tracking the databox as easy as possible. I trust you can find your own way out."

She marches out of the office, switching her biomods on again, primed in case someone's stuck around to make more trouble for her. Nobody's waiting, though, either in the lobby or outside. In case they come back, she won't stick around, either.

The ambient light has deepened to a jaundiced yellow. Her sensors tell her the temperature's only dropped half a degree, but it feels colder.

Closing her eyes, she allows herself one slow, shuddering breath and soft whine, then hurries back toward *Kismet*. She has no idea what to do next, but she's got no time to lose doing it.

Chapter 3

IF YOU DON'T COUNT THE CERES RING, Panorica is the largest arcology in terms of both population and sheer size. It's a cylindrical design like Kingston, but a vast, slow-spinning behemoth. You can dock either at the stationary center or at the rim, where you berth in gravity, start out much closer to wherever it is you're planning to go, and pay twice as much in fees. She can't afford to tie up there but she does anyway, because she's on a schedule. She's here for an appointment with her friend Ansel.

He doesn't know she has an appointment to keep with him yet. But as he would say, that's just an implementation detail.

Keces has a presence on Panorica, but the station enforces strict "public charter" restrictions on companies they contract for services with—she doesn't have to worry about them literally owning the police like they would on Molinar. However, those corporations are required to make video feeds from common areas, like the spartan lobby of the small craft terminal she's hurrying through, publicly available in the name of transparency. If Keces doesn't already know she's here, they will within the hour. Well, screw 'em. She's doing their job. Or trying to.

"Kis, where's Ansel at?"

"His last reported location is Club Acceleration." Of course it is. She knows just which table he's sitting at. She steps out onto the plaza.

Panorica's interior layout forgoes the stultifying squared-off precision of Molinar or the manicured arrangements of Kingston. Instead, it embraces the magnificent ordered chaos of varying city blocks, curved throughways and contrasting neighborhoods. Even when it had been built generations ago, its designers employed most of their artifice to hide just how much artifice a giant arcology entailed. In the intervening years, buildings have been redesigned, repurposed, demolished and replaced, just like—she assumes—a historical Earth city. And the light on Panorica is nothing like other stations, not one uniform ambient glow slowly shifting color. Instead, a yellow-white "sun" moves through the central core, fore to aft, through the daylight period. The sun's almost all the way to the aft end; she docked at the fore, so she stands in deep twilight. Street lamps and business signs and lamps in countless windows glitter before her like docking beacons.

She jogs spinward, toward the personal transport lot. Since she only wants a one-person unit she shouldn't have a wait. And she doesn't—she has a choice between a dozen standing scooters. She hops on one, just a platform between two wheels and a semicircular rail to hang onto. The display lights up to confirm her ID information and the usage charges.

She taps the command button. The display changes to a map, but she doesn't have to look at it. "Take me to the Deck."

"Please hold on," a tinny male voice responds, and the scooter starts rolling forward.

Some streets on Panorica take only pedestrians or transports this size, but this is a wide central avenue with faster, heavier vehicles. The scooter stays to its own lane, quickly hitting its top speed of twenty-five kilometers per hour. Growing up, she didn't understand the Trans-Ring Railway, at four hundred eighty KPH, was sui generis. It wasn't until she began exploring the rest of the River that she realized none of the platform arcologies, even Panorica, were big enough to need anything that went much faster than this.

At least this speed lets her see the city, measure what's changed since she was last here…when was it, eight months ago? Most of the buildings hold apartments, restaurants and the occasional office for companies that need—or just want—separate physical space for their work. Her favorite sidewalk café is still open, she sees, but the little crafts boutique next door has shuttered. Nothing's higher than four stories; much taller and you start noticing the drop in gravity.

And then there's the Deck.

It's a three-story inverted pyramid of a building hung at the top of a metal tripod, about four hundred meters over the floor. It's high enough you can see just all of Panorica—at least all the populated side, as the "top" half of the cylinder is devoted to agricultural and industrial use. Gravity in the pyramid is about point-six g. In addition to the observation deck that gives it its name, there are four bars, three restaurants, and one boutique hotel. All have reputations for being fabulously overpriced and kept in business by tourists (and, in the case of the hotel, honeymooners). Where she's going also gets tourists, but it's none of the above. She's going to what is, as far as she knows, the only low-gravity dance club in the universe.

The Deck wasn't built with the rest of Panorica, but it's at least fifty years old—the architectural flourishes of faux cantilever beams and tall, thin triangular columns along the edges of each level didn't turn out to look so timeless. Yet it's impossible not to be impressed, even as many times as she's seen it before. From an engineering standpoint, it's Panorica itself—hell, the River itself—that's the true marvel, but it's background wonder. The Deck is sheer celebratory hubris made manifest.

Gail hops off the scooter before it comes to a complete stop in the parking lot, earning her a reproachful buzz, and hurries along the short path to the elevator. It runs up one of the legs, enclosed on all sides but the floor by glass. Sometimes she's been able to wangle a ride on the service elevator inside a different leg, which makes the trip in a third the time, but she doesn't see any employees she knows nearby. So she gets in with the tourists—ten total, nine of them cisform—and waits for it to start moving. At least there's only a couple of young kids to enthusiastically smash themselves into other passengers as the gravity drops.

The countdown clock on the wall shows it's not leaving for another two and a half minutes. She leans against the railing. "Kis, Ansel's still in the Club, right?"

"No subsequent locations are recorded." She didn't expect a different answer—Ansel usually stays there late, and while he could have left without leaving a track, he usually leaves his privacy mirror set to share any public stops he makes with friends.

The transform kid flashes her a suspicious look, trying to decide if she's got a communication mod or is just crazy. His body is mostly unmodified human, but he has big cat ears and a tail, both electric blue, matching his mane-like hair. Tattoos cover his arms, abstract patterns in faintly reflective ink. The tail moves all the time, too, and it's nearly as long as he is. She wonders how often it gets caught in doors. He's kind of hot, though. The black pants and half-shirt, both tighter than a fully furred totemic would be comfortable in, don't hurt, either.

Gail nods to him with a slight smile. He relaxes and smiles back, folding his arms loosely over his chest. Okay, more than kind of hot. Also barely twenty. One of the cisform women is paying far more attention to Catboy's butt than she should be. Oh, tailchasers. Her boyfriend's oblivious.

Finally the countdown hits zero, music starts playing, and the elevator starts rising. A recorded voice begins narrating the history of the Deck—right, it's closer to sixty years old than fifty—and warning people to hang onto the railing, which no one does. The ride up takes a full three minutes, which the recording extols as a virtue.

As much as she wants to mimic Catboy's too-cool-for-this disaffection, the view of Panorica slowly unfolding below always catches and holds her attention. Most tourists ride up here during daylight, but that's wrong. Nighttime has magic. The colors mute, streetlights creating bursts of contrast and shadow. The curve of the station comes into sharp focus, making the little world seem impossible, surreal, beautiful. Buildings jut out parallel to the horizon, people walk sideways, creeks flow up into the huge linear parks on either side of the city. Gail has never set foot on Earth or Mars, but she's seen images. Nothing on a planet compares to this.

Soon the recording runs out, and the trip proceeds without narration except from the family with the kids. The mother, a stocky woman with limp brown hair and tired eyes, tries to point out landmarks to them, but they seem more interested in bouncing around in the slowly diminishing gravity. Her eyesight isn't good enough to pick them out at night and it doesn't sound like she's been here before, so she doesn't have a clue what she's looking at. "That's Peters Park," she's saying, pointing at one of the linear parks. Can't get that one wrong. "Pay attention. And that big hexagon building is… uh…"

Gail walks over, with long, pillowy low gravity strides. "The Davison Museum of Art. It's a dodecahedron."

"Oh. Thank you." She smiles at Gail. "I've heard it's a very good museum."

"It is. It's almost worth a visit just for the building itself."

"Why doesn't your tail have fur?" the daughter asks. She has limp brown hair, too, and looks like she's about six. Mom pales visibly.

Gail grins. "Because I'm a rat."

"Why are you a rat?"

"Jennifer," the mother hisses, now looking mortified.

"You've been on a spaceship, haven't you?"

The girl nods. "Uh huh."

"I live on a spaceship." Gail spreads her hands. "All ships need rats."

Jennifer falls silent at that, blinking slowly twice. Mom laughs, then looks self-conscious about it.

The music swells as the elevator platform comes to a stop and the doors open. Gail—and Catboy—wait for the tourists to exit first, the kids bouncing out toward the observation deck, giggling madly. The adults wobblejump their way after them, yelling admonishments. Then Catboy heads off across the polished stone floor, not jumping in his steps but gliding, perfect athletic poise. She's so distracted by the way he moves—the way he looks moving—it takes her a couple seconds to realize he's going the same way she is.

This is the middle floor, above the hotel and under the observation deck, and it's where most of the shops are, the restaurants and bars and tacky souvenir kiosks surrounded by padded railings. The walls are padded, too, although you have to look closely or smack into one to notice. Her path takes her close to one of the cafés; as she passes by, the menu board highlights the pumpkin cheesecake. She hasn't had dinner yet and it's pitching her a favorite dessert? She's not sure what that says about her eating habits, but it isn't good.

The warm grey patterned tiles end at a sunken floor along one wall, glossy black over shifting patterns of glowing light. As she steps down on it, the colors ripple. They flow toward the pitch black doorway at the far end, and as the stream gets closer to the entrance they pulse in time with a driving beat you feel more than hear. Small symbols to the right of the door glow bright white, pulsing in time with the music.

$$\frac{\Delta v}{\Delta t}$$

A full transform tiger, decked out in formal black shirt, jacket and kilt, stands to the left of the doorway. He looks like a polite striped mountain. As she approaches, he nods. "Gail."

"Hey, Carl." He could just be reading her name off a HUD in *his* eye, but she doesn't think he is. She isn't, either. She remembers him. "No line yet?"

"It's early." He waves her in with a sweep of an arm.

The glowing floor is the entrance hall's only light source, the lacquered walls and ceiling reflecting the stream's turbulent dance. Two steps in and she's past the noise cancellation barrier, and the music jumps from conversational volume to bone-shaking.

The hall's just another six slow-long-stride steps long. Then it turns to the left, and all at once you're there. The walls and ceiling and floor go matte black rather than shiny and the ceiling bubbles into a huge dome, and nothing but air remains between you and the speakers. The main floor rotates, a disc about twenty-five meters across, and the club has a projection system like the one in *Kismet*'s cockpit. Look in any direction and you see the stars that surround Panorica. You dance floating in space.

Gail slots people on the floor into three categories: the nervous, the nutbars and the magicians. The nervous step onto the disc and realize they don't have a single clue how to dance in low gravity, and make tiny little petrified moves, not always in time with the rhythm. The nutbars are the ones who have grievously miscounted the number of clues they have. The results range from amusing to dangerous.

Right now there are only five people on the dance floor, three totemics and one who's gone more xeno, iridescent green skin and silver eyes. She's never figured out the xenos. Totemics have a history, a philosophy, even a spirituality, and you might think the spirituality is bullshit but it's *there*. As much as she tries to give xenos the benefit of the doubt, she's pretty sure they're just about looking alien. Xeno guy's a nutbar. Surprise. The cisform woman is nervous, barely moving; her partner's not bad, and the silver vixen moves decently. Maybe the wrong word given the outfit she's barely wearing.

Catboy, though: he's a magician. Whirling in midair, spinning end over end, dancing sideways against the wall, always aware of where that meter-and-a-half tail is, tattoos as much of a light show as the pulsing spotlights swinging around the dome. She stops at the railing by the dance floor and just watches. He's lost in the music, and she lets herself be lost by proxy for a few minutes. When the track changes, one percussion line smoothly melding into the next, she follows the railing up to the second level bar.

The tabletops and the bar itself are high-gloss, reflecting the stars and lights from the dance floor. The underside of the bar glows and flows like the entranceway. It's an oval bar, most of the tables on the side overlooking the club, some on the opposite side with windows looking down at the city. It's still loud, but less than it looks like it should be.

Right where she expects him to be, at "his" table, Ansel's turned to watch the dancers. He's almost certainly watching the catboy—he's cute, and he's the only dancer worth watching anyway. Ansel's a fox, full transform. Every time she sees him he's varied his color scheme. Tonight he's mostly just fox-colored, but the hair sticking out from under his tan driving cap is vivid green, and his claws are copper, glittering when a spotlight catches them. The drink sitting in front of him matches the hair almost perfectly, a snifter full of lime green something on the rocks, garnished with a slice of orange and a paper parasol changing color in time with the music.

Gail hurries over, and as he's turning she's dropping into the seat opposite him. "Ansel!"

His violet eyes—that's natural, or at least it's never changed in the years she's known him—focus on her in surprise. He's not much younger than she is, but still looks like he's barely into his twenties. The guarded expression falling over his face makes him look older, though. "Gail."

"How've you been? It's been a while."

"I've been fine, thanks. I'm not about to wish it'd been a while longer, am I?"

She feels her smile slip. "I hope not."

"Sorry." He holds up his hands. "But when you show up out of the black here without sending me a message first, you usually want something and you figure it'll be harder for me to say no if you're pleading in person."

That doesn't sound either right or fair to her, but it's right this time, isn't it? She laughs self-consciously, looking at the table. "That's not always true."

"I didn't say always, I said usually." Ansel takes a long sip of his drink and pushes the glass aside. "Okay, talk to me."

"I've got a quick job and I need advice from someone who's more technical, and you're the best I know."

"Mmm hmm."

"So. I'm trying to track down a lost databox. I have some information on it—appearance, serial number—and I know roughly when and where it went missing…"

She trails off. The fox's eyes have widened in a deeply unsettling way, as if she'd said *I just need you to help me hide a body.* "A databox. You're tangled up in something that involves finding a databox."

Her ears lower. "Is that bad?"

"Oh, Gail." He rubs his forehead. "Do you know what the payload is?"

"I'm not sure I even know what a databox is, beyond an educated guess. It's a physical data backup, right?"

He wiggles his hand in a *sort of* gesture. "It's not backup storage, it's

29

singular storage. You keep the data from being anywhere but in the box, so you need physical possession of it for access."

She tries to make sense of that. "Data doesn't have a location."

"It depends on the data." He waves his hands around. "Some data stays localized, like your spaceship's 'personality.'" (She can hear the air quotes.) "Most data gets replicated across hundreds of storage nodes. But if you're paranoid, you keep all the copies of critical data physically isolated. That minimizes the chance of unauthorized access, but it makes it possible to lose the data forever. If you want backups, you need more databoxes."

"So how do I find it?"

"You don't. That's part of the point." He leans back and crosses his arms, looking at the ceiling. "Since the databox's owner didn't go to a judiciary, this is something they don't want to attract any attention to. Have you talked with Sky?"

"Why would I do that?"

He drops his head back to look at her. "When you're trying to investigate a crime, why would you talk to your sister the police officer? You're right. I don't know what I was thinking."

She rolls her eyes. "C'mon, you just said it yourself—my client doesn't want a judiciary involved. How do you think they'd feel about bringing in the Ring Judicial Cooperative?"

"I didn't say give her the case, I said ask her for advice. I can't give you some kind of magic databox-finding algorithm. You need a thief-finding algorithm, and that's her department, not mine. And why did they hire *you* to find this?"

"I was kind of in the wrong place at the wrong time. Look, can't you give me any help here?"

"Yes. I'm going to go to the bar and buy you a drink. What do you want?"

"I don't know." She glances at the drink special menu on the table. "A mezcal sour."

"Got it." He gets up.

She doesn't consciously slump as much as let herself go, sliding down in her seat. What had she expected Ansel to say? "Oh, sure, Gail, let's just bring up a map and show you where the thief is." Of course not. But kind of. That's not exactly what an algorithmist does but it's *almost* what one does, just with data instead of crooks, and she knows he's damn good at his job. Find the data, find the crook. Except databoxes don't work that way.

Her plummeting mood—not that it had far to fall—keeps her occupied enough that she doesn't notice Ansel's return until he sets her glass down in front of her with a firm *bang* against the tabletop. He has another one of whatever it was he had before, too. "What you need," he says, "is to narrow down where the thief could be. You can't look everywhere on the River at once."

"Yeah." She sits up and takes a sip of the drink, and grimaces. "This tastes like a barbecued lime marinated in tequila."

"Isn't that what a mezcal sour is supposed to taste like?"

"Maybe." After a vigorous stir the drink is better. A little. "I just don't have a clue where to start looking."

"You still haven't answered the big question. Why you?"

"Because I found the wreck the databox was supposed to be on, and they think I stole it."

He lifts his brows inquiringly.

"I didn't!"

Ansel lifts his hands. "I didn't think you would. But you don't just come across shipwrecks randomly."

"I got a tip from a kid I knew growing up who's a yacht captain now." She takes a longer sip of the drink. Maybe it's not so bad. "If I don't get the databox back to them in three days they're going to report me as *socius indignus*. I could lose *Kismet*."

"Wow." He rests his muzzle in a hand and exhales. "All right. You don't know what's on the databox, but a company's trying to keep attention away from the theft. Maybe secrets they've stolen from another company." He sits up and scratches the back of one ear. "Or secrets they're afraid another company will steal. Who are their competitors?"

She lowers her voice. "It's Keces."

"So their competitors are everyone. You do know how to pick your enemies." He drums his fingers on the table. "I'd bet this involves the energy or transportation divisions."

"Transportation?"

"Moving anything between stations is still expensive."

"It sounded like something more…serious. Cheap freight can't be worth killing over."

"Anything's worth killing over if there's enough profit involved."

"Mmm." She stirs the drink again. "So any other ideas?"

Ansel takes a long sip of his drink, which looks much smoother and sweeter. She wishes she'd asked for one of those. "Figure out where the ship was coming from and where it was going, see what Keces divisions match up with those, figure out their competitors." He empties the glass. "And for Christ's sake, call Sky. She may come up with some defense against the *socius indignus* by tangling everything up with the Ring's crazy communist legal shenanigans."

"They're not communists." It's almost a reflexive response.

"You know what I mean." He waves his hand dismissively. "Look, I've got to get going. I'm on a tight deadline for my current contract and I'm planning to work through the night." He stands up.

That's probably a half-truth: it's likely he has his portable display with him and could work here just fine. She's seen him do it. But she won't press; she's made him prickly enough tonight as it is. Maybe she should have brought a gift, not that she could afford one. "Okay. Thanks for the help you could give." She hopes she made that sound credibly sincere.

Ansel leans over and gives her a hug. "Take care, Gail. Try not to get in any more trouble before we meet again, hmm?"

She grins wryly. "I never try to get in trouble, Ansel."

He laughs. Then he's gone.

Gail slumps back in her seat, eyes closed for a few seconds, then gets up with her glass and heads to sit at the bar. It takes her another ten minutes to finish as much of the sour as she can stand, and she's about to order something else when Catboy sits down next to her. He's still breathing hard from his dancing. That looks good on him, too.

When the bartender approaches, he orders something called a "Livingston Swizzle." The bartender nods and looks at Gail.

"I'll have what he just ordered."

He grins at her, the same grin as he had back in the elevator. "You're not dancing." His smile shows pointed feline teeth.

"I'm not much of a dancer. I came here to meet someone."

"But you're alone now."

"Yeah, we already met. He just left."

"Then you don't have a reason not to come back on the dance floor with me."

She laughs. "Other than the part about me not being much of a dancer? I saw you move. Compared to you I'd feel like a brick." She looks behind him at the huge tail; he's looped it around the stool several times. "Is your tail prehensile?"

"Yes."

The bartender brings both drinks. She takes a sip of hers. It's got citrus and ginger and she can't tell what else, but she's sure it's stronger than it tastes. That's good.

She tilts her head and grins. "So what can you do with a prehensile tail?"

He laughs, and meets her eyes with his as he takes a sip of his own drink.

Chapter 4

WHEN SHE WAKES UP there's a moment of disorientation until she realizes Catboy—she did learn his name, didn't she?—is taking up slightly more than half of her bunk. For a single person it's more than big enough, but not for two. Why did they come back here instead of his place?

Oh, right: because *here* is her own private spaceship. That's still a hell of a pickup line.

He stays asleep even as she carefully unwinds that amazing tail from around her leg and slips out of bed. It takes her longer than it should to locate her clothes, given how small the cabin is. After she's dressed she walks to the beverage station and punches up some coffee.

"Mmm?" Catboy sits up, rubbing his eyes. "Morning, Gail."

Dammit, he knows *her* name. She hurriedly calls up her contact manager, hoping she'd remembered to activate it. Yes! Maybe.

"Adrian," *Kismet* says in her ear.

She gives the cockpit a glare, since the ship doesn't have a face to glare at. "Hey, Adrian."

He stretches, then twists around, pulling his pants off the floor and over his legs. "There's a café just a half a block away if you're looking for breakfast."

"Yeah. Well, a coffee and a donut or something, at least. Gonna be a busy day." It'd better be one—as nice as last night was, she's wasting time. And she doesn't have anything more to go on than she did when she left Molinar.

"Is salvage work that regular?"

"No, it isn't. Sometimes I take odd jobs."

"I guess you don't volunteer for the River Totemic Equality Association."

That's a hell of a weird—oh. She flashes him a wry smile. "When did you get a chance to look me up?"

"After you fell asleep. I didn't know you were from a famous family when we met." There's an anxious edge in his voice, like he wants to reassure her that he didn't try to pick her up *because* of her name. That's happened before; it's common to do a quick search on people you want to hook up with.

It's ludicrous to give her family celebrity status, let alone her, though. "Only mom was famous and I've been a lot happier staying off that radar. Working with the RTEA didn't work out too well for her."

His ears flick. "I'm sorry."

"Long time ago."

"In a sense she's won, though. Maybe there's more active prejudice out on the far fringe platforms, but in the Panorica Federation? I've been transform for five years and never had a problem."

"It's better now. Uh, since I didn't look *you* up, did I ask what you do?"

He grins, moving in front of her and running his claw tips along her sides. She wriggles reflexively. "Work-study program at the university."

About what she'd guessed. So all the time he's been transform, he's been a student, and probably only on Panorica or a platform allied with it. A Panorican college might be the most totemic-friendly environment off the Ring you could find. He'll hit turbulence soon enough. "What's your major?"

"Kinetic arts."

"That's not an academic way of saying 'dancing,' is it?"

He nuzzles one of her ears, making it very hard to focus on his answer. "It's more about putting other things in motion, not me."

She nods, touching her lips to his in a light kiss, and chuckles. "I thought my line of work was volatile. I know artists can make a lot if they get a few good patrons, but…does the university help at all with that?"

He steps away and shrugs. "Their matchmaking service is pretty cheap for students. My parents have been making up the difference between what I'm making now and my tuition, so I won't be in debt when I graduate. And as long as I stay on Panorica the basic income should be enough to at least keep me in a place like this."

She lifts her brows. "Basic income? It actually managed to pass?" The

Ceres Ring has a version of that, but to nearly every other arcology that's near the top of the list of horrifying things about the place.

"It won't come back up for a vote until next year. But it's just about guaranteed to pass then."

Most of the direct propositions can't be voted on by people who don't live on Panorica, whether or not they hold citizenship, so she hasn't been paying much attention. She remembers the battles the first time this came up, though, seven years ago, and shakes her head. "It's hard to imagine enough people voting in a flat income tax. Hell, it's hard enough to get them to raise the VAT."

"It's just two percent. That's less than a quarter of the Ring's."

"Yeah, but the Ring had one from the start."

Adrian shrugs again. "You know the saying. If you don't like where you are, the River's very, very long."

She nods. She's heard it. You can beat Panorica's cost of living elsewhere and you can beat its standard of living elsewhere, you just can't beat both. But if one's more important to you than the other, nothing stops you from moving.

He pulls on his shirt. "So why a rat?"

"That wasn't my choice. Mom liked the symbolism. Resourcefulness, adaptability."

"It's your choice to stay that way, though, isn't it? Nothing stops you from another transformation."

"Other than money and medical risk." She laughs. "But I like the symbolism, too. And, hey, most people don't choose what they are."

"I guess your mother thought of that as a design flaw."

Her eyes narrow, but he sounds curious, not challenging. "She wanted totemics to be able to give birth to other totemics, not cisforms, yeah. But that's been fifteen years out for the last sixty years. Like I said, I don't begrudge her making the choice for me. So why'd you choose a cat?"

"Why a totemic at all? The paradox of advanced technology in the service of atavistic desire, living in outer space with a personal connection to wild Earth. We make better humans than cisform humans do. But as for why a cat, I could say I've always felt feline, and that'd be true. And I like the aesthetic."

"You *are* an artist."

Beedle boop "You have a call from Jason Nakimura of Keces."

He looks up at the hidden speaker. "Is that your ship?"

"I thought I'd introduced you to Kis last night. But hang on, I should take this. Put him through, Kis, direct to me."

Nakimura doesn't bother with a greeting. "You're on Panorica."

"Yep."

"Why?"

"I told you I have people. I'm seeing them."

"You're on one of the few places in the River with both a long-range spaceport and a law enforcement agency that coordinates with agencies on Earth and Mars."

"That's because it's also the biggest metropolis on the River. Look, if I was going to run somewhere to hide behind law enforcement, I'd be making my first trip back to New Coyoacán in a decade."

"It appears all you've done there is visit a tourist attraction, then return to your ship. I have doubts as to how seriously you're taking your task."

She walks closer to the cockpit, both ears and voice lowering. "You're my temporary employer, not my chaperone. I'm researching leads, all right?" Nakimura said "tourist attraction," not "club"; he doesn't have specifics. So that means he's set up searches on public viewfeeds to report on her. Low granularity, but profoundly annoying. "All you need to care about is whether I show up with your widget in two days."

"I also care about whether you're taking that 'widget,' as you put it, to the inner system."

"I told you," she hisses, "I'm following a lead. I'll see you in two days. Until then get off my ass." She disconnects the call before he responds.

"It sounds like your busy day's already started."

"Yeah. I've gotta get going on that assignment." No, don't say *that I've told you about,* since she hasn't.

"I have a class in an hour myself." He steps close, tilting her head up and lowering his own so their noses nearly touch. "Will I see you back at the Club sometime?"

For a while she went there a couple times a month, but that was—longer ago than she'd thought, when she puts a year to it. Recently she only gets there when she's meeting Ansel, but she should try to make it more often. Three days from now, for instance, she's going to want a lot of alcohol one way or another. "You might." She turns the nose-touch into a kiss.

* * *

The breakfast place Adrian told her about turns out to be another Magnolia Café, but this one's set up as the kind of high volume, low cost operation that appeals to students. A single employee behind the counter looks so engrossed by the smartpaper she's holding that someone has to yell to get her attention when a serving station breaks. The coffee's good, though, and the pastry's acceptable.

Christ, what's she supposed to even do now? She's sitting here alone with a bum at a nearby table giving her the evil eye, no closer to knowing where and how to look than she was yesterday evening. How do you find a thief who's left no trace?

By finding a trace of something else. *Figure out where the ship was coming from and where it was going.* She pulls out her smartpaper pad. "Kis, send me a news bulletin about the attacks on Keces that Nakimura mentioned."

After a moment the smartpaper fills with an article. Three separate attacks: offices on Panorica and Lariat hit by EMP drones, and a laboratory floating off Arelia hit with a full-fledged bomb, killing nineteen workers. Nobody claimed responsibility, and Keces made no statements beyond indicating they'd handle it internally. The lab's described only as a "research facility."

She taps the side of her coffee cup. The thieves weren't stealing copies of the databox, they were *destroying* copies of it. But not this last one. So they didn't just want to steal the data, they wanted to make sure Keces couldn't keep using it. "Kis, if that SC71 had set out from Keces' HQ on Molinar, what would its likely destinations be based on its course?"

"In decreasing order of likelihood, Panorica, the Rothbard Republic, New Amsterdam and the Ceres Ring."

"Are any Keces divisions headquartered on Panorica?"

"Keces Data Fabrics, Keces-Okita Transit, Keces Bioengineering, and Freshbright Markets."

"Transit," she murmurs aloud. One of Ansel's guesses. Maybe this really is a clue, but how does she translate that into action? She can't just go in and ask them about the damn thing without Nakimura's help, and he's such an—

"Gail Simmons?"

She almost drops the last bite of her donut, and flicks both her ears—big ears that should keep people from sneaking up on her or what good are they—as she turns.

It's the bum. Okay, not fair: he's not in bad shape. Cisform, white, looks ten or fifteen years older than she is, zipper-down square shoulder salesman clothes that look ten or fifteen years older than hers. But he knows her name? Crap, does she know him? She calls up her contact manager, even though using her HUD when somebody's looking right at her eyes makes her look kinda unfocused-spooky. No hits.

"Tom Laurel." He holds out a hand. "We met when you lived on Carmona." His voice is the sound of a baritone jazz singer who took sandpaper to his vocal cords.

Carmona. She never lived there, technically, but she spent a lot of time docked at that platform the first couple of years she lived on *Kismet*. It seemed like the free-wheeling, lawless epitome of "do what thou wilt," the polar opposite of life with Big Sister. She'd worked in a terrible little café until the novelty wore off, then kept working until she soured on the whole experience. It turned out that most people who insisted on doing what they wilt were kind of assholes.

While his name doesn't come up in her contacts, there's a few hits in public databases—oh, *him*. Speaking of those people. "Yeah. Okay. Hi. You used to come into Brio Coffee." She touches his hand perfunctorily rather than shaking it. "Still in the amp business?" She hopes the man's not about to try to sell her some.

He shakes his head. "Not as a main business. I can still get you some—still good quality—but… Panorica, you know."

She knows. It's one of the few drugs that's tightly controlled on Panorica and the Ring. On Carmona, and most other places across the River, it's not. What you put in your body is your choice. Of course, it's also your employer's choice to fire you faster than a railgun if you work under the influence. She tried amp once (Jesus, was that a mistake) and she probably bought from him.

Images of Tom are beginning to come back to her. He always overdressed, always looked like he'd stepped out of a high-end fashion browser. He's wearing the same kind of clothes now, just well past their recycle date.

She finishes the donut and picks up her coffee, as if she's got somewhere to be soon. "So what are you up to these days?"

"Oh, this and that. Working a few angles, following a few leads. Divest, diversify. Amp's a great business, but it's bad for it to be your only revenue stream. I'd like to get to Rothbard, some other place where they're not locking down freedom, you know?"

Rothbard would be right on board with the "this is good because governments on Earth say it's bad for you" spiel she remembers Tom pitching, but unless you're employed by one of the mega-casinos there you'd better be a billionaire to afford permanent residency. Maybe the casinos hire amp dealers, though. "What was wrong with staying on Carmona?"

He sighs heavily. Whatever's on his breath makes her want to scrub her nostrils out. "It's the business associations, the neighborhood associations. They don't want you to sell in person anymore, don't even want you to sell by delivery. The neighborhood I lived in banned amp! Can you believe that?"

"Rough break." Tom lived in the upscale district Brio catered to—cheaper neighborhoods have mostly automated cafés like this one—and it stayed upscale by promising residents a certain "quality of life" and enforcing it by contract. Honestly the biggest surprise is that they hadn't banned it *before* he'd moved in. He might be the proximate cause for the new rule.

"You were always the best thing about Brio. You still have the prettiest blue eyes I've seen." She remembers him telling her that before now, years ago, and it was just as unexpected and weird then. He grins, more slyly. "So are you still running cons?"

Oh, great, this is either going to turn into an illegal business proposition or a lame blackmail attempt. Just what she needs. She tightens her grip on the coffee and lowers her voice. "I was a waitress, Tom, and now I'm a salvor. Pretty above board stuff both then and now."

He raises his hands. "Maybe I'm misremembering. But there was that, what was he, an otter guy you sold a broken water pump to? Thompson, wasn't it?"

"It wasn't broken, just useless for what he wanted. And he'd been charging his own purchases to Brio's account and the owner didn't want to go to a judiciary over it." She shrugs. "I was just getting the money back." She did, and maybe a little more for herself.

He leans close, whispering in confidence. "I'm sure that wasn't the only time."

Nostril scrub again. She musters a laugh, starting to walk slowly backward. "Look, I'm seriously not in that business. It's been good catching up, but the business I *am* in is waiting for me."

He follows slowly, not taking the hint. "The business you're in. You're a salvage operator, aren't you?"

"Yep."

"So that means you found something. I'm not asking what it is, I'm just saying if you need a buyer, a sales broker, I've got a lot of connections, especially back on Carmona."

"I'm not…" She trails off. She doesn't have anything to sell, no, but maybe somebody does. It's longer than a long shot; this isn't the kind of job you do without a buyer already lined up. But that doesn't mean you're working with the buyer directly. "Brokers, huh? Do you know anyone who might specialize in ferrying something small and discreet from a seller to a buyer?"

"Sure." He waves a hand dismissively. "Even down to handling, you know, *complicated* payment details. I know people in the banking system."

"Anyone you can hook me up with?" She's continuing to walk to the exit, more slowly.

"I can take you to somebody, yeah." He bites his lip. "Yvonne, maybe."

"I'm on a *really* tight schedule. Can you just get me her contact information?"

He draws back, giving her a more guarded look. "That's not how these sorts of deals work. I'm happy to take you to Yvette, but I'm going to introduce you in person."

"What was her name again?" Her eyes lock onto his face.

"Yvonne." His uncertain eye twitch isn't something most people would catch. Not people who can't overdrive their optic system just a little. Just enough. Tom isn't exactly lying, but his memory holes make him even less trustworthy now than he was a decade ago.

She blinks twice rapidly as her eyes resync, then smiles apologetically. "Sorry, I don't have time for this." They're at the door.

"I could do it right now. I mean, it's not far." He steps ahead so he's blocking the exit, standing just ten centimeters away.

He's tall and she's short; there's probably forty centimeters height difference between them. Kilogram for kilogram he might be stronger than she is, but she's in so much better shape that's not a given even without biomods. And, of course, she *does* have biomods. No sign he has any of his own, no sign he's on amp now, even if he stopped being smart enough not to take his own product. Maybe he thinks he's going to get a bolt of inspiration, maybe he just thinks he's going to get her in bed. Neither one is going to happen.

"Tom." She reaches up and puts a hand against his shoulder, and keeps her tone pleasant. "Right now you're my friendly acquaintance the drug dealer, okay? Let's not ruin that good impression." She ramps up her strength just enough that when she squeezes his shoulder it's balanced right between *nice to see you, old buddy* and *I will snap you like balsa.*

He makes a pained noise, stepping back hurriedly and rubbing his shoulder. "I'm just trying to help," he mutters.

"If I make a deal with Yvonne, I'll send you a sales commission for giving me her name." She steps out of the café. "I hope things turn around for you, Tom."

She can hear him mutter *get yours, fuckin' rat bitch* under his breath, but she doesn't turn around.

The "small craft" docks are part of Port Panorica, the official name of the spaceport operation, but they're a separate facility from the real spaceport, the one for long-range passenger craft. Some go across the whole River, and when Earth or Mars and Ceres—the reference point all the platforms match their orbits to—are close enough, weekly passenger liners run to one or both planets. Gail's only been to it a few times. Once she bought *Kismet* she stopped flying on intra-River passenger craft, and she's never been on a long run ship. But she's watching one of them now. It docked last night, a cruiser from Earth or Mars, and it'll be heading out later tonight. It looks like a cylindrical station in miniature; she wonders how many passengers puke when they go from full gravity to zero, then get slowly brought back up to point-eight for the rest of the trip.

She's watching from Kismet's cockpit, knowing this is wasting time and that she needs to do the research she'd hoped Ansel would do for her. Problem: she doesn't even know what she needs to research. Okay, she found Keces-Okita, but so what? What does that tell her? She can't work backwards from where the databox was supposed to be, can she?

Keces-Okita has a few competitors, but they're much smaller, and it looks like most of them actually buy equipment from a different Keces division. Despite Ansel's suspicion, she remains dubious that the transportation industry—at least this corner of it—is a hotbed of corporate intrigue and murder.

Okay. If they knew what it was, this thing would be valuable enough for the dark courier operation to screw their own client. But that's not what happened. The ship's crew was killed. So Keces might have sent someone with the databox on the courier ship, but whoever they sent was actually a double-agent, working for the thieves.

Why the hell leave a wreck at all? Why not wait to steal it after it got to Panorica? That'd be much simpler, much less risky, and it wouldn't attract the attention of, well, people like her. What does having done it this way accomplish?

She rubs her face. What if it was *supposed* to attract the attention of people like her? What if the plan was to focus Nakimura's attention on a salvage operator, letting the real thief get somewhere past Keces' reach while they were busy making her life miserable?

No. No, that would mean Randall was in on it, that he helped set her up. She doesn't know what he's been doing the last twenty years, but even if he'd become a criminal mastermind, she can't imagine he'd come across her name on a list of salvors and think *yeah, why not make my childhood buddy the patsy for all this?*

Gail looks back out at the passenger cruiser. Then she frowns.

Somewhere past Keces' reach.

"Kis," she says slowly, "when does that ship leave?"

"The Starliner Supera departs for Earth at eighteen hundred forty-five, two hours and fifty-three minutes from now. Final boarding is two hours and twenty-three minutes from now."

"Crap." She gets up and hurries toward the ship's door, grabbing her jacket on the way, throwing it on as the door closes behind her. "Send me a passenger list as soon as you can, filtering out anyone who's mentioned the trip on any of their social feeds."

"Yes, Gail."

She's not going through the terminal lobby so fast that she doesn't catch sight of Suspicious Detective out of the corner of her eye. Other side of the open space, different clothes to look less obvious, not quite facing her direction, looking down at a smart paper in his lap as if it's the most interesting thing in the solar system. It's him, though. How long has he been there? Did he report on her going in? He'll sure report on her leaving, running out of her ship like her tail's on fire.

So far he's staying interested in that paper, not so much as glancing toward her, no sign he might follow her out of the lobby. He's just a casual random guy who comes to small craft spaceports to hang out and read.

Is it worth trying to lose him? If he tells her buddy Jason she's going to the main spaceport, he's going to start shitting kittens. But what's he going to do? Order Mr. Detective to take her down? She's not going to go to any ticket counters, not going to make an attempt to get *on* the cruiser. She doubts you can even do that on this short notice. She's just following a hunch. A hunch she can't turn into anything actionable besides "start profiling people waiting for the cruiser to see if they look like thieves," but it's the best hunch she has.

But Suspicious Detective is following a suspect, too: her. Even if she doesn't try to get on board, she might try to hand the databox they think she has off to a partner in crime. Well, let him think what he wants. Losing him would be temporary anyway; the main spaceport is going to be full of public feed cameras. Hell, maybe he's staking out *Kismet,* to see if anyone comes to meet her. She hopes he's disappointed his life choices have brought him here.

Gail steps through the terminal's exit doors and someone grabs her from the side.

"What the—" She can't finish the curse before she gets slammed against the wall. Hard. It's Guy Two, and this time he has his biomechanics engaged. Of course.

"Kind of in a hurry, aren't you?"

"Yeah, I kind of am," she wheezes. If he's got the typical cop package, she knows just how strong he is, how fast, and what other enhancements she's facing. No guarantee he hasn't gone a la carte, but he doesn't come across as the creative type. Unfortunately, since he has the jump on her, she can't strong-arm her way out of this.

"You wanna share where?"

No, of course not, you idiot. Well, no. Maybe she does. Sometimes honesty's the most confusing policy. "To the main spaceport to try and catch the real thief."

He sneers. "Yeah, sure you are. Nakimura's already told us you wanna go there so you can run."

"For God's sake, use your head. If I was going there to run, I wouldn't have just told you that's where I'm going, would I?"

His brow furrows.

"I think *someone's* going to run, but it's not me. You can either let me go, or you can let somebody take your damn databox off the River entirely because you wanna butt heads with me. Which is it?"

He takes a very, very long time to consider that. "Okay, rat girl," he finally says. "I'll go check it out. You stay here."

"You don't—"

Something jabs her in the side. Her vision goes to static and she can feel things in her switching off. Everything turns to blue-white electric pain.

Chapter 5

"—SOMETHING FEEL?"

The words are almost there, her ears are back on, but her eyes aren't. Wait, they are. One is. The left one is. Maybe. The right one gets static.

"Something hear something? Lady? Something?"

She's stuck to a wall. Somebody in front of her's stuck to a wall. She can see their shoes. Gravity's twice normal and sideways. They're nice shoes.

Gail shakes her head and pain lances through her skull, a bunch of hot needles rattling around, but her vision clears. She pushes herself up into a sitting position and everything turns around the right way. She tries to say something floridly, beautifully profane, but all that comes out is a line of drool and "What."

The person with the shoes crouches down. Cisform girl, barely seventeen. Wait, not cisform: she has cat ears. Other people stand nearby, helpfully pointing and watching. "You had some kind of seizure. Your friend said he was running for a paramedic. I don't know why he didn't just call—"

"Because he's not my friend. He hit me with a stunner." Gail wipes off her muzzle. "You see which way he went?"

"Oh, God." The girl looks stricken, and points at the main spaceport.

"Terrific." Gail wobbles to a stand. No more pain in her head. Instead it's just the dull, burning sensation in her side where Guy Two shocked her. "Uh. Thanks." She takes a deep breath. It hurts a little, so she takes another one, then another, until she can tell herself it's not hurting. "Do you know how long I was down for? I'm still coming back online."

The girl looks confused. "Uh, just a few seconds. You were opening your eyes already when I ran over."

"Good." Her HUD switches back on. Catgirl's right—she was down a total of thirty-six seconds. If he hadn't attracted attention, would he have dragged her off, or just kept zapping long enough to do serious damage? She's damn lucky Nakimura hires idiots. Of course, she's one of them, isn't she? Ha ha.

"I'm so sorry—I didn't see he'd attacked you." She lowers her voice to a scared whisper. "This isn't some kind of anti-totemic attack, is it?"

"Huh?" She shakes her head. "No. Being an asshole is just his job."

"Gail?" Kismet's voice sounds in her ear. "Are you all right?"

"Mostly."

Her quasi-feline friend looks puzzled again. "Mostly?"

Gail points to her ear. "Sorry, I was talking to my ship."

That gets Catgirl's eyes to go even wider. Gail can't help but grin, but she manages to suppress a laugh that wouldn't be taken kindly. She takes the younger woman's hand in both of hers for a moment. "Thanks again. I have to get going."

"If you're sure you're okay. Uh, say hi to your ship!"

"She says hi back." Gail starts jogging away. "Kis, did you get that passenger list?"

"Yes. Visual matching will be available through your in-eye display. After filtering there are seventy-nine people left."

Groan. "Thanks." Couldn't it have been just two or three?

As she breaks into a run toward the gleaming white palace of Port Panorica, she pushes graphic but entertaining thoughts about what she could do to Guy Two if she got the drop on him out of her head. She's had to get threatening with people more in the last twenty hours than the previous twenty months, and she might be about to face both Guy Two and Suspicious Detective and, if she's exceptionally lucky, the actual thief.

The parts of the spaceport she's been in before have been repainted since her last visit, but not remodeled, so she knows where she's going. Unlike the small craft terminal, this is anything but spartan: three stories high, panoramic windows affording sweeping views of both the arcology interior and, on the outside wall, space. At least they finally covered the floor with claw-friendly carpet. Most places don't; that's why she wears sandals everywhere. She hurries through it, path cutting across two of the three main concourses, then takes an elevator up to the Intersolar Concourse.

It's smaller than she imagined it would be, but ritzier: wood trim, warm ambient lighting, plush seating in waiting areas. The central plaza has a food court and café, a coffee bar and a few travel shops. There are only two docking bays in the concourse, one locked and gated. They're almost never in use simultaneously.

The other one is well lit but cordoned off, since it's not boarding time yet—but boarding starts sooner than she'd like, in only twenty minutes. A spiral escalator past the bay's entrance heads up to the cruiser's gangway, with a secondary elevator for passengers who need it. While she has free roam outside, she's not going to get into the bay without being a paying passenger, so she needs to stop the thief from getting in. If she can find the thief. If the thief is actually here.

The security here doesn't look tighter than the rest of the port, but that's an illusion. The visible cameras doing automatic sweeps? Those are the ones you're supposed to know about. But those vents there, that doorway, the main information display? Sensors there, too, ones that skirt around the public feed requirements. And there are sensors she can't pick up and probably won't guess, as well as counter-measures against people with biomods like hers. Like stunners.

She detours to the coffee bar to pick up a latte, then meanders closer to the cruiser's loading area, noting anyone who seems to be paying attention to her. So far, that's zero, which is the number she wants.

If her hunch is right, then whoever took the box needed a salvor as a decoy, someone who'd hold Keces' attention for as long as it took the thief to get away. And it means Randall Corbett, a boy she's only thought of a handful of times in the last twenty years, hates her. Does she just remind him about his mother's death? He reminds her of that day, too, but it's not his—

Oh, shit, he's not one of the ones who thinks the bomb was her mother's, is he?

Christ, no time to think about that now. Focus on the passengers.

Focusing on the passengers is boring. They're doing passenger things: sitting, talking with one another, staring at smartpaper, a few just staring off into space—probably focusing on displays within their eyes much like hers. Some sit on benches, hunched over boxes of fast food dinners. That's nuts. They have enough time to at least go to the quick-service place, and it's not like they can't afford it—they have enough money to get a ticket to Earth.

She starts scanning for image matches against the seventy-nine people

Kismet filtered the passenger list down to, and switches on a couple visual systems which scan for biomods, the same thing that spotted Guy Two's cop package. Maybe she can pick up the databox. Somehow.

Matches highlight in her vision, green outlines around faces. Businessman with fashion model haircut. Woman with red dress and artificially lavender eyes. Scruffy young man, cisform except for his sharp, glassy claws. Full transform cheetah with black suit and black sunglasses.

Mara's Blood, where is she going with this? She's getting hits, but it'd have been nice if she'd had enough time to come up with a plan beyond drinking coffee and hoping for inspiration. She could stand up and yell "I know you set me up and took the databox and I'm coming for you, asshole!" and hope somebody starts running, so she can tackle them and hope spaceport security brings them both down instead of just her.

That's a terrible idea. She rubs the back of her ear.

Wait. Someone *is* paying attention to her, and not someone on her suspect list. Cisform, one-point-nine meters high, white but tanned, short brown hair. Square jaw. Grey suit, snappy white shirt, kinda conservative look. He's staring right at her. For just a moment. Does he recognize her, or is she standing out? Shit. Plain clothes security, maybe? The belt holster that his suit doesn't quite hide puts another notch in that column; you can carry anywhere on the River, but it's not too common on Panorica.

She keeps doing what she's doing, not looking at him directly but sweeping her gaze around in a way that happens to include him. Yep, telltale signatures of the cop package. But he's not looking at her anymore; instead he's heading toward the food pavilions. She's being paranoid. Maybe. Keeping on her best disinterested look should he happen to glance her way again, she calls up public records on him.

Nothing. Oh, terrific. If he's connected to all this, where can she dig, quick? There's got to be something. "Kis," she murmurs under her breath, "see if you can find this guy in Earth or Mars records. Check Earth first." You can't get complete records from the inner planets out here without putting in a request, but basic criminal and public employee information tends to be readily available. Even though the search requires an ansible link it shouldn't be *too* expensive; it's just one request out and another back.

Meanwhile, keep walking. No, sit down, so she doesn't look like she's pacing. She navigates to a chair roughly in the middle of the waiting area and sits down. She can't see everything from here—not without constantly twisting around—but it's as good as view as she's going to find. Oh, look, there's Guy Two. She flips him off.

Kismet chimes in her ear. "Based on image matching, the person whose background you requested has the highest correlation to Jack Thomas, an FBI field agent assigned to Interpol."

What? *Interpol?* The Panorica Federation has a Compact of Free Association with a bunch of inner system governments. But that doesn't give Interpol agents the power to arrest people here, does it? Now that she thinks about it she doesn't think they have the power to arrest people anywhere—they leave that to local law enforcement. He has to be working with Panorica Federation Security.

As he gets in line for coffee, she moves to another bench, this one as close to the boarding checkpoint as she can get. Only eight minutes to the start of loading, and passengers have started to line up, even though they're only in line to move to the seats past the checkpoint—it'll take a full ninety minutes to get everyone on board.

Okay, the real question is *why* Thomas is here. Is he here because of strings Keces pulled? Is he here to stop *her*, because Keces thinks she's about to run to Earth, or do a handoff to a partner? Could he be investigating this entirely independently, and have come to the same conclusions she did about where to catch the thief?

Could he be here for something that has nothing to do with the theft whatsoever?

Gail sighs, leaning back and sipping her own coffee, scanning the crowd. She can see more matches highlighted in the group lined up. Middle-aged woman, frustrated, standing with small crying child. Another businessman with fashion model haircut.

Beedle boop "You have a call from Jason Nakimura of Keces."

Oh, for—

"Connect," she snaps.

"You're at Panorica Spaceport," Nakimura says.

"Yeah. I'm at Panorica Spaceport. Are you monitoring the cameras, or did the asshole who assaulted me report back to you?"

"If you're planning to run, Ms. Simmons, I assure you that—"

"No, you idiot, what I'm planning to do is see if I can stop someone *else* from running, with your databox. Tell your goons to either help me or back off."

"You're asking me to extend an unwarranted amount of trust, Ms. Simmons."

"If it makes you feel better, I don't trust you, either. Look, I'm really pressed for time."

"If I find out—"

"Let's just agree that I feel properly threatened and I'll get on with doing your job for you. I'll try to sound more fearful next call, but could you hold off for at least—" She looks at the boarding time indicator. "—seven minutes?" She cuts the connection before he can respond, and goes back to her quick, fruitless scanning.

A teenager. More businessmen. A young couple oozing newlywed—what, they hadn't announced their *honeymoon* on social feeds? Weird.

She sees Suspicious Detective enter, far off to her right.

Another businessman.

Thomas is visible off to her left again, now with a cup of coffee. He's not looking at her.

A cisform human, about her age, pale skin, scruffy hair, burnt orange faux-leather jacket zipped up like he's cold.

Gail furrows her brow. Something about him—she *knows* him. She calls up the record that goes with the image match, just name and residence.

Randall Corbett.

She feels the blood drain out of her ears. Setting down her latte, she gets up, walking toward the crowd. Walking toward him.

He hasn't seen her yet, hasn't turned in her direction. Even when his gaze sweeps over her he doesn't register who she must be. Not at first. Then his eyes widen and he bolts out of line toward the main concourse.

Gail sprints after him, zigzagging through the crowd, then when the path between him and her gets clear she ramps her speed up. She can't run on overdrive like this for more than a few seconds, but bursting from twenty-five kilometers an hour to seventy closes gaps real fast.

She's only doing the high-speed trick for two seconds tops, and she powers off the biomods before hurtling into him like a furry cannonball. They both skid along the carpet a good four meters. Since she's on top that's worse for him than it is for her. He's in too much pain to resist as she gets her hands around his wrists and pins them against the carpet, straddling him.

"Get off me, you animal bitch!"

She slaps him, restraining herself from ramping it up with biomods. "What the hell have you gotten me into?"

"All I did was give you a tip!"

"Then why'd you run?" Her brain's spinning so fast it's hard to form words. "You saw me and ran because I wasn't supposed to have figured out this much this fast." Or lucked into it this fast. Same effect.

He clenches his jaw, but doesn't say anything.

There are shouts, people running toward them. They're making a scene, aren't they? Time's just about out. She leans down, baring her teeth. "Hand it over. Now."

He flinches, then narrows his eyes and spits on her.

She can tell someone's about to grab her the moment before the arms go around her. As she's hauled to her feet she resists the urge to fight; it's probably someone from PFS. She's right. Those arms have a dark red uniform covering them. Another PFS officer, a leopard, is grabbing Corbett.

"Break it up," the man stepping between them says, unnecessarily, hands out. "Break it up."

Handsome, well-dressed, and oh so square-jawed. Jack Fucking Thomas, fucking Interpol agent.

"She's crazy!" Corbett winces; he's still in pain. She's probably ruined his jacket, but better than his back. "I was just in line and she jumped me!"

She wipes off her face. "Fuck you, Randall."

Suspicious Detective stands near but not *too* near, trying to look like he's not interested in what's happening. She wants to stab him with his cutesy tie tack. Guy Two's disappeared.

"What kind of grudge do you have against me? It's been years!"

What grudge does *she* have against *him*? After he—

"You two know each other. Interesting." He gestures between them. "I saw you chase him. Why?"

"He set me up to take the fall for a theft he's involved with."

"A theft of what?"

"A databox. I'm pretty sure it's on him right now."

"I told you, I don't know—"

Thomas holds a hand up to Randall, keeping his eyes on Gail. "Is the databox yours?"

"No, it's my client's."

"And your client is?"

"I don't think I should get into that now." She glances meaningfully at Randall.

"Ah." Thomas seems to mull that. "Could you both raise your arms and hold still for a search?"

"No! I have to be on that ship!" Randall spits. "Why are you *listening* to her?"

"Because I find Ms. Simmons' story fascinating, Mr. Corbett."

"Come on, you said you saw her jump me! That's assault!"

"I saw her chase you *after* you started running."

"She looked like she was going to come after me. And she did."

"Why?"

"I don't know! Her kind just goes off sometimes!"

She stares across at him. "My 'kind?' Are we talking about women, totemics, salvors, or what? I'd like this on record." The leopard cop holding Randall lowers his ears but doesn't say anything. Randall doesn't, either. He just looks away with a stop-putting-words-in-my-mouth expression.

Agent Squarejaw lifts his brows, then waves with both hands. "Arms up."

She runs a brief calculation in her head. If she's right, the databox is either on Randall or in his luggage, but probably on him. If she's wrong she gets cited for the brawl, and faces a judiciary proceeding and restitution fines.

She raises her arms up high. It's depressing that this is the best outcome she could have hoped for, but work with what you have.

Randall, though, stays motionless. "I know my rights. I don't have to do what you say."

"No, it's my understanding you don't have to even do what *they* say." Agent Squarejaw gestures toward the PFS officers. "But in any resulting court case—or whatever the local phrase is—your lack of cooperation counts against you, doesn't it?" He pulls something out of his jacket pocket: a thin, foldable display. Bringing it to within about ten centimeters of Gail's front, he starts panning it around her.

"What is that?" Randall narrows his eyes. "That's not a standard wave scanner."

"Databoxes are hard to track, but if you have their serial number you can get an acknowledgement ping from them if you're in very close proximity." Agent Squarejaw moves around to Gail's back. "And it just so happens I have the serial number of a missing databox."

Gail studies Randall's face for the micro-expression but the flash of fear isn't micro at all. The cisform cop notices it, too, giving Gail a raised-brow glance.

Agent Squarejaw finishes another pass, down around Gail's legs and sandals, then straightens up and looks at Corbett expectantly.

"You don't have permission to search me!"

Squarejaw looks at the leopard. "Check me on my understanding of your laws here. We're acting on a report about a stolen databox, so we have probable cause for the stop."

The leopard nods. "Yes, sir."

"Ms. Simmons voluntarily submitted to a search, which did not turn the box up on her person. She accuses Mr. Corbett of the theft. Mr. Corbett refuses to submit to a search, and he started to run from her when they recognized one another. Where I'm from, that would be enough grounds for holding him on suspicion of involvement and compelling a search; would it be here?"

"We can hold him," the cisform cop says. "We'll have to clear a search but I don't see why it'd be a problem."

"Excellent." He nods toward the exit. "Let's be on our way."

Chapter 6

THEY DON'T CUFF GAIL'S WRISTS for the walk to the substation. They don't cuff Corbett's, either, but the officer walking with him keeps one hand on his pistol. While he mutters under his breath and glares at her occasionally, he doesn't mouth off to the officers any more. For her part, she does her best to radiate confidence that the PFS will see things her way any moment now.

The path leads them back out of the intersolar concourse, back to the elevators, down to ground level, through doors reading "Authorized Personnel Only." The air inside smells of age and antiseptic. They pass by a few other doors and side corridors, by a few gawking spaceport employees, and through a door with the Panorica Federation Security logo—a slight variant on the same logo the Federation uses everywhere.

Gail and Corbett get guided to separate rooms. The one they leave her in is nearly bare, just a table and two chairs. And, a quick scan confirms, full-spectrum monitoring equipment embedded in one wall. They shut the door behind her, leaving her alone. The noise of the lock sounds calculated to be melodramatic.

"Kis?" she murmurs. No response. The signal's blocked.

Sighing, she drops into a seat, crossing her arms. Even assuming they let her go, now instead of getting the databox away from Corbett, she'll need to get it away from the PFS. That's assuming they even find the databox on him. If they don't, she might as well start making shit up to confess to. By now Nakimura's had to have gotten word back that Gail's been hauled off by the cops. Since the entire point of "hiring" her for this was to keep this out of the legal system, he's already setting his hair on fire.

But Squarejaw had the databox's serial number. Nakimura's the only one that could have come from, isn't he? Who else is there? It'd have made a great delaying tactic for the real thieves if they'd gotten him to intercept her *before* she saw Corbett, but if that had been the plan it sure as hell backfired.

It's twelve minutes and thirty-eight seconds before Agent Thomas comes back in the room. She was counting.

"Sorry to keep you waiting. I wanted to talk to Mr. Corbett first."

"The hospital scent isn't as strong in here, at least."

He takes the seat opposite hers. "I can't smell it at all here."

"You have a human nose."

He leans back and gives her a slight, curious smile. "So do you. You've just made yours look like a mouse's."

"Rat. And there's more to it than that. If you're stationed out here I hope you're going to learn more about totemics."

"Totemics aren't unique to Cerelia River space. There's millions on Earth. My congresswoman's a vixen. Third totemic elected to higher office. I voted for her. And I know the basics. You all start as cisform but you get transformed sometime after birth, with some surgery and a lot of gene therapy. In your case that happened right after you were born."

Given her generation—and her age at transform—almost no surgery for her. She folds her arms. Eventually he'll get to a point.

He keeps his slight smile for another beat, then leans forward. "Ms. Simmons, who's your client?"

There it is. What's the best way to play this? Cards on the table, for now. "Keces Industries."

"So rather than going to law enforcement, they hired you to find a stolen copy of priceless data."

This is going to be a repeat of the conversation with Ansel, complete with the skeptical tone, isn't it? "Do you know much about the way law enforcement works when you're *not* in the Panorica Federation out here?"

"Corporate anarchy."

"All right, that's a 'no.' The judiciaries are private, but they talk to one another, right? Keces has their own judiciary, they've probably at least consulted with them about this, but the moment they do anything that brings in another judiciary, they lose control of the information. It becomes public, searchable. I don't know what's on this databox, but they've been going to insane lengths to keep it all quiet."

"So they wouldn't go to the PFS with information about this theft."

"No. So why are you here?"

"What?"

"Interpol. You're, like, an investigation unit from the Earth police, right?"

"Earth isn't one big government, Ms. Simmons. I'm with the United States Federal Bureau of Investigation, and I've been assigned to Interpol, an international police agency."

"Got it. I just don't understand why you're involved with this."

"You and Mr. Corbett were both waiting on the boarding call of a ship bound for Earth. This theft crosses multiple international boundaries." He steeples his hands in front of him on the table. "Keces is the subject of a Blue Notice. That means they're a person of interest—company of interest, in their case—in a crime reported to Interpol. This makes you a person of interest in that crime."

"Discounting orbital mechanics, I've never been anywhere closer to Earth than I am now."

"I'm aware of that. I've talked to Mr. Corbett, and now I'd like your side of the story."

Gail spreads her hands. "I got a tip from Corbett a couple days ago about a wreck, went to investigate it, and learned about the databox being stolen off it. I came to the spaceport because I figured the real thief had set me up as a distraction, to keep Keces from looking for him. You saw the rest."

As she speaks, he crosses his arms; after she finishes he taps his fingers against his elbow, looking thoughtful. "Mr. Corbett gave you the original tip."

"Yeah."

"That contradicts his story. Can you prove that?"

"No. The call was locked against copying." Also, she's a trusting idiot.

"So why you?"

"I'm trying to figure that out. We're both from New Coyoacán, went to the same school. We got along. I haven't seen him in nearly twenty years. His family moved away after…" Her voice catches unexpectedly and she swallows. "After our mothers died."

He studies her intently a few moments, then looks at his portable display, flipping through virtual pages with a finger. "In the bombing on Solera. That was never officially solved, was it?"

"No."

"His mother was traveling with yours to that demonstration?"

She nods.

He flips through more pages, then sets the display down. "In his telling of the story, he ran because he's afraid of you."

"Because 'my kind' is unstable?"

"Of you specifically, Ms. Simmons. You do have an aggravated assault charge from about ten years ago, one he brought up without prompting. And your history with him is…fraught, based on news reports I've scanned."

Oh, she can feel the heat rising in her ears. "That charge was withdrawn, and I don't have a 'history' with him beyond a few playdates. His mother supported mine in the RTEA. That's it."

"Supporting a radical group can mean a lot of things. Was she giving money? Making signs? Making bombs?"

All at once she's on her feet, chair kicked back hard enough to topple it, hands slammed flat against the table top. She manages to keep her voice just above conversation level, but her tone trembles. "It was a totemic rights organization and I don't care what the hell you think you know, my mother did *not* believe in violence."

Thomas goes quiet again, although there's that eyebrow lift. She closes her eyes, breathing slowly. Good job keeping her temper there. She hasn't had a nightmare about that day for years. She's not seeing it again, right now, not in the frozen moment between what she'd thought were fireworks going off and the start of the screams.

"Ms. Simmons," he finally says, "we received a tip about you, specifically, this morning. I'd been intending to go to your ship, but we saw you come to us here at the spaceport instead. My working theory so far is that you were there to transfer the databox to another courier. Maybe Corbett, but probably someone else, and he just gave you an opportunity to set him up as the fall guy when you noticed me."

"That's the stupidest—" She narrows her eyes. "You found the databox on him, didn't you? I was right."

"Or you've made it look that way."

"I'm not the thief!"

Squarejaw rises to his feet, too. "Sit down."

"I'm—"

"*Sit. Down.*"

She pulls the seat back and drops into it hard.

"Let's get something crystal clear here. One or both of you is going to be charged for grand theft as well as any other crimes committed during the course of the robbery. Depending on who we find at the other end of this conspiracy back on Earth, you may be extradited to the United States, where we do *not* have this private judicial crap. You will make things a *lot* easier on yourself if you tell the complete truth."

She can feel herself blanch under her fur, picturing the floating bodies in the SC71 cockpit. "I have been!"

"Assuming that someone else is paying to have the theft carried out, you *both* have motive. But only you have the connections, opportunity, and means to pull this off."

"That's why I was set up! He's probably the one who tipped you off about me! And what do you know about Corbett's connections, anyway? What's his job?"

"Ms. Simmons—"

"Are you sure he wasn't working with the unflagged courier Keces hired? You haven't had time to check that out yet. I think he might have been the inside guy."

"What inside guy?"

"The databox was taken from a wreck of a passenger ship being used as a private courier, right? Someone on that ship staged the wreck and used the escape pod to get away." She tilts her head. "Keces thinks I did that myself, all without leaving any record somehow, then came back to tell them about it. Does that story honestly make more sense to you then somebody else stealing it and setting me up to make Keces—and you—waste your time with me while they made a getaway?"

"No, it doesn't. I'm not sure it makes much *less* sense, though. None of the information I have contradicts your story, but none of it contradicts Mr. Corbett's, either."

"What about him claiming I tackled him in front of you, two PFS cops and Keces' private detective just to plant evidence on him without any of you noticing? Because we both know that's a really fucking stupid story."

Agent Squarejaw frowns. "Keces had a private detective there?"

"Yeah, he was the blond guy in the overcoat that was too big for him."

He taps his fingers on the table. "If you're working for them why are they surveilling you?"

"They're paranoid." She slumps. "Now they probably think I've secretly been working with you all along because Interpol wants to steal the box for a company back on Earth."

"Given what people here think about Earth politics, that wouldn't be surprising, no." He tilts his head. "So what's on the databox?"

"How would I know?"

He does that slight brow lifting thing once more. She's ready to rip his eyebrows off.

"Look, I don't even have a good guess." She throws her hands out to the side. "Keces sure as hell hasn't told me, and I never had the damn thing, remember? I'm not even sure what it even looks like. Ask Corbett what's on it."

"I have. He gave me two conflicting answers." Reaching into his inner jacket, Agent Squarejaw pulls out a thin, palm-sized black square. At first glance she'd mistake it for a portable display projector. "And it looks like this." He turns it over in his hand. "I've only seen one once before, about ten years ago, and it was a lot bigger. I was told that was deliberate—it was designed to be too big for anyone to easily hide." He puts it back.

"What were his two answers?"

He looks at her silently, letting the question hang. He doesn't have any reason to tell her, but she bets he will. He does. "That he doesn't know, and that it's the end of the human race."

Plans for a weapon? Maybe. That'd fit the picture disquietingly well. "Do you seriously think I hid it on him? You know he's been feeding you lies this whole time. I haven't."

"My suspicion isn't that you're lying. It's that you're not telling me the whole truth."

"Look, I don't have the whole truth. I don't *want* the whole truth. I just want to stop being interesting to the wrong people." She sighs. "I think Keces was transferring that databox to a subsidiary on Panorica, and whoever's responsible for hitting them planned to steal it and take out all the remaining copies. They got away with the last part, but not the first." And whatever the data is, someone thinks it's valuable enough to kill for. She nearly says that aloud, but that'll create even more complications for her with both Agent Squarejaw and Keces.

"Guesses are still guesses, Ms. Simmons, and those guesses don't rule you out as a more active participant than you claim. And I'm still puzzled by how you can be helping out Keces while they're treating you as their number one suspect."

"Because helping them out clears my name." She stops herself from adding *you idiot.* "I can share the recording Kis made of my conversation with their guy. I'm just trying to get my life back to normal."

"A life of being a drifter with no fixed address but her spaceship."

"We all have our own normal. Look, Agent Thomas—can I call you Jack?—Jack, you've solved the case. You found the databox on Corbett and you can charge him with the theft and extradite his ass to Earth. If I take the box back to Keces, everybody wins."

The brows go up higher than she thought they could. "You're *not* seriously suggesting I should simply hand the box over to you."

"Well." She takes a deep breath. "I wouldn't want to break your chain of custody, so maybe you come back to Molinar with me this afternoon and deliver it to them yourself. You know it ends up back with the right owners." Also, she gets a whole lot of money.

"It hasn't been definitively proven that this is even the right databox—"

"How many do you think there are?"

"—and as much as I appreciate you telling me how I should do my job while I'm in your part of space, I need to go over a lot of questions with the PFS officers about not just your role in this but Keces's role. This case started well before yesterday."

Of course. Blue Notice. "So what else can I clear up for you?"

He taps his jacket over the databox. "Why not just put this in someone's pocket on a normal flight? It would have been thousands of times less expensive."

"They're really paranoid."

"Yes, they are. They don't trust you. They don't trust your judicial system. I don't know what that suggests to you, but it makes me question whether the databox—or the data on it—was theirs to begin with."

Didn't she already have a headache? Apparently not, because *that,* that sudden stabbing pain right now, *that* is a headache. She rubs her temples. "You're saying they might be trying to get me to recover something they already stole."

"It's possible."

She waves her hands in front of her, fingers curled like claws, her voice rising. "It still wouldn't be my problem, Jack!" She points at the door. "I was hired to bring this box back to them. Period. Yes, it's possible they stole it first. It's possible that it was never on the ship I found in the first place, or that it was but they were the ones who stole it off the ship from somebody else and they were double-crossed by their own man. All sorts of things are possible and all of them would make fantastic crime shows, but they're all shows I'd like to not be starring in!"

As she finishes she's just about screaming. Agent Squarejaw is staring at her as if she's lost her mind. It's possible.

After a couple seconds pass, he speaks more softly. "Ms. Simmons, if your part in this doesn't extend any farther than what you've claimed, I'll get you back on your way as fast as I'm able to. But the databox can only be released to its actual owners. Those owners may be Keces. But one thing that's certain, however, is that they're not you."

He walks to the door. "I need to talk to the officers in charge. I'll be back in a moment."

Gail slumps down in the uncomfortable seat, staring at the wall.

The moment is closer to three minutes, but she'd been expecting much worse. Squarejaw returns with the uniformed leopard guy. "You're free to go," the leopard says.

She leaps to her feet so fast she nearly misses the rest.

"—to have to stay on Panorica while we complete the investigation."

"What? How long will that take?"

"I doubt it'll take more than a day or two."

"I have a deadline of tomorrow to bring the databox back!"

"Keces will have to understand that the situation's changed," Squarejaw says, tone maddeningly reasonable.

"Let's go to your ship so you can get what you'll need off it before we lock it down," the leopard continues.

"Before—" Gail stares. "You're impounding *Kismet*?"

"We have to temporarily disable the pilot controls and AI."

The leopard's the one who spoke, but she looks back at Thomas, stricken. "You can't do that!"

"That's what I'm told you do here in this situation." He sounds genuinely puzzled at her reaction, like he's doing her a massive favor by turning her ship off instead of throwing her into prison. Like they're not pretty much the same thing.

"That's what they do here to criminals. I *live* on my ship."

The leopard sounds apologetic now, a little uncomfortable. "Restricting movement of suspects under active investigation is standard operating procedure, and we have to do this with someone who owns her own ship. Ms. Simmons, we really will try to make it as fast as we can, I promise."

"She's—she's my home. My job. My assistant for everything. I'm talking with her all the time."

"We have to restrict your ship's movement, too, not just yours."

"You can afford a hotel room, can't you?" Squarejaw remains polite but unsympathetic. He doesn't understand what he's doing to her. Or he's just an asshole. Yes, she can afford a hotel room, although it'll mean she'll run completely out of money in one and a half months instead of two.

"Come on, Ms. Simmons." The leopard motions her to follow him out of the room. She does, ears down.

"That's everything?" the leopard says.

It's not like this knapsack is a *small* bag. It's just not huge. But it's supposed to be only a few days. She checks—for the third time—that she has her old viewcard in there; she's been using Kis as her interface for so long she hopes she can remember how it works. "Yeah, that's everything." She looks around *Kismet*'s cabin again, trying to keep the despair off her face. "Kis, I have to let them turn you off for a while."

"Yes, Gail," the ship responds, oblivious to what that means. But what does it mean? It's not as if the ship's going to resent her over this, resent the cops for making her do it. She can't resent anything. Objectively, Gail knows that. Even calling the ship an AI drives people who actually know about this stuff—people like Ansel—nuts. She's an expert system. Kis can carry on all sorts of conversations, can recall things Gail's told her, can make complex associations and inferences. Within her design parameters, she's smarter than any human who's ever lived. But she won't crack a joke. She won't use metaphors. She'll never start a conversation about anything that isn't ship-related, never show volition. She can't.

None of that makes this less painful.

Gail swallows, resting a hand on the aft bulkhead for a few seconds. "I'll see you soon."

She'd argued with the leopard—irony of ironies, his name is Jon Wolfe—on the way over about how this wasn't necessary, how they could just lock the ship down physically or let her disable just the piloting and auto-piloting controls. He'd just kept repeating it was standard procedure to shut the AI down when a ship's under guard, until she'd finally snapped at him. She'd been under suspicion once before, and they didn't do anything this draconian.

"I bet that was before Carilco," he'd responded simply, and she didn't have a comeback. A ship's expert system *is* the autopilot, and soft switches can be overridden. Ships don't have self-destruct switches like they do in action shows, but it's not hard to give one an order that accomplishes the same thing. It might warn you, but it won't stop you. It won't stop you from, for instance, ordering it to throw its engines wide open while it's still docked. The death toll was close to a hundred, and if Carilco's emergency response systems hadn't worked perfectly it would have been in the thousands. It would have been another Alexandria. Or worse.

The hard switches in the system—the switches she leads Wolfe to now—are all or nothing. He crouches and looks at the panel, studying it a few seconds, then unlocks two of the knobs, pushing them in until they pop back out higher than normal and clicking them to OFF.

Nothing visible changes on the ship, but when *Kismet* goes offline Gail feels the disconnect. It's as hard and physical as the switch. It's like having the world suddenly trip from color to black and white.

Wolfe straightens up, then looks down at her with a concerned expression, putting a hand on her shoulder. "You okay?"

She nods stiffly, wondering what in her expression betrays the lie.

"I'll try to make this go as fast as it can, and when we get any news I'll let you know." He leads her away from the ship, back through the port.

Focus on the business at hand. Don't sniffle. "Is it more your investigation than Agent Thomas's?"

"No, but officially it's my responsibility." His tail flicks behind him in irritation. "Thomas is the new liaison with Interpol, and the databox involves both inner and outer system. So he makes the calls. We can override him, though, and not the other way 'round."

"He seems like he has a rod up his ass." She raises her hands. "I mean that in the most complimentary way possible, officer."

The leopard grins. "He cares about his job. A lot." His tone carries an edge of cynical wonder. "First one I've seen like that from Interpol in eleven years."

They've reached the exit to the port. It's well past sunset; the streetlights wrapping around the inside of Panorica remind her of the Ring's hills. For one peculiar moment she's homesick for them. "Call me if you have any questions or problems, or just want a status update. Otherwise, we'll be in touch shortly."

Gail nods, but can't think of anything else to say. Her throat's closing up.

After a moment of hesitation, he waves awkwardly and heads back into the port building toward his office.

She steps outside, then turns around, staring dully backward as if she could see through walls and crowds, right to the dock she'd just come from. Yeah, that's everything.

Chapter 7

THE PRIVACY DOOR GLIDES SHUT as Gail sits down in the booth, clear glass frosting over. She's tired enough that the hard plastic chair bolted to the wall almost feels comfortable, despite having no allowance for tails. She didn't think she could sleep, went back to another Magnolia Café—a quieter one—and stayed up all night alternating between crying into glasses of cheap wine and watching videos.

And now she's here.

When's the last time she's had to use one of these? Six years ago? Seven? When she wanted—or needed—something with a genuine external display instead of her HUD, she always had *Kismet*. She pulls out her viewcard, holding her finger to it for a second until it powers on and recognizes her, then sets it into the booth's holder. The projector snaps to life, a transparent blue curtain of light with a company logo filling the wall. After taking a deep breath and steeling herself, she makes the call.

The display shifts opaque, connection info scrolling in along the bottom. After several seconds it crossfades to a woman's face, from shoulders up. A wolf woman, full transform, grey fur so dark it stops only a couple shades short of true black. Gail used to joke the white speckled highlights on her muzzle looked like stars. Her mane-like hair's cut shorter on the sides than it used to be, but remains longer in the back. Despite little visible background in the picture she looks physically imposing. She is. She'd be at least as tall as Agent Squarejaw if she were standing by him. Even so, her expression's warm and pleasant. "This is—"

She stops in mid-sentence, green eyes focusing on Gail and widening in clear shock.

Gail tries unsuccessfully not to hunch forward, but she manages a very small smile. "Hello, Sky."

69

The wolf remains silent, still, for several seconds. "Hello, Gail."

She swallows. "I'm sorry about not calling. I know we fought last time, but that's not really a good excuse."

"It's not anything new, either. You look like you've been through a war. What's happened?"

Never one for small talk. She wonders if it's just so plain on her face, or if Sky would tell her the same thing Ansel did, about how she only comes by when she needs help. With Sky that's less often true, but it's a few orders of magnitude more humiliating when it is.

"I just haven't slept much since yesterday. Um. *Kismet*'s been locked down by the PFS and I think Keces Industries is going to report me as *socius indignus*. I think …" Her voice cracks. "I think I'm in a lot of trouble."

The wolf stares silently for three full seconds, then closes her eyes. "Mara's Wounds. Start at the beginning."

She does, starting with the tip and the wreck, the meeting with Nakimura, the confrontation at Port Panorica and the interrogation afterward. She doesn't tell Sky about Adrian—that's none of her business—and doesn't tell her about Ansel blowing her off, because she's still annoyed by it and because it'd remind her that Ansel wanted her to call Sky then. Not that the wolf could have done anything for her then. Not that Gail has any idea what she can do for her now.

"All right." The wolf strokes along her muzzle, and her tone slips into the practiced patient-with-everything cadence that drives Gail nuts. "Even if Keces files a *socius indignus* order against you, your judiciary's going to be able to freeze it immediately. The circumstances that led to this Interpol agent taking custody of the databox were well beyond your control."

She looks down, mumbling just above a whisper. "I don't have a judiciary."

Sky's ears lower. "What?"

"Mine went up to twenty-one hundred a month and I was in a pretty tight spot financially last year, and I get basic services as long as I'm paying Panorica's citizenship fee." So she's paying to fund the PFS, but not to have an advocate against it. "I figured I'd restart when things were, you know, better. They *are* better. Or were until yesterday. I just hadn't gotten around to setting it up again."

She braces for the growl and lecture, but what she gets is far worse. Sky just sags in resigned disappointment, beyond anger or even surprise at how much her little sister's screwed things up again. "Oh, Gail."

"I didn't know any of this would happen!"

"You keep a judiciary on retainer because you never know when something's going to happen. That's the whole point." Oh, *there's* the growl. "Engaging one on demand is far more expensive. And isn't that a good price for that on Panorica?"

God, she just doesn't get it. It's not a bad price, objectively, but that's not the point. With docking fees running about thirteen thousand a month on average—and that's avoiding the more expensive ports—you start making tough choices when your income barely crests thirty thousand a few months in a row. "I didn't. Have. The money."

"I know." Sky's tone drops to miserably, maddeningly sympathetic. "I wish you'd stayed somewhere where every little thing isn't tied to your income."

Which means New Coyoacán. It could mean somewhere else on the Ceres Ring, but they both know she means New Coyoacán, with the big sister she's not related to by blood, the big sister she can't possibly live near—let alone with—anymore. They're adults, they have their own lives, and their paths couldn't possibly have taken them farther apart. Their relationship may be more tenuous separated by a few thousand kilometers, but whether Sky sees it or not, it's a lot more peaceful. "I just want to get *Kismet* released. I want to get the hell out of here."

"How can I help?"

Gail tries not to scream. "I don't *know*, Sky. You tell me. *You're* the mediator. I need you to be *mine*, okay? I need you to—" And all at once she can't keep talking, because she's crying. Hard. She wraps her arms around her sides, looking at the scuffed gray floor.

"Oh, Gail." This time when Sky says it she sounds like she wants to step through the connection into the booth and hug the rat tightly. If she were there, she would, despite all the fights, despite Gail not returning her calls until she took the hint, despite them growing from sisters to near strangers. Somehow that makes it hurt worse. "I don't know what I can do, but I'll make calls to the PFS. I'll see if I can get in touch with Agent—what was his name?"

"Thomas." She sniffles. "Jack Thomas."

"And I'll see what I can find out about Randall Corbett." Her lips pull back from her teeth slightly. A full totemic wolf's jaws are only about three-quarters the strength of a real wolf's, but Sky could still bite your arm off. It'd just take her a few seconds longer. As far as Gail knows she never would, but she'd be fine with people occasionally worrying about the possibility. "He's still being held?"

"I don't know. I can't see why they'd release him." Gail throws herself back in the seat—she bangs her head against the booth's wall, but doesn't care. "God. Why would he do this do me?"

"You know a lot of people believe the bombing conspiracy theories."

"Only people who already hate totemics." But she's right. Those people think the bomb was her mother's, and it went off prematurely. Like most totemics, Gail's sure it was Purity's bomb, catching innocent bystanders along with the hated mongrels. According to others, it was the PFS, or one of a half-dozen Earth governments, or a secret society. "Jesus, his mother worked side-by-side with mom. He knew our family. He knows that's bullshit."

"People change. We both know how hard losing your mother that way, at that age, is. Randall left very shortly after that, didn't he? His father moved away from Ceres entirely." Disapproval rings in the wolf's tone, as if leaving the Ring is, in and of itself, sufficient evidence to condemn Corbett of multiple crimes.

Gail can't keep an edge of challenge out of her tone. "I moved away from Ceres entirely, too. Somehow I haven't found myself joining any hate groups."

"No, but you've found yourself in their crosshairs at least once before." She sighs. "And you've spent a decade on the edge of constant poverty."

"I've made good money some years. Can we not do this again for once? It's my choice, just like your life is yours."

Sky shakes her head, looking away from the camera. "You've made a life of not making choices."

"No, I've made a life of not settling down. That's a choice. It's just not yours. Besides, I don't see your spouse and one point three children, either."

"That's not a fair comparison."

"Yeah, Sky, I think it is. You're married to your noble calling and I'm married to my ship." So do your noble job and get my ship out of prison. Please.

The wolf bares her teeth slightly again, but doesn't look at Gail when she does so. She doesn't say anything for a few long seconds. When she turns back to the camera her tone's back to zen calm. "I'll talk to my PFS liaison and, if I can, speak directly with Agent Thomas. And I want you to come here."

Gail squeezes her eyes shut momentarily, trying to stave off wolf-induced headache. "I don't have *Kismet*, remember?"

"There are other ships you can hire. I just think this is the safest place for you right now. If you're here, it's much easier to deal with Keces. The *socius indignus* threat goes away—"

"You know damn well I don't get magic protection from being in New Coyoacán. They'll file it no matter where I am. If I'm there it just means you get to deal with it."

The temperature in Sky's voice rises. "Since you don't have a judiciary, it looks like I'll be dealing with it no matter what."

"Then maybe you shouldn't ask me to do exactly what the PFS and Agent Thomas have told me not to do, all right? I'm a suspect in an inter-solar theft. I'd like to try not to do anything excessively suspicious, like running off somewhere outside the Panorica Federation's jurisdiction."

"I'm just trying to help you, which I remind you that you asked for."

Gail clenches her fists, keeping them too low for the camera to see. Yes, she did, and if she demands Sky only help her on her own terms that kind of makes her a shit. But it's been almost fifteen years since she bought her ship over Big Sister's objections, and Big Sister can damn well get over it. "Sky. I am not leaving *Kismet* behind. That's not an option. Got it?"

Sky turns away and growls loudly. It's not a guttural groan, not a human voice doing a passable dog imitation. It's a full-on, inhuman snarl. It's the kind of noise that reminds you her normal speaking voice isn't *normal* by any conventional definition; canid totemics don't form sounds the way cisform humans and short-muzzled totemics do. It's the kind of noise that, if it's directed at you from right up close, might just make you pee yourself. Gail knows that noise well, and even she can't stop her ears from pinning back.

"Yes," Sky finally says, still looking off to the side. "I'll do what I can to dig you out of your hole from here. Try not to dig any more in the meantime."

"What's that—"

The video abruptly returns to translucent blue nothingness. Sky's ended the call.

Gail stares dully for a few seconds, then slides her viewcard back in her pocket and stomps out of the booth.

*   *   *

Milliaire Park's always breezy. She's never been sure if it's a naturally occurring weather pattern—Panorica's interior is big enough for systems to form, although she's never seen more than a drizzle falling from a haze above—or if it's artificial. She suspects it's artificial, and she wishes they'd turn the damn wind down because her smartpaper keeps trying to blow out of her hands.

She's scribbling down numbers, a quick budget for the next few days. Normally *Kismet* acts as her interface, but since that's not an option now, she's writing commands on the smartpaper itself. While her HUD could display the information, some things are easier to think about when they're in front of you instead of imprinted on your retina.

The paper shows how much money she has on hand, and what the rates are for hotel rooms that are cheap but still in totemic-safe parts of the arcology. That's most parts—nearly all parts—but not all of the safe parts are affordable parts. Hmm. The Martinson. She's seen that one. Edge of the neighborhood Ansel lives in, so it's safe, and at eighteen fifty a night not *too* expensive. Her budget says she shouldn't go over seventeen hundred a night, but it looks like the rate includes a breakfast credit at a lobby autocafé.

She scribbles out a purchase order for three nights. After another second, DECLINED appears by it in red ink.

She stares at it. Declined? She has *way* more money than that. After a moment she scrawls "call" by the hotel name.

Beedle boop "Hello, Hotel Martinson, Tobias speaking. How may I help you?"

Her HUD's displaying his name already, of course, just like his display—probably in front of him rather than in him—shows hers. "Hey. I just tried to make a reservation for three nights and got declined."

"Yes, I see that, Ms. Simmons. Hold on a moment and I'll see if I can find out what happened." A pause for about five seconds. "It looks like there's a restriction on your bank account limiting the transaction amount we can run."

"What? Who put it there?"

"I'm sorry, I don't have that information."

"Can you run it as three separate transactions? One for each night?"

"I can try." Tobias sounds dubious. After another couple of seconds pass she can just about hear him shaking his head. "No, a single night doesn't work, either."

"Can you break it into smaller transactions somehow? I have the money."

"I don't have a way to do that, Ms. Simmons. I'm sorry. Do you have a different line of credit?"

Her credit right now might buy her a sandwich if she doesn't go wild with the condiments. "I'll check and get back to you." She cuts the call off before Tobias says anything else polite, then starts another one, interrupting the voice prompt almost before it starts. "PFS office, Interpol agent Jack Thomas."

Beedle boop "Ms. Simmons," Agent Squarejaw says. "How can I—"

"What the hell do you think you're doing with this block?"

Momentary silence. "What block?"

"The block on my spending account. How am I going to book a hotel room if I can't spend eighteen-fifty at once? I don't even know how low it is. Can I book a flophouse? Can I buy a soda?"

"Hold on." She hears muted voices as he talks to someone else. "I don't have the authority to block your accounts myself, Ms. Simmons, and I haven't put in such a request. Officer Wolfe hasn't, either. Have you tried contacting your bank?"

Wolfe cuts into the conversation. "It looks like it's a hold initiated at the request of a judiciary. You've got a one thousand per-diem limit, and a holder-present requirement for any purchase over two hundred. You don't have any outstanding warrants or judicial cooperation requests, do you?"

"No. No." She tugs on her ears with both hands until it hurts. "It's got to be Keces, then."

"Ms. Simmons," Thomas says, "can I let Officer Wolfe handle this with you? I've got to take an ansible call with my Interpol supervisor."

"Yeah. Sure." While she'd like to yell at him more, an ansible call means serious business; a five-minute voice call costs about as much as a night at the Martinson. If they'd let her book one.

Wolfe speaks again after another couple seconds. "I've pulled up the details on the hold and your account's been flagged for possible fraud. That doesn't mean you're being accused of fraud, it means—"

"I know what it means. It means Keces is screwing with me."

"Restricting outflow is a standard way of handing possible account compromises."

She gestures angrily with her hands, even knowing he can't see it. "My account isn't compromised! It was just fine this morning!"

"Have you tried to buy anything over one thousand dollars recently?"

"I don't know. Not for a few days. But fixing this sort of thing doesn't *take* a few days. It's hours. Come on."

"Usually, but not always." The leopard sounds genuinely apologetic. "I wish I could do more, but this isn't related to any of our actions and you're not even using a Panorican bank."

She isn't using one for the same reason a lot of people don't, because other platforms aren't subject to Panorican banking oversight and offer higher interest rates and bonuses. On the flip side, it might be harder for a Panorica bank to put this kind of hold on her money.

"So I have to find a hotel with rooms under one thousand a night? How?"

"There's some out there." He's clearly doing his best to sound encouraging. "The Travelers' Inn right by the spaceport usually runs a special for nine hundred a night."

The misery in her voice grates on her own ears, but damn it, things are miserable and she's miserable and that's that. "Great. I'm sure their rooms are fantastic." She cuts the call.

Yes. Great. What now? She can call Nakimura and yell at him, but if he's responsible for this he's not going to start playing nice no matter what she says. If he *isn't* responsible, she'll just be antagonizing him unnecessarily. Granted, it's not like they're on one another's good sides now anyway.

She checks out information on the Travelers' Inn. Even the photos that come up on the paper look grey and sad. If that's the best they could come up with for a glamor shot, it doesn't bode well. After another moment, though, she sees it's immaterial: the place is sold out tonight.

This just gets better and better, doesn't it? She groans, slumping back on the park bench and closing her eyes.

The smartpaper blows free from her hands.

"Fuck," she says aloud, without moving.

Has this elevator always made that hum? She doesn't think so. But as it traverses the five floors between the lobby and Ansel's apartment, she picks up a definite soft buzz, kind of a low "C" note, maybe a hundred-thirty hertz. How could she have missed it before? It makes her grind her teeth the whole way up.

The door slides open and she strides down the hallway, hoping that moving with forceful purpose will keep her nerves settled. It doesn't. By the time she reaches his door she's trembling. It takes her two tries to touch her fingers to the calling panel.

A couple seconds pass before the little green camera light, tastefully invisible unless recording, switches on. Ansel's voice comes over the speaker. "Gail? What—" His voice clips sharply enough she can't tell if it's an audio glitch.

"Ansel?"

The door slides open, and Ansel's there, a one-piece turquoise wrap draped over his form in a way only a fashion model should be able to get away with, unfeigned dismay creeping over his face. Before she can say anything he's got his arm around her, guiding her into his living room. It looks like it belongs in a fashion ad, too, straw-blond polished stone floor, color-splash throw rugs, modern furniture that somehow manages to look minimal and plush simultaneously. "What happened?"

Mara's Blood, she must look worse than she'd thought. She thought she'd been holding it together better than that. "They locked down my ship and I can barely get any money out of my bank account and I can't get a hotel room and I almost had the databox but I lost it."

The fox gets her to sit down on the couch. "Slow down, dear. Start over."

Squeezing her eyes shut and forcing herself to take a steady breath, Gail runs through the last twenty hours or so. Ansel looks sympathetic at the right points, although he looks reproachful when she talks about the fight with Sky. Fortunately he's tactful enough not to say anything. Yet.

"All right." Ansel rocks back and forth on the sofa by her, looking at the ceiling as he thinks. "You didn't mention calling your contact with Keces."

"God, what am I supposed to tell him? His damn databox is with the police now. It's not like he doesn't know, anyway. He was having me watched and he's got to have trackers on public feeds searching for me, too."

"First, that's out of your control. Second, for all we know he's the one who called the PFS on *you*, because he thought you were running. If he's not happy they have the box, it's on his head, not yours. You did a much better job than the guys he actually hired, didn't you?"

She runs a hand through her hair. "I guess."

"So call him. Get out of this deal."

She starts to ask Kis to place the call, then remembers. Jesus, she's been through this already once today. Come on. The viewcard gets fumbled back out of her pocket. After it lights up, she gathers her resolve and swipes through her contacts, tapping the voice-only connect button by his name.

It takes longer than usual for Nakimura to answer. He doesn't sound angry this time. He sounds subdued. "Ms. Simmons. I've just finished a conversation with Agent Thomas."

"Since he was there waiting for me at the spaceport, I'm guessing it wasn't your first one. I know you don't trust me, Jason, but today might have gone a lot better for both of us if you had."

"In point of fact, that *was* my first conversation with Agent Thomas. Interpol is involved because a company on Earth claims the databox was stolen from them."

Oh, terrific. Squarejaw's crazy suspicions might be right. "So was it?"

He sighs, long and drawn out. "No, it was not. Quanta Biotechnics has made a claim on the data set the box contains."

"So the *data* was stolen from them."

Ansel tilts his head. He's only hearing her side of the conversation, so this has to be mysterious.

"Again, no. The matter is … complex."

"And you're not at liberty to get into it. Which is fine, because I really don't want to know." She rubs the back of her head. "Look, I did my best, and I'd say I did better than your people did."

"My 'people,' Ms. Simmons, did not start a fight in front of an Interpol agent that resulted in the PFS taking possession of the databox."

Her ears lower. "And if they hadn't been harassing me every step of the way, I might have been able to get the box before Thomas did."

"I fail to see how."

"Look, I'm sorry about the box, but you've got enough information to know I wasn't part of the theft and to know there's nothing else I can do. Are we good now? I go about my life, you remove my account block?"

"Account block?"

"The spending restriction order with my bank."

"Any difficulties with your financial institution are not our doing. Despite what you may think, I would prefer the quixotic mission you profess to be undertaking to be successful. And no, we are not 'good.' You've not only failed to fulfill your contract, you've turned this from an internal affair into a multi-agency law enforcement investigation."

"They were already investigating you!"

"My assessment stands. You have twenty-two more hours."

"Jesus—" Don't panic. Think. "Look. Give me more time. Two or three more days. I've been set up and so have you. And from what you're saying, Quanta's a prime suspect, right? Someone wanted you to focus all your attention on me while the real thief got away. You know that, and Agent Thomas knows that. We just have to get to the bottom of this."

He remains silent.

"At this point what do you have to lose? Wrecking my life doesn't get you any closer to getting your data back, and Thomas has more reason to deal with me than he does with you, because he knows I've been telling the truth." Mostly.

The time between when she finishes speaking and he finally answers stretches out like space between the stars. "An additional two days, then, Ms. Simmons. Understand that if you don't deliver the databox by then, you'll have failed to deliver on this contract twice, and that will be documented when we file the *socius indignus* order." He disconnects.

Ansel's staring at her, expression shocked, incredulous. "Did you just promise to get the databox back from the PFS and delivered to Keces within two days?"

She musters a wan smile. "That's the extension, so I think I have a full three."

He looks up at the ceiling. "Mara's Wounds, Gail."

She covers her face in her hands.

Chapter 8

"How did you learn to *do* any of this?" Gail's leaning on the countertop that separates Ansel's living room from his kitchen, watching him splash golden wine over chicken and mushrooms and trying not to drool at the scent billowing up with the steam. She'd forgotten his apartment had a full, real kitchen, although she recalls—now—that she's had the same *oh my God, your apartment has a kitchen?* reaction each time she's noticed before.

Ansel looks up from the stove. "Haven't we had this conversation before? Your house on New Coyoacán had a kitchen? How much you loved your mother's, what was it, Pasta Aztec?"

"Pastel Azteca. Yeah, although at this point I barely remember much more than the name. Still never saw it on a menu out here, Sky never learned to cook it, and once we moved we just had your standard little kitchenette."

He wrinkles his muzzle as he stirs the chicken. "With just a combochef, yes." He holds up a hand. "And they're fine if you're going to live just on prepared meals, and I'm sure they're a step up from whatever cartridge-based monstrosity you have on your ship. But you need a real meal."

"Hey, those prepared meals are real." She sags. "And I need a real drink."

"I'm going to pour you a nice glass of wine to go with your chicken marsala and you're going to enjoy both of them."

"Yes, sir."

He waves his stirring spoon at her. "Sit." She does.

In a few more minutes he's got two plates on the counter, the marsala over pasta, broccoli on the side. Even the broccoli smells delicious and she hates broccoli. Either Ansel should be running a restaurant, or she's so starving she'd eat cardboard. A glass of white wine gets set down next to her plate, another by Ansel's. Then he sits down on the stool next to hers.

She takes a sip of the wine; it's good, fruity and a little caramelly without being candy sweet, but she doesn't have a very educated palate. The chicken, though, is good beyond words. She hasn't been able to afford food like this in months herself, and she doesn't have any friends who cook.

Wait, that can't be right. She has a lot of friends. Some of them must cook. Does she just never visit them?

"Hmm?"

Gail turns at Ansel's questioning noise. "What?"

"You're frowning. Don't you like it?"

"Oh, God, I love it. Your cooking is amazing." She starts to add *I should come over more often,* but he already thinks she takes advantage of him, doesn't he? And she kind of is right now. Again. She'd do the same for him if their situations were reversed, but he's never going to be in a situation like this.

Okay, while he's beaming, she should change the subject to something that won't give her a chance to wallow in self-pity. She takes another bite of chicken, then waves the fork. "How's your contract going?"

"It's … I suppose it's coming along splendidly, it's just deathly boring. More marketing mining work."

"That's most of what you do, isn't it?"

"I'm afraid so. They're the people who pay the most, because they're the ones who need to keep adjusting the tuning all the time."

That's a war that started generations before either of them were born: finding new ways to get ads in front of people who keep finding new ways to stop ads from being put in front of them. Ansel's worked both sides of the fence.

He gets through about two-thirds of his meal—he's eating faster than she is—and then leans back, sipping his wine and looking thoughtful. "On the call with your contact, you said 'Quanta.' Quanta Biotechnics?"

She nods. "Yeah. You've heard of them?"

He laughs. "So have you. You've just forgotten the name. They were the original biomodification company."

That was at least a century ago, around the time the unmanned asteroid mining that led to the River had just started. She thinks. It's not like she'd ever been a good history student. She starts to reach for her viewcard, then remembers. Her eyes widen. "They transformed Mara."

He nods. "It was about half surgery back then." He shivers melodramatically.

"And effectively no surgery by our generation. I guess that's why they lost out to Keces and others."

He waggles a hand in a sort-of gesture. "They didn't lose to Keces, they sold the business to them. And while Keces has made a lot of refinements, there haven't been huge leaps in decades. Quanta's still giant, but just in the inner system. Government contracts. Defense and medical."

She frowns again, and sips her wine, mimicking the way Ansel does it, with the little swirl. He makes it look elegant, but she's pretty sure she just looks goofy.

Finding you, specifically, involved after multiple attacks against Keces, all focused on this project…

Her, specifically, the daughter of a totemic rights activist. This project, with the two most important companies behind transformation technology fighting over it?

"This has something to do with us, Ansel. With totemics."

Ansel gets a brooding expression. "Maybe. It doesn't have to be that specific. There's a lot of other ways the work that went into making us could be used. But none of the patents from back when they divested that group are still valid, even on Earth. Unless they're licensing new work to Keces, they're trying to get their hands on research that isn't theirs."

"Yeah." She rubs the back of one of her ears, then her eyes widen. "Shit. And that's what the Blue Notice is for."

"The what?"

"Plan A was getting Randall on that ship back to Earth. Plan B is convincing Interpol that the databox belongs to Quanta and having *them* take it back to Earth."

The fox raises his brows. "Huh. Or Interpol knows the truth and doesn't care. Earth states are legendary for taking orders from big companies."

"Either way, it's a genius plan. Get the police to steal something for you."

"You sound envious."

She grunts. "It's a brilliant con. It's the part about it destroying my life I'm less thrilled by." This all fits, but would Agent Squarejaw go along with it voluntarily? Wolfe said Thomas genuinely cares about his work. If he's truly honest, he's the key to turning it around. How can she convince him he's being used as a patsy?

Now Ansel's expression gets thoughtful-moody instead of broody-moody. He gets up and heads over to his desk. As he sits down, the curved holographic display flickers on, and his hands play over the control keyboard.

Gail follows him, carrying her wine glass. "What are you checking on?"

"I want to see if I can find anything recent that connects Quanta to either Keces or your friend Mr. Corbett. Meanwhile, you still haven't talked to your bank about your account restrictions, have you?"

"I hate talking to my bank. Unless they call you, you just get an automated assistant."

He rolls his eyes. "Oh, you have one of *those* banks."

"There's no fees!" That's not true, strictly speaking. There's a sliver of a percent charged by the bank for any transaction that involves currency conversion, and only about half the River's adapted the Panorica dollar. But it happens so transparently nobody pays much attention.

"And this is why. Pull up a chair and use your own window if it's easier."

Sighing, she does so, using her viewcard to make the connection.

The bank's expert system expands on the story she got from Officer Wolfe. Her old bank on Carmona reported her account as involved with fraudulent activity, but there's no detail about whether they think she's perpetrator or victim, so her bank's limited access to "protect" her funds. Apparently her lack of judiciary hung the process until she got upset enough to follow up.

The resolution form is simple to fill out but tedious, filled with incorrect assumptions, starting with the notion that she's either a Carmona resident or regularly does business there. She hasn't been back in years, though, not since—

"Tom." She groans, holding her head in her hands.

"Who?"

"Tom Laurel. An amp dealer who used to come into the coffee shop back on Carmona. I hadn't seen the guy in years, not until breakfast yesterday morning when he spotted me and tried to get in on the scam he thinks I'm running. I blew him off, he *really* wasn't happy about that, and this block comes up a day later based on reports from a bank where?"

"Carmona." He shakes his head. "Does he really have that kind of pull?"

"He 'knows people in the banking system.'" She makes air quotes with her fingers. "He probably dealt to somebody in the fraud department. On top of everything else going wrong over the last two days, a guy I barely know is screwing with me because I hurt his little drug-addled feelings. Jesus."

"I know you don't have a judiciary on retainer anymore, but there are charity ones who can take this on for you, especially if you can make the case this is based on prejudice." His ears perk. "Call the RTEA. They'd bend over backwards for you."

They'd try, but this is out of their bailiwick. She could ask Sky, because *that* will go well. "I'll see who I can find. Have you got anything on Quanta we can use?"

He looks back at his windows. "Not yet, honestly. There's nothing public that connects them to Corbett. He doesn't work for one of their subsidiaries or affiliates."

"There's got to be one. What company does he pilot for?"

He swipes through a few windows. "He's not a pilot at all. He's an antique furniture restorer on Solera."

She feels her face blank out. "He moved to the platform our mothers were killed on."

"It could just be a coincidence." Ansel's bushy tail droops.

"No." She shakes her head. "Solera's always been one of Purity's biggest strongholds. Sky was right—he blames my mom for the bomb. And me. That's why he dragged me into this."

Ansel snorts. "Well, that hasn't worked out for him too well yet, has it? But so far I can't connect him to Quanta, and I don't see anything that connects him to Purity, either."

"It's there, trust me. They're mostly quiet under their own name, but front groups pop up."

He tilts his head. "I thought you made a point not to keep up with this."

"I make a point not to be involved with the politics, but I also make a point not to be a target. That hasn't been working out for me too well, either."

He grins wryly, and keeps scanning. "Hmm. Corbett keeps his privacy mirrors pretty open, but there's nothing obvious here. He attends a church that isn't known for being anti-totemic, he's a regular at a bar that must be near his home, he volunteers with the Lantern Foundation."

"Which is?"

"Hold on." More swiping and scrolling. "A charity. They give out grants on historical preservation, medical research, and social welfare."

"Dig into them." What else is she missing? "And I want to find out more about the courier company. Somebody working with Quanta got on that ship and got the databox to Randall."

"What's your 'friend' at Keces told you about that operation?"

"Almost nothing. But I don't think he's lying when he said they didn't own the ship. They just hired it."

"So he can tell you the courier company."

"If he knew it, he wouldn't have agreed to let me help."

"How could he not—"

"Pay through a laundry relay, transfer the databox using a dead drop somewhere with no public feeds. It's all set up so that nobody ever has to meet in person or do anything that leaves a verifiable data trail."

"I don't want to know how you know this, do I?"

She grins. "I'll spare your delicate vulpine sensibilities."

"Ha ha. If it's all set up so neatly, what's there to take a look at?"

Good question. What else… hmm. "Physical evidence. We have the wreck itself, right? So maybe we start there." She calls up the video and telemetry info from her data store—accessible from anywhere, since she's not paranoid enough to use a databox. She wonders if she will be before much longer.

As Ansel scans the data, his expression grows exasperated. "There's no identifying information here."

"Kind of the point of an unflagged courier."

He sighs exaggeratedly. "Yes. Thanks." He flips through other windows from her data. "Now this might be identifying information. The pilots."

She frowns, looking over his shoulder. Shit, why didn't she think of them? She never even looked up the taxi service one worked for. "So what can we connect them to?"

"First, see if we can connect them to one another." His fingers start flying over control panels, windows whizzing around. Sometimes she thinks he does that more to show off than to be useful. "This ship had to have been berthed somewhere. If we can put them near one another and near it, we can correlate them with possible candidates for our inside man. But how do we find a dark courier's home port, Ms. Salvor? Look for reports of ships with no registration showing up at docks?"

"Maybe, yeah. Only a few ports would be willing to handle that, it won't be an operator that has offices in Panorica, and it's sure as hell not going to be a Keces-run port. And you only need to look for SC71s."

He types out a few commands, leans back, and waits. And waits. Just as she gets antsy enough to think about saying something, he shakes his head. "Nothing."

"Okay, that means they have their own private port. I kind of expected that."

"So what now? Trace every single SC71 built from the day they left the factory to today?"

"Can you do that?"

Ansel grimaces. "I was being sarcastic. But let's see." He taps on his keyboard, swipes more windows around with his hands. "This will take time. They've been making the SC71 for over four decades and they've made over two thousand."

She gets up and looks over his shoulder. "No, you're looking at the total for the whole SC7x line." She points. "Don't look at the SC70 or SC75, and this one was built for River use rather than inner system, so it's an SC71-200."

"Okay, captain." After a moment he leans back, frowning at a window. "That's still a little under five hundred ships, and there's three hundred fifty-four in service." He pauses and looks at Gail. "But it's going to be one of the ones that *isn't* listed in service, right?"

"Right. And not documented as definitively sent for scrap. You need to find the ones in limbo."

"Documents can be faked, so I'd need to look for anomalies."

She nods, leaning over his shoulder again.

Ansel reaches up and touches his finger to her nose. "This isn't just pressing a button, dear. I'm going to have to build a data constraint set and keep fine tuning it as I go."

"That's what you do, isn't it?"

"Yes, and if you weren't a friend I'd be charging four thousand an hour for it. This is going to run late, and I'll warn you that I *am* going to go to sleep in"—he looks up at a circle on the wall over the desk—"two and a half hours."

She looks at the circle, too. She's seen it before but she's never *looked* at it. "That's a clock?"

"You've never seen an analog clock? The short needle points at the hour and goes around twice, the long needle—"

"I know how they work." She still has to study it a few seconds to figure out what it's telling her. "That's a really imprecise way to say it's twenty thirty-five."

"Sometimes imprecision is just what you need. You're welcome to go watch a video or something to pass the time."

That's Ansel-ese for *please stop sitting here bothering me while I work.* Got it. "Okay, thanks." She gets up and heads back to the sofa.

Buzzbeep

Gail's eyes drag open. Is that an alarm, something wrong with the ship she needs to tend to? No, she's not on her ship. It's not an alarm.

At least, it's not an alarm she's used to. That doesn't mean it isn't one.

She sits up. She'd fallen asleep on Ansel's couch after watching the most recent episode of *Other Suns,* and the mild annoyance that his sofa feels more comfortable than her bunk on the ship returns. When this is all over she'll buy a new mattress.

Buzzbeep

She can't tell if they're coming at regular intervals, but she doesn't think so. That's the third alarm chirp she's heard, and the first two were closer together than the second and third. So these are individual events.

Ansel's not at the desk anymore, but he's walking out of his room, wearing a bathrobe and a worried expression. He glances up at the wall clock, and she follows his gaze. It's…six…eleven…six fifty-five? No, the short needle moves continuously, just really slowly, right? So five minutes until six. That is *such* a stupid way to tell time.

He glances at her now, and she keeps her voice low. "What is that?"

"Someone's trying to physically break in. Each of those beeps is a vulnerability probe against the lock software." He heads past her toward the desk and sits down. After a few seconds of his fingers flying over the control surface, a display window flickers on, showing the view of the hallway outside. Empty. "Hmm. They've got to be somewhere close by, or have someone working with them who is." The camera view changes to other angles on the hallway, then the ground level elevator foyer, just as empty.

Buzzbeep

Ansel types something. The light in the room changes; it takes her a second to realize the indicator lamp by the door has shifted from red to green. Oh crap oh crap. "They just unlocked the door!"

"No, I did. But hopefully they *think* they did."

"I hope you know what you're doing."

"So do I." He brings up four of the camera view windows in a two-by-two grid. "I'm glad I have you here to protect me."

Before she can figure out an appropriately caustic response, she sees in his expression that he's not kidding. He really *does* expect she can protect him. So she just takes a deep breath and nods.

Someone appears on one of the cameras, hurrying out of a stairwell she didn't know existed. They're wearing a black hoodie and looking down, so she doesn't get a chance to see the face, but they look—familiar.

Ansel's hands swipe over the surface. The green light flickers to red again.

Barely two seconds later, he's in front of the apartment door, reaching out to put a hand on the lock panel. He doesn't look directly ahead, but enough of his face is visible for her to make an ID.

"That's Randall!"

"What? Isn't he still being held?"

Corbett tries the touch sensor several times, getting visibly angrier, less careful. His full face is visible for a second when he raises his fist like he's about to pound on the door, thinking better of it at the last moment.

"He should be." This can't—Agent Squarejaw knows Corbett's with the real thieves. He *knows* that. Does that mean Squarejaw's with the real thieves? Was he just lying about it all? But if that's the case, he could have found an excuse to just keep holding her. Even though you can't do that in Panorica, there's got to be some kind of damn Earth law he could—

The touch on her shoulder makes her jump, but of course it's just Ansel. "He's gone."

"But he's out and he was *here*. What the hell is he coming after me for? How did he find me here?" She's standing up, voice rising. "You have your privacy mirrors wide open, don't you?"

Ansel's ears lower. "Compared to *you*, yes, but I don't broadcast who's sleeping over. Anyone doing a search on you might find you in my history at Acceleration last night, and if they're searching for you they might be watching me. Or put a watch for you on publicly accessible cameras around this area."

"He's not smart enough to figure that out on his own." Is he?

"That's only one level of association. I can think of a dozen off-the-shelf trackers that can do that. And I hate to point this out, but you haven't seen him since you were both teenagers. You don't know how smart he is."

"That's great. Thanks. That's great." She wraps her arms around her head, bending her left ear painfully. That's okay. It makes her more awake. "God. I need to—" Need to what? How does she feel safe now, no matter what she does? Go back to New Coyoacán somehow, despite what she said to Sky, despite knowing how it'd look to the PFS? How it would look to Keces?

She strides back to the couch and rifles through her jacket for her viewcard, activating a link to the PFS station, again barely waiting for the prompt. "Officer Wolfe."

Ansel gives her that raised-brow *oh, really?* look. Before she can decide how deep to make her scowl, a cheerful female voice comes on the line. "Panorica Federation Security, front desk. Officer Wolfe isn't on duty currently. How can we help you, Ms. Simmons?"

"Then get me Agent Thomas. The Interpol liaison."

"He's not going to be in for at least two hours, Ms. Simmons. What can I help you with?"

"Maybe you could find out for me why the thief you were holding yesterday for extradition back to Earth is out now."

The woman's voice stays polite but gets much less cheerful. "I'll see what information I'm cleared to give you."

"Why don't *I* give *you* some information? Like how he was trying to break into where I'm staying right now about five minutes ago."

She can just about hear the woman's mouth opening and closing. "Are you—may I pull up a feed from the closest exterior cameras?"

Gail swipes on her card to bring up output controls, and switches the audio out of her ear and into the desk speakers. "Ansel, can you send her a shot of Corbett at the door?"

The fox nods. "Sure." He brings up the video window again, swipes his finger in the air along the image's base until it's showing Randall approaching. Tap, swipe forward a few seconds, tap. Then he types something. "Sent."

"It should be on its way."

Officer Frontdesk sounds mumbly-flustered. "Thank you. I'll send this to Officer Wolfe. And to Agent Thomas. Can you stay on the line?"

"It's not like I'm not going outside any time soon."

She clears her throat. "Someone will be with you in just a moment." Music starts playing.

Ansel makes a face and lowers the volume. "Are you sure looping them in this was a good idea? These are the people who let Corbett go and who think Quanta's the victim instead of the perpetrator. They're not on your side."

"I don't know if anyone's on my side. But they're the only ones who know why that lunatic is out there," she stabs a finger at the door, "instead of with them."

The music keeps playing. Gail grunts. "I'm gonna get some coffee, if that's all right."

"What do I say if they come back on the line?"

"Say I'm getting coffee." She heads to the kitchen, ignoring Ansel's pointed sigh, and rummages through cabinets until she finds a mug to shove at the beverage dispenser. He insists coffee tastes better in ceramic, so his machine doesn't deign to print containers. It's a wonder it's as automatic as it is.

Its display comes on, but nothing happens. She leans over, squinting at it. Voice command. "Coffee. Uh, black."

The machine responds in a chatty-cheerful male voice. "Central American, African or Mountain style?"

Seriously? From her time back at Brio she knows those refer to geographic regions on Earth, even if "Mountain" seems suspiciously generic. But if this coffee isn't synthetic, it's from the Ceres Ring. None of the arcologies grow it and importing it from Earth would be insane. "What's the difference?"

The machine doesn't answer. *Kismet* would be able to, and you'd think the expert system in a coffee machine would know more about coffee than the one in a spaceship. "Central American." She's thinks that's the darkest roast.

Satisfied, the machine chimes an acknowledgement. The display lights up with the words INFUSING: 90 SEC LEFT. It didn't take that long at Brio. God, even Ansel's coffee machine is a prissy perfectionist.

She pokes her head back out of the kitchen. Ansel's reading a display. The hold music's still playing. The coffee has another eighty-two seconds.

After the drink pours out into her mug, she stomps back toward the desk. "You have the slowest coffee machine I've ever seen."

"There's only so fast you can make coffee."

"*Kismet* makes coffee in ten seconds!"

"She makes bad coffee in ten seconds."

"C'mon, this isn't that much better." She takes a sip and her brows go up. Annoyingly, it *is* that much better. It's better than the non-espresso coffee they served at Brio. Ansel doesn't say anything, but his expression is pure smug vindication.

Another two sips of coffee and the music abruptly stops. "Ms. Simmons." Officer Wolfe. "What's happening?"

"Other than you guys letting Corbett go so he can stalk me? Not much."

"He was still in custody when I went off-duty yesterday." There's some frantic tapping noises. "We were told Corbett wasn't a person of interest in the case Interpol was investigating, but we were holding him in our investigation. He was released on bail around midnight last night."

"Someone paid bail for him? Who?"

"Even if I had that information I couldn't tell you. But keeping his distance from you was an explicit condition of bail."

"The guy who framed me for theft and murder isn't following the law? Who could have seen *that* coming."

Ansel stifles a snicker.

"I'm sorry, Ms. Simmons. I'm going to put watches on public feeds for Corbett. That recording of him trying to break into the apartment you're staying in is enough to hold him under *our* jurisdiction and deny any further bail."

"Do you have eyes on him anywhere now?"

"No, but when he's in custody we'll let you know."

"Share the watch with me."

"I might have to clear that with Agent—"

"You're pulling from public feeds and everything you guys do is required to be public too, so tell Agent Thomas to get used to working in a transparent goddamn society."

"We're having some—conflicts over jurisdiction and procedure." The leopard clears his throat. "I'm sending our endpoint to you."

Ansel looks up at Gail after a second and nods. He's got it.

"Okay. Call me if anything changes, unless I call you first." Part of her hopes he's not going to get pissed off that she's speaking to him like she's his superior officer, but given the monthly assessment fee she pays to maintain her citizenship, he *does* work for her. Sort of. Right?

He doesn't challenge her, though. "I will, Ms. Simmons. And Agent Thomas may want to speak to you again."

"Terrific."

Beedle boop

Gail closes her eyes, counting to five silently, then leans over Ansel's shoulder. "Can you tell if Corbett's still nearby?"

"The check's running now." He examines a window full of incomprehensible text. "A good match for our hooded figure was last seen a block away from here and moving downtown. That was four minutes ago. He hasn't passed another public feed since, so he's likely keeping to residential neighborhoods."

"Naturally." Most—although not all—businesses set cameras watching areas like streets and walkways to be public, but you need explicit permission to access ones around private housing. Stifling a sigh, she takes a seat. After a few seconds, she says, without looking over at him, "This *is* really good coffee."

"Thank you. I suppose that means you don't want to try to get back to sleep."

"With Randall out there? How?"

"I don't think he'll be coming back, and we'll have a lot of warning now if he tries. And if he shows his face—which he might, because with any luck he thinks he just bought a bad door hack and wasn't actually caught—he'll be in PFS custody by noon."

"Assuming the PFS is really on our side."

"Now you're sounding like me." He laughs. "I wanted to take you to Porter's for breakfast, and they won't be open for another two hours."

"As long as we both feel safe enough to leave."

He smiles lopsidedly.

Chapter 9

"I TOLD YOU the pancakes were terrific."

"I didn't doubt you." That's a lie. As a kid she liked Panorica-style pancakes a lot more than she does now, coming to diners with her mom when they were here for RTEA meetings. (Never with dad, but she was too young to recognize that as a marriage heading for trouble.) Instead of a stack of three or four centimeter-thin cakes, they make one airy, spongy one, four or five centimeters thick and stuffed with something sweeter than civilized people should face before noon. But Porter's has a slightly sweet batter matched with a lemon ricotta filling that merges seamlessly into the cake. It's almost like a breakfast pastry, but with a pancake's texture, and with the golden pomegranate syrup it's amazing.

But the pancakes aren't the best thing about being at Porter's, or the coffee, or anything else the cute partial transform cat waitress has brought over. She and Ansel sit outside in cool "fall" morning air—she still can't think of any of the arcologies doing "fall" without the air quotes, even though the seasons aren't any less artificial on the Ring—enjoying the street bustle as the overhead glow brightens. At this moment, her life feels normal again. That's the best thing.

"Did your algorithm pare down the possible ships?"

He nods, swallowing a mouthful of his own pancake. "Down to four, but I haven't looked at those to see if we can zero in on just one." He waves his fork. "But I'm wondering if this is really following the right course."

"What do you mean?"

"Your goal isn't to find this ship, it's to get the databox back to Keces."

The chair's not friendly to her whiplike tail; she can't imagine how uncomfortable it is for Ansel's fox brush. Sky used to whine—literally—at chairs with solid backs. "And we're following this lead to prove that

Quanta's behind the wreck and the theft."

"I know. But why isn't Interpol interested in Corbett?"

She shrugs. "Quanta doesn't care about him now. He failed. They just want the databox."

"They could have just left him in PFS custody, though. But they didn't. I think either he has some other part to play, or they're worried that he'll end up talking to the wrong person and they'll find themselves in a real investigation, not a sham one."

She hadn't threaded the logic out quite this far, but it makes sense. But how does it help? "And?"

"That means you should find the wrong person. Whoever they don't want Corbett to talk to is exactly who you want to talk to." He finishes off his pancake.

She slumps in her seat, thinking. "Wolfe thinks Thomas really cares about his job."

"That doesn't mean he isn't conscientiously crooked. There's reasonable suspicion the databox belongs to Keces, not Quanta, but it looks like Interpol started out on Quanta's side here. The PFS isn't under legal obligation to do them any favors."

"No, but they're not going to screw them if they want cooperation the next time they've got a problem that goes back to the inner system. And Wolfe's not the one who's gonna be making that call. It's got to be coming from higher up than Wolfe is."

"Then go higher up."

"Oh, *that* should be easy. I'll just get the chief on the line when we're finished here."

"Look, dear, you're the one who promised the impossible, so you'd better be prepared to do the unlikely."

After the waitress clears the plates away she pulls out her viewcard. The call starts as a nearly word-for-word repeat of the one from a few hours ago: ask for Officer Wolfe, get Officer Frontdesk, express urgency, get the brushoff. "Can you at least give me a status report on Corbett?"

"I don't have any information on that."

"Lucky for you, I do. I'll tell you what. I'll just head to the station office and wait for Wolfe. I have some things to talk about that might be better in person anyway."

Frontdesk remains polite but sounds more strained. "He's in the field and it might be some time."

"That's fine. I mean, since you don't know if the person stalking me is still out here, there's probably no safer place to be than in your lobby, right?"

"I may have to clear that with—"

"Thanks. See you in about fifteen minutes." She disconnects.

Ansel's lowered-brow look makes her parry with an exasperated one. "What?"

"I'm sure there's some age-old warning about walking into the lion's den."

"I'm pretty sure that's a prerequisite to parlaying with them. Besides, I dated a lion once. They're okay."

He gets up, putting his cap back on. "Do you want me to go with you?"

The *oh please don't say yes* in his tone is so close to the surface she's not sure it still qualifies as a subtext. "It sounds like it's going to be a lot of waiting. I wouldn't mind a walk to the station just in case, but you're off the hook after that."

"Deal. I'm not sure what case you're thinking I can be helpful with, but I'll try."

She grins. "Just an extra pair of eyes."

They walk along in silence for about five minutes, heading toward Port Panorica. She scans the crowd occasionally, but doesn't see Corbett anywhere. It's nearly ten in the morning and she'd wager if he's not in custody yet, he's not going to be. Getting someone past the PFS and off Panorica isn't easy, but there are ways. She's done it once.

Who she does see, though, is Agent Squarejaw, walking down the other side of the street. He doesn't look like he's seen her yet. She has her vision ramped up two-x, and he probably doesn't. Her whiskers twitch. "Crap."

"What?"

"Up ahead. Thomas."

His ears fold back. "Is he looking for you?"

"Probably."

"In here." He ducks into a storefront, and she follows. It's not until they're inside that she sees it's a lingerie store. All at once Ansel looks self-conscious in a way she doesn't think she's seen him do before; she can't help but grin.

"They must have told him I was on the way to the station." She subtly motions for him to follow as she pretends to examine a rack, lowering her voice. "Which means he wants to find me before I get there."

"That's ominous."

"Maybe." Mostly, though, it's curious. If he wanted to have her arrested, it'd be easier to do it at the station. Same if he wanted to do her harm—he could take her to some back room and arrange an "accident" of some kind. Or he could just wait until she went back to Ansel's place; they know that's where she's staying now. So why come out after her here?

Because he wants to stop her from talking to the PFS.

Maybe that's ominous, but maybe she doesn't have the right read on him. From what Wolfe said he's not the one who decided Corbett wasn't going to go back to Earth, and he's not the one who decided to let him go, either. Maybe he wants to say something where it's not going to be monitored. Searching through publicly accessible feeds might show that he talked with her, but with no audio, they'd have to take his word on what they'd talked about.

But why wouldn't he trust the PFS? Ansel would tell her it's because they'll object to Interpol's plan to send the databox back to Earth. But they already know that plan, and they haven't objected yet. What she's planning to tell them might change that. If he wants to talk to her off the record, though, something's already changed.

She touches Ansel's shoulder. "Maybe not, though." She moves toward the exit.

"Gail!" Ansel hisses.

Opening the door, she motions for him to follow her, but doesn't wait to see if he does. She steps out onto the sidewalk and waves toward Thomas, but she doesn't need to. He's crossing the street. He's already seen her.

"Ms. Simmons." Squarejaw's dressed much the same as he was yesterday, but the suit under the overcoat looks more rumpled. "You're on the way to the PFS substation?"

"Yeah."

He glances at Ansel, who hasn't completely stepped out of the lingerie store. "Mr. Santara." He looks back at Gail. "I'd like you to take a longcut with me." He gestures back the way he'd been walking—the way Gail and Ansel came from, away from the station.

Ansel steps out of the shop fully. "Is that an order?"

"No."

Gail tilts her head. "He wants a conversation that's not being monitored by the local police."

Thomas raises his brows, then gives a confirming nod.

She starts walking, motioning for him to follow. He walks beside her, a slow ambling gait rather than the purposeful stride he'd been walking with earlier. Ansel follows a step behind, looking worried. "You know *I'll* be recording it," the fox says.

"That's fine. You're not contractually bound to share your recordings with the PFS or Interpol."

She thrusts her hands in her pockets, keeping her tone nonchalant as she powers up her biomods. There's a small but non-zero chance she's about to get into a serious fight. "You think your agency's working for Quanta Biotechnics, don't you?"

He looks down at her, and this time his brow furrows rather than lifts. "Do you?"

"I'm pretty sure the databox belongs to Keces and Quanta hired Corbett to steal it. I screwed that up for them by almost catching him, but they had a backup plan. They don't need Corbett anymore—they got him released because they don't want him sticking around in PFS custody. Now they just have to wait for the databox to be sent back by *your* agency. That's a lot better than a sketchy civilian guy, right? Are they going to have you bring it back yourself?"

Ansel's ears have folded back into his hair. She supposes she *did* just implicitly accuse Agent Squarejaw of being in on an intersolar conspiracy that's left nearly two dozen people dead already, but that wasn't her intent. She's accusing someone he *works* for of being in on the conspiracy and using him as a dupe.

"That hasn't been decided yet." He looks like he's about to say more, but instead he falls silent, looking away.

She keeps silent, too, just walking beside him. He's the one who wanted to meet this way, so he'll say something when he's ready. She glances back at Ansel, gives him a surreptitious thumbs-up sign. He looks like he's ready to sprint off at high speed.

Eventually Thomas speaks. "The warrant for Mr. Corbett signed this morning was rescinded."

"What? Why?"

"All I've seen is the cancellation notice." He thrusts his hands in his coat pockets. "Within minutes of that cancellation, he showed up in public view again, at the spaceport. He's caught a shuttle to somewhere called the Rothbard Republic."

Gail groans. "So you've lost him." With a population of barely twenty thousand, "Republic" is absurdly grandiose, but the residents are in on the joke. The platform's famous for two things: being the biggest, most lavish tourist trap in the universe—only a couple cities on Earth might give its casinos, clubs and shows competition—and for refusing to cooperate with anything they consider a "state power," which includes the Panorica Federation.

Ansel mutters something that sounds like a complaint about using Rothbard's name in vain. When Squarejaw turns with a quizzical expression she holds up a hand. "Don't get him started." Ansel sighs theatrically.

She powers down her biomods. Not quite all the way, but enough that she's not going to exhaust herself in another few minutes. "So you didn't answer my question."

"Whether I think Interpol is working for Quanta Biotechnics." He shakes his head. "No. There's still no conclusive evidence the databox belongs to Keces Industries, either. But it certainly seems like someone's trying to quash any investigation into Mr. Corbett."

"What about Purity?"

"What about them?"

"Randall lives on Solera."

"So do a lot of people who aren't involved with Purity. But I've looked into his past and yours, and yes, that struck me as well. It also strikes me that you're doing investigation with Mr. Santara on your own."

The fox's ears flat. "Since you and the PFS haven't done any to speak of, who else is going to? Someone has to be on Gail's side."

It wasn't just in her head that he'd been standoffish a couple days ago, right? Now he's rallying to her. It's good to have the right enemies.

Thomas looks like he's concentrating hard to understand Ansel. Has he really been around so few canid totemics that he hasn't learned their speech quirks? After a moment he nods. "I'm only trying to get at the truth, Mr. Santara. But I'm hampered in a way you aren't as long as I work this through official channels."

"Are you saying you want to work this through non-official channels?"

He looks straight ahead. As he speaks his voice slows, like he's carefully considering every word. "I'd like to perform some independent work outside the PFS facility. It's my understanding of our cooperation agreement that I have the authority to seek contracts with outside assets as long as I have Officer Wolfe's approval, which I do."

"Assets."

Ansel snorts. "He means you, Gail."

"Actually, Mr. Santara, I'd like to include you and Bright Sky as well."

She bites her lip. When a break seems unbelievably good, she's inclined not to believe it. If she asked Ansel he'd tell her this had to be some kind of weird elaborate trap; by his standards Panorica's already too much of a state as it is, and adding in an Earth agency makes it authoritarian madness. But getting the databox requires getting it out of the station first, and wait, did he just say— "Sky?"

"Is that her first name? I assumed either 'Sky' was a surname, or 'Bright Sky' acts as a mononym."

Her voice drops to low gravel. "What the hell does she have to do with this?"

"She called to speak with me yesterday on your behalf. We talked about what it is she does in New Coyoacán, since it's not a judicial system I'm too familiar with. They've worked with Interpol in the past, but don't have formal agreements with us." Infuriating brow-lift. "Which may be an advantage in this case."

"And what is it you want me to do?" Ansel's ears fold back. "You want me to crack the databox, don't you? Oh, *hell* no. Do you have any idea what that would do to my reputation?"

Screw Ansel's reputation. What's Sky's angle? Yes, she said she'd call and she'd help, but this isn't just about getting *Kismet* released.

"Not necessarily. I want to keep pursuing how Mr. Corbett's connected in with this. But I do want to know if we can find more definitive information about the box's source without compromising its contents. Is that possible?"

"I couldn't tell you that without having the box to examine, and—"

Oh, of course. That's it. Single-minded Sky. "She wants you to go to New Coyoacán."

Ansel's rising-pitch rant ends in a choked gargle. "What?"

"It's an option Bright Sky brought to my attention."

"No. Absolutely not." The fox looks like his tail might be about to spontaneously ignite. "Even if I had the equipment I'd need there, which I doubt they'll have given that Gail's spent ten years telling me the place is a gray featureless shithole, I'll be damned if I'll get involved with the basket case government there. Especially to help an agent from the only place I know of in the universe with a *worse* government. No offense."

"None taken. But from a legal standpoint, you wouldn't be involved with their government at all. I would. I know how unorthodox this idea is, but politically speaking, the Ceres Ring might be the best place to do this work. They're not hostile to Interpol, and while they're not hostile to the PFS, either, they won't just give them jurisdiction."

Ansel's ears remain flat. "But *they* don't have any jurisdiction."

"No, but as long as Ms. Simmons remains a potential target, they have a legal interest."

Gail gives him a sour stare. "So you're using me as a shield to hide from your own damn agency while you finish an investigation they're trying to cut short."

"I'd put it more diplomatically than that."

"Look. If you bring that damn thing to New Coyoacán, that means handing everything over to the Ring Judicial Cooperative."

"Not in Bright Sky's telling."

"Jack, trust me when I tell you that if you take this thing there she'll personally be running your investigation within twenty-four hours tops."

"If I—we—go forward with using you as independent contractors, it's to keep agencies, even mine, from having too much control over this. We'll manage the same with the RJC."

If she understands Squarejaw's crazy plan, it makes a lot more sense than hers. To the degree she even has one. God, is she talking herself into going back to the Ring after all this time? Why not, though, if it's the best way to salvage her rapidly crumbling life? And even in the most cynical case—that Thomas is playing some kind of long con—it means getting the databox away from the PFS without having at least two security forces chasing after her. That's a huge step toward getting this whole damn affair over with.

"I'm going to need to call Keces in a day or two and either tell them I have the databox or give them a *real* good reason not to ruin my life. You're going to have to help me with that." God knows how, but burn one bridge at a time, or whatever the saying is.

Squarejaw nods. "I'll do everything I can."

She takes a deep breath. "Okay. We'll do it."

Ansel splutters. "We? *We* most certainly will not."

"Ansel—"

"Gail, no. I'm sorry your life's upside down right now, but I'm not upending mine as a gesture of sympathy. I am *not* going to New Coyoacán on the off chance we can find a way to discover information about the stored data that doesn't involve breaking its lock, even if you pay me *over* my standard rate. Look, if you can get the databox to my place I can take a look at it with the tools I have there. But I'm not going to touch the encryption."

"I'm sure you can do that without leaving a trace if you have to."

He rolls his eyes at her. "No, I can't. That's why you use quantum encryption. It's like putting a physical seal over a door lock—even if you fail in breaking and entering, the property owner is going to know somebody tried."

"There's all sorts of ways around that trick."

Squarejaw lifts a brow.

She clears her throat. "From what I've heard."

"It was an analogy," Ansel snaps.

"I know your reputation, Mr. Santara, and I suspect you're capable of bypassing that metaphorical seal given the right resources."

The fox's tail droops. "Possibly, but not without attracting a great deal of attention."

"We'd attract less of that on New Coyoacán, wouldn't we?"

"I don't know, but since we're not going there, the question is moot."

Gail grits her teeth.

"Then I'll work with what I have. I'll let Officer Wolfe know I'm following up a lead in the field."

"If you must."

"Legally this is his case, not mine."

"Are we doing this now? Right now?"

"I'd appreciate it." Squarejaw gets out his own viewcard to message Wolfe.

Gail pats Ansel's shoulder, trying to be reassuring. He glares at her. They trudge on in silence toward the transit lot a block away, hopping into a four-person tram. Ansel shoves his cap in a hip pocket as the tram picks up speed.

The silence lasts for about five minutes, about two-thirds of the trip. Then Ansel frowns, looking at the display on his wristband—he uses it instead of a viewcard. Gail's tried one, but decided she didn't like things on her wrist. From his expression, it's telling him something unpleasant. "Is your man going to my apartment?"

"Officer Wolfe? I didn't request him to and he hasn't told me otherwise. What's wrong?"

"I'm getting multiple alarms. This time they're trying to break into my personal data histories, and someone *may* be doing it from inside my place. The traces say they are, but the interior camera says no one's there. So at least one of those feeds is being tampered with."

She looks at Squarejaw. "You said Corbett was off Panorica!"

"He is."

Ansel grunts. "That's why I asked if Wolfe might be there already."

"If he were there he'd have let us know if something was amiss."

"Unless he's what's amiss." Ansel stabs at the tram speed buttons, but it's already going as fast as its autopilot is going to.

Squarejaw looks mildly affronted. "You don't think Wolfe's breaking into your data."

"Maybe not. All I know is, *you* don't trust the PFS in this matter, and I'm more cynical about police than you are."

Thomas shrugs with his brow-lift again, as if to say *point conceded.* "When we get there let me go in first."

Ansel snorts. "I'd be happy to."

When they reach the hallway to Ansel's front door, it's empty. No Corbett, no Wolfe, no mysterious persons hidden in shadow. Blissfully, worryingly empty. The fox twiddles with his wrist display, studying the tiny text scrolling past with a furrowed brow. He keeps his voice at a whisper. "Still contradictory signals." When he motions toward the door, Agent Squarejaw steps forward to stand in front of it. Gail stands behind him, ramping up her hearing just enough to pick up the subtle whine of his biomods coming on. She leaves hers off. She doesn't know if he knows she has any—he'd have to have dug into her history better than Nakimura's goons did. He might have heard them engage earlier, but only if he'd had his own mods engaged; baseline human hearing isn't good enough to pick that up, especially over street noise.

Ansel steps up behind them, just close enough to the door to trigger the lock. They all move to the side as it swings open. Squarejaw leans in just enough to do what she guesses is an infrared scan—it's what she's doing, at least. Nothing.

He takes a slow, silent step forward. Gail follows unbidden. Ansel takes a couple seconds to follow, wisely waiting to make sure nobody inside starts shooting.

"See if anything's disturbed." Thomas heads toward the bedroom, still scanning.

Ansel darts his gaze back and forth, tail curled around his left leg. "There's no alarm lights on, and nothing's obviously missing." He hurries to his work desk. Displays flicker to life above the surface as he sits down.

Thomas walks back up. "There's no signs of anyone here. You're sure about your signals?"

"Yes." He points at one window as evidence, although from Squarejaw's expression it's no more helpful to him than it is to her. "These are the last searches in my history, with times recorded of under ten minutes ago—and the location column says they were made from here."

"Someone broke in to do data searches and left without touching anything?"

"No, I don't think they broke in physically." He swipes around on the windows, then types furiously on his keyboard. "They bypassed my first-level security and forged location data to try and open my data vaults."

She grunts. A data vault is what she'd *thought* was the most secure way to store data before she'd heard of databoxes—an extra security layer that requires you to access them from specific locations or devices. She has a data vault that requires her to access it through *Kismet*, although she doesn't have much in it.

The fox scowls. "This is fairly sophisticated code. If it had worked, it'd have cleaned up after itself. My security's just better than what they'd accounted for—their system got locked out before it finished."

"Can you tell who they were, Mr. Santara?"

"No, but I see what they were searching for." He looks puzzled. "Something called 'Shakti.'"

Gail squints. "What's that?"

"A Hindu goddess of creation and change."

Both of them look at Squarejaw.

He shrugs. "I know some history. So nothing you've been working on involves that name?"

Ansel shakes his head. "No. I've never heard the word before."

Gail exhales sharply. "That's what's on the databox."

"You said you didn't know what was on it." Brow-lift, very high.

"I don't *know* know. But think. The two most important companies in the history of biomods and transformation? The goddess of creation? That's a project code name."

"That's a plausible interpretation."

"Is 'Kali' another Hindu word?"

Squarejaw looks at Ansel. "She's another Hindu goddess, of time and death. That's also a search term?"

"Yes. And there's a few other terms that seem less … code name. Gail, is this the databox's serial number?" He zooms in on one line of text.

"Yeah." She runs a hand through her hair. "They either think we already have the databox, or they were checking to make sure we hadn't cracked it."

"Creation and destruction." Thomas rubs his chin. "That's unexpectedly poetic."

Ansel grunts, bringing up more display windows. "I think you mean 'ominous.'"

"The keys to heaven and hell." Gail bites her lip. "That's what Nakimura said when we first met."

"Ominous-er." The fox leans back, staring at the ceiling. "I've already started security audits, but I'm going to have to do some manual reviews and see how they compromised my system. Until that's done it's not safe to work on the databox here."

"I'm not sure it's physically safe for you here either, Mr. Santara."

The fox closes his eyes. "Dammit, they want your databox. They want Gail. I should *not* be sitting here worried about someone trying to break into my place."

"You can post a guard outside or something, right?"

"Not without justifying it, which means aborting this side investigation before it starts."

Ansel slumps down further, covering his face.

She clears her throat. "This might not be a bad time to consider a trip to New Coyoacán after all." God, she doesn't sound like she believes that. She *does* believe it. She thinks. But her tone says she'd rather be hung by her tail.

The fox sits up again, staring at her morosely. "Jesus, Gail. I don't want to get involved, any more than I am already, in a political fight that spans the entire damn solar system. And the best argument you two can make is that it might be safer because people might come after me to—to do what? Torture me for information I don't have?"

"If it was me, I'd think that was a pretty good argument."

Squarejaw clears his throat. "I did mention we'd pay your full consulting rate, didn't I?"

Ansel pulls his tailtip into his lap, twisting it.

"And there's the challenge."

He pauses and looks at her.

"Have you ever tried to get this kind of information out of a databox? Figuring out how to break that seal without anyone noticing? That's got to be the kind of challenge the best algorithmists on Panorica would shake their heads at and walk away from."

Ansel glares. "Oh, don't even try this game. I'm one of those people on Panorica walking away." He lets go of his tail and makes walking motions with two fingers.

"But you're already thinking of ways you could do it, aren't you? You've been thinking of them from the moment we got into the tram."

"Well, I—" He makes an affronted *chuff* noise. "I figured we'd be—yes, of course, but…"

Gail leans forward. "How many ideas for it do you have already?"

He covers his eyes.

Chapter 10

ANSEL'S COLLECTED WHAT HE NEEDS in a small and tasteful traveling bag; Agent Squarejaw directs the tram to a hotel not too far from the spaceport so he can pick up his own suitcase. The hotel looks like one Gail could afford even with her purchase restrictions. Is PFS the agency cheaping out, or is it Interpol? Probably more polite not to ask.

As they head out, Gail asks a leading question. "So how do we fly to the Ring without using the PFS?" Use *Kismet*, of course. She's been going over the case in her head. Since the whole idea is to minimize PFS influence, then depending on them for transportation isn't just nice to have, it's essential. Even if you don't trust her, Agent Squarejaw, you'll be with her. What's she going to do, kidnap you? You can sure as hell trust that she wants this resolved even more badly than you do.

"The best way would be to take your ship."

No, look, we should—

Her breath catches, for just a moment, and her ears come forward. She can't help it. Thomas sees it, she can see it in his eyes but she can't tell if he's thinking *that's cute* or *damn crazy animal people* or what and it doesn't matter. "You're releasing her?"

"I'm going to try."

"Contingent on me helping you?"

"If I'd been planning to use your ship as leverage with you, I'd have told you this a half-hour ago, rather than after you'd already agreed to help."

Ansel snorts. "But you wouldn't have released it if she hadn't."

Gail swears that Thomas looks like he's counting to five under his breath. Then he turns to look at the back seat, directly at the fox. "Mr. Santara, I'm about to take a trip with someone Interpol still considers a person of interest, bringing the central evidence in that investigation with me outside of PFS jurisdiction. Do you know how my supervisors are likely to react to this?"

The fox's ears lower. "Not well?"

"Not well. My sincere hope is that we'll clear the databox to go back to Earth as scheduled, because if Ms. Simmons's conjectures are right, I should probably start applying for work on the Ring myself."

As the tram approaches the station wall and navigates into the same transit lot she'd walked out to when she landed a couple days ago, her brooding stops. She's almost—almost home.

Officer Wolfe waits at the port entrance for them. He gives Gail a surprisingly warm smile as they approach; she can't tell if he's flirting or he's feeling apologetic about the last time they met. She guesses those aren't mutually exclusive.

Before he says anything and before she thinks of anything to say herself, Thomas steps up. "Everything's all set?"

"Set as it's going to be, sir."

"I'm not sure how to interpret that."

"All the standard records have been updated, and nothing's been forwarded to the liaison office other than automatic actions. This—candidly, this isn't the kind of scheme I'd expect from you."

Thomas strides forward, making them all hurry to keep up. "I think of it as conducting an independent investigation. I'm sure everyone out here should approve of independence."

Ansel mutters under his breath.

Wolfe grunts. "I'm being dead serious here. I can tell when I'm being kept out of the loop, but I can't tell whether it's because you don't trust me, don't trust the PFS, or don't trust your own damn agency."

"From what I've seen of you, I trust you. I know from experience that both the FBI and Interpol do good work, and I have no reason to doubt the PFS. But it's my sense that someone's trying to close this case too fast."

"You think someone's trying to cover up something."

"I think…I think bureaucracies treat 'go along to get along' as a bedrock value, and someone's afraid to open the wrong doors."

The leopard's tail lashes. "If this databox's chain of custody is broken it's my ass in the sling, too."

"It's remained entirely under either your control or mine since we obtained it. I double-checked this morning, and involving private contractors isn't considered breaking that chain as long as the work's performed under our supervision—well, mine—or a private judiciary's. Correct?"

"Under some circumstances." Wolfe narrows his eyes.

She glances up at Thomas. "The Ring Judicial Cooperative isn't private, technically."

"Wait. You're going to the Ceres Ring?" Wolfe sounds even more agitated.

"It sounds like an excellent place to disappear for a few days. And functionally the RJC and a private group are the same in the eyes of the PFS, aren't they?"

"To some degree, yes, but…" The leopard gets the look of someone trying to do differential equations in his head. Yes, going through New Coyoacán will make the communication slow and prickly. The leopard's expression shifts to a silent *ohhh* as he solves his equation: slow and prickly is the entire point. "Sir, they can co-opt your investigation if they decide it's in their interest. It's happened before."

"If they do, I promise I'll step in front of the plasma for you." When they reach the top of the escalator that heads down to the small craft level, Thomas stops. "If anything comes up, keep me in the loop."

"I will, sir." He reaches into his jacket pocket, pulling out a smartpaper pad. Thomas takes it, scribbles a signature, and hands it back. Wolfe studies it, puts it back in his pocket, and seems to steel himself. Then he holds out the databox. "Sir?"

Thomas takes it. "Thank you. And yes?"

"Watch yourself." His tone's genuine concern, not veiled threat.

Thomas nods thoughtfully, and steps onto the escalator. Ansel and Gail follow.

It's only a minute walk to *Kismet's* berth. The cisform officer stationed there gives Thomas a curt nod and Gail a suspicious glance as he makes the agent sign yet another form, then makes Gail sign one, too.

When Gail steps in front of the ship's entrance hatch, it takes her a second to remember it's not going to open for her automatically. She takes out her viewcard and flips through its control set to find its key function.

She's rewarded with the sweet familiar sound of the lock disengaging. The hatch slides open.

Before the lights have come up to their full level she's beelined to the ship's power panel, sliding back the cover plate and switching the knobs back to on. An indicator light comes on, but nothing else happens for a second. Then a three-tone chime sounds, followed by the same three tones at slower, irregular intervals as integrity checks run. Cabin lights come up, circulation systems start whirring.

Ansel and Agent Squarejaw enter behind her, both looking around. She knows Ansel's been on the ship before but he has his judgmental look, like her housekeeping isn't up to par, even though nearly everything's still stowed. The bed isn't made, though. Her ears flick down a moment; the sheets might still smell a little of Adrian. If she'd been able to, she'd have asked Kis to inject a little more of that citrus air freshener into the system.

A final chime sounds, all three tones at once as a major chord. Finally, *Kismet* speaks, as melodious as ever. "All system checks are complete. Good afternoon, Gail."

She lets out the breath she's been holding. "I've missed you."

"Thank you. I have missed you, too."

She beams.

"You know that's just a stock response." Ansel's mutter doesn't quite stay under his breath as he takes a seat.

Gail glares.

"It was turned off." Ansel gives her an exasperated look. "Even if it was capable of missing you, which it isn't, how could it have?"

"It's a nice touch, either way." Squarejaw's looking around at the ceiling, as if trying to find the speaker. "That's not a stock voice for an Arcturus, is it?"

"You're that familiar with the line? Mittelbach's a River-based company." She heads toward the cockpit, motioning him to follow.

"They licensed the Alphaliner 200 from Red Sun Engineering back on Mars, including the software, if I'm not mistaken. I didn't think the voice was adaptive."

"It's not an Alphaliner, though. And everything about her's adaptive." She ignores Ansel shaking his head behind her and takes her customary cockpit seat. Thomas sits in the other one. "Strap in." He does. "You've been in zero g before, right?"

Squarejaw nods. "Yes."

"So you're not gonna puke, right?"

"Right."

"Because I don't like floating vomit."

"Noted."

"Okay. Kis, let's plot a course to New Coyoacán."

"Yes, Gail." After a short pause the ship continues speaking. "The flight will be approximately eight hours thirty-six minutes."

"Let's have the full view projection."

Suddenly she and the agent are sitting in two seats floating in space. The docking platform spreads out in a vast curve to the left, above, behind. Under them: stars. She knows Earth skies are nothing like it is out here, not even what they call a night sky. They just have a scattering of weak white dots. Here, this far from the sun, you *see* the stars. Colors across the spectrum, some steady and some constantly shifting, many faint and many blazing like guidance beacons, all against a background of the highest grade, purest blackness nature allows.

Squarejaw sucks in his breath, looking down over the edge of his seat but otherwise remaining still, as if he might fall out if he leans over too far.

Gail arches her brows. "Don't you get this kind of view on the long haul ships? I figure they'd have to have observation decks."

"They do, but they don't do that." He points down at the floor.

"You're not gonna puke, right?"

He gives her a reproachful look.

"Okay. Kis, let's go."

The floating status windows fade in around Gail's seat, virtual indicator lights and meters flickering. Then the ship's engines come online. The deep thrum's the most beautiful music she knows. She keeps her hand by the throttle, but *Kismet* is flying this one on her own.

"Signaling departure from Panorica," says the ship. A series of clunks and rattles follow as physical connections disengage. "Casting off." The engine's pitch changes subtly, and the station recedes from overhead.

Jack looks nervous, gripping the armrests, and she recognizes the look as the one she wore for about the first two years of being a pilot: your eyes tell you that you're falling, but your body tells you that you're upside-down and accelerating. She grins. "Don't worry, it'll just be relaxing microgravity soon." The feel's already changing as the direction of thrust changes; now they're being pressed back in their seats. You could almost mistake it for being in a vehicle driving along on a surface, although if you unstrap you won't fall to the floor.

"It's a eight hour trip, she said?"

"Eight and a half."

He nods, looking like he's making an effort to get comfortable. "I'm mildly surprised they standardized on Earth time out here."

Ansel chimes in. "It'd be awfully inconvenient if we picked something else."

"That's why I'm surprised you didn't."

"Very droll. We're nothing if not pragmatic."

"That's not the first word that would have come to mind, Mr. Santara."

"You're just conditioned to think that if you're not living in an authoritarian state like Earth, you're living in chaos."

He twists around in his seat to look back at the fox, visibly straining against the ongoing acceleration. "You *do* realize that Earth isn't one state."

"It might as well be for all the difference it makes."

"That's—"

Gail raps her armrest loudly. "If you two plan to talk politics for the trip, I'm going to make you take it outside."

Ansel throws up his hands. "Sorry, captain."

They all fall silent until *Kismet* levels off her speed, transferring the duty of holding them in their seats from acceleration force to their four-point harnesses. True to his word, Thomas doesn't look like he's going to throw up. He fingers the harness release, but doesn't press it.

"I didn't mean to needle you, Mr. Santara. The River's a set of radical political experiments, from virtual anarchy to minimal states to at least one command economy. And they've mostly all been successful. I'm interested both in what's stayed the same since the founding of various platforms, and in what's changed. And why."

The conversation's off course now from the argument, but she'd like to keep it steered away. "Is that why you volunteered to come out here? Or were you assigned? I can't tell if being a liaison between Interpol and Panorica is a top-notch gig or being banished to the fringes."

"That was a matter of debate at the office. It's a fourteen-month posting with a guaranteed four-month paid vacation afterward, and total pay of two years' worth of my normal salary. But it's considered a high stress assignment. You're isolated from the chain of command, but you're not given any breaks because of it. And yes, I volunteered. You don't get opportunities to travel to new worlds too often."

"So kinda for the experience and kinda for the money."

He nods, and for a moment looks like he's going to say more. What's he leaving out? The expression that flickered through his eyes for a half-second makes her less worried than curious. It's not something about this case, or even about the job; it's something personal. And, yeah, none of her business. Maybe she can find a way to ask without seeming like she's prying, but she'll table it for now. She's still suspicious he might be playing her—but if he's telling the truth he has every reason to be suspicious of her, too.

"Well, make yourself comfortable." She waves back at the cabin. "There's a combochef back there and I'm pretty sure all the ingredient cartridges are full, and I have a few beers. Unless you don't drink on the job. Assuming you're on the job now."

"Saying 'I'm always on the job' is a cliché, but it's going to be accurate the next few days. I'd rather just get a ginger ale than a beer for now, if it can do that."

"It should, yeah, although it'll mix with low carbonation. Bubbles don't work well in zero-g."

He clicks the harness open and pushes off from the seat, sailing gently toward the cockpit roof.

"Careful there, flyboy."

"There's nothing fragile to bounce into." He bumps into the roof and pivots back with too much force, nearly crashing back into the seat he'd just vacated.

Gail flinches away. "*I'm* something fragile to bounce into."

"I have my doubts about that, Ms. Simmons, but I'll try to be careful." He makes his way to the cabin like a skydiving frogman.

Ansel watches warily. "I could have just gotten something for you."

"I may not be an old hand at this like you two are, but I don't think I'm doing that badly, and I can only get better by practicing." He hangs onto a handle by the combochef, putting his feet on the ground. He doesn't hold himself down with enough force to keep from slowly drifting aftward, a sign the ship's still very gently accelerating, but he doesn't seem to be bothered. Or maybe he doesn't notice. After a touch to the display he speaks the order aloud. "Ginger ale."

After a beep of confirmation, the machine goes to work, printing a zero gravity cup while another part of it mixes a flavoring syrup. He scans through the menu selections on the display idly while he waits. "This is all junk food."

Ansel's ears come forward. "Still? I've told her about that before."

She rolls her eyes. "It is *not* all junk food. It's got what it needs for dough, meat, vegetables, and spices. It may not be gourmet, but it can make a lot."

He keeps flipping through the sections. "Unless you're pretending the mushroom pizza counts, I'm not seeing the vegetables."

"Jesus. You've gone from my arresting officer to my abuelita in under twenty-four hours."

"I'm just making the observation." The machine chimes, its door sliding back to reveal the filled cup. He picks it up and studies it.

"Sip from the side with the groove," Ansel says.

Thomas nods. "I've seen cups like this, but I haven't used one." He takes a seat on the bench opposite Ansel. More accurately, he positions himself against it, then starts a slow drift.

She gets up and pushes off, settling by Ansel and latching the belt around her hips. "Remember, you're not sitting, you're just touching your butt to the cushion. If you want to stay there, put on your belt."

He puts on the belt. "When's the last time you went back to New Coyoacán?"

Maybe an idle question, although he might know the answer already—he looked up her history before the interrogation. But no, he couldn't have had time to get more than the major beats; putting together a travel history from public records isn't a casual action. He talked to Sky, though, and that might be the first thing she'd bring up. "Twelve years. Did you already know that before asking?"

"No, but it's what I'd have guessed." He doesn't look ruffled. "You don't get to be a detective without learning to pick up subtle cues, like you having spent ten years telling Mr. Santara it's a gray featureless shithole."

Ansel stifles a laugh.

"Yeah, well. He kind of misquoted me. The *sky* is gray and featureless. The Ring itself is much more like a planet than an enclosed arcology."

"It's actually open at the top, isn't it? And the sky is Ceres."

She nods.

"But it must rotate much too fast to let the side of Ceres you're facing determine the day and night cycle."

"Yeah, a full rotation takes about twenty-five minutes. There's a lot of reflectors and floating particles and…" And what? She doesn't remember how it works, exactly. "Maybe that's it. Anyway, the light and dark cycles mimic an Earth day, but it's lighter when you're facing the light side of the surface and darker when you're facing the dark side. It doesn't have sunset and sunrise the way Panorica does."

He laughs. "The way Panorica does." She thinks he's going to shake his head patronizingly, but he just looks thoughtful again. "Some of it has to be artificial light, though."

Ansel cuts in. "Much less than you think. It's amazing engineering work."

"I've heard it called one of humankind's thirteen wonders. Also, I think that's the first positive thing I've heard you say about the place."

"Communist dystopias can still have brilliant architecture."

Gail rolls her eyes. "Knock it off."

"If I'm stereotyping your homeland I apologize, but you haven't said much over the years that contradicts my impression."

"I don't talk about the politics with you. You're the one who goes off on tax rants, not me, remember? Most of what I hate about the place isn't…isn't the place."

Ansel furrows his brow.

"Look, it's complicated. I'm just not comfortable there."

A chime sounds and *Kismet* speaks unexpectedly. "Another craft has approached within three hundred kilometers on a non-standard course."

Gail frowns, unlatching and pushing off back to the cockpit. Squarejaw follows. "What's that mean?"

"I don't know. Kis, zoom in on the ship."

The whole starfield wheels around and it looks like they're flying sideways. Thomas hasn't taken his seat yet, and instead ends up gripping the back of the chair tightly, making an *urp* noise.

"No floating vomit, I mean it." She leans forward, looking at the dot circled in red. "It's paralleling us."

"Why's that raising your hackles?"

She reaches around to the back of her neck.

"Metaphorically."

She grunts. "See the ID for the ship in that red circle? Any text at all?" "No."

"That's what's metaphorically raising 'em."

A second chime signals another inappropriately calm report from the ship. "The other craft has altered its course, and is projected to intercept ours in twenty-eight seconds." A new display appears floating in front of

Gail, showing two dots moving along two lines: *Kismet* and its projected course, and the approaching ship and its course.

She raises her voice. "Both of you, four-point harness. Now." She presses a button, restoring the starfield display to straight ahead travel. "Kis, turn away and accelerate. Hard."

Kismet immediately begins to pivot. The lines diverge, then converge again at a different point.

"Are we about to be in a dogfight?"

"Since I don't have any guns, I sure as hell hope not. But they're not firing, they haven't hailed us, they're just—"

The split second she realizes what's going on is the same split second *Kismet* rings like she's been hit by a giant hammer. "Fuck." Gail snarls, grabbing for the manual stick and yanking it all the way to the port side. The ship pitches sharply, and for a moment they see the attacking ship less than a kilometer away: little more than a fat, short cylinder, all engine and cargo space.

Ansel shrieks. "Now they're firing!"

She keeps her eyes on the course display as she pushes the throttle open. "Those are grapples."

Squarejaw stares. "They're trying to board us?"

Even though she isn't looking at him she can hear Thomas's brows lift all the way off his forehead. "Hook us. Missiles damage cargo."

"Pirates?"

"Maybe." She pulls up another display in front of her, a rear view, zooming in on their pursuer. The two dots on the first display are converging again, even though she's zigzagging.

"Can you shake them?"

Good question. The attacker looks like a modified Allister CH-9. A lot of power, not much maneuverability. "They're flying under computer control."

"Then why aren't we under—"

She cuts the thrust off and twists the control stick and *Kismet* spins around with it, flying backward and facing the other ship. The grappling hook rockets past the cockpit in complete silence, seemingly meters from their seats. If she hadn't spun the ship around, the hook would have hit the stern.

"And *go*." She pulls the stick back toward her and jams the throttle forward full. She and Thomas slam back into their seats and Ansel makes a pained noise. At least she thinks he does. The engine becomes so loud inside the cabin they have to raise their voices to talk over it.

Thomas wheezes. "Good lord."

"That's why we're not under computer control."

"Because computers aren't insane. Copy that."

The Allister has to reel in its hook each time it misses, so she has a few seconds to change course. But she can't keep doing this the whole damn way to the Ring. New tactic. "Kis, get us in parallel with the attacker, close enough to fire tow cables. Fast."

Thomas stares at her again. She ignores the look.

Closer, closer, before they get the hook in—perfect. "Fire the tow clamps at the grapple." The clamps "fire" at a claw-bitingly leisurely pace. One catches the grapple—and sticks. The other two of them bounce into the pirate ship's hull, only one of them latching on.

"Ms. Simmons—"

She takes *Kismet* into another barrel roll. This time the ship's shudder sounds like ripping. Discordant alarm chimes start. "Cut the cables!"

They feel the snaps. She shoves the throttle forward again, and more alarm chimes start, matched with a brief but ominous hiss. "Kis, what's going on?"

"A section of outer hull plating has been breached. The inner hull is intact but compromised. The temporary seal should be replaced as soon as possible."

"Fantastic." She zooms the display back in on the attacking ship. It's slowed down, tumbling awkwardly, the grappling hook—with the tow clamp still hanging on—trailing behind it. With any luck, she's broken more than the chain motor. Fuckers.

Yet another alarm starts somewhere. "Slow down!" Ansel screams.

Gritting her teeth, she eases the throttle back. The distance between *Kismet* and the CH-9 is growing rapidly; they're out of danger. Probably.

Squarejaw swallows, taking a deep breath. "Is there a chance this is just a random pirate attack?" She can tell he already knows the answer.

"Pirates don't operate this close to Panorica unless they're after a very high-value target." She points at his jacket pocket.

"No one knows this is on your ship right now."

Ansel sounds weak. "Officer Wolfe does. Anyone either you or he had to clear this with does, too. I think I sprained something."

"You can't believe the PFS sent pirates after us."

"Given the way my week's been going, I can believe a lot." Gail runs a hand through her hair. "Kis, is that ship disabled?"

"They do not appear to be operating under full power. Its course is diverging from ours."

"Where are they going?"

"Their current course has the highest probabilities of being toward New Amsterdam or Solera."

"Of course. Christ." She throws herself angrily down in the seat, then hangs on to keep from ingloriously bouncing off the cushion.

Thomas's brow furrows. "Where Mr. Corbett is from. But he couldn't have gotten from the Rothbard Republic to Solera that fast."

"He's not running this operation, and he can't be the only flunky Quanta hired. But I want to know what the hell is happening on Solera. Again. Still." She closes her eyes. "Kis, get back on course for New Coyoacán and get there as fast as you think it's safe."

"Yes, Gail." The ship picks up speed and, with a gentle grace quite unlike her owner's piloting, arcs up and starboard.

Chapter 11

After her standard reassuring announcement chime, *Kismet* speaks. "We will be under gravity in three minutes. Please secure any loose items."

Gail stirs in her seat. She didn't manage to fall asleep, but she got close. Squarejaw, though, stares ahead wide-eyed.

Astronomers describe Ceres as a dwarf planet. Even though they're still far enough away to see the pronounced curve of the horizon, nothing looks small about it. *Kismet* speeds high above a vast rock and glacier field, neither featureless nor entirely grey; craters and mountains and color striations are easy to spot. Surface mining operations are easy to miss, squat structures spreading thin, delicate tendrils of piping across the ice.

But what seizes your attention, what you can't look away from, is the Ring.

Take a metal belt eighteen kilometers wide and bend it into a circle big enough that if you wrap Ceres with it, there'd be a hundred kilometers of space between the surface and the inside of the belt. Build walls many kilometers high, high enough to keep the atmosphere in if there's gravity, and top them with an elaborate system of mirrors, shades and light concentrators. Then fill the space you've created with soil and trees and "natural" water formations, and use technology indistinguishable from magic to make the whole thing spin.

On approach, the side facing away from the planet looks like the top, a dull metal surface like Panorica's hull. But it's the other side with farms and fields, research stations and ore processors and water plants, towns and cities. As *Kismet* gets closer to the Ring, flying over it now, she matches speed, dropping closer still, and Gail feels the pull—a slight one, but well past microgravity—from the planet.

Then, as she synchronizes her speed, *Kismet* barrel-rolls to fly upside down with respect to the planet and drops up into an open bay, the angular velocity of her flight mimicking the Ring's spin-induced gravity, moving from outer space to underground. Gail holds her breath as the operation completes, unable to exhale until the sound of the docking clamps echo around the hull. There's a small chance she could pull off that landing manually if she had to, but she hopes she never has to find out.

Squarejaw unhooks his seat restraints even before the ship gives the all clear chime. There's a difference between the gravity here and the gravity on platforms, even the ones like Panorica, that she'd almost forgotten. The platforms have a slight, subtle pull counter-spinward. On smaller platforms like Molinar you can even see it, if you drop a ball straight down and watch closely: the ball doesn't drop straight. The Ring, though, is so damn huge that you'll never feel it, let alone see it.

But she's not in any hurry herself. By the time she's standing, they're both looking at her expectantly, although Ansel keeps gingerly rubbing the base of his tail. That's what he's worried he's sprained, she guesses.

She grabs her bag and follows the others to the exit, but pauses by the hatch, looking back at the cabin. "Kis, I'll arrange for repairs immediately, okay?"

"Yes, Gail."

She nods, but stays where she is. What's the damage like? How long will it take to repair? It doesn't matter—it'll take as long as it takes. How's she going to pay for it when her bank account's still locked? Who knows? Some things you can't control, and trying to pretend otherwise just drives you nuts.

"Ms. Simmons?"

"Come on, Gail. You're only going to be stuck back home for a little while."

"Home is *Kismet*. New Coyoacán is just where I'm from." Before either of them can respond with some helpful aphorism, she moves past fast enough to take the lead.

The interior of the docking bay sports the gray industrial walls so many others do. But things take a more colorful turn when they step into the wide exit hall: bamboo floor and ceiling tiles, warm indirect lighting illuminating riotous painted wall murals, some of stylized scenes she recognizes from New Coyoacán, some from other places entirely. The slight bounce from the floor's claw-resistant coating triggers more memories; it's rare everywhere else on the River, but *de rigueur* here. There's only a few other people here, all totemics, including the full transform vixen standing with hands clasped in front of her watching them approach. Her light green dress looks hand dyed, not too far off from something Sky would wear; the only thing that marks her as an official is her cloisonné pin: blue ring around white dot.

"Welcome to the Ceres Ring and New Coyoacán. And welcome back, Ms. Simmons." She smiles brightly.

Gail can't muster a return smile, but she manages not to scowl. She hopes. Ansel looks both unsettled and a little smug, like this is *just* the kind of state-in-disguise intrusiveness he'd been expecting. But official greetings aren't standard procedure: the vixen's here because of Squarejaw. "Thanks. I'm sure being back will be an experience."

The vixen's smile grows fractionally worried. "I hope a pleasant one. It's quite a thrill to see you return, even if it's for a short visit."

Her ears splay. Oh, God, she's *not* here because of Squarejaw. "Uh. Thanks." She clears her throat. "Do you know if Kingsolver Repair is still open? We had a little event on the way here and my ship needs some work done." She also needs new tow cables and clamps, but those will have to wait. Even if she could get into her bank account, there's not enough to cover the full repair bill as it is.

"Yes, they are. Give your ship permission to talk with them and we'll give them access." She motions them to follow her up the hallway. "Agent Thomas, are you here on Interpol business? I know you've been in contact with one of our mediators."

"Not exactly, ma'am. I *am* working on a case with Panorica Federation Security, but it doesn't involve New Coyoacán."

Her tail swishes back and forth as she walks. "Then if I may ask, why here?"

"I'm hoping to get some advice on the case from your mediator. She seems quite sharp. I also expect to get more work done with my consultant here than I might be able to there. You could call it a—hmm. Is 'skunkworks' offensive?"

She laughs. "No."

"Good. In any case, I'm sure Bright Sky will make sure the case doesn't impinge on New Coyoacán jurisdiction. Beyond that, I'm here for a quick vacation."

The vixen smiles, tension and ears both lifting. "That's good to hear. New Coyoacán is the loveliest city on the River."

Another ten seconds of walking takes them to the top of the incline and the spaceport's main concourse. Ansel looks winded and grumpy. Maybe he's thinking there isn't a moving sidewalk or other tram because New Coyoacán can't afford modern conveniences, but one glance around the spaceport would dispel any thought the city's short on money. The treated bamboo floor continues throughout the whole area, the ceiling high above supported on natural wood beams. Nearly every exterior wall's a floor-to-ceiling window. At least a third of that ceiling is windowed, too, bright pale light drifting down around sales stalls peppered across the open space. Even though the spaceport's just as busy as Panorica's, it doesn't feel crowded. Nearly everyone else she sees is a totemic.

The vixen stops, hands folded in front of her again. "I hope you all enjoy your stay. I don't know if you have lodging arrangements already, but there's a wonderful hotel that opened a few years ago overlooking the Sonora River. It's only three dozen rooms, and it's quite romantic."

"Hey, we—"

"That sounds lovely. Thank you very much." Squarejaw smiles. The vixen nods in the kind of not-quite-a-bow way that Ring-folk have when they're being formal, and he returns it passably.

As soon as she walks off, Gail hisses. "Flirting with the vixens? That's record time for going local."

"I'm simply being diplomatic."

"And what the hell do you mean, 'that sounds lovely?'"

Thomas shrugs. "Doesn't a romantic hotel overlooking a river sound lovely to you?"

"You've probably made her think we're a triad!"

"It's possible."

Ansel snickers. She narrows her eyes.

Squarejaw keeps his voice absolutely deadpan. "Now, don't be like that, honey. I admit I'm very curious about what a riverside hotel here will be like. Also, what did she mean that seeing you was a 'thrill?'"

Oh, now he's discovered his sense of humor? She keeps her clenched fists at her side. "My mom's still remembered around here, I guess."

"I guess, too. We should get in touch with Bright Sky now that we're here, though. You never answered if that was a monoynm. Did she take your family's last name?"

"No. 'Bright Sky' is the only name we've ever known for her."

"Is she Native American?"

"I don't think so, but we didn't know her before her transformation." Sky had been broke after her passage to New Coyoacán, and broken after whatever trauma had led her there; even after she grew into her new life, she never shared the whole story. As a young girl, Gail thought that was the coolest name ever. Later, she realized it was what a pre-teen might pick if she thought it was the kind of name a totemic should have. "You handle coordinating with her, and we can check out accommodations in the area. What's your expense budget like?"

He looks at her askance.

"I mean, to cover hotels for a few days." Sky might already be preparing a bedroom for her, and she doesn't want to get steered in that direction. But she can't pay for a hotel herself with that account lock. Interpol, though? They can.

"Moderate."

They step out of the building into daylight. With chagrin, she realizes she thinks of this and only this as *real* daylight: the brilliant ice of the Ring's filtered sky. The wisps of dark grey cloud against it are real, too. She hasn't seen an actual damn cloud since she left. To Squarejaw, though, this has to be unfathomably alien. She can't even guess what Ansel's thinking beyond his now very wide eyes.

The spaceport sits near the center of New Coyoacán, and whether or not it's the prettiest city on the River, it's unlike any others. They stand at the side of a wide paved road, a similar plastic-carbon material as roads on Panorica. That's where the resemblance ends. The buildings along the road, along the roads down visible intersections, all sit low, rarely more than two stories—and they revel in wasting space. Lawns and gardens and trees separate building entrances from sidewalks. Some buildings have grass between them. And the buildings themselves seem oversized, wood and stone rising from the grass to meet slanted roofs of wood and red tile. Half-doors, bottoms latched but tops flung open, are unheard of elsewhere on the River but common here. And now she can guess what Ansel is thinking, and maybe what Squarejaw is, too: this is the only place on the River where houses blend into the landscape, because it's the only place where they can. It's the only place that *has* landscape.

The road runs down the center of a valley; technically, this valley runs all three thousand, seven hundred kilometers of the Ring, but not all the space is terraformed. The streets and the city aren't perfectly level, but the hills are small, gentle. To either side lie bigger hills, forests in the distance. A block away there's an urban park, a pond she remembers feeding fish in. A few blocks in the other direction the buildings become set even more widely apart, shifting to a more residential area, and there's a wildflower meadow creeping up a much steeper hill.

After several seconds of open staring, Squarejaw folds his arms. "I confess this doesn't match the image of New Coyoacán that you two painted for me."

Ansel makes a displeased noise. "It's beautiful but it's creepy. All—all the edges and curves are hidden. Is this what being on an actual planet is like?"

"It's closer than anywhere else I've been out here."

While they speak she calls up local information guides, information bubbles overlaying across her vision to show accommodations. "There's a hostel about two blocks away."

Squarejaw shakes his head. "We need more secure accommodations than that. If we're allowed private rooms, we should take them."

"'Allowed?' Look, stop listening to Ansel. We're 'allowed' whatever we pay for, just like everywhere else. If you want to spend the money on private rooms, let's do it."

"Then let's take the riverside hotel."

She grits her teeth. "It's going to be fairly far out of town." She adjusts the search parameters of her display, looking around, then sees the proper tag. She points. "That way, about a kilometer and a half."

"About a twenty minute walk? I'm willing if you are."

"Fine."

Ansel glowers.

As they walk, Gail remembers a word she learned from the inner system: *rural*. The Ceres Ring looks—she thinks—rural. Geographically New Coyoacán's borders encompass almost a million people, but less than half live in what she would call "the city." And even in that city core, the lack of density she grew up with and thought of as normal for her first two decades seems shocking now. Pedestrian traffic flows in leisurely clumps instead of hurried streams, and vehicles are fewer but larger, designed for longer distances.

The agent checks his viewcard every so often, occasionally tapping on it. Looking up references? Playing tourist? Even though retina implants have been around for decades, few people get them. She can't imagine why more people don't at least use display eyewear, though.

Soon the street turns more residential, and Squarejaw puts away the card. He gestures at one of the buildings to the right, a house at the top of a hill a good five meters over the street level. "I'm still trying to understand property here. Does the state own that house?"

"Yes," Ansel says, looking at Gail for confirmation.

She shakes her head. "No. Well, sort of. The Ring Collective owns all the land, which is what they mean by 'property.' And legally we're *all* the Collective. Anyone who builds a house gets homesteading rights."

"But they could still kick you out if they wanted."

She shrugs at Ansel. "Maintenance crews on every platform have the authority to kick people out of buildings. I know philosophically that's not the same, but I've seen that happen on Panorica. Never seen anyone lose a house here."

Squarejaw nods thoughtfully. "It's just interesting, given how fiercely anti-state so much of the Cerelia River is."

"But that's still true here, too. The Collective isn't a state, right? The argument against private property is that there's no way to create it without state coercion. If you go back far enough in any piece of land's history, you'll find a claim built on either force or the threat of it." She grimaces inwardly. She sounds like her mother all of a sudden, right down to the cadence.

"On Earth, maybe. If there's any piece of land that couldn't be applied to, it'd be land that literally *was* created." He waves a hand around.

Ansel grunts. "You'd think."

"I guess they wanted to be consistent. Anyway, it's pretty much that philosophy that made them the best for running the Ring. The River can't exist without the mining and water extraction, and giving the bid to the one group that'd run it as a non-profit was a way to head off fights about profiteering."

"It wasn't a bid!" Ansel throws his hands in the air. "It's like—like—everyone wrote political philosophy term papers and a committee awarded the Ring to the group with the highest grade."

Squarejaw makes a thoughtful noise. "The River's grown much faster than even its initial supporters thought it would, though, so it clearly worked."

"But did it work because of this model, or in spite of it?"

She grins. "Always the principle with Ansel."

The surroundings grow still more residential, still more open. A bird cries in a nearby tree and receives a distant answer. After a quick double-check of the directions, she points at a gravel path to the right, leading down into a forest. "That way."

Ansel groans, hefting his own bag as if it were full of lead bricks. "This is going to kill my paws."

She points at her sandaled feet. "Sandals, Ansel. Wear sandals."

"I hate footwear."

"At risk of asking a gauche question, is that a totemic custom? About half of the ones I've met are barefoot—barepawed?—and I've never seen one wearing full shoes."

Ansel sniffs. "We don't need shoes."

"Says the fox bitching about walking on gravel." Gail chuckles. "I think some of it's kind of aesthetic, but some of it's practical. Shoes and fur aren't a comfortable combination."

"I'm still trying to get a sense of what animal characteristics totemics have adapted and why. I can read your emotions through your ears. And tails. But I'm presuming that while Ansel has better hearing and smell than I do, he has full color vision, isn't allergic to chocolate, and doesn't have any other drawbacks from canine/vulpine genetics mixed in."

Ansel grins. "That's an advantage to being able to mix and match genes. On the flip side, cisform humans can wear clothes that fur makes impractical. And they don't get fleas, mange, or other furry problems that can't be addressed by flipping a genetic switch."

"Hmm." He nods again.

"Are there many totemics left on Earth? I always thought most of them moved out here."

"That was generations ago. There's at least two million there now. Most Earth countries have stronger legal protections for totemics now than I think it's possible to have out here. Your system doesn't have the tools for anti-discrimination laws."

The fox grunts. "Our systems, plural, rarely do, true. But they also don't have the unintended consequences of those laws. Your cures are frequently worse than the diseases."

"I'm not convinced of that." Squarejaw glances at Gail.

Her ears lower. She knows exactly what he's thinking. "I can't see how anti-discrimination laws would have stopped someone from bombing my mother's speech."

"They wouldn't have." He leaves the *but* unspoken; her brain fills it in anyway. *But they wouldn't have been allowed to turn her away from the hospital. They wouldn't have been allowed to let her die.*

Thomas speaks again after a few seconds. "I'm enjoying the walk. I could almost mistake this for an undeveloped area near where I used to live."

"There are parks like this on Panorica."

He shakes his head to Ansel. "There's a few spots carefully maintained to look wild. Here, you can tell they built it and just let it go."

"This is what a lot of Earth is like, then, isn't it?"

"Some parts. I'm not sure I'd say a lot."

It takes another three or four minutes of walking before the forest gives way to a meadow. The gravel path meets a paved road after one more minute's walk. The road follows the bank of the Sonora River.

Squarejaw comes to a full stop this time, staring at the water. They can hear it from here. "It looks completely natural."

"It is." She waves a hand. "I mean, obviously they decided to put in a river when they were building the Ring, but they let the water seek out its own channel."

The river's over a hundred meters wide here. A dozen or so buildings sit facing them on the far shore, a handful of skiffs tied up to a long pier running along the shore. Her dad sometimes used to take her out on the water. She'd loved swimming and diving, and he'd joked that rats were just better swimmers than humans. He almost never said transform or cisform—he'd say the animal name and human. She knew that was one of the things he and mom argued about. Back when he still took Gail out in the boat they were only arguments. Later they became screaming fits.

God, she's been here an hour and she's opening doors in her mind she keeps closed for a reason. She loved living here. She hates being here.

The road follows the bank for another half a kilometer, then pulls away as it reaches a cluster of waterfront buildings. A boardwalk continues on right over the river bank. She points ahead. "The inn's one of those."

Her memories of the river as gentle and clear are true to the reality; you can see into it nearly a full meter. Piers jut off the boardwalk, the wood weathered by water and wheels and feet. The boardwalk takes them in front of a riverfront café. Wrought iron tables and chairs sit on a tiled patio between the boardwalk and the building proper. Again, nearly all the patrons are totemic. After more than a decade away, that seems unnatural.

Ansel's looking down at the water with a dubious expression, holding onto his cap as if it's in danger of falling in. He was born on Arelia, the next largest arcology behind Panorica, and he's lived on Panorica since college and transformation—nothing in his experience matches this. She looks to Thomas curiously. "How close is this to a river on Earth?"

"Remarkably. Incredibly." He hesitates. "Inefficiently. Panorica feels like a dense, lived-in metropolis—it has that sense of changing over time in a way I don't think most of the other platforms out here have the physical leeway to do. But they still manage resources there down to the milliliter."

"It's big enough that this is the most efficient way to manage our— their—resources. Instead of algae farms and scrubbers, they use fields and forests. And rivers."

"It's too open." Ansel looks up at the sky, squinting at the brightness, then blinks furiously as he looks away. "And I think the design is a philosophical statement, in line with a lot of Mara's original thoughts about totemics. Merging technology and nature."

Gail waves a hand. "This thing took five countries, a dozen corporations and a half a century to build. It ain't all about philosophy."

Squarejaw laughs. "No, but you know there's still fierce arguments over whether these projects ever paid off, economically. The consensus is they didn't."

"*Your* consensus," Ansel sniffs.

"An inner system one, yes. But maybe it succeeded on a philosophical level, by creating a new frontier. And it surely did that. It's impossible to tell we're on a ring circling a planet." He looks down at the river. "The water flow seems just a little unusual, though. Is that from the spin?"

"I don't see anything odd."

"You grew up with it."

She frowns, and walks on in silence.

After another dozen storefronts—coffee shop, candy store, more than one art studio—they reach the Sonora Inn. Three stories high, floor to ceiling glass windows everywhere, stone walls and wide, rough-hewn wooden beams jutting out. It's all straight lines and right angles. Squarejaw studies it with his typical fascination. "They're using cantilever construction. What was this called? The Prairie School. It's beautiful, although it's quite a shift from the Spanish influence in the city. I'd expected that, but not this."

She tilts her head. "The city looks Spanish?"

"Just touches. But the names are geographic references. Sonora. Coyoacán."

Ansel laughs. "There's a platform out here called 'Amsterdam Mission' and another one called 'New Mumbai.' It doesn't mean much in practice."

"It meant a lot to someone. The murals we passed by in the port were in Diego Rivera's style, and I can't imagine that's mere coincidence."

The fox gives Squarejaw the furrowed brow look of someone who's suddenly lost. She isn't, but explaining that New Coyoacán's name was inspired by radical leftist artists will just provoke a new rant. "It's not," she says. "But I don't think the city has much more of a Latino population than anywhere else on the River." Despite her grandmother's ancestry, she feels about as much connection to Mexico as she does to Mars. She never met her grandmother, anyway.

Thomas reaches the entrance to the building ahead of her and Ansel, but takes a moment to realize the door's not automatic. Ansel's looking at the door handle like it's an ancient artifact of evil. Right, the guy with the analog wall clock can't deal with a door that doesn't go *whoosh* for you.

They step into a long hallway delineated by low half-walls on either side, an upscale restaurant to the left and a lounge to the right. The whole place has the same squared-off but warm look: wooden floors and ceiling, stone walls, predominant colors brown, tan and black. It smells like...ash? She sniffs, whiskers twitching. A fire? No, a fireplace.

Squarejaw comes to a stop in front of it, staring. "That's *not* burning real wood."

She watches the flames flicker and listens to the cinders pop, and dredges through her memory rather than looking it up. "Kinda, yeah. Compressed wood. The ash gets reprocessed into something, too, but I don't know what." Other scents lie under the ash: whisky and citrus from the bar, spices from the restaurant kitchen, a faint cedar perfume she suspects they've added to the air conditioning.

Two people stand behind the desk, both full transform, one fox and one squirrel. She doesn't see many squirrel totemics on Panorica. Not many rats there, either. You see the less common species choices when you're living around thousands of others, and sure, there are thousands of totemics on Panorica, but…it's different. There are totemic neighborhoods there, like there are on Carmona and Kingston, but here everything's—God, wait, there might be cisform neighborhoods in New Coyoacán, mightn't there? She doesn't remember it that way, but she was so young.

"Welcome to the Sonora Inn." The squirrel's stepped up to greet them, beaming a huge square-toothed smile. "How can I help you, Mr. Thomas?" Her eyes flick down momentarily to read his name off her display.

"Thank you. I'm looking for a room or suite with three separate beds." He gestures to Ansel and her.

Tufted ears flick, and she glances down at a display in the counter, swiping finger pads across it. "All right, sir. There's a junior suite available, or two separate rooms, although it doesn't look like we have two adjoining rooms available. The suite will be less expensive."

"Let's go with that, then."

"And for how many nights?"

He hesitates for a second. "Three."

"Your preferred currency is the North American dollar?"

He nods.

"Very good." Another swipe, a few taps. "The junior suite is five thousand eight hundred per night, with a ten percent manager's discount. So the total will be fifteen thousand, six hundred sixty dollars."

Gail watches Squarejaw's expression move from *that's a bargain* at the first number to *or not* at the "per night." Well, hell, Interpol can afford to send him halfway across the solar system, they can afford a damn hotel suite, right?

"How nice there's a discount." His tone's drier than normal. "Let me set up the payment." He pulls out his viewcard and fiddles with it.

"Excellent. Thank you, Mr. Thomas." A section of the counter in front of them lights up with the charges. "Could all three of you confirm the room rental so we can key the room for you?"

"Yes." They all touch the display; it flashes green when Ansel touches it last.

"You'll be in room nineteen, just down the hallway." The squirrel points. "The bar opens at fifteen o'clock, and the restaurant serves dinner between seventeen and twenty-one. It's open for breakfast between six and ten." She glances down at her display and her eyes widen for just a split-second, but she recovers nicely. "I hope you enjoy your stays in New Coyoacán,

Mr. Thomas and Mr. Santara." When she looks to Gail it's with an expression a touch too close to reverence. "And it's very nice to meet you, Ms. Simmons."

"Thank you." She tries to keep from sounding too guarded. The nebulously-named "manager's discount" might be a "we recognized your name" discount. But they couldn't have already known—

"When Bright Sky arrives, should I send her to your suite, or will you meet in the lounge?"

—unless they were told in advance. "She's left a message?"

Squarejaw waves his card. "I've been handling coordination with her, as requested."

Gail's ears lower. "That's great. Thanks."

He gives her a steady look. "You're welcome."

The squirrel clears her throat.

"I guess we'll meet in the lounge."

She nods. "I'll let her know."

"No need," a voice calls from the opposite direction of the lounge, from the front entrance. "She's here."

Chapter 12

EVEN IF YOU DON'T COUNT THE EARS, Sky stands taller than Agent Squarejaw by several centimeters. Her casual but conservative outfit— dark green buttoned shirt, matching slacks, gray jacket—isn't at all the colorful look Gail remembers her favoring. Her own style of shorts (usually black), halter (usually black) and open shirt (usually loud) hasn't changed much since her early twenties.

The wolf woman smiles as they approach, ears forward, no teeth showing. "You must be Agent Thomas." She clasps his offered hand in both of hers. "Bright Sky."

"Pleased to meet you. You can call me Jack." Gail picks up on the slight hesitation as he works through the wolf's speech; her canid "accent" is stronger than Ansel's.

She nods. Then she's got the fox's hand in hers before he offers it. "And it's good to meet you in person finally, Ansel."

While he's not quite staring up open-mouthed, he's clearly been struck with temporary loss of suave. "Uh. Thanks. Yes." That's close to the look he gets when he thinks someone's extraordinarily attractive, but she doesn't think he's bi. This may be an *oh God please don't eat me* look.

Then Sky turns to her. Gail starts to raise her hand but she doesn't get it all the way up before the wolf pulls her into a crushingly tight hug. "It's been far too long since I've been able to do this."

Gail puts her arms around the wolf, then squirms. "Jesus, you're going to break my ribs." At least part of the wheeze is genuine.

Sky doesn't let go for another few seconds. When she does, she looks down at their bags. "We should go to your room. Where is it?"

Ansel points. "Nineteen, just down that way."

She nods and strides in that direction, motioning for them to follow.

Maybe ninety seconds at most and she's already in charge of everyone. Naturally.

When Agent Thomas drops in behind Sky, Ansel right after both of them, Gail briefly toys with the notion of heading for the lounge instead. By the time they notice she might already have a drink in hand. Sigh. No. Be good.

The door unlocks at Squarejaw's touch, but like the main entrance, they have to push it open manually. She doesn't remember this being a standard around the city; maybe doing more work holds some kind of high-end appeal. Maybe she's supposed to be employing someone who opens doors for her.

Straight across the room, a floor-to-ceiling window looks out across the river. It's the best view yet of the green hills rising up toward the north wall. God, she's forgotten so much about the landscape. After a few seconds of staring, the furnishings filter in: two sofas, electric "fireplace," work desk, kitchenette. Openings on either side must lead to the bedrooms. The hardwood floor's covered with a protective layer like the port's, but thicker, with more give. Nearly as warm as carpet, too.

Gail drops onto one of the sofas. Both have a good ten centimeters between the lower cushions and the back, letting Ansel's bushy tail pass through easily as he sits at the other end. Squarejaw heads toward the other couch, settling beside Sky.

"So." The wolf's eyes settle on Gail. She has a way of looking directly at you without blinking for what seems like hour-long stretches, like a real wolf tracking prey. Growing up, Gail thought that must be part of the lupine transformation, subtly encoded in genetics, but she's never met another wolf totemic who had quite the same knack. "What have you learned since we last talked?"

She fidgets, then launches into a brief recap. Keces and Quanta both want the databox. The data on it might be from either company or a mix of both. What's on it probably involves totemics, and they've found two code names, so two projects.

Sky remains silent until Gail gets to the part about leaving for the Ring. Then she looks at Thomas. "Do you have any idea who the leak in the PFS may be?"

"I'm not positive there's a leak."

"If you weren't positive, you wouldn't be here."

"I'm just taking precautions."

Gail snorts. "Pirates, Jack? About eight hours ago?"

Sky's eyes widen. "You were attacked by pirates?"

"I hadn't gotten to that part yet. Yeah, someone came after us on the way here, and only the people Agent Thomas has been working with knew our destination."

"Anyone monitoring Port Panorica departures would, too," he says.

Sky takes a slow breath, looking out the window. "And Randall Corbett's involved, and is the reason you're involved."

"That's about the course of it."

Squarejaw steps in. "We still haven't found how Mr. Corbett's connected, though." He and Ansel take over the narrative.

Sky lids her eyes, falling silent several seconds, then looks at Ansel, wolf gaze on full power. He shifts like the couch has suddenly grown spikes. "You said Randall worked with a charity. Have you looked into them yet?"

"Uh, Lantern. The Lantern Foundation. No."

"Then I suggest you start now." The gaze of skewering shifts to Squarejaw. "And begin forensic work on the databox."

"That was my plan. Mr. Santara and Ms. Simmons were also trying to draw a connection between the wreck she found and Quanta or Lantern."

Sky looks back to Ansel. Gail finds it weirdly relieving to watch both of them get as nonplussed as she does—it's not *just* the family relation. "Can you perform both analyses concurrently?"

His ears fold down. "Maybe. I mean, yes for the data reduction tasks, but there's a lot of work that's manual, and I have to do it serially."

"What can I provide that will help you?"

"If there's somewhere I have at least tier two data access, I have *nearly* everything I'd have at home. If you're stuck on tier three I can probably muddle through."

"All of the Ring is tier one." Sky's voice remains level.

"Oh. Well, uh, if you have local calculation engines you can make available that I can allocate securely, that would speed things up."

"Done. What else?"

"They need to be isolated, so nothing can get off the box into publicly accessible dataspace."

"Of course."

"Of course," he repeats, then sighs. "I can't think of anything besides that. Thanks."

The gaze shifts back to Squarejaw. "And is there anything I can provide for you?"

"I don't think there's anything else you *should* provide to me, since the Ring Judicial Cooperative isn't officially involved."

Sky clears her throat, a bass rumble very easy to mistake for a canine warning growl. "Your work is being done in our city, at my invitation, to provide cover for you and legal assistance for Gail. We're not officially participating, but I'd say we're officially involved, wouldn't you?"

His brows try to vault off his forehead. Gail doesn't get much of a chance to smirk before Sky's looking back at her, though. "Are you planning to stay here, at the inn?"

"Yeah. I figured that was easiest."

"You know I have space."

"I know you could make space, sure, but..." She waves around. "I don't want to put you out. And I mean, Interpol's already paying for this, right? I don't want to make them waste it."

Sky's ears lower a fraction and she looks away. "No. Of course not." The hesitant softness in her voice startles Gail. That's not the woman who was just here a second ago, not the one she grew up with. Is it?

"Hey, we'll still get a chance to catch up." Come on, the distance isn't new. It shouldn't surprise her, dammit.

Sky nods, and takes a deep breath. "Would you come home with me tonight, at least? We can talk over dinner. It's been a very long time since we were together."

Crap. Gail glances furtively to both Ansel and Thomas; they're both making a point of looking somewhere else. Not that they'd be able to give her an excuse to say no. If she doesn't want to, she should just say that on her own, anyway. Sky will understand. Probably.

"I...uh." She runs a hand through her hair. Oh, come on, get the words out.

Sky stands. "It doesn't have to be tonight. Or any night, I know. But the offer's open as long as you're here." She starts to turn away.

"Yes," she blurts.

Sky's ears lift and she turns around again. Her tail starts wagging. Gail smiles weakly. She says something to Ansel and Squarejaw as she follows the wolf out of the room, they say something back. She hopes her once and future big sister is willing to call a tram, because right now she's feeling kind of faint.

* * *

"Thank you."

Gail looks over at Sky. Naturally, the wolf *had* walked here, but she'd consented to summoning a two-person standing scooter to ride back into town, following a paved road rather than the wooded trail. After they'd gotten underway, neither of them had spoken. Until just now. "For what?"

"Coming along. I know you didn't want to."

"It's not that I didn't want to." Isn't it exactly that, though? No, it's not that simple, yet she doesn't have an answer to—

"Then what was it?"

—the obvious next question. "It's...it's complicated, Sky. Everything's complicated. I wouldn't even be back here if I wasn't in trouble."

"I know. I just don't understand why that's the only reason you'd come back."

"Because this isn't my home anymore."

Sky turns to look at her, but doesn't say anything. The scooter's reached the edge of the city proper, meadow transitioning abruptly to a neighborhood of densely packed freestanding homes.

"Look. I..." I don't see what's hard to understand here. I left. I left a long time ago. I left that little apartment and I left this city full of people who don't see why anyone would ever possibly want to live anywhere else and I left everyone who didn't see *me* when they looked at me but only saw a symbol, a child of a martyr, some kind of holy rodent for them to rally around. The here and now is tough enough to navigate as it is without lashing myself to someone else's cause. "I left."

As the wolf's gaze lingers on her, it's less piercing than searching. "I understand you think of *Kismet* as your home now. I just want you to understand this is also your home."

No, it isn't, and also that's insipid. "Yeah."

Sky's ears flick and she turns away again, hands tightening over the scooter's rails.

The vehicle turns left down another street, and the standalone homes give way to row houses, three stories high. It's neither the neighborhood she grew up in nor the one she last lived in. She knows Sky's lived somewhere new for years, long enough that it's not new. But she's never seen the outside, just a few shared pictures of the living room and kitchen. Isn't it bigger than these places? Isn't it a full house like mom's? Maybe they're just passing through.

No, they're not. The scooter glides to a stop and Sky steps off. Gail follows; the scooter chimes and rolls away to find its next passenger. The wolf heads toward a staircase alcove.

At the top floor—of course—she walks down a shadowed hallway and faces the second door on the right. When it slides open the way a door's supposed to, Gail can't stop herself from commenting on it. "I was starting to wonder if New Coyoacán had banned normal locks."

Lights switch on as Sky steps in. "I hope that's a joke. Take off your sandals by the door."

"Yeah, just a joke." Slipping off her sandals, she starts to set them down on the carpet's edge, then sees the wooden rack for them, Sky's bigger sandals already lined up just so. The wolf always went barepawed growing up—she'd said she hated the feel of even the lightest footwear. Maybe walking back and forth to work finally convinced her otherwise, although Gail's not sure how much of an office job being an RJC mediator is.

The place is big after all. The living/dining space has to be twenty-four or twenty-five square meters, at least a third more than the old place. How large was her family home? It seemed huge when she was nine or ten but she'd assumed that was just the child's-eye view. It wasn't as big as the homes she's seen from the outside today, but this flat is bigger than Ansel's.

After tossing her sandals on the rack, she crosses the carpet and perches on the sofa. It faces a long coffee table, looking toward the kitchen; when she twists around, the wall behind her is a sliding glass door opening onto a garden. Maybe that's where the flower arrangement on the coffee table is from. Non-flowering plants sit at the room's corners. "This is a nice place."

"Thank you." Sky heads toward the kitchen. "Do you still like ginger apple?"

She can't stop a surprised laugh. "I haven't had it for years. Uh, sure, thanks."

Nodding, the wolf touches the beverage dispenser's control panel. "Two ginger apple sodas."

Sodas? Right. Sodas. God, it's like being fifteen again.

The machine clunks and whirrs and hisses, quickly printing two clear glasses, filling them with ice and bubbly gold liquid. Sky brings them over, setting them down on the coffee table, then sits down in a chair at one end of the couch instead of by Gail, like she's worried the rat will bite her.

"So. My job and your ship."

Gail pauses as she reaches for the glass, looking up.

"You said I was married to my job and you were married to your ship. I've been thinking about that." Sky picks up her own glass, with the wider brim that dips down to a spout-like point on one side, and takes a careful sip. It's more like dripping it into her long muzzle.

"Sorry." She suppresses a sigh. "I was kinda angry."

"You were also right." Sky laughs, but there's melancholy rather than humor behind it. "I didn't even know if I'd stay in New Coyoacán after I grew up."

"Really? I couldn't imagine you anywhere else."

"I'd already moved to Lariat before the bombing."

"But you were just there setting up the RTEA office. You weren't going to live there, were you?"

"No. I thought I'd be doing that for other offices, leading protests, following in Judith's footsteps. Then at some point the battle would be over and we'd all be equal, and I'd settle down somewhere and start a family." She laughs, then furrows her brow, looking into her glass. "Then I came back here."

She came back to settle Judith's affairs, and found herself becoming mother to her adopted sister, even though they were barely six years apart. Gail was too young to fully understand what Sky was giving up—and hell, Sky was too young to understand it then, either. She finally takes a sip of the drink. Yes, she still likes ginger apple soda, even if right now a splash of rum would make a great addition. "I think you're doing pretty well." God, that sounds forced.

"I am. Thank you. I—I still wish you were doing better."

She tries to summon a reassuring smile. "Normally I'm doing pretty well, too."

"Are you? You're always lurching from crisis to crisis. Don't your docking and fuel costs add up to more than you'd pay in rent?"

"Depends on where I dock. But look, there are years I've made more than you." That's a guess; she doesn't know what Sky's income is, but she's paid by Ring Services, the nonprofit group that Ansel would point to as the State By Another Name when he got halfway through his third

Electric Lemon Sour. She also knows the rest of this conversation with Sky, word for word. *I just wish you'd find a way to be more stable.*

"I just wish you'd find a way to be more—more stable."

This is the next branch point in the conversation tree. Touch here for *So you want me to sell my ship?*, here for *This is what I love doing. Don't you want me to be happy?*, or here for *I'd like it to be more stable, too, but what do you expect me to do?*

Or she can short-circuit the script. "Maybe not everyone's meant for a stable life. I've seen a lot more of the River than you have now, Sky, and I'm not even sure stability's the norm. I think I know exactly one person who's been in the same job for more than five years and isn't working for themselves: you. Maybe two if I count Agent Squarejaw."

Sky laughs. "Don't call him that."

"Come on, the man has the squarest jaw in the solar system."

The wolf shakes her head, taking another pour-sip of her drink and grinning. "But here you'd have the living allowance. Is New Coyoacán really that unbearable?"

"No, it isn't." She never got that allowance, but Sky had, and it made the difference between eating into the inheritance and insurance money and conserving it. It's what allowed her to have enough money to buy *Kismet*, over Sky's objections that it would leave her essentially broke. "It's just…" Just what?

Sky looks at her expectantly.

"I know you're happy being in one place with one job, but I don't know if I ever could be. You know that about me. And I can think of a few people who've destroyed their lives trying to find stability. Hell, that's what Dad did, right? He couldn't stand the uncertainty of living with an activist, fled back to the inner system, and spent the rest of his life drifting miserably. I'm drifting happily. I think I'm doing it right."

Sky's gaze grows unfocused, like she's looking at a point somewhere very far off the Ring. "You're right. Life isn't stable. But you know I can't help but worry about you." The focus returns. "We're the only family both of us have."

Yes, that's true. That's the whole damn problem: they *are* family. If they'd met under other circumstances, met later in life, they'd have been easy friends. It's not nearly as easy when you know one another this well. "I know. I worry about me, too." She smiles. "But I've made it this far."

"I know. I just want you to remember that you have help." Sky bites her lower lip, two fangs gleaming against black flesh, then sets down her glass and gets up. "I need to start cooking."

Gail grins. "Before I left, most of your dishes involved pressing combochef menu buttons."

"Honestly, most still do. But I've learned to cook for friends. You remember Travis and Nevada, don't you?"

"Travis Duarte? *Oh* yeah." The stag transform had been both the first hoofed totemic she'd ever met and her first crush. She still doesn't see many hoofed animals used for transformation templates; it's about the most difficult and expensive transform to do short of faking nonmammals, and creates a host of practical problems ranging from hoof care to how you deal with narrow or low doors—or chandeliers—when you have goddamn antlers. She didn't know any of that then, though. She just knew she liked watching him. A lot. And after she got up the nerve to speak to him, more than watching. It was almost too bad he'd been her first kiss: nobody since had measured up. As most teen romances did, theirs had plummeted from the highest highs to the lowest lows in a ludicrously short stretch. Later they'd become friends again, and kept in touch after she left New Coyoacán, for a while.

But Nevada? "I don't remember a Nevada growing up, though."

Sky pauses in the kitchen, tilting her head. "No, she wasn't here then. She said you met her on Panorica. She used to be…oh, what was it. Linda, I think? Linda Lamport. You *must* have kept in touch."

She can feel her eyes widen, her ears stand straight up. "The cisform woman I rescued from Solera." She'd been working at a salvage yard Gail's boyfriend managed; when Gail went there to buy her first tow engine, she learned Leon's father, the yard's owner, was pathologically anti-totemic. The aggravated assault charge Squarejaw had brought up came out of the resulting standoff. So had Linda.

They'd become friends, but Linda seemed fixated on totemics and New Coyoacán and maybe just a little on Gail specifically. Their relationship hung in an uncomfortable quantum state for a while, until the rat moved onto *Kismet* full time and the waveform collapsed. "Uh, no. We didn't keep in touch very well." It's not a surprise she's ended up here—tailchasers often do, although they rarely stay—but taking a new name suggests more than infatuation. There's no legal requirement to do that after a transform, but many people do. "What's her form?"

Sky's in motion again, getting down kitchen utensils, pulling out ingredient packets and setting them on the counter. "Vixen. Gray fox. She's very pretty."

Of course. Those are the pictures she kept coming back to in fashion magazines, the examples she'd ask about. God, Gail should have given her much more support. Something else to feel guilty about. "No problems from transforming as an adult?"

She shakes her head. "None I've heard about. You didn't know about any of this? It's been years."

"No. Honestly, I didn't think she'd want to see me again. Are she and Travis a couple?"

Sky nods. "Married, and both of them want to see you again."

"What, did you just casually tell them I'd be in town for a day or two?"

The wolf snorts, dumping a couple of the packages into one of the two sauté pans she's set on the cooktop. Onions and garlic, from the scent. "No, I did not. But you *do* come up in conversation."

"I can't imagine I come up very often."

There's the reproachful big sister look. "You could make the effort to keep in touch."

Dammit, she will not react to that she will not react to that her ears just lowered, didn't they? "So could they."

Now Sky's ears lower fractionally, and she looks down at her cooking without responding. Pureed tomatoes join the other vegetables.

Gail wriggles her nose and watches as butter goes into the second pan, along with squash and corn and mild chiles. "This is starting to look complicated."

"It feels like it is, even though it never looked that way when mom made it."

The scent's becoming something new, something specific. No, not new. Old. Familiar. It doesn't click until Sky takes the casserole pan out and starts layering ingredients. Sheets of tortilla, filling from one pan, filling from the other, drizzle of sour cream, sprinkle of salt and pepper, repeat. "Oh my God. You're making Pastel Azteca."

"It's not Judith's recipe. I never had that." Sky bites her lip again, without looking over. "But it's as close as I've been able to get." She slides it into the oven.

"I haven't had it since… since I was twelve."

Sky straightens up and flashes Gail a self-conscious smile. They'd looked for packaged versions when they lived together, but never found one. Then the wolf had gotten hung up on some meat-centric diet fad and stopped looking. Gail had tried making it on her own once, and had ended up with a screaming fit, two ruined pans, and an order for a combochef the next day.

"I don't know if anyone on Panorica has ever even heard of it." Gail shakes her head. "I looked a couple times, but I didn't know it was as rare as it is."

"I hope you still like it."

She takes a deep breath, and memories rush in with the scent: a seat at a wooden table in the kitchen, high and huge to a girl of ten, looking across at her new and strange and impossibly tall fifteen-year-old wolf sister, both sets of young eyes lighting up as her mother sets down a steaming baking dish. "I do." Her throat's threatening to close up, but she's not crying, not at all, she just has to dab at one eye.

If Sky notices, she doesn't say anything.

Chapter 13

SQUINTING, GAIL PUSHES HERSELF UP on her elbows, then sits up the rest of the way, kicking off the sheet and sniffing at the air. The sheet slides off the sofa to puddle on Sky's floor.

The last time she'd woken under natural light streaming in from a window had to be the day of their last big fight over *Kismet*, shortly after Gail's nineteenth birthday. That night she'd slept on her ship, and the next day she set off for Panorica, paying movers to collect her belongings and ship them after her. She hadn't spoken to Sky again for over a year.

What's woken her, though, is the smell of coffee, a dark roast and strong brew, saturating the air like over-applied perfume. There's a thick, sweet undertone to it which takes her a moment to place: sweetened, condensed milk. Her mother never drank coffee at home without adding a spoonful, and Gail started drinking it like that very young—it wasn't until years after she'd left that she ever tried coffee straight, and not until years after *that* that she learned to like it for what it was on its own.

She rescues the sheet and folds it. She recognizes this one, the worn light violet floral pattern, the scents of three homes and two owners. When she'd moved to Panorica she'd found sheets that looked almost the same, but hadn't known that she'd need to buy ones labeled as claw-safe. She'd woken up to half a sheet and a dozen cloth strips.

"Good morning." Sky's voice comes from the kitchen area.

Gail stifles a yawn as she pulls her shorts back on over her underwear, stands up and finds where she's put her shirt. "As far as mornings go, yeah. I shouldn't have let you talk me into sleeping here."

"We were up past midnight, Rattie."

"Yeah." For the first time in a very long time, no fights. Shared memories, at first carefully chosen to avoid pulling one another's triggers. That somehow led to talking about mom's vintage cloth dolls, at least two generations old if not three, and Sky's insistence that Gail should finally take them. That led to more than one cry, more than one hug, and more than one glass of wine.

She woke up once during the night and stared at the ceiling and thought: what in the hell are you doing here? This is exactly what you didn't want. You haven't been called *Rattie* in nearly two decades and you haven't missed it. But just what is it you don't want, Rattie? To have her ask why you've kept a hundred-odd thousand kilometers between you and the one family member you have left in the entire fucking universe?

"Are you going to wear the same clothes again?"

"Unless we go back by the hotel, yeah. They're clean."

"I still have those old clothes of our mother's in the back closet. I can't wear any of them, but I'm still sure you could."

Still? Like the dolls, Sky wanted to send them to her years ago and she said no. She wouldn't be able to wear them either, not because they wouldn't fit but because, like the dolls, she'd burst into tears if she looked at them. "It's okay, really. These are fine."

"All right, if you're sure. I thought we could meet Nevada and Travis for breakfast, then get a status report from Jack and Ansel." She walks around the divider wall, carrying a tray with two mugs.

"Wow. Okay."

Setting down the tray, Sky lifts her brows. "We don't have to meet them if you don't want to."

"No, it's okay, really." She's just having a whole lot of past broadside her in a very short amount of time.

The coffee's good, although not quite as good as Brio's and nowhere near Ansel's, and the condensed milk makes it taste like hot melted ice cream. It's markedly better than what she stocks on *Kismet,* and she's going to have to kick Ansel's ass for making her aware of that again. She doesn't have the income to be a coffee snob.

Income. Money. She feels her whiskers droop. Wasn't the bank supposed to get back to her already? No, they didn't promise anything beyond sending the case to the resolution department.

"What's wrong?"

Damn whiskers. She can tell from Sky's tone that the wolf figures it's something about her, or New Coyoacán, or the coffee, or something else

that'll lead to a fight. "Nothing. Um. Well, thinking about financial—
issues I need to deal with."

"Worry about your job after this is over."

"It's not that. Somebody I used to know on Carmona accused me
of fraud, and *he's* the one committing fraud but it seems like he's got
somebody at the bank in his pocket. I'm kinda stuck until the resolution
department gets back to me."

The wolf lap-sips some coffee, looking contemplative. "I'd try to help,
but Carmona doesn't hold Ring mediators in very high regard, and even
if they did I can't testify to any business you conducted then. Please tell
me you had a judiciary while you were there?"

Did she? She squeezes her eyes shut, thinking. "Yeah. Yeah, I'd joined
up with the one on Panorica by then."

"They're the ones you had on retainer until you stopped paying them
this year."

"Right. But—how do they help? I *did* stop paying them."

"All they need to do is provide archive access to your accuser's judiciary,
to show your side of any disputed transactions."

"How's that do anything for me? Tom's probably accusing me of something now."

Sky shakes her head. "If he was it'd already have been thrown out,
unless you did business with someone on Carmona without knowing it.
It has to be something that your bank couldn't immediately disprove."

"Huh. I didn't know judiciaries would do that for former clients, just
current ones."

"They'll charge you a processing fee."

"Terrific. All right. Kis, you there?"

Of course she is. She always is. "Yes, Gail."

The wolf's ears perk up. Can she actually hear that? No. She's just
reacting to Gail suddenly speaking to her imaginary friend.

"Send all my old account information with Lopez and Bowens to my
bank, and attach a note saying to contact them for the dispute resolution
with the judiciary on Carmona. Ask them to deduct the processing fee
directly from my account with them, but ask me for clearance if it's over
five thousand. And copy Sky on everything." She bets they won't limit
what *they* can withdraw from her account.

"Yes, Gail."

That was easier than she thought it'd be. That almost certainly means it isn't going to be easy at all, but maybe it won't boomerang back for another day or two.

Sky's still giving her an odd look.

"You know I can do that with Kis. It's not that weird to have a vocal interface implant."

The wolf grins in a way that sets her at ease despite showing way too many teeth, an expression Gail used to think of as the Canonical Sky Smile. "It's you using her as a personal assistant."

"She's a pretty good one. More functional than any home hub I've seen other than maybe Ansel's, and his isn't nearly as usable by people who, well, aren't like Ansel. Uh, you're not upset I copied you on it, are you? I figure you might be able to catch something fishy I miss."

"No, that's fine."

"Great." She takes another sip of coffee. "Have you gotten in touch with Travis and Nevada yet?" Nevada. Nevada. That's a name she'll have to get used to.

"I told them we'd meet them there at nine."

"Oh." A glance at Sky's sensibly digital wall clock reveals it's already eight-thirty-five. "When do we have to get going?"

"The café's in Midtown. It's on the way to your hotel. Sort of. We should set off in ten minutes."

Which Sky will measure to the second. "Got it."

If Midtown had been called "Midtown" when Gail was growing up, she never noticed. The businesses all look new, but in a shabby/chic new-place-in-old-building fashion she sees a lot on Panorica. Just like there, it's fallen out in a typical mix of boutiques and restaurants and workspaces. The Starlight Café takes up a corner facing two streets restricted to pedestrians and personal scooters; a sign outside proudly announces its upcoming fifth anniversary party, a week from next Saturday.

Gail pulls up Linda's presence information in her HUD to see if she's already at the café. It's only after it works—redirecting the lookup to "Nevada Argent"—that she realizes it shouldn't have. Not Linda anymore. Is she that public about who she was? No, not if she's changed her family name, too; you do that if you don't want it to be trivially easy to find who you were. Gail must still be on her priority list. Way to make her feel just a little crappier about herself: if Nevada was still on *her* priority list, she'd have known about the name change when it happened.

Also, Argent? Really? How many other gray/silver foxes and wolves have that somewhere in their name? Not that any other gray-furred totemic couldn't use it, but it sure seems like a dog thing to do.

Anyway, L—Nevada, Christ, do *not* screw up and use her old name—Nevada's here. Travis is here with her. Somewhere. She stops at the café entrance and scans around, but Sky strides on past her, waving.

The restaurant's interior is bright and open, high ceilings, dandelion yellow walls and polished stone floor, round wooden tables with metal chairs. About three-quarters of the tables are full and about three-quarters of the clientele are totemics. Sky's waving at someone. Someone's standing up and waving back. Nevada.

As they approach, the vixen smiles broadly, but her blue-gray eyes betray her uncertainty. "Gail. It's been…a lifetime ago. Almost literally." If she hadn't known who Nevada was—used to be—she couldn't have connected that smoky voice back with Linda's, but it's the same cadence she used to have. And the same nervous laugh.

"Yeah, it has been. I'm sorry I didn't…" Didn't what? Didn't know what to make of her obsession with totemics? Didn't recommend someone for her to talk with about species dysphoria? Didn't do a better job of being that person herself? "You're absolutely stunning." That, at least, is unequivocally true. She takes the fox's hands in hers and leans up, kissing her nose.

Nevada's ears shift forward and her tail starts to wag.

"And you're still as attractive as I remember you, Gail."

She hasn't looked to her right, but she knows the voice—deeper and richer than she remembers, but unmistakably Travis. Older, yes. But she'd still recognize him in an instant. He hasn't aged well, he's aged spectacularly. Broader shoulders, bigger arms, bigger pecs, a face that's gone from youthfully round to handsomely chiseled. Those magnificent, absurd antlers are bigger too. As he stands up she wonders if he has trouble fitting through some doorways, but he looks strong enough to just shoulder his way through.

"Thank you. You're, uh…wow." That was kind of a flirtatious opening, not just because it's been fifteen-odd years but because his wife's sitting right next to him and God his wife had a crush on Gail way back when and this is all beyond awkward maybe she'd just better not say anything.

Also the only thing in her mind right this second is more *wow* which is a whole lot less witty than she wants. "It's really good to see you—"

She gets cut off by the stag pulling her into a hug, her cheek pressed against the fabric over his chest. "It's great to see you, too."

When she's released, Sky's giving her a look that might reflect disapproval or might reflect amusement. Or both. Damn enigmatic wolves.

As they sit down again, Gail picks up the menu, glancing over it. She starts to select the orange juice, then sees they have mimosas. It's a mimosa morning. She circles that with her finger.

Nevada leans forward. "So you're still a salvage operator? And you're living on…um…the *Kismet,* isn't it?" The vixen has a mimosa already. Travis has a big glass of boring unadulterated orange juice.

"Yeah." She flips the menu over. *True vat-grown bacon,* a footnote proclaims. "As opposed to what, fake vat-grown bacon?" she mutters.

Travis laughs. "As opposed to plant-based. A lot of the meat off the Ring has little or no animal protein in it. Vat-grown meat takes up more resources, and—" He stretches his arms out, as if embracing all the resources they have here that the rest of the River doesn't.

"Travis is an agronomist." Nevada sounds very proud of this.

"Does vat-grown meat count as a crop?"

He grins. "It involves a lot of the same work to produce."

"Do you think it's better? I guess I don't remember the meat here growing up being that different from what I get anywhere else." She likes the food on Panorica just fine, thanks, and there's a *terrific* steakhouse she knows on Rothbard.

"I think so, yeah. It's more the mouthfeel than the flavor."

"It's better," Sky chimes in. Of course she says so. It's New Coyoacán, therefore it's better.

"Mmm." She circles the short stack of the batter-toast, the bacon, and a pomelo cup. "So, um." She wants to ask *when did you transform?* but that sounds so gauche. "How long have you lived on the Ring, Nevada?"

"Four years. Five in May. I love New Coyoacán—it's so, so, so green. So open. Everyone is so friendly. Not like Panorica and definitely not like Solera." Her ears lower on that name, but flick forward again quickly. "You told me it was nice, but I don't think you did it justice."

Sky turns toward Gail, expression comically startled. Mara's Blood, Gail said nice things about where she grew up?

Travis helps. "I can't imagine living anywhere else myself. I've been to

Panorica, Santa Esmeralda, Arelia, even Mars. They're all nice, but this is like living in paradise full time." Thanks, Travis.

"Well, there's almost always something, you know, something interesting about anywhere you go." A waitress—a cisform woman, tall with straight black hair—appears and sets down Gail's glass, along with whatever Sky ordered. Looks like another coffee. She takes a quick drink of the mimosa, deeper than she should, barely managing not to choke on the bubbles. "The River's huge. I mean, if you add up all the area it's much smaller than Earth, but it's so varied." She's pretty sure Squarejaw would lift his brows at that if he were here, but all three of them nod. Good. She feels her words growing warmer with the sparkling wine. "And that's what I love about what I do. Every year I go places I'd never thought I would."

"So work's good?" Nevada's expression glows with unfeigned interest. Travis looks sincerely interested, too.

"Yeah." She doesn't risk a glance toward Sky. "There are long slow stretches—really long ones—so I do other work sometimes. But the payouts can be pretty big when they happen."

The stag chuckles, lapping at his orange juice. Oh, that tongue. "I always kinda figured you'd get into sales."

"Me? Sales? God, no. Retail's close enough and I haven't had *that* slow a stretch in a decade now."

"Yeah, you, sales. You're a smooth talker. You could sell life vests to otters."

Gail snorts at that. Nevada giggles in a way only someone who'd never heard that line could.

The waitress returns with all four plates. The kitchen must have held Travis and Nevada's food so everything would come out at once. The server isn't strictly cisform, she sees now, but she's not a totemic, either; she has a short, reptilian-looking red tail with a spade at the tip, and stubby horns almost hidden by her hair. Cute. She's heard of people who tried for wings—not to fly, but just for the aesthetics—but hasn't heard of any successful attempts. Adding one tail to two legs and two arms may not be *easy,* but adding another pair of limbs goes beyond resculpting the musculoskeletal system into completely reimagining it.

"So what do you do now, Nevada? I know you were thinking of going back to school."

"I did. I went back to school to go back to school." The vixen laughs again, cutting into her chicken-stuffed cornbread. "I'm a teacher."

"Which stage?"

"I started with first, but this year I'm teaching fourth."

Gail nods. Almost every student takes at least one of their five stages in a classroom setting, usually two or three. She'd ended up taking the last half of third stage and all of fourth and fifth out, too, to save Sky's sanity. "Neat. I hope."

"Oh, it is. It's so different from what I grew up with. Solera doesn't have an out-of-home school program at all, and there's no stages. It's all about test levels there."

Gail wrinkles her nose. "That figures. They like doing first stage out of home here because it's best for socialization, which I think Solera's philosophically opposed to."

Nevada laughs. "Now, I *did* have friends growing up."

"But no totemic friends," Travis says.

She shakes her head. "No. There was only one totemic family in the neighborhood, and their child was already full transform." She smiles humorlessly. "Which my family thought was awful."

Gail has some of the toast. It's prepared well, the batter crispy enough that it cracks under the fork while the bread inside has turned meltingly soft. "That's still a huge argument here."

"I know. We talked about it back on Panorica, remember? I understand the idea of choosing what you are. I mean…" She waves at herself. "But I know if I could, I'd want my child to be born totemic. Transforming early is as close as we can get."

She nods. Sky strongly feels the same way; so did their mom. If she hadn't, Gail probably wouldn't be a rat. "So no kids yet yourself?"

"No. But we're planning for one."

Travis grins. "And trying hard. We're not sure which species, though."

That's a common dilemma for mixed couples. "Fox with antlers," she suggests.

Nevada chokes, but Travis's grin just grows more. "That could be pretty sexy when he gets older."

The vixen elbows him. "Or her, and she might not look good with antlers."

"*Everyone* looks good with antlers."

Sky's pulled her viewcard out, holding it at arm's length and scrolling through its display with a finger. As slight as the frown on her face is, it's growing. "What's wrong?"

The wolf shakes her head, and rises to her feet. "Excuse me a moment." She walks away from the table.

"So what made you decide to visit again after all this time?"

Gail looks back to Travis, startled. Sky didn't tell them—well, no, she *wouldn't* tell them why Gail was here and Gail would be pissed if she had.

"I mean, it could be that you finally got homesick, but I don't think you do that." His grin crooks into an accusing smirk.

"No. I mean, there are things I miss. People I miss." She raises her hands apologetically. "People I should stay in better touch with."

"You should." Travis nods. "How long are you staying for?"

"I don't know. A few days."

He gives Nevada a prompting look. Uh-oh. What's this about?

Nevada bites her lip. "If you have time, can I ask you to do something?"

"Uh. Sure."

"Could you come speak to my class?"

What— "About what?"

"About your mother, about the RTEA and everything they did. Everything they still do. We've been talking about equality issues recently, and …" She takes a deep breath. "I'm kind of out of my depth."

"God, and you think I wouldn't be? I can talk about antique spaceships, but the only thing that qualifies me for talking about old social problems is my family name." She gestures over at Sky. "Why not get her?" As she speaks she looks at the wolf, who's talking with someone via the card. She's keeping her voice very low, but her expression's shifting from merely upset to positively furious.

"Because as much as I like Sky, you're …" Nevada seems to catch herself, then looks down at the floor. "You're the reason I've become who I am now."

Gail swallows. God, that's not a good reason. "I don't know, Nevada. Like I said, I'm only going to be on the Ring a few days."

"Just speak for a half-hour. I'll set it up quickly. The day after tomorrow."

Travis joins his wife in looking at her pleadingly. Nobody says *it's the least you can do* aloud, but they don't have to.

"Sure." She tries not to sound resigned.

Nevada's ears lift and she beams, but abruptly Sky stalks back to the table. "I'm sorry, but I need to leave on a work emergency." The viewcard gets shoved back into her pocket with enough force Gail's surprised it doesn't rip through the cloth.

"Do I need to come with you?"

The wolf hesitates.

"Does it involve what we're working on?"

"Yes."

Nevada's wide eyes become worried again. "Are you in some kind of trouble, Gail? Is there anything I can do to help? You did so much for me—"

"No, I don't think so." She gives Nevada's cheek a kiss, then Travis's. "Send me details about the school visit, Nevada."

As they walk off, she murmurs to Sky. "How serious is it?"

"Officers from the Panorica Federation are here to take the databox back from Agent Thomas."

"Terrific."

When they arrive at the hotel, they're met by a rabbit woman and a raccoon man, both wearing simple outfits and both adorned with the blue-ring-white-dot cloisonné pins. Sky nods to them and waves a follow-me motion, without breaking stride. The wolf's putting on her own pin as she moves. Given the ferocity in her scowl, it's a marvel she has the control to keep from slamming the room door as she flings it open.

In addition to Ansel and Thomas, there's two uniformed PFS officers: Wolfe and a balding cisform man only a few centimeters taller than Gail. The balding man turns abruptly as the group enters. When he finds himself looking up to meet Sky's eyes, he looks momentarily nervous. Good.

She launches into the silence. "I'm Bright Sky, with the Ring Judicial Cooperative. These are my associates, Karen Dupree and Robert Bunten." She indicates the rabbit and raccoon respectively. If she catches the microsneer he flashes when she gives her own name, she gives no sign, but Gail's clenching her fists. "I must have missed the communication the PFS surely sent to the RJC before arriving here. You are?"

"Captain Taylor. With all due respect, Ms. Sky, I'm not here on business that involves the RJC. I'm here to ensure that property in an ongoing PFS investigation isn't compromised."

"We know." Dupree speaks, her voice mild. "However, this is not only occurring on the Ring at this very moment, it involves a Ring citizen." She gestures toward Gail.

Taylor shoots a venomous glare at Gail. She volleys one back.

"And I'm here to resume that investigation, in the jurisdiction where it belongs." The glare shifts to Agent Thomas. "You had no authority to take crucial evidence off Panorica and you knew that full well." He points accusingly at Wolfe. "And so did you."

"This is Interpol's case, not yours, Captain Taylor." Jack lifts his brows. "I determined that I no longer directly wanted to work with the PFS to complete the investigation."

"Interpol's already determined the disposition of that damn thing!" He points at the databox now. It's on the desk, sitting on top of other bigger, sleek boxes Gail can't recognize. Holographic windows float through the desk's airspace, ghostly cybernetic flotsam and jetsam. "And how dare you criticize the PFS after we've—"

"Released the guy who had the stolen databox on him when you found him and rescinded the warrant for him after he came after me?" Gail throws her hands in the air. "Yeah, you're doing a fucking terrific job. Have a cookie."

While Taylor looks livid enough to spit, she can tell he's processing that. "That release order was a mistake. The PFS still intends to pick him up. None of that changes the legality of bringing evidence we need to return to Interpol *here* without authorization."

She points at Squarejaw. "He's Interpol! It's with him! Job done!"

Wolfe shakes his head. "Interpol wants it back with us."

Squarejaw's voice remains mild. "Captain, right now you have as much evidence supporting Keces' claim to ownership as there is Quanta's. What we have that you don't is evidence connecting Quanta Biotechnics to Mr. Corbett. The investigation I'm doing here may *make* this your case. If the databox goes back to Earth, your jurisdiction goes with it."

What? They've made the connection? How?

Sky's the first one to speak. "Explain this."

Taylor holds up a hand. "Whoever ends up with this case, it's not going to be the RJC."

Dupree clears her throat. "As I said, this involves a Ring citizen. Two, counting Mr. Corbett. Wouldn't it be easier to informally share information now?" She smiles brightly.

Agent Thomas nods, and gestures at Ansel. "Mr. Santara?"

"Right." The fox points at an open display window. "We've been following up on the Lantern Foundation, the charity Corbett's done work for. It turns out they fund a lot of studies about the dangers of genetic transformation."

Sky looks over his shoulder. "Like totemics?"

"Like totemics. Now, they've gotten almost two-thirds of their funding over the last decade from the Thomas and Cathy Burke Foundation on Earth, and share three board members with them." He scrolls the window. "Thomas Burke is the former CEO of the Burke-Weaver Group, a holding company. Thirty-three years ago, Burke-Weaver bought a huge biotechnology firm and took it private. Guess which one?"

Gail closes her eyes. "Quanta Biotechnics."

"And as soon as he did, he appointed Thomas Burke Junior the VP overseeing R&D, and his first act was to sell the totemic division to Keces."

"So both Burkes look kinda anti-totemic."

Ansel snorts. "There's no 'kinda' about it. Lantern's funded just about every pseudo-intellectual argument against transformation out there, from 'genetic pollution' to critiques of our spirituality."

Taylor's been listening with a furrowed brow. "All right, but that's a damn circumstantial connection between Corbett and Quanta. And what does it matter if this think tank is allegedly 'anti-totemic?'"

Sky points at the databox. "It makes the analysis of that box even more critical. The creators of transformation technology and their successor, both involved in a theft tied to anti-totemic activists?"

Taylor's scowl immediately returns. "You do *not* have authorization to tamper with it in any way."

As another argument picks up, Gail runs a hand through her hair. *The goddess of change. It's a project code name. Defense and medical.*

The keys to heaven and hell.

"I think I know what's on it." They don't hear her until she almost shouts. "I know what's on it!"

Everyone falls quiet.

"Kis, call Jason Nakimura. Connect the call to the room speaker, but only take my input."

Kismet speaks over the hotel room's audio. "Yes, Gail."

Beedle boop "Ms. Simmons." Nakimura sounds guarded. "You're calling from New Coyoacán, yet the databox is on Panorica."

"It's here with me. Long story, but I think I'm close to returning it to you." She ignores Thomas's brow lift and Taylor's eye narrow. "But I need to ask you something."

"And that is?"

"Shakti is your project, and Kali is Quanta's. They're both based on technology used for totemics. I'm guessing Kali is a bioweapon. Shakti is about creating—what?"

Now everyone in the room's staring at her. Sky's ears fold down.

"If you have opened that databox—"

"I'm trying to prove we don't need to."

It takes him several seconds to speak again. "Your conjectures are mostly correct. The projects are two applications of the same biomedical technology to target specific genetic markers. Our work on Kali, however, is years ahead of Quanta's. As for Shakti, it performs genetic modifications that allow inheritable *in utero* transformation."

Sky's eyes grow wide and she begins to tremble.

No. Holding this damn promise out again— "We've been hearing that for generations."

"The theoretical solution is older than totemics, Ms. Simmons. What we've addressed is the failure in practice, and we're months away from productization. Or were, until coordinated attacks against us destroyed all but one copy of a crucial data set."

"This copy."

"Without it, Shakti will be set back at least five years, more likely over a decade, as will any countermeasures to Kali." He sighs audibly. "To celebrate our new spirit of openness with one another, can you elucidate just why you and the databox are on the Ceres Ring?"

"To give Thomas enough time to figure out who really owns it. And as much as I know now, that part's still surprisingly fuzzy. I'll call you back."

"Agent Thomas is with you?" Nakimura sounds dismayed.

"Yeah, he says hi. Gotta go." She cuts the call.

All the totemics in the room—even Officer Wolfe—have taken a seat or leaned against something. Dupree looks like she's crying. Sky's whispering to herself. "They've achieved Mara's dream."

Ansel takes a deep breath and smiles lopsidedly. "That explains the value. God, I can only imagine how much they're going to charge, given that it stops us from being recurring revenue."

Sky's expression of shocked joy turns to shocked affront. "This is—our future, Ansel. Our children. Not inventions to sell and fight over."

"We *are* inventions, Sky. We've always been inventions."

Taylor cuts into the ensuing silence with a heaving sigh. "Now that you're finished helping us all violate the privacy of Quanta or Keces or both, Simmons, legally we're still where we were ten minutes ago. The databox is still evidence in both a physical theft out here and a data theft on Earth. It's still been taken to the Ring against orders. And it still has to come back with us."

"It's not going anywhere." As she whirls on him, Sky's voice could shatter steel. "This situation directly involves the welfare of a Ceres Ring citizen, and we are asserting our jurisdiction. The databox's disposition will be determined by a Ring Judicial Cooperative tribunal."

The other Ring officials nod assent, giving Taylor challenging looks. For a rabbit, Dupree's got almost as solid a *cross me and I will cut you* glare as Sky does.

At once Taylor's back in spitting livid mode. "You can't just—"

Thomas folds his hands behind his back. "I believe they did just."

When the raccoon speaks his tone remains pleasantly mild. "If you wish to appeal, you're welcome to go through our embassy on Panorica."

Taylor visibly forces his voice to be level. "We'll see about that. And your role in all this will be highlighted, Agent Thomas." He stomps out of the room, motioning Wolfe to follow.

Squarejaw and the Ring judiciary officials look at one another. Gail drops down into a seat and stares at the ceiling.

Chapter 14

WHEN GAIL SLIPS OUT of the room it's only a few minutes after Captain Spitty's grand exit, but everyone else is too distracted by Sky giving orders—mostly to Ansel—to notice. Is it too early to drink? No, since she had a mimosa with breakfast. But she thinks she just wants a coffee. She gets one at the lounge, then takes a seat where she can look out over the river.

She's barely taken a sip before Agent Squarejaw comes in and gets his own coffee. He approaches her table, then hesitates. "May I?"

"Sure. But shouldn't you be working on your case?"

He sits down opposite her. "If it were still my case, yes. I'm feeling somewhat at a loss now that Bright Sky's taken over."

"Welcome to my teenage years."

He smiles crookedly. "You know more of the legal system here than I do. What does a tribunal involve?"

"Let me think." She drums her claws on the table, sifting school memories. "Every involved party in a case chooses one mediator as a representative, and the rest of the panel's filled out by a pool of citizens a majority agrees to. You need at least five people on a tribunal and the neutral panelists have to be a number greater than half of the parties in the case. So if you and I were suing one another, we'd have to both agree on three others. Then together we all hear evidence and a four-fifths vote decides the resolution."

He frowns. "Who are the parties in this case? Quanta, Keces, the PFS, Interpol, you, Mr. Corbett ... ?"

"Depends on who the RJC decides has standing." She sips her coffee. "I hope to hell they get Keces in, because it might stop Nakimura's damn destroy-Gail's-life clock."

"Do you still believe it's theirs?"

"Yeah. Do you?"

"In part. I think Keces stole work from Quanta as a base for their projects. So they're *both* guilty of theft. I don't know where that leaves us."

"I don't, either." She sets her mug down and leans back, staring at the ceiling. "Quanta's version of Kali isn't very good, though, and the databox is the only copy of Shakti."

"Assuming Nakimura told you the truth."

"Assuming Nakimura told me the truth." She sighs.

"Here's something interesting. We couldn't find any evidence of payments to Mr. Corbett from Lantern or any group they fund."

She straightens up. "So?"

"I'm trying to understand why he's here. Purely for ideology? He said it was about the end of the human race."

"That's just old bullshit Purity arguments. They accuse us of setting ourselves up as new, improved humans, twist everything we say or do, and if any of us say 'that's not true,' our denials are just proof of how deep the conspiracy runs."

"So you think it's solely irrational hatred."

"Mom always said hate isn't irrational, it's childish. It's pointing at something—a person, a company, a group, a government—and saying, 'Everything would be better if it wasn't for them.'"

He nods thoughtfully, and takes another sip of coffee. "But isn't it about to be true?"

She stiffens. "What? No. What do you mean?"

"Shakti."

Oh, come on, that's—that's—that's correct. She stares into the distance, feeling sucker punched. "We'd turn into actual new subspecies of humans."

"I think stopping that is what this operation's about. At least from Mr. Corbett's point of view."

She nods, digesting that. "But it's crazy to think they've gotten the company that created totemics on board with that."

"Someone at one of these two companies had to get information to Mr. Corbett, and perhaps Purity, about Shakti. Quanta may have been driven by Burke's anti-transformation stance in the past. It's also possible they're simply using Mr. Corbett to advance their own agenda, rather than sharing his."

"Yeah, but this whole plan just seems so…so baroque if it's only about getting Keces's improvements to Kali."

"Was anything else stolen from Keces?"

"The databox is all they asked about." She shakes her head, then sips her coffee. "I'm impressed with your whole chain-of-reasoning detective thing."

"That's why they pay me the big dollars."

"Do they pay you the big dollars?"

"No."

Laughing, she sets down her drink again. Then yesterday's conversation on *Kismet* drifts back to her. "Well, I guess they're big dollars as long as you're out here."

"In a relative sense."

"I'm sorry I've made your posting so interesting right out of the dock."

It's his turn to laugh. "I admit I expected things to be…quieter than they've been. From what I've heard they usually are at this station, at least for liaison officers."

"We don't have a lot of crime."

"You don't have a lot of crime that requires Interpol. Statistically, there's more crime per capita across the River than there is on Earth."

"Huh. I wouldn't have honestly thought that."

He shrugs. "I think it's unavoidable. The median cost of living out here is higher than it is anywhere on Earth. Most of the costs are technically voluntary, but in practice you're just choosing who you pay most of them to—choosing *not* to pay them isn't viable."

"No, but we can choose to pay less than you do for a worse service, or pay more for a better one, right? Even on Panorica and the Ring."

"That doesn't help people who can't pay. The Ring's the only settlement here with a true safety net."

He's right, but that still seems awfully reductive. "You think that's responsible for a higher crime rate?"

"I'd be wary of drawing a simple straight line between the two, but I'm not the only one who's asked that question."

"I can see the correlation, sure. But, I mean, it's not like you don't have crime under your system, or you'd be out of a job."

"We have crime. And a lot more bureaucracy." He shakes his head. "Between the FBI, Interpol, and whatever foreign police agencies I'm working with, the only way I get anything done is finding mutually unacceptable compromises between everyone."

She laughs. "I like that phrase. There's a saying I've heard out here that runs something like, 'Any political system works if everyone agrees to it, but you can't make a political system everyone agrees to.'"

"That sounds like a folksy version of... what was the actual social science hypothesis? The Miller Paradox?"

"The Miller Limit. He studied the River and hypothesized there's a point after which no society can be completely non-coercive. Sometimes people quote a number, but he just said it was when the second generation fully comes of age."

Thomas furrows his brow, then has an *oh, I get it* look. "Because they weren't a party to any of the implicit social contracts."

"Right. If you grow up and agree with everything that your parents signed on for, great, but if you don't, then either you have to leave, accept something you don't like, or try to change a status quo that the older generation's going to fight to keep. No matter how things shake out, somebody's going to feel forced into a choice they didn't want."

"So after a few generations, you end up with societies where most people agree with most things but almost no one agrees with everything."

"Yeah, and they all change over time." She chuckles. "So maybe not that far off from Earth after all, these days."

"With magnitudes more people and centuries more time to argue, sometimes it feels like no one agrees with anything. You might wonder why everyone hasn't moved out here." He looks out the window, across the river.

She grins, looking out, too. As much as she hates to admit it, it really is a stunning view. "We don't have the space."

"No, and immigrating from Earth or Mars to anywhere on the River is tightly regulated. On this end, too, you know. It's my understanding that the Ceres Ring gives priority to totemics."

"Huh. Well, it is..." She trails off, surprised by the words she's about to say, but they're true. "It's as close to a homeland as we have."

"It's a beautiful place." He looks out the window again. "I'd love to be stationed here instead of Panorica. I could imagine Laurie here, swimming with the otters."

"Laurie?"

"My daughter."

Daughter? This is something Squarejaw hasn't talked about before. Not that he'd have had reason to, but being sidelined seems to have made him chatty. "Huh. How old is she? And that river doesn't have otters in it, does it?"

"She's ten." He points at a building across the river. "The otters run the canoe rental place over there."

"Oh." Right, that kind of otter. But if he has a kid, why the hell—that's too personal a question to just throw at him. Dammit, she wants to know, though. Maybe she can put it delicately. "I didn't know you had a family."

"We really haven't talked about anything but your case until…well, until now. And they're a very long way away."

"Are you still married?"

"We're separated."

She's dancing around the question in her head, still. "That's a long time for a daughter to be away from her dad. She understands you're coming back, right?"

He gives her a sharp look. Okay, she's not being as delicate as she hoped.

"Of course." His brows sink rather than lift. "I hope she does. And I hope I am. That's not entirely up to me."

"So you're not just…" No, don't finish that with *just walking out.* Talk about being indelicate.

"Just?"

She shifts awkwardly in her seat and tries to pick a path out from the conversational minefield she's led herself into. "Sorry. This is a tough topic for me. My dad left when I was ten and I haven't seen him since."

"I admit I've wondered how you ended up being adopted by your adopted sister. That's very unusual."

"Unusual, that's our family." She bites her lip. "I should have been sent to live with dad, you know? Wherever he was living on Earth. Somewhere in Europe. At least then. I think. They told me that he said he couldn't take me, and I imagined it was some kind of emergency, some horrible situation, something temporary. It wasn't until I was sixteen that Sky told me she didn't know why. All she knew is he said no."

Thomas looks shocked.

She takes a deep breath. "Even after that I kept looking for explanations that weren't him just not wanting me. But I never found one and he never gave me one. So after a while I just stopped trying. He should be the one to reach out, to say why, you know? He never has. I don't think he ever will."

It takes him a few seconds to respond, voice getting softer but less studied, more direct. "I'm sorry."

She shrugs, smiling awkwardly, not sure there's a response. Neither his fault nor his problem.

He sips his coffee, letting the silence grow, then looks out the window again, speaking slowly. "I didn't leave my family because I wanted to. I'd do anything for Laurie. I'd still do anything for Claudia. But what she asked me to do for her was to go away."

"So that's why you volunteered to come out here?"

He doesn't turn to her, but he smiles faintly. "Are you imagining I might have had an argument with her that ended with me screaming, 'You want me to give you space? How's *this* for space?'"

"No." She keeps her eyes on him, though, letting the *but did you?* hang unspoken.

"I didn't, but I thought it. I was just smart enough to keep it to myself." He takes a long sip, enough of a slurp to make Gail's ears twitch. "Unfortunately, I wasn't smart enough to think better of it until I was already on the ship out here."

"Oh."

He gives his own shrug. "Now I'm out here, and they're still there. I told Claudia she and Laurie could come out for a visit, but they can't. I know that. Ten to fourteen weeks each way, only during launch windows. You don't visit here, you move here temporarily, and Claudia doesn't have the kind of work that would let her do that even if she wanted to."

Most kinds of work wouldn't let you do that, she guesses—keeping in touch with the inner system gets either very slow or very expensive. And Claudia wouldn't want to even if she could, not for Jack, would she? Not right now.

What leads a couple to a point where one of them thinks it's a good idea to go halfway across the solar system and the other agrees? Did he cheat on her? Did she cheat on him? There's nothing she can add to the conversation and apparently nothing else Jack wants to volunteer. She finishes her coffee in silence.

Kismet chimes in her ear unexpectedly. "Kingsolver Repair would like you to come by their facility to check on my progress and arrange payment."

Payment. A really big payment. Which her bank will still block. "Terrific."

She's alone enough of the time that she forgets talking to Kis looks like talking to herself. Jack can tell she's not addressing him, so he just looks confused. "Uh, I need to go check on how *Kismet* is coming along." She stands up.

"They didn't give you bad news, did they? You look worried."

"I'm still having that, ah, issue with my bank. I sent them the info they need to clear it up this morning but I haven't heard back."

"I hope it goes smoothly. I'm going to get another cup of coffee, and maybe go see if I can impress Sky with my chain-of-reasoning detective thing."

She chuckles. "Good luck."

Gail picked Kingsolver Repair for *Kismet* because they did the initial inspection for her when she bought the ship, and also because she doesn't know any other repair shop here by name. New Coyoacán and Panorica are two of only three ports on the River with privately-owned repair bays by the docking facility. Anywhere else, you either pay to have a crew come to you or drag into one of a few dozen free-floating stations, mostly ones that double as salvage yards. She knows all of them by reputation and most of them through direct business.

Her regular mechanic's damn good, but his place always looks like the aftermath of a comet strike. By comparison, Kingsolver's bay looks supernaturally neat. Every tool has its assigned place, all of them are in good shape, and judging by the display she's looking at—an overlay that stays perfectly matched to *Kismet* while she's looking through a physical window at the real craft—they're state of the art. None of this bodes well for her bank account.

"So we've melded in new inner hull sections here and here," a mechanic's telling her. The mechanic is a coyote totemic, lithe and beautifully androgynous. Tan and warm gray fur pairs with an iridescent red undercoat that shifts and shimmers mesmerizingly as they move. They move an awful lot. Is the red natural, or a dye? Probably not appropriate to ask, and definitely not appropriate to keep staring.

The coyote points at the appropriate areas of the overlay as they speak, each section lighting up when their claw tip touches the virtual space.

"The new plates for the outer hull have been printed, but they're not out of verification yet." Their voice is a melodious alto. Walking to the rear side of the display/ship, the mechanic touches near the exhaust port. "And, we found fractures in the exit cones of nozzles two and three. We've taken care of those already." Despite being in overalls laced with the scent of machine oil, there's faint undertones of lavender and some other herb, like they've used a nicely perfumed cleaning powder.

"What caused them?"

"Might be just a mix of normal wear and tear and the banging up that you took on your way here. You know, I've never worked on a ship that was attacked by pirates before."

"I've never piloted a ship attacked by pirates before."

"Did they know who you were?"

What? They knew her ship had the databox on it, but—right, that's not what the coyote means. "I don't know, but it wouldn't have mattered. They weren't after me, they were after my cargo." And from the way things are looking, if they did know, that would just have been more of a reason to attack, not less.

"Still. That's…that's so…" The coyote shakes their head. "I shouldn't expect pirates to have much of a conscience, huh?"

"No, they're with whatever gets them the biggest payout." She shrugs. "And, look, I'm just the daughter of somebody who's famous here. And famous on Solera for the opposite reason. Go anywhere else on the River, though, and they won't have heard of my mom, much less me."

The coyote stops and looks at her directly. Those are the most beautiful green eyes Gail thinks she's ever seen. "You're wrong, Ms. Simmons. Go anywhere in the solar system there are totemics, and they'll have heard of you."

"Not me. My mom. They'll have heard of Judith Simmons. Maybe." She taps her chest. "But not of me."

The mechanic walks out past the display onto the dry dock floor, motioning Gail to follow. "Well, we've heard of you. *I've* heard of you. And I know I said this already, but it's really an honor to meet you."

"I kinda wish people would stop saying things like that."

"Sorry." Their ears fold down and they flash a sheepish, disarming grin. As far as Gail knows every coyote she's met has been perfectly trustworthy, but this is still the first coyote smile she remembers that hasn't made her want to check her pockets.

This is a view of *Kismet* she hasn't had since she bought the ship: the view you get when you can physically walk up to her, not see her through a window or on a monitor. Floor-mounted braces, wall-mounted struts and ceiling-mounted cranes suspend her in the air about five meters off the bay's floor. The coziness of the cabin belies the ship's true size, twenty meters from bow to stern. Most spacecraft enthusiasts refer to the Arcturus, with its weirdly ovoid nose and boxy back end, as "ungainly," and that's when they're being tactful. They're wrong. She's beautiful.

"Kis," she says aloud. "How've they been treating you?"

"Repairs are progressing on the schedule the repair company provided, Gail."

"Everyone's been following the right procedures? No shortcuts?"

"The service has been at a very high standard so far."

The coyote's ears are perked up, and the smile is back, even broader than before. "You're really having a conversation with the ship AI?"

"Don't tell me I'm the only pilot you've met with transducers for this."

"No, you're not, but most of the pilots I've met with implants still just use viewcards when they're not on board."

"Why? Kis makes a better interface for, well, *everything* than a view-card."

"I can see that. But it's your style," the coyote says, simultaneously with *Kismet* replying, "Thank you, Gail."

Wow. That's not the first time the ship's responded when she didn't expect her to, but it still throws her for a loop. "Um. My style?"

"You're not saying 'ship, give me the current status,' you're asking her how she's feeling."

"We have a good relationship. So you think everything'll be finished by today?"

"It might be tomorrow, but no later. Which brings me to the part where we have to talk about payment." The coyote's voice becomes studiously offhanded, but an ear flags. "Something came up doing a pre-payment check I need to clear with you."

Of course it did. She doesn't trust herself to sound equally offhanded if she tries to speak, so she grunts inquisitively. "Mmm?"

"Your bank indicated we wouldn't be able to complete a transaction for your first installment amount."

"There's, uh, I've been working through a kind of bank error they've had. It's a little complicated." She stops herself from blathering details;

the mechanic can't help, and explaining that the mistake involves a fraud accusation won't do her any favors. "I'll check with the bank again. I think everything should be fine by tomorrow."

"I can talk to the accounting department for you if you need to set up some kind of alternative payment plan."

"No." She shakes her head. "I mean, thanks, but you shouldn't need to."

"Okay." The coyote smiles again. "If there's anything I can help with, let me know."

"Thanks again. Uh, I didn't catch your name?"

"Dani. D-a-n-i." The coyote's smile gets more impish. "I'm surprised you didn't ask your ship. She knows me pretty well by now."

Gail laughs. "You make that sound kind of saucy." Dani's smile grows more, maybe because she's looking right into the coyote's eyes. She clears her throat. "Anyway, thanks. Uh—" Oh, hell. This has been bothering her since she got here. "How do you—"

"Singular they."

What? Oh. Gail laughs. "I was curious, but that wasn't what I was going to ask. How do you—I mean—people don't, like, learn my mom's name in school or something, do they?" Nevada's students might, but that's Nevada being Nevada, isn't it?

Dani's head tilts. "I guess it'd depend on the school. But when I learned about institutional prejudice, how River society deals with totemics … I learned her name. And I learned yours, too."

Gail gives the coyote another weak smile. God, she's going to need a history lesson in her own life, because the class she's agreed to speak to in two days may know more about her mother than she does.

Chapter 15

"I TOLD YOU, I haven't been on Carmona in years."

Gail's back to the Sonora River Inn, but hasn't gone in yet. She's pacing on the boardwalk in front of it, speaking with a real live person at her bank. They called her. Initially she'd thought that was a good sign; now she's not so sure.

"I understand, Ms. Simmons, but as I said, the disputed transactions are from nine years ago."

"Oh, come *on*. How can that even happen?"

"It's rare, but it's not unheard of."

"After *nine years*?" She grips a wooden dock piling with both hands, glaring into the water.

"It's not unheard of," the voice simply repeats. "Can you tell me anything about a sale you might have made in this time frame for thirty thousand six hundred dollars?"

That's all? "No."

"It was a private transaction, if that helps jog your memory. Equipment?"

She tries not to scream. "If you know what it was, just tell me!"

"Used equipment sold to a private buyer."

God, how is she supposed to remember anything from nine years ago—wait. She sighs heavily. "A water pump?"

"Yes. Can you tell me anything about that transaction?"

"What am I supposed to have that you don't? They're your records!"

"As I said earlier, we don't have the records to disprove the allegation, Ms. Simmons, because you weren't our customer then. If you can just send corroborating information from your previous banking partner, we can move the resolution process forward."

"I asked my former judiciary on Carmona to get in touch with you. Haven't they?"

"I don't have that information."

"Well, what makes you think I do?" Silence. "And they waited nine goddamn years to file a complaint? You don't think that's kind of odd?"

"The transaction has been flagged as fraudulent. That doesn't mean the flag was triggered by a complaint from the original customer, Ms. Simmons. This came up in an internal review."

She rubs her face. "So should I talk to my old bank, not just my old judiciary?"

"It might help."

"Fine. I'll talk to that bank. Meanwhile, you have to lift the spending restriction on my account."

"I can do that as soon as the dispute clears—"

"Look, I need to pay an unexpected repair bill tonight. It needs to be lifted tonight."

"We'll clear it as fast as we're able to, assuming the transactions check out, Ms. Simmons."

"Which needs to be *tonight*."

"I'll note that in the dispute log, Ms. Simmons. I can check on extending a line of credit to you in the meantime, if you'd like."

"Yes, fine."

Another few seconds pass. "I'm sorry, I can't extend your credit past where it already is. Is there anything else I can help you with?"

There's nothing they've helped her with yet, so why start now? "No." She disconnects the call and channels the energy she was going to put in the scream into slamming her hand against the piling repeatedly. On the fourth slam she gets a sharp jab in her palm. Cursing under her breath, she stomps into the inn, using the side of her index claw to work the splinter out of the pad.

When she opens the room's door, Ansel and Sky are still arguing. Jack's looking between both of them with a weary expression. Mara's Blood, it can't be the same argument, can it?

It isn't. Rather, it is, but the tenor's changed.

"—all the engines in the damn solar system and it's going to be a month if you're lucky." Ansel's ears are flat.

"Only if you care about doing it undetectably."

"I *do* care about that, and even if I didn't—"

"Hi, Gail," Jack says loudly, stepping around the other two and walking toward the rat. Both fox and wolf stop and look over at her.

"Hey. Should I come back in a bit?"

Sky looks up at the ceiling, closing her eyes. "Every time Ansel describes the databox's encryption he makes it sound more uncrackable than the last time he described it."

Ansel makes an exasperated groan. "No, I described it as impossible to break this morning. You just didn't want to hear it then, and you still don't want to hear it."

"And Agent Thomas doesn't want to see the box unlocked at all, despite knowing what's on it."

Jack lifts his brows. "I don't want to tamper with evidence in an investigation Interpol still *does* have direct involvement in."

"Of course not." Gail rubs her temples. "Have we ruled out just returning the thing to Keces and calling it a day?"

Sky and Jack speak at the same time. "That's not an option." "We can't do that yet."

Gail groans. "Of course not." She drops into a seat. "You know that *socius indignus* order is going to be filed against me tomorrow, right?"

"It will not." Sky's voice is firm. "Both Keces and Quanta will have representatives here in the morning."

She looks up. "What?" She feels the blood leave her ears. "You've told Nakimura *you* have the databox?"

"We'll have a meeting tomorrow, select two neutral parties to fill out the panel the next day, and hold the tribunal a day or two after that. Mr. Nakimura can't hold you responsible for returning the databox now."

"No, he can hold me responsible for handing the databox over to you!"

Sky tilts her head. "You didn't. Agent Thomas did."

"Not helping, Sky. Not helping."

"I think we can convince Mr. Nakimura your role in this is largely over." Jack sounds soothingly reconciliatory. "Assuming he's told you the truth, he's likely to get the databox back."

"That's not a best outcome, but it's preferable to giving it Quanta." Sky's tone seeps with bitterness.

Jack furrows his brow. "Those are the only two outcomes."

"Perhaps."

"Oh, Mara's Blood." Ansel leaps to his feet. "If you're even *thinking* about co-opting Shakti in the name of some greater totemic good, you're going to do it without my help."

"Why isn't that an option?" Sky's voice grows just as heated. "We know—at least on the Ring, we know—that some things *should* be owned by everyone. And if there's anything, *anything*, that applies to most of all..." She trails off, shaking her head.

"Clean air and water? You can make a great case for that. But transformation is not a goddamn public good. Totemics have gotten along since before the River existed and we'll keep getting along just fine choosing whether to transform ourselves or our children."

"That's not what we've wanted for—"

"That's not what *you've* wanted. You don't speak for every other totemic, Sky. If I was going to violate my principles by not returning Shakti to Keces, I'd rather do it by shooting the fucking databox into the sun. Excuse me." He storms out of the room.

Jack runs a hand through his hair. "I'm going to go to the front desk and see if they have an ansible available. As much as I've been avoiding the home office, I think it's time to bring them in." He heads out, too.

Gail swallows, watching her sister quiver with rage, the wolf's eyes squeezed tightly shut. Sky slowly sinks into a seat on the sofa.

After a few seconds, Gail gets up and sits down by her, touching her hand to Sky's lightly.

Sky takes a shuddering breath and looks down at her. "I'm wrong to have even mentioned that, aren't I? Maybe I'm wrong to want it."

"I..." Gail shakes her head. "This is all heavy enough to be way past my tow rating. I don't think anyone can blame you for what you want. But I don't know if we can just say 'hey, this invention of yours that people have literally been killing each other over is too important to return to you.'"

"It's something Earth governments do all the time."

"Isn't that why we're out here and not back there?"

Sky summons a brief, sad smile. "I'm not used to you being the one to talk sense into me."

"I'm sure it won't happen again. Will Agent Thomas be on the tribunal?"

She shakes her head. "The three parties will be Quanta, Keces and the Ring."

"That's going to make both Interpol and the PFS real unhappy."

"It might." She shrugs, then stands up. "I don't think there's anything I can do here now. I'm going to go by the RJC office and then go home." She starts to walk to the door, then turns. "Are you going to spend the night here?"

"I don't know. But I want to come by to talk with you about what I'm going to say to Nevada's class, and if you're gonna be up to your whiskers in tribunal stuff tomorrow maybe we need to do it tonight."

Sky smiles. "I'd like that."

Once she's alone, Gail looks around the hotel room. It'd be nice to just nap. Maybe she'd better make sure that Ansel hasn't spontaneously combusted, though.

She finds him—naturally—in the bar, with some kind of outrageously orange drink in front of him. He still looks pissed. She sits down by him and he doesn't say a thing.

The bartender comes over to her. How adventurous is she feeling? Not at all. "Rum and Coke." He nods, moves off, returns with the drink a minute later.

She takes a sip, then another. Ansel still hasn't spoken. Okay, up to her. "I didn't know you felt that strongly about *not* having inheritable transformation."

He takes a too-long sip of his drink through the straw, then coughs. "I didn't, either." At least now he just looks morose. "There are so many mixed-species couples. What's the child of a rabbit and a fox look like? What would you have looked like, with a rodent totemic mother and a cisform father?"

"I guess we can ask whoever Keces sends to the tribunal."

"It's rhetorical. I mean, it's important, but it's just…God."

"You know, if someone's born a totemic and wants to be cisform, they could just get a transformation to do that."

"A reversal is always more expensive and more complicated."

"But it wouldn't be a reversal, it'd be a first transformation. And even if losing fur is harder than adding it, the cost would come down, assuming enough people say, 'No, I'd rather have duller senses and exposed skin.'" She touches his shoulder lightly. "You know, if Jack can't use you and you won't work for Sky, you can probably bail now. You've gone above and beyond already."

He snorts. "Even if I'm not working for her, I may still be a witness at this tribunal, so I shouldn't leave. Besides, until this is all over I don't know if my apartment's safe. Quanta knows I'm involved, and as much as I hate to say it, I distrust the police *here* a little less than the police on Panorica. So I may be on vacation in New Coyoacán for a while."

"It's a prettier place than I remember."

"It's a prettier place than you told me. You really undersold it." He sighs. "You also undersold how much of a force of nature your sister is."

"Some things you can only learn by experience."

He laughs, finally cracking a smile.

"So." Sky sets down two mugs of coffee she's made on the table in front of the sofa, then sits down beside Gail. "What have you been thinking about telling the class?"

"Let's see." She pulls out her viewcard and pretends to read notes off it. "What I have so far is 'something mom something RTEA something something something any questions.'"

The wolf picks up her mug. "That might need some more work."

She puts the card away. "No kidding. I met the mechanic who's working on my ship and they said they learned about mom in school. In school! She's a lesson, Sky!"

"We learned about totemic history in school."

"But this isn't history, this is—this is our mother. I mean, I know she's important, but what am I going to tell them that's new? Mom stuff? 'Well, she wasn't really the best housekeeper, and I bet she let Sky and me play outside unsupervised way more than your parents do.'"

"That might be a start." She smiles. "You're the only one who knows about your relationship with her. You know that even better than I do. And have you kept up at all with the Equality Association?"

"Less than you have, I'm sure. I mean, it's not that I haven't been interested. I've kept tabs, I've sent money sometimes. I even volunteered at outreach days a couple times on Panorica when I still lived there." Only to humor then-Linda, but she probably doesn't need to mention that.

The wolf leans back, cradling her coffee loosely and looking thoughtful. "You didn't get involved when you were young the way I did."

"You came to New Coyoacán to meet mom. You were a radical at fourteen."

"I was a radical at twelve. By the time I was fourteen, mom had talked sense into me." She turns, giving Gail a curious smile. "You know she wasn't that radical, don't you? There are a lot of voices that say otherwise, but I was there. She was the voice of moderation a lot more often than I think people know."

"You were there and, even though I'm her daughter, I really wasn't." She shakes her head. "I told Nevada you should be the one speaking."

"I think you'll do a wonderful job, but you're right, you're going to have to learn more about what you missed."

Gail smiles wryly. "I haven't missed it at all. You know I hate politics."

"I know you keep saying that. Then you go and get shot at by old guard Purity, do smuggling work around Lariat—"

"I was a courier!"

"My point is that for someone who says she hates politics, you haven't done a good job of staying out of them. Look at what's brought you back here now."

"Intersolar corporate espionage and an old schoolmate with a pathological grudge?"

"Mmm. If you're going to speak about mom, you're going to have to know not just what it was like for her to be your mother, but what it was like for her to be an activist." She picks up a tablet from the end table and starts tapping on it. "So you're going to watch this with me."

"What, we have home videos?"

"No, but we have public appearances. This is one I've watched…I don't know how many times. I don't even know how I came across it when I lived on Earth, but I saw it when I was eleven."

A rectangular part of the wall they're facing darkens, then brightens again as the video starts.

"I know this show," Gail says after a moment. "'Crosstalk.' It's still being produced. I hate it."

"Shush."

She *does* hate it. It's less an interview show than the host and a panel of three other people arguing about a timely topic. Of course, on this video it's a different host, a cisform woman who looks Spanish or Mexican. Not a New Coyoacán connection, though; the show's from Panorica. Two of the three panelists are totemics, full transforms—

One of them is Gail's mother.

At first it's like seeing a slightly younger version of herself: rat woman, about the same build, about the same height. Darker hair, more of a honey blonde. Longer.

The host introduces everyone, then the panel topic: the RTEA and its "controversial" tactics. When Judith launches into a casual but practiced response, Gail realizes it's one she recognizes. Not word for word, but she's heard it. She might have heard a version of it just before her mother was killed. She shivers.

And Sky was right: it's not the fiery speech of a mad bomber. It's all careful, acceptable, non-confrontational language. Yes, everyone has the same rights, and as insightful as it might be that rights aren't granted by a state, if you take the state out of the equation what happens? A state can use brute force to police rights, but on the River we can't. We have to use education and demonstration. In the long run, our way's more effective because it's about changing attitudes.

Gail figures the one who's going to speak against her—on Crosstalk, that's the whole point—will be the cisform guest, but it isn't. It's the other totemic. She thinks he's a horse. He's got a kind of creepy-looking biomod job; equines are hard to do well. "That's what you say, but it's not what you do. You're just appropriating the use of force for yourself. The whole premise of your group's actions is extortion: give us what we want, or we'll make your life difficult. We'll scare away your customers, we'll block access to your business, we'll vilify you in the media." Scattered audience clapping. "How is that any different from a protection racket?"

"This is one of the things I find fascinating and frustrating about the River," the cisform cuts in. He's got grey hair, looks like he's in his sixties; he was introduced as a famous novelist from the United States, although Gail has never heard of him. "You take some very noble, worthwhile ideas—like this strong stance against coercion—and apply them with no sense of proportion."

The horse splutters, but the host holds up her hand. "What do you mean, John?"

"Well, take the argument that taxation is theft. I hear that out here so much. It's taken as a given, like water is wet. Theft is obviously coercive, and taxation is obviously coercive, so they must be the same. But in every other detail—implementation, risk, individual cost, intended benefit—they're nothing alike. It's like saying a cat is a mammal, a dog is a mammal, therefore a cat is a dog. Our friend here," he gestures at the horse (who snorts), "and I think he's like a lot of the River's founders, wants to argue that coercion renders everything else irrelevant."

"They're not identical, but they're still on the same continuum."

Judith spreads her hands, in a gesture very similar to the one Gail makes when she's making a point. "If you ask my daughter, telling her to eat her vegetables is coercive."

The host laughs, along with some of the audience. Sky glances in Gail's direction with a smirk. Gail's ears lower. Oh God, she's an example.

She goes on. "But we don't really consider that coercion, right? Because we don't want our moral code to be something you can reduce down to 'never make somebody do something they don't want to.' Sometimes the right thing to do is something you *don't* want to do. And if we say, 'oh, if it's even slightly coercive we can't do it, end of discussion,' that makes us have to rationalize really stupid positions in the name of consistency. We can argue about which side of the line things like taxation and mandatory insurance are on, but only idiots would argue that 'give me all your money or I'll kill you' and 'eat your vegetables or you're grounded' are on the same side. Idiots and political theorists, I guess."

The laughter makes Horse scowl more deeply. "But that's not what we're talking about with the RTEA, we're talking about you stirring up mobs to bring pressure on people you don't like. We're talking about you potentially putting people out of business or even putting them in harm's way."

Judith remains unruffled but firm. "No, we're talking about forcing— and yes, I'll own that word—forcing people to face how their attitudes affect others. You may technically have a right to discriminate against me, but I damn well have a right to let everyone know that's not acceptable."

"But you don't have any right to force me to stop."

"Me saying things you don't want to hear isn't coercion. Me saying things you don't want *other* people to hear because they might agree with me and stop agreeing with you isn't coercion, either, even if it makes you feel threatened. Don't try and argue that me holding a protest rally is functionally the same as me holding a gun on you. It just isn't."

The cisform cuts in. "You've been attacked before physically, haven't you?"

"Regularly." She laughs. "Three broken ribs, a dislocated shoulder, broken foot, bruises in places I didn't know I had."

The horse crosses his arms. "No one's defending that kind of behavior. But we have to defend people's freedom to express unpopular thoughts."

"These aren't just thoughts. They're actions. We're being denied housing and jobs and credit. You're telling me that I shouldn't make anyone feel threatened or uncomfortable, because that's interfering with their right to discriminate."

"That's not—"

"Yes, it is. Look. If you spin this story to make us into the aggressors, that makes the other side into victims. When they shut us down, when they meet our protests with actual violence, they're just defending themselves, right?" She spreads her hands. "I'm sorry, but that's not the kind of people we should be. That's drawing the line between coercion and non-coercion in the wrong place."

Most—well, at least half—of the audience applauds. "I think Judith just told you to eat your vegetables," the host says to the horse. His snort gets drowned out by laughter.

Gail smiles a little at Sky. "Maybe I should be taking notes." She means it to sound lighter than it does.

"Maybe," Sky agrees.

Gail sighs, leaning back against the wolf. Sky puts her arm around the rat's shoulder as they keep watching.

Chapter 16

THIS TIME WHEN SHE WAKES UP on Sky's sofa she's disoriented because it doesn't feel strange. Getting used to couch-crashing with her sister? No. Tomorrow she's going back to the hotel.

Instead of waking to the scent of coffee, though, she's waking to the sound of Sky arguing. Gail can only hear her sister's side of the conversation, so the wolf must be using an earpiece.

"Warrants from the PFS only apply to Panorica. Here you need—"

Gail sits up, rubbing her eyes. Sky's pacing in the kitchen, tail bristled.

"I don't care what you call it, Captain Taylor. You know full well you wouldn't allow me to execute a raid on—"

Sky's lips pull back in a silent snarl. Gail stands and pads over toward her.

"I don't care if you call it a raid or a recovery operation or a fucking hula dance, you're going to show us the respect you'd expect—you'd *demand*—from us if we were operating in your jurisdiction. You *will* go to the RJC building right now, you *will* wait for me, and everyone *will* tell me you've been on your best behavior, or I will personally send you back to Panorica by railgun." She stabs her viewcard hard enough to flex it, cutting off the call.

"So, good morning." Gail forces her voice into exaggerated humor.

"Somewhere, I'm sure." She pulls the speaker clip off her ear and tosses it onto the dining table. "Taylor showed up at your hotel room trying to take the damn databox back. Again."

Oh, God. If it goes back with him she's screwed seven ways to Neptune. "He can't just—Jack wouldn't give it to him just like that!"

"He couldn't even if he wanted to, since it's not in your hotel room. Karen took it back to the RJC office. All Taylor's done is make Agent

Thomas more annoyed with him, and probably scared the hell out of Ansel."

Good. Not that getting it back from the RJC will be any easier than getting it back from the PFS, but there's a much higher chance she can start gluing her life back together this way. "So you said he came back with a warrant from Panorica? How'd he even get back here this fast?"

"I don't think he ever left, he just waited here for new orders. And it's not even a warrant, it's 'authorization for an out of jurisdiction investigation.'" She makes the air quotes with her claws. "Permission from the PFS to take any action he deems reasonable, as long as it doesn't compromise our property rights. Which they don't fully recognize."

"So he's claiming permission to do anything, basically. Terrific."

Sky growls. "I wasn't planning on leaving for the RJC quite yet, but I'm going to have to leave immediately. The tribunal representatives from Quanta Biotechnics and Keces Industries should be here by ten, and you should be there, too."

Gail's ears skew. "Why? I'm not on the tribunal, right?"

"No. I'm representing both you and the Ring, unless Karen decides that's a conflict. But there might be questions for you, Ansel and Jack as we set the scope. You'll also need to be at the tribunal itself, of course."

"Of course. Uh, okay." She glances at the clock. That early? She's so looking forward to getting back to a late to bed, late to rise sleeping schedule. "I'll catch up with you in three hours. Maybe I'll try and meet Ansel for coffee somewhere."

Ansel meets Gail at a Magnolia Café a few blocks from the Ring Judicial Cooperative building. She knows she was in this neighborhood a few times when she lived here, but she doesn't remember it being this nice. It's as urban and crowded as New Coyoacán gets, and she's still debating with herself about how normal this does—or doesn't—feel.

"So is dealing with the PFS always like this?" Ansel hands her one of the cups of coffee he's holding. She can't imagine it's up to his standards, but so far he hasn't commented.

"Hey, you live on Panorica, not me. Before now the most I've done with them is defend a salvage claim or two. But I think they're like any fully private judiciary. You're paying for them to do whatever they can to get the upper hand."

"Yes, but I don't pay my own judiciary to advocate against me. Anywhere but Panorica, Quanta or Keces would have to spend a lot to do this. Well, anywhere but Panorica and here."

"Don't worry. I'm sure they're both paying a lot to pick up where the PFS is leaving off."

He sighs. "Thanks for that ray of beautiful starlight."

She chuckles. They finish muffins in silence, then head back out.

"I can't get over the way the city here mixes in so much greenspace." Ansel waves around. "They plant bushes down the middle of the street. There's grass and trees everywhere."

"When I moved to Panorica, it seemed like you kept the grass and trees in little boxes. City all on one side of a giant cylinder, all the fields and industry on the other, hard lines between them, no countryside."

"As God intended."

Like the buildings closer to the spaceport, the ones here are mostly stone and glass. The RJC's office makes their devotion to transparency painfully literal: the front is entirely see-through. You have to look close to see the translucent framing, to tell it's not just one pane two stories high and sixty or seventy meters long. You can see into offices, into conference rooms, into the café. It has to be acutely uncomfortable to work there. Maybe it's a deliberate way to select people who have the temperament for it.

Ansel stares as they get close. "Surely their walls aren't glass."

"Transparent aluminum, maybe. I'm sure you can't just break in by throwing rocks."

"Still, that's awfully trusting. I can't imagine the PFS ever doing this."

"No, but I can't imagine Captain Spitty smiling and waving to people and having them smile and wave back."

The reception area's pleasant, polished beige concrete floors coated for claws, pale green walls, totemic-friendly couches. A few people mill about, but nobody she recognizes.

The receptionist—guard?—at the desk is a cisform man, who looks up at Ansel and Gail as they approach, down at his screen, then back up at them. "Good morning, Ms. Simmons. I'll let your sister know you're here."

"Thanks."

After about a minute someone who isn't Sky walks through an open doorway behind the desk: Karen Dupree, the rabbit woman from their first encounter with Spitty. Somehow Gail had gotten the impression of her being close to the age her mother would have been, but she looks like she's only a year or two older than Sky. Unlike most—well, maybe two-thirds—of totemics, she doesn't have human-style hair; there's an eternal background debate in the community as to whether that's more "true" to the animal nature. In practice, it's usually aesthetic preference.

"Ms. Simmons, Mr. Santara. It's nice to see you again. Sky's still in a meeting with Captain Taylor and other PFS officers, but she's expecting to be able to let you in when the others arrive."

To be able to let them in? She *can* let them in now, unless there's conversation happening she doesn't want them to know about. More likely it's Captain Spitty who doesn't. Since violating protocol didn't pay off, he's probably standing on every millimeter of it he can right now. "People from Quanta and Keces?"

"Keces is on their way. Quanta may only join us by video. If at all." She makes a disdainful *chuff* noise. "So far the extent of their response has been a statement that, if I remember their phrasing, 'strongly rejects the ridiculous accusation that Quanta Biotechnics has been involved in the criminal activity we reported to Interpol ourselves.'"

Put that way, it is a ridiculous accusation. She wonders if that's one of the holes in the story Jack wants to fill.

"If you'd like to take a seat, it should just be a few minutes." Dupree gestures at the back wall. "We have coffee if you'd like a refill."

"Thanks." Gail heads to the nearest couch, sprawling across it. "I remember being in this room before, long ago. When I was twelve."

The rabbit gives her a smile. "I remember that, too." She steps back through the door.

Gail straightens up and looks after her. Dupree—Karen—has been working here that long? The woman who played cards with her to keep her entertained while Sky was in another room, being told that their father couldn't be found—that woman had been a rabbit, hadn't she?

Ansel walks up to the outer wall/window, looking out on the street. "There's no way to adjust the transparency?"

She shakes her head. "Not for us."

He pokes at the glass with his claws a couple times, then gives up the investigation and heads to the far interior wall, sliding his coffee cup into the dispenser and letting it fill back up. When he gives it a sniff he makes a sour face.

It's only another ten minutes before Dupree comes back yet again, still longer than Gail had been expecting. "They should be arriving now. We can meet them at the elevator."

They get up—Ansel still has the coffee cup, so it couldn't have been *that* bad—and walk back toward the elevator foyer. When Gail sees who's there, though, she stops stone cold mid-step.

Jason Nakimura turns toward her and lifts his brows, as if he's just as surprised to see her as she is to see him.

"Well, well. If it isn't the bionic rat girl." She'd been so stuck on Nakimura she hadn't even noticed Suspicious Detective standing behind him, still in his overcoat, although he's at least lost the tie. This day gets better and better.

"Ms. Simmons." Nakimura returns to his customary stoic expression and inclines his head. "I hadn't been told to expect your presence, but I suppose I can't say I'm shocked by it."

The rabbit woman presses the elevator call button. "This way."

"You're the one they sent for Bright Sky's tribunal, huh?" Gail follows along, but keeps her eyes on Nakimura.

"Who is this?" Ansel murmurs.

"Ms. Sky demanded the presence of a representative from Keces. Given that I'm the most familiar with the circumstances of this case, it's logical that I be that representative." They step into the elevator.

While she's pretty sure he was answering her, Ansel nods in understanding. Then the fox's eyes narrow. "He's the one who got you into all this?"

Suspicious Detective snorts. "She's the one who got her into all this."

"No, Randall Corbett is the guy who got me into all this. You know, the guy you saw me tackle at the spaceport, the one who was actually carrying the databox you accused me of stealing. Has it seriously not sunk in yet that everything I've told you and your boss has been the truth? Or are you just sulking because you got punched out by a rat lady?"

He narrows his eyes. "You're lucky we're at a police station right now," he mutters.

Dupree gives him a sharp look.

Gail puts her hands to her head, staring at Nakimura. "Jesus, where did you *find* this guy? Why's he's still working for you?"

"Mr. Nelson is an approved contractor," he replies curtly. "While he may have a blind spot with respect to you, he's done good work for Keces in other matters, and has been involved with this case from its start."

The elevator doors open. The second floor has such an open design that at first glance it's hard to spot any floor-to-ceiling walls, just dividers separating departments. The air smells of over-applied citrus deodorizer, masking the scents of all the employees save for momentary bursts, like whispers you're not sure weren't your imagination. There's not a single uniform in sight, either, beyond the cloisonné pins. When she left the River, discovering that most judiciaries fielded uniformed deputies surprised her. Again, what had been normal for her as a child has become alien.

They're led deeper into the building, toward one of those few real walls and through a door into a larger meeting room. The deodorizer isn't working as well here, losing its battle with human sweat: mostly Captain Spitty, from appearance, but at least one of the women standing there in a PFS uniform is sweating, too. Okay, she should think "cisform sweat," not "human sweat," but sometimes it seems like the smell's at least as much of a difference between totemics and cisforms as the obvious appearance changes—totemics not only smell different from base species to base species, they just don't sweat as much. Still, she knows there's more effective skin deodorants than whatever Spitty's using. Did he charge in here screaming demands? Given the beaten-down look in his eyes, probably. Oh, that would have been so much fun to see.

As everyone turns to them, Dupree speaks. "This is Jason Nakimura of Keces Industries, and his associate, Blake Nelson."

Sky's dressed in a better-tailored outfit than Gail ever remembers seeing her in, a dark blue sports jacket and white blouse. She looks imposing. "Thank you for agreeing to come." She gestures at a seat. "This is Captain Taylor of Panorica Federation Security, Officers Canales, Jollenbeck and Wolfe, and Agent Thomas of Interpol."

Jack nods. "Good to finally meet you, Mr. Nakimura."

Nakimura takes a seat and laces his hands together in front of him on the table. "It was my understanding that Quanta Biotechnics would also be sending a representative to this tribunal."

Sky starts to speak, but Spitty talks over her. "So far they've refused." His tone is dry, matter-of-fact. "They don't recognize the Ceres Ring's claim for jurisdiction in this matter and they're relying on the PFS and Interpol to return their stolen property to them."

"It is true that the Ceres Ring's claims seem dubious." Nakimura tilts his head fractionally, studying Sky.

"Ms. Simmons is a Ring citizen, and she alleges extortionate behavior from you and your associates on behalf of Keces Industries."

"I see."

Spitty cuts in again, tone louder, more heated. "This isn't about Simmons, it's about the RJC acting like they get special jurisdiction because the technology affects totemics."

Dupree holds up a hand. "We haven't made any special—"

"Oh, come on!" He gestures accusingly toward Sky. "Is anyone in this room seriously going to claim we'd be here right now if that databox didn't have plans for making animal-people babies?"

When Sky speaks she keeps her voice level, but the tremor belies how difficult it is for her. "Our jurisdiction is no—"

"Speak clearly."

The wolf glares at him, and speaks each word like a slow dagger. "Our jurisdiction is no more 'special' than yours. The databox's contents are a concern, yes, but the circumstances are extraordinary."

"Those circumstances only exist because you and Thomas conspired to bring the databox here in the first place."

Jack stiffens. "I 'conspired' to investigate the theft properly." He gestures toward Nakimura. "If it wasn't for me, no one would even have looked into Keces' claim, which appears much stronger than Quanta's."

Nakimura nods to Jack, then looks to Taylor. "I share your reservations about the Ring's interest. However, someone executed attacks on Keces Industries, *not* Quanta Biotechnics, to ensure that this databox was the only surviving copy of critical project data, then arranged an elaborate theft. You know this, yet you insist the databox should be sent back to Earth."

"Quanta is an Earth company!"

"Given that they have a legal presence here while we do not have one in the inner system, this jurisdiction is more equitable. And can you explain how Quanta even knew about this databox to tip Interpol about it, given that it was being moved between Keces facilities on a private, unannounced transport?"

Jack answers. "By your own admission the databox contains Quanta's work, so it's reasonable to assume they have spies within your organization just like you must in theirs. A lot of the difficulty in this case stems from you and Quanta both being bad actors."

Sky holds up a hand. "This isn't the tribunal yet."

Taylor shakes his head. "I don't even know why I'm here."

"Then let me clear that up for you, Captain Taylor." Dupree drums her fingers on the table. "From a legal standpoint, you and I both know that your orders to take back the box might as well be scribbled in purple crayon. The only reason I haven't handcuffed everyone in this room wearing a PFS uniform is because Bright Sky, the woman you've been lobbing accusations at the last two hours, talked me out of doing so. You're a centimeter away from talking me back into it."

He straightens up, crossing his arms, but looks away.

Nakimura leans forward. "I would like to return to the matter of Quanta's representative to this tribunal. If I understand your process correctly, they must be represented by someone."

Sky sighs. "They can explicitly waive their right to representation, but otherwise you're right." She goes over the tribunal system with him again, nearly word for word the way she'd explained it to Gail earlier.

"If they do not have a representative on the way yet, I do not see how the tribunal can hold to the rather aggressive schedule that was outlined to me."

"That's a valid point." Taylor isn't raising his voice now, for once. He doesn't even sound that aggressive. "I need to talk to the PFS, and Interpol, about this. Since Quanta indicated they're still expecting us to return the databox, they might permit me to be their representative. If you will, that is."

Dupree frowns. "I think we can take a break for now, then." She looks to Sky. The wolf nods.

"All right." He pushes back from the table and motions to the other PFS officers. "We'll be back within the hour if at all possible. I may have a lot of arguing ahead of me."

"Should I join you?" Jack starts to stand.

Taylor looks at him. "No, I don't think you'll need to." He heads out, the rest following. Wolfe gives Jack an apologetic glance but stays silent.

Nakimura's the first one to break the silence. "What is Ms. Simmons' role in this tribunal?"

"She's a potential witness." Sky gives Gail a slight smile. "And we need to determine what the appropriate redress for what you've done to her is."

Gail clears her throat. "That does remind me to ask about the *socius indignus* threat. The deadline's, uh, more or less now."

"Given the extenuating circumstances, it would be unfair to hold you to that contract, Ms. Simmons. We will release you with no obligation for further service on your part."

That's it? That fast? Of course, he's in a less than friendly legal environment. "What about paying me for transferring the salvage claim?"

"We will not pay you for services not rendered, Ms. Simmons."

"Thank you, Mr. Nakimura." Dupree tilts her head. "However, the tribunal must determine whether compensating her for her time and expenses is appropriate."

He purses his lips, then turns to Sky. "It is my belief that Ms. Simmons is personally apolitical. You, Ms. Sky, are not. I have some concerns that your sense of justice will not be assuaged by Keces commercializing Shakti as we intend."

"I doubt it will." She folds her arms. "The Ring has no legal basis for taking ownership of the work, if that's what concerns you, however."

He steeples his hands. "That is somewhat reassuring." Then he stands and inclines his head to Sky. "I believe I should take this time to consult more with Keces' legal counsel. While they approved my participation on the tribunal, I would like to confirm they are aware of the stakes." He leaves the room. Suspicious Detective pushes himself away from the table with a grunt and follows.

Jack turns to Sky. "Is a tribunal here legally binding for both Quanta and Keces?"

"Yes. Keces's judiciary will hold them to the tribunal's decision."

"That's one."

"If Quanta wants to continue doing business around the River, they'll follow suit."

Ansel clears his throat. "Your answer about ownership seemed very carefully worded."

Sky sighs, glancing at Gail, then at Ansel. "I'm not just bound by law here, Ansel, I'm an officer of it, and I take that seriously. Beyond that, I'm not irrational. Even if we had a legal mechanism for nationalization, which we don't, we don't have the resources that Keces does to deploy this. I intend to recommend compulsory licensing of their patents to other providers, but also to give Keces time to set themselves up as the premier provider of the service. And I may not get my way. Keces and Quanta will likely vote against that, so the other two tribunal members would need to side with me."

Ansel nods, but doesn't look mollified.

"I'm surprised you've reserved even that power." Jack lifts his brows. "It's so very…state-like."

"It is." Ansel sighs. "But intellectual property is a compromise to start with. You can make a case that if you're going to have patents at all, compulsory licensing strikes a better balance between inventors and producers."

"We discourage patents on the Ring, but we respect them." Dupree laughs. "Despite legends to the contrary." She pauses and looks down at the wrist band she's wearing. "You'll have to excuse me; I have to join the video call with Captain Taylor, it seems."

"Good luck," Gail mutters.

She smiles, standing up, then waves around at those still seated. "Gail, Ansel—you don't have to stay for the rest of the afternoon if you choose not to. If we have any further questions for you before the tribunal, we'll be in touch."

After she leaves, Jack folds his arms. "I'm beginning to wonder whether I need to stay for the rest of the case."

Sky tilts her head. "Until Interpol officially drops it, it's still your case, isn't it?"

"Yes, it is. I just don't know what I'm going to do at this point other than offer moral support."

Ansel snorts. "Hopefully part of what else you're going to do is make sure someone's still covering my fees. And lodging. And let me know when I can go the hell home."

"I'll do what I can. Meanwhile I suspect your home's no longer in any danger, and it doesn't seem like I'll have any further need of your services. I imagine you can go home at any time unless Sky says otherwise."

Ansel looks toward Gail.

"I guess he's right. I mean, if things go according to schedule the tribunal's going to be in just two days. But you…" You should stick around even if you don't want to because I want you to, even though I think we're not nearly as close as I've been fooling myself into thinking we are and you have already gone *way* farther out on a limb for me than I have any right to expect and all I've done in return is turn your life into a radioactive dump.

She bites her lip, then summons a casual shrug. "You don't have to stick around."

He's looking at her very carefully. Maybe she doesn't have the poker face she thinks she does. "Okay. I'm not on a deadline, I don't have to rush back, but I needed to know if something more was expected of me."

"I don't think so."

Jack stands up abruptly. He's holding his viewcard, clearly reading an alert. "I'll be back in a few minutes. I have to follow up on this." He hurries out of the room.

Now it's just her, Ansel and Sky. The wolf's let her guard down enough to look dazed; she's been riding a rocket the last couple of days and maybe it's catching up with her.

"Hey." She gets up and touches Sky's shoulder. "Can I do anything for you?"

After a small sigh, the wolf puts her hand over the rat's lightly. "No, but I appreciate you asking. There are just … so many questions I have about Shakti."

"Like whether Nevada and Travis really get an antlered fox kid?"

She laughs. "Yes. For one. But more—what it means to turn us into a race. Or many races." She looks over at Ansel. "And how our own people will react to that, not just cisforms."

"It sounds like it's finally moved from 'if' to 'when.' But you don't understand why I'm so wary about going down this path, do you?"

Gail scratches the back of her head. "I don't think I do, either."

"What do you think the defining characteristic of totemics is?"

"Merging human and animal."

"Physically, yes, but we do that for dozens of different reasons. Spiritual, philosophical. Sometimes it's pragmatic. Sometimes it's just aesthetic. There's no one reason someone becomes a totemic. What links it all together? It's not tails and fur and pointy ears. It's choice."

Sky furrows her brow.

"The way I see it, we're already a race. Maybe we chose it, maybe our parents chose it, but it's that choice that makes us unique, that makes us different from any other race before us. If Nevada chooses to have her child transformed *in utero* with Shakti, that's still a choice—but that child won't have a choice any more than cisform humans do." He shakes his head. "I know that's what Mara dreamed of all along. But maybe what we're losing is more than we gain."

Sky's frown deepens, but she doesn't say anything. Nobody does.

Gail clears her throat. "I know it's a little early, but I'm kinda starving, so I'm gonna go get lunch."

Ansel manages a faint smile. "Sometimes I envy your lack of strong opinions, Gail."

She frowns, echoing the wolf's look. She can tell he's not intending to be insulting, even though he's tacitly agreeing with Nakimura: she's apolitical. But that's not the same thing as being a blank display. Sure, she's never thought of herself as opinionated, but it's not like she just has white noise between her ears.

"There's just a lot to think about here," she says, knowing how thin that sounds. She stands up.

Ansel stands, too. "Can I come with you? I feel like I need to get out of here for a while."

"Sure."

"I have more work to do here. I'll keep you up to date." Sky stands as well.

When they're in the elevator, Ansel turns to Gail. "Didn't Jack say he'd be right back?"

Chapter 17

JACK ISN'T IN THE LOBBY, either. What does this mean? Has he gone off with Captain Taylor? He couldn't have gone off with Nakimura, surely.

She doubts he's got his privacy mirrors very open—she's never had reason to check before—but there have to be public-access street views here. And New Coyoacán being New Coyoacán, the RJC office should give public access to cameras that aren't explicitly set private. She pulls out her viewcard and swipes the speaker on so Ansel can hear the ship, too. "Kis, where's Agent Thomas's last reported location?"

"Agent Thomas has not granted you access to his location information. He is no longer in the Ring Judicial Cooperative building."

She sighs. "I figured that out already. Do you see him anywhere?"

Ansel gives her an amused look. "That's a pretty non-specific way to ask that."

"She knows what I mean," Gail murmurs.

After a few seconds, *Kismet* responds. "He may have entered the Blue Coyote Café two blocks east of your location along Second Street."

"Thanks." She puts the card away, looking smug.

"He 'may' have entered? Mara's Blood, you've somehow trained your ship's computer to be as noncommittal as you are."

"She just means she can't make an absolute confirmation from whatever street views caught him."

"Fine, fine." He holds up his hands in mock surrender, tail swishing. "But what's the plan? Go down to this café, peek in and see if he's meeting someone sinister-looking?"

"Well, we'll..." She shrugs and starts walking. "Yeah, I think that's the plan."

After a block the street gets more commercial-residential again. She picks out a half-dozen restaurants without even trying, and all of them look full service. The buildings are all two- and three-story, the upper floors apartments. One across the street sounds like it's having a midday party.

The Blue Coyote's small but appealing, with the Spanish-style decor that Jack had said he'd expected in a city with a name like this: tile floor and tabletops, rustic wood trim, wrought iron accents. The air carries an odd mix of coffee, cinnamon and corn.

Jack's at a table by the street-facing window, a painted ceramic mug in front of him. He's alone. They're definitely in his line of sight as they walk up but if he sees them, he doesn't give any sign. He looks—unhappy? No. Yes, but in the specific numb way you get when an unexpected crisis you can't even process has dropped on you. She recognizes it because she's pretty sure she's had that expression a lot the last week.

"Do you think we should bother him? He looks like he wants to be alone." Ansel's tail curls down.

Gail bites her lip, then shakes her head. "No, we should at least check on him." She heads in before Ansel has time to muster a plausible counterargument.

Jack doesn't look up as she approaches, but his brows lift, just a hair. "Hey. You kinda disappeared."

"Were you worried about me, or worried I'd gone off to report to my secret masters?" His voice is amused, not bitter, but sad. He sips whatever's in his mug. It's not just coffee, but it doesn't smell alcoholic, so at least he's not gone to before-noon drinking.

"I dunno. So far you've been pretty up front about reporting to your masters. And about avoiding them. Hey, is that a Café de Olla?"

"Yes."

"I haven't had one of those in years. Are theirs good?" Mom didn't let her drink coffee at all, and Sky worried—with good cause—that the blend of strong coffee, cinnamon, and dark brown sugar could lead dangerous places when mixed with hyperactive young rat girl.

"I like it. I've never had one before, though, so I don't have anything to compare it to." He takes another sip, then sets down the mug. "Anyway, as of today, I don't have masters, secret or otherwise. Interpol's put me on suspension."

"What? Jesus." Her ears lower. "That's Captain Spitty's doing, isn't it?"

"Captain…" He smiles faintly, looking down. "I'm sure his recent reports haven't helped my standing, but it wasn't his call. And I can't say I blame him. In the process of conducting my own investigation, I've done multiple end runs around his department, stretched the chain of custody past its breaking point, knowingly violated the spirit and possibly the letter of my orders, and seriously strained Interpol's relations with both the FBI and the PFS."

She takes a seat by him unbidden. "So now what?"

"Now I kill time until the next ship back to Earth. At least I'm suspended with pay. For the time being."

Ansel crosses his arms, looking sour. "So your job is at risk because you've been trying to do it too well?" Apparently the way for the agent to finally earn the fox's trust is to lose the trust of his superiors.

"Go along to get along." Jack lets out a short, humor-free laugh, looking out the window rather than at them. "During one of our last big fights, that's what Claudia told me I always did. My defining character flaw." He furrows his brow, shifting his gaze to look into the mug like it was a scrying pool. "I joined the FBI, and later Interpol, because I believe in the job. But going after drug traffickers is one thing, going after politicos and corporations is quite another."

Gail nods. She sees the shape of this now. "This time you didn't go along."

"This case—after questioning you that first time, I started to see it wasn't the simple theft it was being presented as. The more I learned, the more the PFS seemed to be trying to deflect me instead of helping me, the more insistent I got about not just going along this time."

She lets out a sigh, scratching the back of one ear, then looks to Ansel. "It looks like they do counter service here. Can you get me a Café de Olla? And a pastry or something so we're actually eating."

Ansel looks momentarily shocked that he can't just order off the viewcard, but nods. "Sure. I'll get us some real food. I imagine you could use some too, Jack."

Jack grunts.

"I'll take that as a yes." The fox heads to the counter.

"So what do you do until the ship home? Stay on New Coyoacán, or head back to Panorica?"

"I don't know yet. I think I'm expected to go back, but Sky may still want me at the tribunal, even if Captain … Spitty objects. And I like New Coyoacán more than Panorica, even though I'm not as comfortable here."

"That sounds like something I'd say, except without the liking it more part." She grins.

"You're uncomfortable here because of your past, and because of your unwanted celebrity. Everywhere you go, someone's looking over at you, wondering if you're Gail Simmons. I'm sure there's someone here wondering that right now."

Her ears splay and she sinks down a centimeter or two lower in her seat. Thanks for calling attention to it. "So why are *you* uncomfortable here?"

"Because I don't have fur."

Inappropriate jokes leap to mind. Hey, I can get you a coat! There's a good clinic a few blocks over that might be running a special! But she's learned some of Jack's expressions by now, and that isn't the little smile of sly joke, it's the little smile of wry truth. "You're not telling me you're feeling discriminated against, are you?"

"People have been perfectly nice to me, and if anyone's muttered 'prim' under their breath they've done it too softly for this prim's ears to pick it up." That's more of the sly joke smile, although hearing him use *prim* even in jest makes her squirm. "But there's at least one person everywhere *I* go looking over and wondering just what I'm doing here. Do I want to be transformed? Am I a tailchaser? Am I just here to gawk at the strange animal people?"

"That's not really fair to us."

He shakes his head. "It's not a criticism. They're all reasonable reactions. It's just that I feel like I'm traveling in a friendly country where everyone else speaks a language I don't, and it's a language that's literally impossible for me to learn without changing myself."

Ansel reappears, setting down a tray with two more steaming mugs on it, as well as a plate with six sopaipillas and dishes of honey and sour orange marmalade. "It sounds like you just haven't been around many totemics before." The fox grins as he takes a seat.

"I suppose only one or two at a time. Totemics are a minority everywhere but the Ring, and they're a small minority in the inner system. But there was a full transform raccoon and two partial transforms—both feline, if I'm remembering right—in my class at the FBI Academy. I've been paired with a cacomistle agent for an assignment. For a few years I worked out of a field office whose secretary was a jackal." He looks at the pastries. "I've never seen those before."

Gail takes one and spoons some of the marmalade on top, smearing it a bit. "Really? Sopaipillas? I know they're from the Americas. They're delicious."

He picks one up, too, and carefully adds a little marmalade. "'The Americas' is a very big target area. As much cross-cultural pollination as there is, not everything in Mexico is known in Philadelphia and vice-versa."

Ansel laughs, taking one and drizzling honey over it. "Yes, we know, Earth is big and not one country. Isn't the River still more diverse, overall?"

"I don't know. There's more countries on Earth than there are independent platforms out here, but there's more… hmm. More experimentation here. We have a long history of first fighting against diversity, then fighting to expand it. You don't have that history, but it's because you started from a more idealistic place."

Gail chuckles. "Is that actually a compliment?"

He takes a bite of his sopaipilla, finally. "Wow, these *are* terrific." After another bite, he looks back to Gail. "I admire the idealism, but I don't admire all the ideals."

"You don't understand them." Ansel shrugs. "You work for a state."

Her first sopaipilla's already gone. She picks up another one, hesitates, then tops it with both honey and marmalade. Why the hell not. "If you don't get reinstated on the secret agent gig, maybe you and Ansel could do a political debate show together." She waves the pastry around. "But I want to bring the conversation back to what you're going to do for the next few days. Is Interpol still paying for the hotel suite?"

"The tab is on my account, not theirs. I can't be sure whether they'll reimburse me now. Given the way this has played out they may not reimburse me for anything on New Coyoacán." He sighs. "Maybe we should be looking for cheaper accommodations."

Well. So much for going back to the hotel tonight. "That's fine for me. I can keep staying with Sky." God, she needs to leave before this place feels too much like home. Not that she can leave without paying *Kismet*'s repair bill. Not that she can do that until she calls her bank. Again. Which she should have done several hours ago.

Jack nods, sitting back in his chair, wriggling once. Maybe it's uncomfortable if you don't have a tail? No, that doesn't make sense. Does it? "All right." He looks over at Ansel. "If you're staying on New Coyoacán, you may need to start footing your own bill from this point on."

"As much as I hate to say it, I want to stick around to find out how this all ends." He leans forward. "This might be a touch indelicate, but I still do expect to be paid for my time up to this point."

If Jack had the right ears for it, they'd have just gone down. "We'll talk about it."

"So it sounds like you're both deciding to stay here, not go back to Panorica?"

When they both nod to her prompt, it relieves her more than she'd expected it would.

"I might try and see more of the Ceres Ring, though," Jack adds. "I'd like to ride the trans-ring rail. It's not underground the whole trip, is it?"

She chuckles. "No, it's elevated most of the time. The rail's on the Ring's north rim. I remember riding it sometimes just for the view—it's amazing nearly all of the way. Cities, forests, fields, hydroponic farms. Even the industrial sections are pretty cool. And there's some great places to take a day trip to." She scratches her ear. "Although I think New Coyoacán has the highest cisform population of any of the Ring cities. Some of the smaller towns are entirely totemic." Coming right out and saying *so you might be uncomfortable* sounds weirdly prejudiced, but, well, he might be uncomfortable.

"I'll make do. Maybe I'll spend a day canoeing with the otters, too."

She smiles. "That sounds neat. Uh, this may be weird to ask, given our whole suspected thief and arresting officer relationship. But I hope you'll come to the tribunal even if Sky isn't requiring you to be there."

"I'll do what I can, then. Let me know if the schedule changes, so I know when to come in." He finishes his Café de Olla. "And I'd like to be there one way or another. I want to stick around for the ending, too."

Now that she's finally trying their mixed drinks, it turns out the hotel bar is pretty good. Expensive, but Ansel—Mara hold him—covers her this afternoon as they sit waiting for Nevada to meet them.

Gail's let him drag her into trying to explain the difference between the Ceres Ring's medical insurance pool and an income tax. She's not doing a good job. She'd like to blame that on her being well into her third drink, but the truth is she probably couldn't have done it sober.

"I'm not saying it's an income tax, I'm saying it amounts to the same thing."

She looks at her glass. The limelo-infused martini's strong, but she bets the nitrogenated marasca sour is the one that really kicked her ass. "No…no." She holds up a finger. "It's like, every platform other than here—since here isn't a platform—has, has resource fees. Right?"

"Right, but the Ring rolls that into its crazy land fees. It's just a different name. But insurance isn't the same. You and I can choose how much coverage to get and who we're going to buy it from. Sky doesn't have a choice and she has only one insurer."

"You can buy extra private insurance here if you want." She looks toward the hotel lobby as she speaks. "And I can only choose the insurance I can afford, which is pretty…" She sets down her glass, leaning forward. "I think that's Nevada."

"Where?" Ansel looks, too.

He's never met her, has he? Neither in this life nor her previous one. "There. The vixen." She stands up and waves broadly.

The vixen's gaze sweeps past her, then returns to the rat. She waves back, breaking into a smile, and hurries toward the bar area.

"Gail! I'm glad you could meet me. Is this where you've been staying? It's lovely."

"Yeah, well." She laughs. "Sky shanghaied me and I actually never got to sleep here, and we've already checked out. But I'm glad we found the place. I know this didn't exist when I used to live here."

The vixen nods. "I think it's about twelve or thirteen years old. It was here when I moved to New Coyoacán, but I've never been in the hotel before." She turns toward Ansel.

"This is my friend Ansel Santara. He came with me from Panorica. Ansel, this is an old friend of mine, Nevada Argent."

Ansel's already holding out his hand. "It's very nice to meet you, Nevada." He smiles brightly. It's a shame Travis hadn't come with his wife—she'd like to see if he left Ansel even more tongue-tied than he leaves her.

He motions to the table. "Pull up a chair. Gail was just arguing for how wonderful everything is around here."

She pffts. "That's not what I've said at all."

Ansel ignores her protest. "I have to say, she's made quite a turnaround from the way she's talked about the Ring over the last decade, in only…" He makes a show of checking his wrist display. "Forty-six hours, give or take?"

Nevada laughs, but her gaze focuses on the rat as she sits down. "I do remember Gail being more ambivalent about New Coyoacán when we knew each other on Panorica. She'd make it sound like the nicest place on the River until I asked why she left."

"And then suddenly it would be hell incarnate." Ansel smirks. Nevada laughs.

Gail tries not to sink under the table. "Ha ha. I've had my problems with the place, but they're more, you know, personal history. Objectively, it's like any other place. Good parts, bad parts. Not too different from Panorica."

"Which one do you think of more as home?"

"Neither."

Nevada tilts her head, smiling. "All right, then, if you were asked where you were from, which one would you answer?"

"I'm…" She sighs. Great, she's drunk and she's being ricocheted from political debates to personal prying. "New Coyoacán. I mean, what else could I say? Around here, everyone would answer that for me anyway."

Nevada's ears flatten.

Gail puts her hand over the vixen's. "Sorry. I don't wanna sound like I'm upset with you. It's just been…kind of a rough week."

The ears go up again, and she nods sympathetically. "You didn't answer when I asked if you were in some kind of trouble, but I could tell. Is it anything you can talk about?"

She takes another sip of the martini. "I don't honestly know. The longer this goes on the crazier the truth sounds."

Nevada lowers her voice. "It doesn't involve Purity, does it?"

"It involves the company that created totemics and the son of someone who died with my mom, somehow connected through a think tank which increasingly sounds like Purity shoved in a nice business suit."

The vixen's ears lower once more and her eyes get wide.

"I told you it was crazy."

The waiter, a handsome tiger who looks to be a few years older than Gail, comes by before anyone else speaks. Picking up Ansel's empty glass, he exchanges it for something pale purple in a stemmed cocktail glass. She didn't see the fox order anything new, but he's pretty fast.

Nevada points at the drink. "What is that?"

"It's an Aerospike, miss."

"I'll have one of those."

"Very good, miss." He heads off.

The vixen turns back toward Gail. "If there's anything I can do to help, you must let me know."

"I appreciate it, but I can't ask—"

"You saved my life, Gail."

She looks away, fidgeting, then picks up her martini.

Ansel stares. "She did what?"

"I was working at Emerson Salvage, off Solera, and the owner… recognized Gail when she came in, I guess." She looks down at the table. "I'd heard him talk about Purity occasionally, but I didn't know he was that involved with them. He tried to kill Gail, and later went after me."

Gail clears her throat. "She's leaving out that they were going after her because she kinda rescued me first."

"It ended in a gunfight." Nevada lowers her voice to a conspiratorial whisper. "Between the owner and Gail."

Ansel's muzzle has been open for several seconds at this point. "Oh my God. How come this is the first time I've ever heard about any of this? And how come Purity keeps coming after you? I've never even *met* someone in Purity, at least who admits it."

"I shot the owner she's talking about, I didn't kill him, and I haven't heard a peep from Purity after the suit he tried to file against me got bounced."

Her glass is halfway to her muzzle, but the vixen sets it back down again without taking a drink. "Charles Emerson tried to sue you?"

"Yeah, he claimed I stole the tow engines. Which I didn't, technically. My judiciary pretty much told him that he could consider the engines payment for me not going after him for trying to kill both of us, or we could both go after one another and he could spend *way* more money to lose both cases."

Nevada bites her lip. "I'm so sorry. I can't imagine him even daring that. I'm surprised you *didn't* go after him."

Ansel studies the vixen a moment, tapping his chin. "You grew up cisform, didn't you? I know that's indelicate, but a Purity follower wouldn't hire you. The you you are now, I mean. You were cisform when you worked there."

Her ears drop, and she gives an almost imperceptible nod.

"Ah." He grins wryly. "That's why you can't imagine it."

Her expression grows uncertain.

"Have you ever had the experience of seeing someone just on the edge of your vision giving you a nervous glance or making a mocking face? The funny-not-funny jokes about fleas and shedding, the 'small talk' with the undercurrent of 'what kind of crazy person makes himself look like an animal?'"

As Ansel goes on, Nevada squirms in her seat. "I didn't run into that on Panorica." The worry that maybe it was there and she just didn't notice shines like a distress flare in her eyes.

Gail leans forward. "Panorica's pretty good for totemics, but I travel a lot. Anywhere I go about half the time the chairs will suck if you have a tail, the sound system will have a weird buzz cisforms can't hear, hotels will only have water-based showers and handheld dryers, and if you say anything people get huffy about 'special treatment.'"

"Oh, *that* I've experienced. I mean, a little. I spent a week on Ferran visiting friends, and strangers would come up and—and just *touch* me, and ask all sorts of personal questions. My friends couldn't understand why I didn't like it. 'Oh, I guess you get that all the time. You must be used to it, right?'" She shakes her head. "The hotel made me put down extra deposits in case I 'damaged' anything *and* charged me extra for housekeeping every day." The litany ends, and she takes a sip of the Aerospike. "This drink's really good."

"Ansel knows his alcohol." So Nevada has only been a totemic for a few years, Ansel's been one most of his life but remembers being cisform, and for practical purposes she's never been anything but. Does that make these little humiliations easier for Nevada, or harder? She's had less time to accumulate grudges, but less time to build up resistance. And the memory of what life's like *without* facing them remains sharper and brighter. "So you wanted to talk about what I was going to say in class and make sure I wasn't going to embarrass you, right? I hope I haven't made you come far out of your way."

Nevada waves her free hand. "Travis and I live on the east side, so it's not too far. And I haven't seen you in years until yesterday. I'd hoped Travis would come out, too, but he's on call tonight." She lowers her voice, and grins impishly. "I think he's worried you'll get nervous if you're around both of us together."

"Why—what, because he was my first crush? We've both been past that for a long time, I promise." God, he's past it too, right?

But the vixen just laughs. "I know. I'm not worried. But you've been close to both of us at different times."

Ansel's ears come forward. Gail stifles a sigh. "Yeah, but you and I weren't dating."

"No, but you know I had a hell of a crush on you." She laughs again, more sheepishly.

Gail smiles back. It's weirdly relieving to hear Nevada confess that out loud. Sussing out romantic intent has always been one of her blind spots. Intents like Adrian's, those are easy: hey, that cute young guy is up for sex with a middle-aged woman! It's when someone wants to go deeper than that she hits a brick wall. With—well, with Linda—she wasn't absolutely sure.

Maybe she didn't really want to be sure, though. If Linda had been Nevada then, would she maybe have been more open? God, is she really that shallow? Linda was cute. Nevada is hot. Okay, yes, apparently she's that shallow. "I kinda guessed, yeah. But I was pretty set on not settling down. So, uh, I'm not going to make things awkward by trying to be friends with both of you now, right?"

Nevada laughs. "No." She takes another sip of her cocktail, then folds her hands on the table. "But instead of making us both feel embarrassed, I wanted to tell you about the class you'll be speaking to tomorrow morning, and answer any questions you might have." Her cadence shifts as she speaks, hitting the conversational-but-instructive tone Gail remembers from nearly all her teachers.

Ansel stares again. "You're bringing in Gail to talk to your class? About what?"

"About her mother, about the RTEA. About—well, about what we were talking about just a few minutes ago."

"You learn about activist groups in school here?"

"We teach the history of totemics. By fourth stage they've already learned about Mara, about the symbology she was striving for, about the Ranger movement that grew up around her. And about the Purity counter-movement and her assassination."

"We learned that on Arelia, but it was just a class or two. I don't think we were even tested on it."

Nevada looks down. "We learned all of it on Solera, but we learned it differently."

His ears flag.

"So." Back to Gail. "The presentation's going to be to the fourth stage students, mostly in second and third year. They've learned a little about the RTEA and about your mother, but to them this is all kind of ancient history."

"Ancient? The Solera bombing was barely twenty years ago."

"Twenty-one, so seven or eight years before most of them were born. At that age, that seems ancient." Nevada laughs. "And remember, most of them were born *here,* with a totemic majority population, and might never have been off the Ring."

"Fine, it's ancient. I'll bring a cane to wave around." She rolls her eyes. "Anyway, so I'll come in and talk about my mother and how she got involved with the Equality Association. As crazy as it might sound, I've been studying for this."

Nevada smiles warmly. "Don't let this be too stressful. I know you weren't ever involved with the RTEA yourself."

"I was, kind of. I mean, I went to meetings with mom, and sometimes protests. I understood what was going on." Why does this make her bristly? "But, I mean, yeah, I know you want history, not, like, a call to action. But what if they ask about me? What if they have questions?"

"Answer them." The vixen pats her hand. "You can always say you don't know, or don't have the answer, or that it's too personal."

"Any tips?"

"Just try and be entertaining."

"You're losing an audience if they're looking around and coughing." Ansel tilts his head. "Is Sky coming with you?" His tone makes the question into *Sky's coming with you, right?*

"No, she's going to be really busy tomorrow morning, remember?"

"Oh. Of course."

She takes a sip from her drink and half-smiles. "That's not a confidence-building question."

"I didn't mean it that way." He waves a hand. "Sky has more background in what the RTEA is doing now—at least, I'm guessing she does—but I think you'll be a hell of a public speaker."

Really? She's heard that twice in as many days. If it was true, she'd have been able to sell her bank on unlocking her account, or Dani on letting her skate by *without* unlocking her bank account. "I don't know why people think that."

"Because we know you." Nevada grins. "I think you'd make a good teacher."

"A teacher." Oh, come on. The vixen might as well say she would make a good concert pianist.

Ansel strokes his chin. "Hmm."

Gail downs the rest of the martini.

Chapter 18

NEVADA'S STARING AT HER with embarrassingly open admiration. "Gail, you look beautiful."

"Thanks." After agonizing over her clothes this morning—casual but not too casual, colorful but maybe not so space bum—she thought about her mother's clothes that Sky had saved, the ones she'd refused to take, and rifled through them. Finally she'd settled on a moss green dress, short-sleeved and dyed with batik. After she'd put it on she'd thought it looked ridiculous, but Sky had told her she'd looked stunning, too.

As she follows Nevada into the school, the panic she'd predicted when they spoke last night doesn't hit her *quite* as hard as she'd feared. But isn't this school bigger than the one she went to? Bigger and nicer: rich mahogany walls, colorful (if scuffed) flooring, a woodsy-floral scent that makes her think more of hiking than it does of young teens in need of baths.

"So this is just fourth and fifth stage students? Mine had all the stages."

Nevada nods. "This is one of six upper schools around New Coyoacán, and there are ten lower schools. We try to get about three hundred students per school now." They enter the building through a small foyer, clearly not the students' entrance, and head right into a teachers' lounge.

Two other teachers—she guesses—sit in the lounge, a stout white tigress with short-cropped head fur and a partial cat transform who looks just enough like Adrian to make her think inappropriate thoughts. They look up as she and Nevada enter. "Gail, this is Tabitha," she gestures at the tigress, "and this is Enrique."

Gail waves. "Hey."

Tabitha's already standing. She looks like she's come to attention, eyes wide, expression nervous, like she's meeting a star. Oh, God. "Ms. Simmons. It's an honor."

No. Just no. Don't start that. "Just Gail. Please."

Enrique stands, too. "Nice to meet you, Gail."

"It's nice to meet both of you, too. So, uh, Nevada warned you that I don't have a prepared speech, right? People keep telling me I'm good at extemporaneous talk, but I think that's—" No, not an appropriate word for school, ratface. "Uh, overly generous."

"That's fine. Just talk about you. Your mother. The River Totemic Equality Association." Tabitha's words tumble out so fast they barely stay in the correct order.

Enrique smiles. "Just introduce yourself and tell them why they might be interested in you, and let them lead the conversation."

"Really? Uh, can they?"

Nevada waves a hand. "They're teenagers. Couldn't you lead a conversation with an adult when you were that age?"

"Does sulking in your room and shouting *go away* at your sister before you turn up your music count as conversation?"

Enrique laughs and walks toward an interior door, motioning Gail to follow.

Well, she signed up for it, and compared to her last week it can't be too difficult. She follows the catboy (oh, God, he *is* a boy, isn't he, she might be a full decade older than he is, is he even qualified to teach these kids) down the hallway. She peeks into a room of fifteen or sixteen older students clustered in small groups, poking at holographic displays together. That part hasn't changed much since her day, at least. The displays might be higher quality.

They turn a corner and step through a set of double doors—manual ones, propped open with rubber doorstops. The space beyond is much larger than she'd expected. Tables fill about two-thirds of it; the other third, the third she's stepped into, has cushiony plastic seat-mats rolled out. Dozens of students have gathered into a rough semicircle. Many dozens. A few sit at the tables behind the mats, too shy or too cool to join their peers. A half-dozen teachers sit farther back. All hundred-odd turn to look at her as she enters, with expressions ranging from curiosity to canonical teen boredom.

Gail stops dead. "Is this all the fourth stage students in New Coyoacán?" she hisses, trying to keep her voice low enough not to broadcast her discomfort directly to the students.

"No, silly. Relax," Nevada murmurs, patting the rat's shoulder reassuringly.

She grunts, and lets Nevada lead her toward three chairs in the center of the semicircle. Enrique and Tabitha take the two to either side, leaving Gail the middle spot. Nevada pats her shoulder again and heads toward the back.

Enrique, thankfully, begins. She can't tell where the spot microphones are, but his voice rings with low amplification. "How many of you are studying River history right now?" About half the hands go up. "And how many of you have heard of the River Totemic Equality Association?" Most of the same hands stay up; about half of the rest rise, too. "And how many have heard of Judith Simmons?" About half the hands drop again.

"Today we're lucky to have Gail Simmons, Judith's daughter, here to visit. She's not here as a lecturer, so don't get too worried." He spreads his arms. "But since you don't often get a chance to talk to someone who actually *lived* through your history lessons, her friend Ms. Argent asked her to come chat a little while with you." He looks to Gail expectantly.

She clears her throat and looks out over the audience. At a guess, she'd say three-quarters are transforms, mostly full rather than partial. The cisforms are a disproportionate number of the ones who look like they want to be somewhere else.

"Hi. Uh, so." She looks around, then scoots her chair forward so she's closer to the students. "I feel like I should start by admitting that I haven't been involved, uh, involved much in activism since I was younger than you are, so I guess I'm mostly here to talk about my mom."

She pauses and glances around. Well, at least most of the eyes are on her. She glances at the teachers, hoping she doesn't look too lost.

Apparently she looks just lost enough for Tabitha to give her a prompt. "Some of the class is studying what happened to Judith, but tell us more about her life. Your life. What was it like living with her?"

Gail leans forward, resting her elbows on her knees. "To me she was just my mom, you know? So it was like living with your mom. I mean, I can tell you she wasn't a great housekeeper, but I wish I'd gotten some of her recipes. Maybe I'd be a less terrible cook."

That gets her a few hesitant smiles from the students. Okay, good sign.

"Honestly, I didn't pay much attention then to what she was doing. I just knew she was away a lot and that she was a hero to a lot of people, but I didn't understand why. I mean, she just stood up and talked in front of crowds, didn't she? I saw her on the news sometimes leading protests and chants and sit-ins. That was weird.

"Then she came home from a rally on Panorica when I was…seven, I think it was, with her ribs cracked. That was my first clue she made some people really angry. And that totemics made some people really angry. Up until then, I'd never had to think about that." She sighs, smiling wryly. "And I asked her why. Why would they hate us that much? She said it was fear, the fear that totemics *are* better than cisform humans."

"Not that Ms. Simmons is saying that they are," Enrique cuts in.

Really? Is he seriously worried she's a totemic supremacist? "Uh, yeah, I figured they'd probably pick up on me not having actually said that."

That gets a laugh from more of the students. A cisform girl raises her hand. She's got dark brown skin, matching eyes, hair in frizzy ringlets. "What made your mom an activist?"

"Wow." That's a great question she hopes she can come up with the answer for. "She was Riverborn, but she grew up cisform. And she grew up with a lot of the assumptions we all kind of have. One of those assumptions is that state power tends to, uh, enforce discrimination by drawing lines. This group can vote, that group can't. This group can own property, that group can't. You get legally protected discrimination. If you don't have a state, or you have a very limited one, you can't have that. It doesn't make discrimination go away, but it takes away its protection. You should have a more egalitarian society, right? And that's what she was taught.

"But when she was eleven or twelve she learned about totemics, and she realized something weird. Where she lived, there weren't any. She'd never met a single one. And the adults told her the animal people just must not like it on Solera." Some of the kids murmur at the name, and she grins wryly. "Yeah, you're ahead of me. Most people wouldn't rent living space to totemics, or let them eat in their restaurants, or even sell them groceries. So she wondered how this could happen without a state."

"There's no state to outlaw discrimination, either," the girl says.

A mouse kid sitting behind her says disdainfully, "It's not the same thing. You're free to do business with whoever you want."

"Freedom of association. Right." Gail spreads her hands. "We've structured almost everything around market transactions. Contracts. But what she realized—at eleven, which is just amazing to me—is that those have a hidden bias toward whoever's starting with the power. Usually, who is that?"

"The seller," a rabbit girl says. She looks familiar, although Gail can't quite place why.

"Exactly." Gail points at her. "I don't like people with fur, so I'm not going to sell to you." She points at the cisform girl. "I *only* like people with fur, so I'm not going to hire you." At the mouse boy. "I'm fine with most totemics, but I'm a self-hating rodent, so I won't rent to you." Some of the kids laugh.

"Some people came out to the River—even helped start it—to avoid discrimination, but some people also came out here because they wanted to be free to discriminate. Hate groups that were illegal on Earth aren't here, right? We've decided that's an acceptable cost for free speech and free association. Usually nobody questions that, but my mom asked the most uncomfortable question you can ever ask. She asked *why*. Why does having that freedom mean we can't do anything about discrimination?"

"So that's why she became a totemic?" The rabbit girl tilts her head.

"Well, no, I remember her strongly identifying with Mara, with the idea that instead of constantly fighting for dominion over our ecosystem we needed to integrate with it, fuse with it. She really loved what she saw totemics representing. But her answer to her 'why' was that without a state, you equalize the power balance in other ways. She came in and said, look, just asking people to stop being mean to one another isn't working. She started leading sit-ins and boycotts and blockades. She went to platforms and even just neighborhoods where totemics weren't treated as equals. She said, okay, we don't have the power of the state, but maybe we have the power of shaming combined with the power of hurting your business."

Nevada's looking at her with wide eyes. God, she's screwing this up, isn't she? She told her—no, the vixen's giving her an encouraging smile. She thinks.

"But isn't that coercion, too?" the mouse says.

Gail tears her eyes away from Nevada and clears her throat. "I asked myself that then, and I don't think I had an answer. But I think I do now." She takes a deep breath, looking back at them, meeting as many eyes as she can. "If someone's going to have the freedom to discriminate against me, then I have to have the freedom to call them on it. To stand up for myself, and for you. To tell them they're wrong. And to tell everyone *else* that person's wrong, too. If that's coercion, then maybe there are some kinds of coercion we need."

Some of the students clap, although the noise dies quick, stifled by teenage self-consciousness. The cisform girl raises her hand again. "But how can you measure success when there's no laws to overturn or get passed?"

"Well, like I said, I'm not in the RTEA myself, so I can't tell you what they do. But I know there's a lot of data points you can track, and there's also—well—the feel. I mean, I've lived on Panorica, I'm still there a lot, and I don't worry about what neighborhoods I can go into. Not much, anyway. Thirty years ago I might have felt like I needed to be more careful. I've also lived on Carmona, and I'm *really* sure I'd have only stuck to certain places there thirty years ago."

The mouse doesn't bother raising his hand. "So do we still need the RTEA?"

What kind of a question is that? She bites back a sarcastic response. But she doesn't want to give a glib answer. Maybe it's a good question.

He goes on. "I mean, I know there's still discrimination. But you didn't join it, and you're not worrying about having your ribs broken or being blown up or something. I never hear about it except in history class. I don't think Purity is even still around."

"They are. At least they were around ten years ago when one of their leaders tied me to a chair and threatened to cut off my ears."

Most of the students gasp or wince.

"I understand your question, though. I'd have asked it a few years ago, even after the tied to a chair thing. Hell, I'd have asked it a few weeks ago. Can I say 'hell?' Sorry.

"I guess I stayed away from the RTEA because I lived through what happened to my mother, right? And that was the worst attack from them, but not the only one. I hope none of you will ever have to face people that crazy, but here's something to think about. How many of you—and I'm speaking just to the totemics now, sorry—have ever been walking down the street and noticed cisform people giving you a wider berth than other totemics do?" About two-thirds of the totemics raise their hands, including Skeptical Mouse. He looks dismayed.

"How many of you have noticed ones you *know* doing that, like your classmates?" Nearly half the hands stay up.

"I'm not going to ask cisform students to raise their hands. But as long as a majority of those hands go up when somebody asks that question—maybe even if just a single hand does—then I think the RTEA still has a point to make. As for Purity, honestly, I don't know how much of it might exist under that name anymore. But their ideas are still around, and after—" Whoops, she needs to be careful where she goes from here. "If circumstances change, they might get more popular again. If more people become totemics, for instance."

This sparks quiet conversation for a few seconds across the whole group. Then a lanky cisform boy in the front, short black hair and skin the color of the Ring's sky, raises his hand. "So was the bomb your mother's?"

The room explodes in angry noise. Gail's ears flush.

"Hey!" Tabitha stands up, raising her hands over her head. "Settle down!" She turns to Gail. "I'm sorry—"

"Don't be." She levels her gaze at the pale kid. "He's not the only one who wants to ask that. He's just the only one who had the nerve to."

He shifts in his seat, but keeps his eyes on hers. He doesn't look mocking. Doubting, maybe.

"In the time I knew my mom—and in everything I learned about her later, from my adopted sister who worked with her at the RTEA, coworkers, even my dad before he left—she was brash, direct, sometimes confrontational, and she didn't give a damn about ruffling feathers." She pauses. "First 'hell,' now 'damn.' I'm a terrible role model." Most of the kids giggle. So does Nevada, although Enrique and Tabitha both twitch.

"But here's the thing. I've seen news images of her being beaten, when they cracked her ribs. Instead of fighting back—" She hugs herself. "She did this. And she let herself get beaten. She could have died *then*.

"And it's not that she was some supreme pacifist, that she was against fighting back. She knew that any violence a totemic commits just becomes ammunition. 'See, they don't just *look* like animals, they *act* like animals. They think they've gone and made themselves more than we are, but really they've made themselves *less*.' She would have rather died than give someone that ammunition. Eventually, she did."

He looks down, shamefaced.

There's a few more questions, none as challenging, before Tabitha gives everyone leave to head to lunch. There's a round of applause that makes Gail's ears color. Afterward, some of the students come up to shake Gail's hand. One of them hugs her, then runs off looking mortified. She can't help but smile, although it's as much bemusement as amusement.

"Ms. Simmons? Good luck with whatever you're doing at the RJC tomorrow."

It's the rabbit girl. What? How does she know about that? "You're—your mother works there, doesn't she? Ms. Dupree."

The rabbit nods. "Yes. She's an arbiter there. She knows your sister. Um, adopted sister. She really likes her."

Gail smiles. "I like your mom, too. What's your name?"

"Josie." The girl smiles shyly, like she wants to say something more, but after a moment she just shakes Gail's hand, too, and follows her classmates.

As they walk back to the teachers' lounge, Tabitha puts her hand on Gail's shoulder. "Thank you so much, Ms.—uh, Gail. You're really inspiring."

She stumbled through about fifteen minutes of quasi-speech and mostly just demonstrated how little she actually knows about the RTEA. Inspiring to who, exactly? She turns to look up at the tigress, and the sincerity in the woman's eyes makes all her snark shrivel away. "That's not something I'm used to hearing anyone say."

"Oh, don't sell yourself short."

Nevada laughs. "She does that all the time."

Gail's ears fold down. "You're gonna make me blush. Look, my mom's the one everyone cares about. I wouldn't be famous here if it wasn't for her. When people come up and gush at me about how great it is to meet me, I cringe inside. I don't *do* anything. I don't *know* anything."

Tabitha's started to look nervous as Gail's little depressive rant picks up steam, but Nevada slips her arm around the rat's shoulders. "Do you remember what Ansel said yesterday? Did you hear anyone cough?"

"I don't remember."

"I didn't hear a single cough."

"You're a natural speaker, Gail, trust me." Enrique shakes her hand. "If you want to come back next year, or do—well—anything with the school, we'd love to have you."

Nevada's tail wags. Gail stammers something noncommittal, pleasant enough to make both Enrique and Tabitha look happy before they head off.

"And I'd love to take you out to dinner before you leave." Nevada tilts her head. "You're appearing before the RJC tomorrow? I overheard Josie."

"Yeah, it's that thing I've darkly hinted at but haven't explained. I'll stick around until I can take you up on that dinner offer, though, I promise." She gives Nevada a hug. "Thanks."

The vixen hugs her back, tail wagging harder.

"God, how can this be so difficult? I got the information you said you needed from my banking partner back on Carmona to you yesterday!"

When she'd left the school, a simple thought had hit her like a cargo hauler: everything but the tribunal lies behind her now. Her life is almost back to normal. Instead of feeling relief, she just feels like she's got an extra knot or two in her stomach, though. Maybe it's the unresolved bank screwup. Her life can't get back to normal until she can fly *Kismet* out of dry dock, right? So that's what's led her to screw up her lunch at Blue Coyote by calling her bank.

"Our dispute department's reviewing that information now, Ms. Simmons."

"Come on." She groans. "How much reviewing can this take?"

"I can connect you with them directly if you'd like."

"Yes, I'd like."

"Just a moment." Hold music starts playing.

What's on her plate claims to be a vegetable enchilada, but it's lying. It's diced vegetables cut in precise cubes, with a light beige creme drizzled over them in precise rings, mounded on a corn tortilla cut to a precise square. It's undeniably artful, and the vegetables have a super-intense flavor that must come from compression cooking. But she wanted an enchilada. This is an enchilada construction kit.

"Ms. Simmons? This is Kimberly with the dispute resolution group."

"Hey. So...?"

Kimberly has the decency—or the acting ability—to sound genuinely apologetic. "I'm sorry this is taking so long. You've been over the case information with one of our other representatives, correct?"

She sighs. "More than once."

"I understand. Your previous banking partner on Carmona has confirmed the transactions we've requested information on, but your account's still flagged for hold. It looks like we haven't been successful in getting in touch with the independent auditor who initiated the complaint for his client."

"Would that 'auditor' be a guy named Tom Laurel?"

"I don't have that information."

"Look, Laurel isn't an auditor, he's an amp dealer."

"Even if that's true, if the client's chosen him as an independent auditor, we have to give him time to respond, Ms. Simmons."

"You don't understand. There is no client. It's Laurel and someone working with him at your bank."

"I'll note your assertion for the investigation. Either way, his deadline to respond is tomorrow morning. We should be able to lift this by close of business tomorrow either way."

"That'd be great, because I kinda need access to the money *yesterday.*"

"I'm sorry, Ms. Simmons. I can check on extending a line of credit to you in the meantime, if you'd like."

"Don't bother." She disconnects the call and covers her face in her hands for a few seconds, then goes back to the deconstructed enchilada.

Lunch is just about finished when she sees Suspicious Detective across the street. Oh, you've got to be kidding. Could it just be a coincidence? Sure, technically. But he could trace her here just as easily as she traced Jack—the guy might not be a great detective, but he's probably not *completely* incompetent.

Okay. She could make the effort to try and ditch him. If the restaurant has a back exit, it'd be pretty easy. But even if he doesn't know where she's staying, he knows where she's going to be. Ducking out would only be a delaying tactic. On the other hand, if he's looking for a fight he's got to have brought a weapon. He's not stupid enough to want a rematch.

Beedle boop "Call from Blake Nelson."

"Who the hell is Blake—" She looks across the street. Mr. Nelson. Oh, Mara's Blood. "Fine. Connect him."

Suspicious Detective doesn't start with any small talk. "We need to have a conversation."

"Shouldn't I be having a conversation with your boss, not you?"

"This isn't a conversation that involves him."

Her ears lower. "Since you're standing across the street, I'm guessing you want it face to face."

"Smart rat."

"We're like that." She disconnects the call, then gets up and walks to the café's exit, steps onto the sidewalk, and faces him, hands on hips.

When he sees her he acknowledges her with a sneer and a *heh* she sees rather than hears, and he saunters across the street. As he approaches he raises his hands. "I'm not armed and I'm not looking for another fight."

"Good."

He points back in the direction of the RJC building. "Let's walk and talk."

She falls into step by his side. "About what?"

"You've made things a lot more difficult for us than we'd planned. You weren't supposed to figure out it was Corbett, or to get there in time to catch him. And if he'd just played it cool he might have gotten away with the thing then." He shrugs, hands in his coat pockets. "Or if I'd figured out a way to block you before Thomas got there. Heard he got suspended. Where'd he go off to?"

He sounds like he's unhappy Corbett didn't get away. "How should I know? He was investigating me, not the other way 'round. Look, the most likely outcome here is that Keces ends up with their databox, Quanta gets nothing, and everybody who's supposed to goes home happy. Quanta's claim is pretty tenuous, and Sky may not love Keces' plans but they could be a lot worse."

"That's not the outcome I need, rat. My organization needs to get that databox before this charade of a tribunal gets underway."

She comes to a stop, staring at him. That's why this doesn't involve Nakimura. Nelson's working for Quanta.

He turns to face her, crossing his arms. "Look, I was there when you got into this whole thing. You're no moral crusader. You're in it for the money. We have money. You help us, you get money. It's that simple."

This is ludicrous. She almost laughs, but it's not funny ludicrous. "Even if I wanted to, which to be clear I absolutely don't, what the hell do you think I can do? Steal the databox back from the RJC?"

Nelson shrugs and starts shambling down the street again. "You stole it from the PFS once already."

"No, you idiot! It stayed with Agent Thomas the whole time!" she hisses. "Christ, if it'd ever been in my hands it'd already be with Nakimura."

"If you'd gotten it to him earlier I could have handled it, but you didn't, did you? So now we gotta get it back from that wolf woman, and the only person who can do that is you. You're about the only one she trusts."

"It's not getting it from *her*, it's getting it from *there*!" She stabs a finger in the direction of the Judicial Cooperative's office. "And how much do you think she'd trust me if I managed to do this?" Now, after she's spoken to her sister more in the last couple of days than the last year, after their relationship is less broken than it's been for a decade, you want her to smash it completely?

"If I was you, I'd be less worried about keeping her happy than keeping her alive."

Her blood freezes. "What does that mean?"

"You know they've killed people for this already. Do you think they'll blink at doing it again? Everyone between them and the box is expendable. You, Bright Sky, your fox friend, Agent Thomas, Taylor, Nakimura." He snorts. "Me."

Her fists clench hard enough to drive her claw tips into her palm. "If you hurt anyone I care about, I *will* kill you."

He stops walking and looks down at her. "You might think you understand the lengths they'll go to for this, but you don't. You have no idea. And you have no idea how much some of them would love to hurt you specifically. Hate me all you want, but I am throwing you a goddamn lifeline here."

She closes her eyes. Take a deep breath. Stay calm.

"And if you figure out some way you can help us, I'll see what we can do to help you."

She doesn't say anything. She's still focusing on calm. It's not happening yet.

After a couple seconds of silence, he goes on. "I saw you're having financial trouble. More than your usual cash flow problems. Account locks, high repair bills. Tough combination. Even if that lock gets lifted, from what I hear, you don't got much more money than what you need for your first payment. What about the second? Third? How many installments are there gonna be?"

"From what you hear, huh."

"I really am a detective. We hear things."

"Detective, extortionist, double agent. You get around."

He sighs. "We can pay it all off for you, all at once. You go back to drifting around like you want. And I know what Keces offered you for the wreck. We can match that."

"Even if I *could* steal it, which I can't, I don't trust you. I don't trust Quanta. I know they don't want to beat Keces to market with Shakti. Is this all just about stealing the better version of Kali?"

He snorts impatiently. "That's not your business, or mine. Just trust me about the consequences. Either you choose to get a lot of money, or you choose to let people die." He pulls out his viewcard and taps on it a few times. "I've sent you my contact info. Let me know what your plan is before the tribunal. And if you try and tell anyone about this…" He shrugs.

How the hell is she supposed to come up with a plan and pull it off in an evening? "I can't do this. Please." Something painful and cold twists up inside her.

"You can. Be creative." He shrugs again. "We're gonna have to figure out how to get the databox out of this damn asteroid belt with two or three law enforcement groups trying to grab it. So I think you've got the easy part here, right?" He starts walking away. "You told me you were better than I am and you know people better than you. I got faith in you, rat."

Gail watches him cross the street, her vision blurring, then sits down on the sidewalk, leaning against a building wall and staring up at the ice sky. The scream comes out as a quiet choke.

Chapter 19

WHEN SKY AND GAIL ARRANGE to meet Ansel for drinks, they learn he's relocated to a hotel near the city core, both cheaper and, as he puts it, more urban. The little bar they meet at is right across from his new lodgings; Sky knows it, although before they get there she confides to Gail she doesn't think it's worth the price.

Ansel seems impressed, though, by not just the drinks and the bar menu but the whole neighborhood. "I have to admit the club next door looks interesting, too."

Sky chuckles. "You sound almost regretful about it."

"No, I'm happy I found it. I've just been … surprised exploring the city today, I guess. Are you all right, Gail?"

"Hmm?" She snaps back to attention. Now isn't the time to be thinking of ways to break into the RJC. Is that even possible? Maybe she wouldn't be trying to steal the databox, she'd be trying to talk someone into giving it to her. God, that's insane.

Ansel's still looking at her, waiting for a response. She forces a smile. "Uh, yeah. Just kind of a stressful day."

"You said the talk at the school went well." Sky tilts her head. "Although you haven't said much else."

"It did. I mean, I think I kind of stumbled through a lot of it, but I guess …" She trails off. "I guess I found a voice I didn't think I really had."

"You're not going to start sounding like Sky, are you?"

Sky crosses her arms. Ansel gives the wolf a studiously innocent look.

Gail sips her yerba mate soda and smirks. "I don't have the gravitas. Anyway, I see you found a new hat."

Instead of the cap he's been wearing, he sports a woven straw hat with a wide brim, shaped to fit around his ears. "I don't think I've seen a handmade hat designed for a totemic before. This is what I mean about being surprised. I hadn't thought about what a difference it makes to be in a place that treats us as the norm rather than the exception. I love my neighborhood on Panorica, but some of the cultural differences tip in New Coyoacán's favor." He waves a hand. "Look at places like this. It's not much more expensive than most Panorica pubs, and it's fully staffed. I've seen more waiters in two days here than I have in a month back home."

"Maybe if you went more places than Acceleration you'd see more full service restaurants."

"Come on, the difference isn't my imagination."

"No." It isn't. She's noticed it, too. "You sound like you're warming to the place."

"Don't think that makes me less skeptical of the politics. You know what props this all up, don't you?" He points overhead. "Ceres. The water, the minerals. The Cooperative may be a non-profit in name, but without that revenue stream, you'd all be paying much more for all the social services."

Sky's ears go back.

"Not to change the subject, but where's Jack? You just said he was 'out.'"

"That's all I know. He checked out of the Sonora River Inn when I did, but he said they couldn't book him on the next Earthbound ship, so he's here for another week. When I last saw him he was heading to the canoe rental place."

She laughs. "Of course." Then she glances at Sky. "So how did, uh, tribunal preparation go?"

"The panel selection went surprisingly smoothly. Captain Taylor was less…obstreperous than I'd been expecting, and Nakimura was confident enough in Keces' position to not object repeatedly. So we're ready to go for tomorrow."

Gail's ears lower. So much for the hope she'd have an extra day to strategize. She should just tell Sky about Nelson, right now. She should tell Nakimura about Nelson, too. He knows Quanta has spies in Keces, but doesn't have any idea the biggest one is someone he's personally contracting with.

And if you try and tell anyone about this… God, why didn't she think to trigger Kis's recording when he was threatening her? That'd still be telling people, though, wouldn't it? Just backing it with evidence.

"You're looking a little peaked. Are you sure you're all right?"

"Yeah. I am." She forces her tail to stop twitching, and looks from Ansel back to Sky. "So that'll be held at the RJC building?"

Sky nods. "There are tribunal rooms on the first floor."

She runs a hand through her hair. "Visible to the public, I'm guessing."

"Open to the public." Sky tilts her head questioningly.

"Like everything, right." She doesn't have to make a big confession, she can just guide her sister. This is what she's supposedly good at. "I'm just…I don't want to sound paranoid, but I'm worried about security. Neither Keces nor Quanta wants to be here, they've both engaged in skullduggery—"

Ansel lifts a brow. "Skullduggery? Really?"

"It's a terrific word. The point is we're relying on them to play nice."

"I see your point." Ansel looks between her and Sky. "But—I mean, what are they going to do? They're holding this at a police station."

What are they going to do is the question she doesn't want an answer to. "No, it's going to be at a Judicial Cooperative building, which makes it more like—like a judiciary's office than like even a PFS substation." Gail sighs and looks at Sky. "I'm just suggesting you should consider ramping up security for this one."

Sky looks nonplussed. Maybe the *like a judiciary's office* line; the wolf's always found the notion of privatizing law to be kind of nutty, even if she'll admit it works in practice. But in this case it's absolutely true: the Ring employs few armed officers, and as much as they consider that a point of pride, right now it doesn't feel like an advantage. Although maybe Sky's wondering if this is another crazy scheme of Gail's she doesn't understand, but doesn't fully trust. Finally, she sighs. "I'll call Karen tonight."

Right. As much as Sky may act like she's in charge of everything, she's just a mediator. "Okay." Gail nods, and again barely manages to keep her anxiety display limited to her tail. She remembers Jack's conversation a few days ago about totemics keeping animal advantages while discarding the disadvantages. Right now she'd like a sharp word with whoever thought physically broadcasting their emotions belonged in the advantage column.

"Relax." Ansel pats Gail's hand. "You should come to the dance club with me tonight."

"You know I don't dance."

His tail wags. "You know that's immaterial."

She half-smiles. "Maybe tomorrow." *Assuming they're all still alive, and all still speaking to one another.*

"You're more subdued than usual."

Gail looks across the table at Sky, giving her a weak smile. This is the third home-cooked dinner she's had in four days, and while this one isn't as elaborate as the other two—a homemade spice mix rubbed over chicken, finished in the combochef along with a couple of pre-made side dishes—she can't remember the last time her diet's been on such a streak. She eats out a lot; even cheap restaurants cook better than she knows how to. After these last few days, though, going back to that's going to be depressing. Cheap restaurants don't cook better than this.

When she doesn't say anything, Sky tilts her head questioningly.

"You know I have a lot on my mind right now. Bright and chipper isn't on the star map." *Hey, you know that databox? You didn't happen to bring it home with you, did you? Leave it some place that isn't locked?*

The wolf smiles reassuringly. "I don't think you'll have much to do at the tribunal, other than answer questions about your involvement. Remember, you're not being accused of anything."

"It sounds like it's all kind of a foregone conclusion anyway, isn't it? I mean, we know who owns what on the databox, unless Nakimura's lying."

"We can't discount that 'unless.' And we don't know how convincing a case Quanta's going to make."

"How convincing a case can they make? They hired Corbett to steal the box in the first place."

"Captain Taylor is right about all our evidence being circumstantial." She sighs. "And Quanta's not the group whose paranoia made this data vulnerable to being physically stolen, or who were transporting the last copy in as untraceable a fashion as possible, or who bullied you into helping them recover it. Everything Keces has done makes it look like *they're* the ones dealing in stolen property."

That's true, and—oh God, this is an opening, isn't it? If they decide in favor of Quanta, she doesn't have to steal the box. But she's been arguing for Keces all this time, and Sky would still say they're the least worst outcome. They probably are.

But Gail knows her big sister. If she argues strenuously enough against Quanta, then Sky's going to at least talk her through the opposing side.

"Okay, sure. But what about Quanta's Purity connection? If there is one, this is like … well, like handing a weapon to your worst enemy."

"That's another big 'if.' I've looked into the Lantern Foundation myself. Purity's been laying low for years, but Lantern feels like—like their academic successor, offering up a pseudo-scientific basis for why they were right all along." She takes a big bite of the chicken, barely chewing. She always ate faster when she got exasperated. "But we barely have enough to connect them with Quanta."

"We have Thomas Burke."

"And his son. I know." Sky sighs. "The theory you and Jack have fits the facts. But as much of an ass as Taylor is, he raised a good question today. Why not just have destroyed all the copies of the databox? That stops Shakti."

"But then Quanta loses the advances Keces made on Kali, too, though."

"Is that enough to go through all this?"

"Nakimura doesn't seem surprised by it."

"Given the way he's treated you from the start, I can't say that I trust his judgement."

"Paranoia's probably what makes him a good businessman." She polishes off the last bite of her own chicken, and keeps her voice casual-to-morose. "What would make you decide in favor of Quanta?"

"Personally?" Sky leans back, frowning thoughtfully. "Proof their claim is legitimate, and definitive proof Keces has been lying to us."

Quanta isn't here to provide proof, and she doubts they've told Taylor enough that he can. She might be able to affect the other side of the equation, though. If Sky's already suspicious of Nakimura, what can she do to tip the scales?

But Mara's Blood, if she figures out a way to throw the trial and Keces knows she's done it on purpose—and they will—she might as well light out for the fringes right now. If Quanta pays her what Nelson says they will, maybe she can flee to Rothbard and drink enough to forget everyone she's screwed over. Not just Keces, but Sky. Ansel. Hell, even Nevada, a friend she didn't know she had until a few days ago.

"Hmm?"

Sky's noise jabs her. She refocuses on the wolf, raising her brows inquiringly.

"You had an odd expression. Sad. Now you look like I just woke you from a daydream."

She shakes her head. "No. Sorry. I'm getting lost in thought." She bites her lip. "So is Quanta really letting Taylor be their stand-in?"

"Yes. They've been one of the most frustrating companies I've ever dealt with. I'm almost—almost—sympathetic to the Captain. It's clear they feel he should just be able to order us to stop playing cops and robbers and hand the databox over to him, and they're putting a lot of pressure on both Interpol and the PFS."

"They understand that not only could they lose the databox, but they might actually face charges for the theft, right? I mean, that could happen. RJC investigations lead to actions on other platforms sometimes."

"Quanta could have a *socius indignus* order placed against them and need to pay reparations. I don't know what they'd face on Earth, though. The organizations that would have to investigate them seem more interested in protecting them."

"Even so, I think they'd take this more seriously."

"I don't think they take *us* seriously. Not just totemics, the whole River. We're a bunch of lunatics who made ourselves look like animals and went to live on artificial worlds with minimal governments." She crosses her arms and half-smiles. "Agent Thomas has joined our side and I'm fairly sure he still thinks that. How do you think people who've never left Earth see us?"

She flashes the expected wry grin in response. But is that it? If they're pulling Lantern's strings and Randall works with Purity and the whole theory she and Jack came up with is correct, Quanta's highest executive levels don't see totemics as crazy furry space libertarians. They see them as an existential threat.

She can't figure out how to reconcile that thesis with them deputizing Captain Spitty, though. They don't care enough to even send over Nakimura's equivalent. That's a blow-off, a corporate hand wave. That's Quanta saying "ha ha, crazy furry space libertarians."

But maybe not. Maybe it's them saying that as far as they're concerned the game's fixed, that they can't win. That's why they're having Suspicious Detective put the screws to her.

Sky stands up. "Are you finished?"

Gail nods. "Yeah, thanks." She stands, too. "I think I'm gonna go for a walk around the block."

"If you wait for me to load the dishes, I can walk with you."

"No, that's okay. I just want to clear my head a bit."

Sky tilts her head, but nods.

Gail gives the wolf a hug before heading out, holding it until Sky's tail wags. "Thanks."

It's just past dusk, the sky filtered down to a dim orange, the few wispy clouds glowing from behind. She stops about a block away at a tiny park, walking into the grass, sitting down and looking up. The sunsets on Panorica look more natural to her now—silly, since this is at least natural light. But it's two "sunsets," effectively, the light brightest on the edges of the horizons by the Ring's rims.

Is a true horizon sunset—the kind you can only get on a planet—prettier? The light filtered by immense, thick clouds, the sun sinking behind mountains thousands of meters high or into vast oceans? Earth life sounds so incredibly strange: all that physical space everywhere, hundreds of millions of square kilometers, gravity so strong it makes getting back into space frightfully difficult. Maybe if she'd been born there, she'd be piloting atmosphere-bound ships. Or ocean-bound ones. Maybe she'd just be running a junkyard.

Maybe she'd never have come to a point where she had to decide between betraying her adopted sister and—if she can believe Nelson's threat—risking her life.

"I wish you were better at giving advice, Kis." She says it out loud, just above a whisper.

"I can weigh probabilities."

"Only when you can attach numbers to them."

"That is true." Gail fancies she hears a tone of regret in the ship's voice. "Are you sure there is no way to do that?"

"I don't think so. On the one hand I can try and throw the tribunal and send the databox back to Quanta, which is what Nelson's trying to force me to do. There's no guarantee I'll succeed if I try, but even if I fail, I'll leave Sky and pretty much everyone I know hating me. On the other hand…" She shrugs. "I confess this all to Sky, or just do nothing, and risk that they'll try and kill my family and friends. Or worse."

"What must happen for the tribunal to be thrown?"

"Captain Spitty's going to vote for Quanta and Nakimura won't. So it'll come down to getting two other votes to go with Quanta—either Sky and one of the two pool members, or both pool members."

"How difficult will that be?"

"I don't know."

"In the first scenario, the positive outcome is uncertain, but the negative effect of everyone you know hating you is guaranteed. In the second scenario, both outcomes are uncertain."

"So statistically, the second scenario's a better choice. I get it, but the negative outcome from the second one is people dying. I'm screwed either way, but in the first scenario I don't bring others down with me." She drops onto her back, staring up at the sky. It's black in the center now, orange retreated to the edges of the horizons. "I don't know which one's going to be easier to do. Or easier to live with."

"I do not, either."

She lets another minute pass in silence, then pushes herself up to a sitting position, taking out her viewcard. She doesn't know why she doesn't want to ask *Kismet* to run this message for her, but she doesn't.

> *I can't physically get the databox. But I think I can throw the trial in Quanta's favor. Ok?*

She stares at the text. Simple. Straightforward. Just like signing an indentured servitude contract. There's still time to back out, until she touches send.

She touches send, then closes her eyes.

After she lets another minute pass, she stands up and walks back toward Sky's place.

As she walks back in, the wolf looks up from the couch. Something on Gail's face, in her expression, must give away how miserable she's feeling. She musters an almost-relaxed smile, but it's too late.

"Did you clear your head? You look more troubled now than you did when you left."

She laughs weakly. "No, I think I've gotten some things straightened out."

The viewcard pings in her pocket.

"All right." Sky looks unconvinced, but lets it drop. "Would you like some coffee?"

"Sure. Thanks."

As Sky heads into the kitchen, she pulls out the card and looks at the one-word reply.

> *No*

She puts it back in her pocket and tries to keep from shaking. She can't.

When Sky returns, she frowns, setting both coffees down and dropping into a seat by her sister, putting her hands on her shoulders. "Gail, enough. Tell me what's wrong."

Taking a quick breath feels like rocks in her throat. "I—Sky, do you trust me?"

The wolf's brow furrows. "Of course."

"I know it sounds crazy, but I think—I don't think the tribunal's a good idea. I don't think we can let a committee decide what happens to the databox. They're going to end up giving it to Keces and you're right, they *aren't* trustworthy."

Sky looks bewildered. "But that's what the tribunal is for. To decide that."

"No. You don't understand. We can—just get it to…" She stops. She doesn't know where she's going with this, what she can say without letting what she knows tumble out. Without putting Sky in danger.

Sky's hands drop off her shoulders; she looks at Gail with a baffled expression, then a hurt one, then a measured, doubtful one. "Get it to who?"

"People—its rightful—God." She rubs her face. Yes, she'd be so terrific at sales. Come on. Stop panicking.

"What are you trying to say?" The wolf's eyes narrow. "Are you trying to make some side deal?"

"No! I mean—it's not like what you're thinking. Sky—"

"Mara's Blood!" She clenches her fists. "It's barely twelve hours until the tribunal starts! Do you think I can just tell everyone 'sorry, my sister's decided she knows better than our legal system, so I'm taking the databox and going home?' What game do you think you're playing?"

"I'm not—"

"This can't just be about you, Gail. For once. Too much is at stake." She stalks toward the door. "I'm going to go clear *my* head, and you'd better damn well try harder at clearing yours."

"Sky, please—"

Her sister slams the door behind her.

She slides down on the couch and shrieks into a cushion. God, what game *does* she think she's playing? She could hardly have made things any worse if she'd deliberately tried.

Maybe there's a way to salvage this, to stop the tribunal first, then to confess everything to her. To apologize. She doesn't see how, but she's faced tougher problems. She must have.

Sky isn't back before she falls asleep, still with no answers.

Chapter 20

"You're very jumpy."

Gail twitches when Ansel puts his hand on her shoulder as he speaks. Thanks, body, good timing. "I had a really bad night."

He tilts his head, giving her a worried look. "You and Sky didn't come in together."

"We kinda had a fight."

He pats her shoulder. "You're just getting to know her again after a decade. There's going to be bumps. But it's been amazing watching you over the last few days, you know. You're like a different person."

Well, she'll have fixed that in a couple hours, right? Back to the same old con artist deadbeat who puts Ansel on guard when she approaches his table at Acceleration. God, she's burning bridges while she's still standing on one.

Adjudication rooms on Panorica look ostentatious and imposing, modeled (she thinks) on British or American courtrooms. But this room keeps with New Coyoacán's cherished, infuriatingly casual style. Sky, Nakimura, Taylor, Dupree, and two others—a cat totemic who looks like he's in his seventies or eighties, and a cisform woman with reddish skin—sit around a semi-circular table in front of the room facing the gallery, three rows of seats. Gail and Ansel sit in the front row; Jack got in later than they did, and found a seat in the back. He's dressed less like a cop and more like a tourist, denim blend jeans and a colorful print shirt of the kind Gail favors. Ironically, she's not wearing anything like that now. She's wearing her own slacks and a red blouse of her mother's. She thought she'd have to sit at the table, too, but Sky curtly informed her they'd call her up if they had questions.

What truly makes her jumpy sits on the tribunal table, right in front of

Karen Dupree: a transparent case, with the databox inside it. Is it locked? Not like she can ask without Sky growling at her. "Why do they even have that here?"

Ansel shrugs at her mutter. "It's a connected table, I'm sure. They might ask Nakimura or Taylor to do something with the databox to substantiate Keces's or Quanta's claims."

She swallows, glancing around and settling her eyes on Nelson again. He's sitting in the second row, pushed all the way to the left side so he's not too near anyone else. Maybe so he can get to an exit quick. He hasn't looked at her once, not even when she's stared at him painfully obviously, like she's doing right now. Is he planning to take it? Does he still expect her to? The weekly flight to Earth departs tomorrow. Did they think she was so damn good a thief she could steal it without anyone noticing until the flight had left?

But it doesn't matter now. It's out of her hands, and it's out of his, too.

If he was telling the truth about that. Or about anything. God, why didn't she just go to Sky about him? Hell, if she didn't want to go to Sky, she could have gone to Nakimura. Hey, do you know your right-hand man's been feeding everything to your corporate nemesis and still wants to steal the databox from you? I told you he was an asshole, but did you listen to the rat? No. No, you did not.

And what makes her jumpy, too, is this. If this is the Ring's idea of heightened security, she'd hate to see their idea of lackadaisical security. The back wall of this room is an outside wall, and yes, it's transparent aluminum or reinforced glass or something, but it's visible from the street. There's nothing secret about where they are, and little secret about what they're doing. Passersby can and will be watching. And are there any guards? The partial transform vixen standing by the interior door there is armed with an electric pistol. So is a middle-aged cisform guy standing in the back. As far as she can tell that's it.

"Good morning," Karen begins. "I'm Karen Dupree, and I'm the appointed arbiter for this panel. We have two connected orders of business before us, both tied to this." She indicates the databox and its case with both hands. "A databox, and more broadly the data that it contains.

"The first issue is whether Keces Industries, represented on the tribunal by Jason Nakimura, used unethical measures to compel Gail Simmons—Gail, could you stand up?"

Gail swallows, standing for a scant second and dropping back down.

The rabbit smiles, then continues. "To compel Gail Simmons, represented on the tribunal by her mediator Bright Sky, to retrieve their allegedly stolen property via unconventional means. The second issue is the disposition of the property itself. It has two claimants, Keces Industries and Quanta Biotechnics, represented on the tribunal by Panorica Federation Security Captain Simon Taylor. In addition, we must consider the implications of the technology and whether it's both in the interests of, and within the power of, the Ring Judicial Cooperative to impose conditions on its use. We'll start with opening statements on the first issue from Bright Sky and Mr. Nakimura."

Sky laces her fingers together. "In the Ceres Ring tradition, mediators for individuals rather than organizations are often chosen among extended family. While Gail and I are not blood relations, her mother adopted me when I was young and in need of a home, and we bonded as sisters." The wolf doesn't look over at Gail as she goes on, describing the way Nakimura sent her after the box, all the while believing she was the real thief he was setting a trap for.

After she finishes, Dupree looks toward Nakimura. He merely inclines his head. "We have no cause to challenge any of Ms. Sky's characterizations."

Sky continues. "And we know now that the databox had never been in Gail's possession. It had been stolen by Randall Corbett, acting on behalf of Quanta Bio—"

"Objection," Taylor snaps, then looks uncertain. "Is that what you say here?"

Dupree shakes her head. "No, but all that's relevant to the first case is that Ms. Simmons never had the databox in her possession. Agent Thomas, could you quickly review how you intercepted the databox?"

Jack stands up, clearing his throat, and sketches out a mercifully quick review of Gail tackling Randall at the spaceport. Afterward, Dupree grills everyone on the panel to see if they need clarifications, and if they agree that Gail never had the databox in her possession. Even as efficient as the rabbit is, Gail starts drifting toward worrying about Nelson, until they get to the part about compensating her.

"Twenty-five thousand dollars per diem," Nakimura responds when Dupree prompts him. "We engaged her for six days, so we shall offer one hundred fifty thousand dollars."

Hardly the payoff she'd dreamed of, but for six days she could do worse.

Sky, though, shakes her head. "That's not at all acceptable. You've put her very life at risk, in some cases from your own operatives."

"What would you consider acceptable, then, Ms. Sky?"

"Three million, coupled with a formal apology."

Is she crazy? Gail tries to catch Sky's eyes, mouthing *are you crazy?* to her.

Nakimura's frown deepens and he drums his fingers on the table. At length, he says, "We shall admit no malicious intent toward Ms. Simmons and, further, agreeing to those terms will require this tribunal find no malfeasance on our part with respect to the dispensation of the databox."

The cat raises his hand and speaks hesitantly when Dupree nods at him. "Isn't that the second case?"

"Mr. Ritchie is correct." Dupree nods to the cat. "We can't agree to pre-decide any of the next part in your favor."

Nakimura drums his fingers a few more seconds. "I shall recommend this settlement to my employers, then. Understand that it may take some time to be finalized, and that process will not be under my control."

That translates to *our lawyers will drag this out for years.* Naturally, even though three million might as well be a rounding error to Keces, and it's a far cry from the original promise of half the SC71's fair market value. But it's more than three years' typical income for her. She can be patient.

"Now we'll move onto the next part." Dupree starts to review the story of the databox.

"Are they always that fast?" Ansel whispers to her.

"I have no idea." The last time she was involved in a case at an RJC center it was over her legal guardianship when they couldn't find her father.

He looks over at Jack. "Are they that fast in *your* courts?"

"Sometimes," Jack whispers back. "But very rarely. How about Panorica's?"

"Sometimes." Ansel grins. "But very rarely."

As Dupree invites Nakimura, Taylor, and Sky to speak in turn, Gail tries not to completely tune Nakimura's drone out. She's heard these arguments *way* too often over the last few days. He gives an overview of the work, patiently explaining that Shakti and Kali aren't separable projects, but applications of the same data set. Under questioning from Ritchie and Ms. Saganey, the cisform woman, he makes the case that *all* the work is original to Keces, legally speaking—while parts are based on Quanta's work, Keces considers those to fall under Quanta's original licensing.

She glances toward Suspicious Detective again. He remains disengaged, restless. Is he waiting for something?

Captain Spitty keeps quiet until Dupree turns to him, even though it looks like he's literally biting his tongue to stay silent a couple times. "Okay, let's work backward from what Mr. Nakimura just said. If Keces had no concern about this project's legality, why would they be using a dark courier? Everything they've done—and I do mean everything—tells me they treated this as a criminal enterprise. They treated this work as if it were smuggled contraband."

More or less what Sky said to her the other day. And, yeah, all true. His review lays out an argument that the case for Quanta's involvement in the theft relies entirely on drawing a tenuous, circumstantial connection from them to Corbett. Yes, Corbett did volunteer work with the Lantern Foundation. Taylor's rebuttal boils down to a simple question: so what? Why would Quanta go through all this trouble to steal a databox containing a mix of data they already have and data they don't want?

"But we know why." Sky gestures toward Gail. "We know Corbett hates totemics. He *especially* hates my sister. The Lantern Foundation is a front for Purity. As Captain Taylor himself just said, Quanta's former CEO funds it, and his son still works as a Quanta executive. They have ideological reasons to want to make the bioweapon better and to destroy Shakti. And commercial reasons, if Shakti is based on unlicensed Quanta technology."

Saganey raises her hand. "I don't think I agree that the Lantern Foundation is a hate group."

"Did you all see the selected list of presentations from Lantern I sent?" Sky looks around the table. "There's a *lot* of anti-transformation sentiment there."

"Anti-transformation sentiment isn't in and of itself an endorsement of terrorism." Saganey leans forward, looking directly at Sky. "My family has avoided biomods for generations because we're concerned about the safety. And the Navajo have never been pleased with the appropriation of the word 'totem.'"

Sky gets an uncomfortable look. She and Gail have had that discussion before—it came up once in a while at RTEA meetings—but no alternative suggestions ever took off. To Gail, it's obvious *totem* and *totemic* diverged a long time ago, and while she knows symbolic associations for rats, she never thinks of rats as her "totem animal."

Ritchie clears his throat. "I understand what Kali is, but could you explain Shakti again?"

Nakimura sighs thinly, hands steepled on the table. "It's technology for stable *in utero* modification, and while it is based on *legally* licensed work from Quanta Biotechnics," he glances at Taylor, "the work is primarily ours."

Murmurs start in the room. "So applying this technology to a child *in utero* would allow the child to be born as a totemic. And that child would give birth to totemic children, not cisform, without needing any more genetic work performed?"

"The answer is too complex to be a definite yes or no, Mr. Ritchie. But, in general, yes."

Saganey looks at Nakimura. "How can that possibly even work? I see totemic couples of different—is species the right word?—all the time."

"Species is fine," Sky says. She looks at Nakimura, too, though.

"Our tentative answer, based on simulations, is that if the base species could form hybrid offspring in the wild, totemics would have hybrid children. If they could not, one of the species will prove dominant. If a rabbit totemic and a wolf totemic had a child, the child would be either a wolf or a rabbit totemic. Our data suggest that certain combinations of parental species are more likely to produce certain kinds of offspring, but not in a consistently predictable fashion. And some genetic modifications— unnatural fur colors and patterns, for instance—are not transmissible."

Saganey frowns. "And if a totemic and a cisform human had a child, the child would be…?"

"Almost certainly totemic."

The murmurs stop being murmurs and start being conversation. Loud conversation. Arguing. Dupree holds up her hands, trying to yell over the room to bring it back to order. "Quiet. Please! Quiet!"

"And *that* is why Quanta wanted to stop this at any cost." Sky's almost shouting. "Purity ideology."

Taylor slams his hands on the table. "Purity is not Quanta!"

"The Lantern Foundation—"

"They're not Quanta, either! There's one retired executive, and allegedly one current one, in common. You're making a connection that simply isn't there!"

Is he being disingenuous or just naive? Surely…

Mara's Blood, what if he's right? If Quanta isn't behind the wreck, if they just see this all as a business dispute, that explains a lot of their behavior. Suspicious Detective never said he was working for Quanta, just for "his organization"—and if his organization is Lantern, that's why throwing the trial isn't good enough. Corbett wasn't going to deliver it to Quanta, he was going to deliver it to Lantern. She was never supposed to stop him, but Nelson was there with Nakimura just in case she managed it.

And they're not interested in getting the improved version of Kali to Quanta. They want to get it to Purity.

She turns to Suspicious Detective's corner and—

He's not there.

Gail bolts to her feet, looking around the room with a rising sense of panic. She switches all her biomods on, speeding up her senses, her motions. He's not anywhere. Not inside, not on the street, not visible through the transparent wall.

"What is it?" Ansel looks up, puzzled. "You're moving weird."

"Where did Nelson go?"

"Who?"

As Dupree tries to shout the room back in order, Gail waves at her frantically.

Sky stands up, bangs both fists on the table hard enough to shake it, and snarls. *"Quiet!"*

It doesn't produce absolute silence, but the volume drops in a hurry. Both Saganey and Ritchie scoot their chairs back from her.

Gail raises her voice to a yell. "They're going to try and steal the databox!"

Everyone at the table—everyone in the room—stares at her. "What?" Sky and Dupree both say simultaneously. "Who?" Nakimura says. "Quanta?"

"No. Lantern." She points at where Nelson had been sitting. "Your hired detective, Nelson. He's with—he works for—Lantern, Purity, someone who isn't you. But he was here, and now he isn't, and whoever he works for is about to do something *now.*"

Dupree runs a hand through the short hair between her long ears. "Mr. Nakimura's assistant? You're going to have to start over."

"We don't have time, but he threatened his employers would kill people if I didn't cooperate. I *thought* he meant Quanta, but I think Taylor's right. It's not Quanta, it's Lantern acting alone."

"If you didn't cooperate by doing what?" Sky's voice is low, dangerous.

Her ears fold down and she forces her voice not to crack. "If I didn't steal the databox for him. They're desperate to get it back to Earth."

The wolf's expression goes flat. She knows why Gail screamed at her to get the databox now. God, does this make things better, or worse?

Ritchie's ears have gone back. "This is an RJC facility. What do you think they're going to be able to do?"

"Look, they know exactly where the databox is right now, and exactly how protected it is."

Nakimura's expression shifts from his typical annoyed weariness to thoughtful worry. "As much as I would prefer not to prolong the proceedings, perhaps adjourning to a more secure room is appropriate."

Dupree looks between the five tribunal members. "Those in favor of adjourning?"

Nakimura, Saganey, Ritchie and Taylor all raise their hands. Sky remains perfectly still. She hasn't stopped staring at Gail.

The rabbit looks mildly surprised. "Very well. I'll ask what's available. We'll take an hour recess."

Most of the people in the gallery get up and meander toward the exits, talking excitedly. Dupree taps on her bracelet, and her eyes lose focus as she studies whatever's coming up on her HUD.

Jack makes his way to her side, looking angry. Great. Sky's hurt, he's angry. "Nakimura's hired help was a mole for Purity, and you knew?"

"Don't say 'mole.' It's offensive." Ansel looks at Jack, then at Gail. "But why didn't you say something before now?"

She hasn't shut off her biomods yet and they're starting to hurt. "Because he threatened me, okay? He threatened all of you—"

Something moves outside, on the street, and she isn't sure what it is but it's not right. She slams herself to the ground, pulling Jack and Ansel with her hard and fast enough that she probably hurts them.

Two deafening, simultaneous cracks sound: one behind her and over her head, one in front of the room. Then a flash. A dull bang. Fireworks.

Screams.

The room fills with white smoke. It's sour, acidic, poisonous. Tear gas? There's a loud bang right behind her, more screams. Street noises.

Jack wheezes. He sits up, then sinks down, coughing. She can't see. Is his head bleeding?

Her muscles *really* hurt. Other things hurt. Maybe she's bleeding too. No. It doesn't matter. Something's on fire. Retune her vision, shift spectrum, she needs to get to the table—

People are running. In? Out? Light behind her. Part of the wall's come down. Small, sharp pops from an electric pistol. There: infrared. It helps a little. She turns to Ansel. He's terrified, trying to cover his muzzle. She catches his eye, puts her hand down low to the floor. *Stay down.* He nods.

Then she starts crawling forward, keeping her hand over her nose, her mouth shut. Jack's beside her. He moves like he can see as well as she—right, he has biomods too. She's just never seen him have to use them before.

She can see the table. It's burning. Dupree is the only one still there, slumped forward, head resting where the databox had been. Eyes open. Oh God. Blood's running down her leg and she isn't moving. Nakimura's sprawled under the table. Ritchie, the old cat, is crumpled next to him.

what's going on I can't see where mom fell somebody help

People scramble out, other people scramble in. As the smoke clears she can see they're Ring security forces. And PFS. She thinks she recognizes Wolfe, but it's hard to tell. Keeping her eyes open rubs sandpaper on them. Alarms ring buzz shriek inside the building and out on the street.

Nakimura's bleeding. Side? Arm? It looks bad. She scrambles toward him—

She sees Sky. Mara's Wounds. Her sister had tried to get to the gallery rather than trying to get to an exit.

To get to Gail.

"Sky." She drops to the wolf's side. Bleeding, too, from wounds on her back, across one side of her face.

Her nerves scream at her. She's past the limits for keeping her biomods ramped up like this. She shuts them down and instantly pain floods her body, not just from the sudden crash but from her own cuts there and there and there and—

No time. She has to trust nothing she has is serious. She checks over the wolf's body, looking at the wounds. Medics should be here by now. Why aren't they here yet? No. They are here. She sees them. Is Sky breathing?

what's wrong with mommy she isn't

Yes. She's breathing. She thinks. "Sky." She says it louder, trying to keep her voice from sounding high and fluttery and shaky, and she cradles the wolf's head in her lap. "Sky!"

The wolf's eyes open. After a second she focuses on Gail.

She lets out a sharp, ragged sigh. "Jesus. It's okay. It'll be okay." She looks around frantically. "Hey! She's wounded!"

"Everyone's wounded," someone yells back. She isn't sure if they're a doctor. Dammit, that's not—

Sky makes a noise, a groan, a whisper, like she's trying to say something. But the sound is wrong. Gail snaps her attention back down.

"I..." the wolf chokes out. "G..." Pink foam dribbles out of her mouth, and she convulses.

Gail trembles violently. Then she starts wailing.

Chapter 21

As far as waiting rooms go, this one is visually nice, at least as nice as the teachers' lounge. Much more cheerful and less institutional than the hospital she's been to on Panorica. But the air cleaning system runs so hard it feels like a faint breeze, and it's cold. It doesn't smell like citrus or floral "neutral" scents; it doesn't smell like disinfectant, either. It smells like nothing. It's like distilled water. It's unsettling.

Jack has contact bandages in a half-dozen places and he's limping, but he's been talking with Wolfe and Jollenbeck, conferring with doctors. About ten minutes ago he ran down a hallway that they won't let Gail go down, not yet. Apparently, everyone's forgotten he's been suspended. Maybe Taylor's the only one who'd have put up a fuss, and he's in a bed down that hallway. So is Nakimura. And Ritchie and Saganey.

And Sky.

When her eyes blur with tears—again, dammit—Ansel squeezes her hand, but doesn't say anything. He's more banged up than Jack is. For that matter, so is she. It's been about two hours since they treated her, just one of nearly two dozen with minor physical injuries. She can feel each individual cut and gash they've squeezed bandage cream into, especially where a piece of shrapnel sliced her tail. They told her she was lucky it hadn't been taken clean off; the therapy for that is longer and more painful. The goo's supposed to be an anesthetic, too. If it is, she can't imagine how much pain she'd be in right now without it.

A doctor, a tigress a good fifteen centimeters taller than Gail, walks toward them from the don't-go-down-there hallway. She has short black hair and vibrant green fur that looks subtly slicked down. Gail remembers hearing somewhere that totemic doctors use special treatments to keep their fur in place, rather than letting it float merrily into places it shouldn't be. She smells faintly of antiseptic. Jack's following her a meter behind. They pull up chairs.

Something in her face must have just fallen, her ears flagged, because Jack quickly says, "Sky's still alive."

She lets out a breath, nodding numbly.

The doctor speaks in that gentle please-don't-make-a-scene way a true professional has when she's telling you unpleasant things. "We've been able to talk to Mr. Nakimura, as you suggested."

She didn't suggest it, she screamed it. They didn't understand what she meant until Ritchie—not Saganey, not Nakimura, not Taylor—showed the same symptoms. "And?"

"We won't be able to confirm if Sky's been poisoned by Kali until laboratory technicians from Keces arrive, but we're following their treatment protocol until then. Hemodialysis, fluids." The tigress takes a deep breath, looking frightened herself for just a moment until the calm veneer snaps back into place. "We're trying to stave off multiple organ failure. The therapies we have for this are slowing it down. But they're not stopping it."

"And Ritchie's showing the same thing."

"Mr. Ritchie was older, and he took more physical injuries than Sky did." She sighs. "That complicated his treatment. He passed away an hour ago."

She closes her eyes. Saganey is the most badly injured, she'd heard—except for poor Karen Dupree, dead before the medics even arrived. But Saganey isn't poisoned. Saganey isn't a totemic. "No one else is showing signs of…whatever it is?" Like Ansel? Like Gail herself?

"Three others." She stands up. "The techs from Keces won't be here for another five hours. We can call you as soon as they get here, but you don't have to stay if you don't want to."

"I'll stay." If she was the one in the hospital bed, Sky would be sitting guard over her no matter how many doctors tried to keep her away.

The tigress nods. "I'm Doctor Allen. If you need anything—or if any of your injuries start causing you any more pain than they are now—ask for me."

When she leaves, Gail stares up at the ceiling. "This is my fault. That's what everyone says at a moment like this, right? That's so melodramatic. But it really is my fault."

Ansel puts a hand on her shoulder. "You're not the one who launched a mortar attack."

"I could have warned them earlier."

"You could have, yes. But would that have stopped them? Maybe they'd have gotten bigger explosives and there'd be dozens dead instead of just two. And I don't think there's any reason not to think they wouldn't have still gone after Sky in retaliation. And maybe Nevada and her husband. Maybe me."

She rubs her face. That all makes sense, but none of it helps. "God. Why aren't my organs failing?"

Ansel winces. "Don't say that."

"No, no, I don't mean it that way. I mean, why is it just the ones who were sitting close to the bomb who got contaminated? Why aren't *we* poisoned, too?"

His ears pin back.

"We'll ask Quanta when they get here."

She looks up at Jack. "You mean Keces."

"I mean Quanta. Getting them to be more cooperative only took them facing charges for terrorism, murder and attempted murder from both the RJC *and* the PFS."

Gail closes her eyes again, shaking her head. "I don't think they did any of this."

"I know what your theory is. But if what was used in the attack was really Kali, there are only two sources we know of."

"Yeah." She slumps in her seat. "Did they get *anything* from video?"

"Not enough. It looks like the strike team was only four people wearing photocamo and they didn't stay together."

She groans.

Jack leans forward, looking at her worriedly. "Are you sure you don't want to go home?"

Home. Sky's place? Dani might let her go back to *Kismet* and curl up in a little ball. But she shakes her head. "I'm going to stay here until…until we know something."

"Then you're all coming with me to get food in the hospital cafeteria."

Ansel smiles weakly. "Hasn't the day been hard enough?"

Gail shakes her head. "I don't want food."

"None of us have had lunch, you and I have both run on biomods longer than we should have, and it's past fifteen o'clock. You want food. And Doctor Allen says the food's pretty good for a hospital cafeteria."

"That's a four-star recommendation if I ever heard one." Ansel grunts and gets to his feet, putting his hat back on, and holds his hand out for Gail.

"No."

"Yes." He wiggles his fingers. "Jack's right and I'm prepared to be annoying about this until you give in."

Sighing, she takes his hand, allowing herself to be led down a different hallway toward the cafeteria. Here, at least, there's scent again. It smells good. Maybe she really is starving.

For a hospital, the food's good. She thinks. She's not paying that close attention to it.

Around twenty o'clock Gail falls asleep for about a half hour, waking up with a crick in her neck and a momentary terror that she'd been woken up by a new alarm, a scream, a cry for help. But nobody's screaming, nothing's buzzing. It's just her by herself in the waiting room, soft music playing somewhere. Ansel's fallen asleep two seats away.

She gets up, wobbling. Her tail still stings, but none of her other injuries hurt at all, the nanobots in the bandage cream mostly finished with their work. The bioplastic skins should dissolve by tomorrow. She got obscenely lucky. Almost everyone—except for the ones right at the front—did.

None of the doctors seem to be around. She heads down the hallway she's not supposed to go down without permission.

Glances into the first couple of rooms she passes show them empty. The first occupied one is Nakimura's. Two people she's never seen before hover over him: cisform, one man and one woman, both wearing white coats and thin blue surgical gloves. It looks like they're talking with him rather than checking on his condition. Doctors, or Keces' lab technicians? Maybe they showed up and Doctor Allen didn't call her. Or maybe they're from Quanta, there to make sure he doesn't recover. If her hypothesis from earlier about how all the pieces fit together is true, that would make no sense, but she's just about given up on worrying whether things make sense at all today. She watches a moment. It doesn't look like they're doing anything nefarious, but she doesn't really know what she's looking at.

"Can I help you?"

Startled, she turns to look up at the nurse who asked the question, a young cisform who looks like he could be Nakimura's son. "I—I was looking for Bright Sky's room. I know it's down this hallway."

He checks the smartpaper tablet he's carrying. "This is room 112. She's in room 115, so two doors down on the other side of the hallway. But she's not accepting any visitors."

"I know. I mean, I know she's not in any condition to see me. But I want to see her."

He hesitates. "I'll have to ask Doctor Allen. If you can wait back in the waiting room?"

"Sure." She points into Nakimura's room. "But are the people in there talking to him from Keces Industries?"

Now he looks bewildered. "I don't know, ma'am. Do you know this patient, too?"

"Yeah. You could say he's an old boss. Can I say hi?" Without waiting for permission, she opens the door and sticks her head in.

Abruptly, the two white-coated people stop talking and turn. One's holding a metal case. Both their coats sport embroidered Keces Biotechnics logos.

"Didn't mean to interrupt. Just checking on how Mr. Nakimura's doing."

"Ma'am," the nurse says from behind her, "you can't—"

"Ms. Simmons. I should recover, thank you," Nakimura murmurs, barely above a whisper. "My associates and I are finished with our conversation, and they are here to assist Doctor Allen."

Gail turns to the flustered nurse. "You heard the man. Is Allen in with Sky?"

"She should be."

"Great. Let's all go to room 115."

The nurse swallows and hurries down the hallway ahead of them.

As the two follow Gail out of the room, she points at the briefcase. "Do you have the countermeasure to Kali in there? Or whatever it is Kali produces."

They exchange brief glances with one another.

"I know it's top secret, but I'm pretty looped in."

"Yes, we've been told about you." The woman answers. "We…might. The most current batch of Kinetitox we had was destroyed in the attacks on our facilities, but we still had a few vials of an older run. How well it'll work depends on the version deployed here."

Doctor Allen's striding toward them from Sky's room. "Kinetitox?" She lifts her brows skeptically.

"Not our name. We're not the marketing department."

"Can you tell me more about the exposure?" The man addresses Allen, not Gail.

"The RJC forensic team found three shells. One they described as a phosphorus grenade, another as a CS gas grenade. The third has our mystery agent in it, and we think the reason we've only had six cases is that it didn't disperse properly." She holds the door of room 115 open.

"We need to analyze that to confirm it's Q200."

Q200? The weapon Kali produces is called Q200? The code names were *so* much cooler. Before she can say anything flippant, though, Gail walks into the room and her heart leaps into her throat.

If you want to make someone look fragile, no matter how strong they are, how indomitable, put them in a thin green hospital gown, stretch them out on a metal-framed bed, and run a network of tubes between their body and bedside machines. This room doesn't smell like the rest of the hospital, the carefully controlled scent of nothing. This room smells like chemicals and fear.

Sky's eyes are closed, body perfectly still but for very slow, shallow breathing, an occasional whisker twitch. Even without all the medical equipment surrounding her, you wouldn't look at her and think "pleasant sleep." She looks troubled. She looks like someone chained by nightmares.

"She's on strong sedatives." Doctor Allen puts her hand on Gail's shoulder briefly. "She's resting as peacefully as she's able to."

Do not say that. That's what you say about people who are dying. She's going to be okay.

The woman from Keces sets the case down on a counter and opens it, revealing a set of dismayingly ordinary vials. No glow, no odd colors, just clear liquid. The man's already studying a display projected over Sky's bedside, swiping through the revealed data. "Got it. It's Q200. Ah…" He glances at Gail, then motions the other tech closer.

She looks over his shoulder. "Fuckers," she mutters. "So it hits totemic signature tags just like Shakti."

Totemic what?

Even though the tigress has walked to Sky's bedside, she registers the rat's confusion. "Companies that perform the genetic work that goes into totemics leave genetic signatures."

"Are you saying my DNA's been rewritten to have 'Copyright Keces Industries' in it somewhere?"

"In a sense, but it's less for copyright protection than for medical diagnostics." As the man speaks he steps away; his partner takes over the data swiping.

Doctor Allen nods. "With the myriad of potential transformations, it's useful to get an instant record of them from the patient's body. I'd never thought of that as a potential attack vector." She sounds tired.

"It wasn't the intended design." The woman's tone is positively dehumidifying. "The nanobots find those signature tags, decode them, and write a new program for themselves to modify a fetus *in utero*. It's the most complicated biotech we've ever produced. It's frankly amazing. The weaponized version just lops off everything after the decoding step and replaces it with a bacterial payload." Her tone makes it clear this is the scientific equivalent of urinating on a Picasso.

Bacterial? Gail stares at the woman, then at Sky. "That's just a bacterial infection? Is it contagious?"

"That," the technician sighs, turning to look at the wolf as well, "is a variant on toxic shock syndrome, which is so rare now most doctors won't ever encounter it outside training sessions. You can't treat toxic shock effectively until you remove the source of the infection, but as long as the Q200 is still operational in a patient's system the source can't be removed. The countermeasure variant finds the Q200 and, with any luck, shuts it off so conventional treatments start working." She looks to Allen again. "I trust you *are* treating all her fluids as transmission vectors."

Allen nods.

"With any luck?"

She looks back to Gail, pursing her lips. "This is our first field test." She turns to Allen. "You have organ-printing facilities here?"

It takes a moment for Gail to process that. Sky's going to need new organs? God, she's on dialysis, they said. By the time her ears fold down, Doctor Allen's already answering. "Yes, of course." She sounds offended at the question.

"Not every clinic I've been to has them on-site. Are we ready?"

Doctor Allen nods. She puts on gloves as well, then takes one of the vials and inserts it into one of the machines by Sky's bedside at about eye level. The machine beeps, its display changing subtly as the—what was that stupid name? Kinetitox—flows into the saline solution being steadily dripped into the wolf's vein.

The woman moves to another monitor. Allen joins her. "How fast will we see a response?"

"It should be within a minute."

Silence falls, the background noise of soft clicks and whispering fans moving to the foreground.

After a minute passes the man frowns and changes some of the displays he's looking at. No one says anything.

The tigress breaks the silence after another minute. "I'm not seeing any change."

Gail clenches her teeth.

The woman sighs. "Give her another vial."

It's clear from Allen's expression she's not pleased with that advice, but when she turns to the rat her voice is soft, sympathetic. "There's nothing you can do for her staying here. I'll give you an update as soon as I have anything to tell you."

Deep breath. Nod. She makes it out of the hallway and back to the waiting room without feeling like she's going to hurl, at least.

Ansel's awake now. "Hey."

"Hi." She slumps down by him.

"How is she?"

"They're giving her a countermeasure, but ..." She shakes her head. "It doesn't look like it's working."

He sighs, patting her shoulder again. "She's strong."

"I don't know if that's enough." She rubs her eyes. "I'm going to go back down to the cafeteria again for some coffee."

"Do you want any company?"

"Sure."

When they get there, though, Gail finds Jack standing by a corner table, along with the raccoon—Bunten?—she remembers as a Ring official when Sky claimed jurisdiction of the box. There's another cisform, his black suit and tie making him look more like an Interpol agent than Jack does right now. Or maybe like an undertaker. No, don't be morbid. But the man's pale white, balding, with the kind of face that looks permanently fixed in a frown.

"Ms. Simmons." The raccoon waves her over.

The man looks up as Gail approaches, but neither stands nor offers to shake hands.

"This is Mr. Alfred Sidgemore, Vice President of Internal Affairs—did I get that right?—of Quanta Biotechnics. Mr. Sidgemore, this is Gail Simmons."

Her mouth opens, but she can't get any words to come out. Is he part of the Lantern/Purity group within Quanta? Assuming there is one, under Burke Junior. Assuming it's not the whole company.

Sidgemore looks surprised at the introduction. "I see. Yes." Then he nods to her curtly. "I hope your... sister... is recovering."

Gail closes her mouth and swallows. Don't show any emotion. Okay, her hands are clenching into fists. That's an emotion. Don't punch him, though. Too much emotion. "She isn't. The stuff they've brought with them to counter your damn bioweapon isn't working."

"'Our' bioweapon? Whatever Keces may have told you—"

Gail slams both her hands down on the table, making both Bunten and Sidgemore flinch. Coffee sloshes over the rim of a mug. "I would like someone," she says flatly, "to stop pointing fingers and give me fucking answers."

Jack picks up the mug. "Gail, maybe you're a little too close to this to—"

"Shut up."

Jack frowns at her, moving away from the table.

"Ms. Simmons, as of this morning we can still account for every milligram of Q200 we've produced. Our research has diverged from the Keces lines, but the countermeasures are still fundamentally keyed to specific production runs. Either you reverse engineer them from a sample, or you make the countermeasure at the same time you produce the weapon."

She closes her eyes. "The Keces medical tech just said a minute ago it was from a very recent run."

"I don't doubt them. But it wasn't ours."

Gail clenches her fists hard enough to hurt. "You're claiming it's Keces's version, but their own fucking antidote doesn't work?"

He spreads his hands.

She laughs bitterly, just once; it threatens to become a sob. If Nakimura lives through this, she's going to kill him.

Ansel had been standing silently, almost motionless, this whole time, but he clears his throat. "I don't understand why Purity didn't just take your copies of Kali, since they're being run by one of your vps. Is the Keces variant that much better?"

"They would say so, we would disagree." Sidgemore sighs. "But there might be a more practical reason to target them. Mr. Burke, Junior, has been under suspicion of corporate espionage for nearly a year, along with several of his associates. We've kept the investigation secret, but we've tightened both our data and physical security considerably since it started. River-based corporations like Keces are comparatively lax."

Ansel grunts. "And it might also deflect suspicion from him, at least for a short while, if attacks are using Keces's designs."

"Mara's Blood." Gail looks away, then back at Sidgemore. "How can you have been investigating him for a year without doing anything? He can't be acting alone, can he? How many people sympathetic to to Purity are in your company?"

"Not many. But some." He falls silent a few long seconds, then speaks softly. "I knew Mr. Burke—Senior—when he still worked at the company. The values he instilled in Quanta, his uncompromising standards, have been invaluable. We're much larger as a defense contractor than we ever were focusing on the aesthetic transformation market." He shakes his head. "But he became increasingly..."

"Reactionary?" Ansel suggests.

"Obsessed. He encouraged our direct corporate support of the Lantern Foundation, but as they started to take increasingly strident stances against all biomodifications, the board began to balk. When we lost a *very* large military contract due to concerns over our long-term commitment, we had to make a sufficiently public severance with Burke."

"But you still left his son as a goddamn executive?"

"It was a calculated choice. Some shareholders signaled they preferred we keep a connection with the family, and until recently, there'd been little evidence that Burke Junior shared his father's ideology."

"There's only one good reason to be going through all this trouble to get this thing to Earth. He doesn't just want to stop Keces from having Shakti or a quick antidote to Kali. He wants to produce Kali there."

"I can't say one way or another, Ms. Simmons. My concern has been with what they do within the company."

"They won't make it to Earth." Bunten sounds reassuringly firm. "We'll be monitoring the passengers *very* closely on ships bound for the inner system and the seasonal launch window for those trips is closing in only three weeks."

"So we're supposed to just wait and hope?"

Sidgemore purses his lips. "If I were you, I would press your contacts at Keces for more active assistance."

The man has a point. She spins around and heads back to Sky's room. She has no idea where Jack's gone. Hopefully she didn't piss him off too much.

The scene hasn't changed, except that Allen and the two technicians look more frustrated. "Ms. Simmons," the tigress says. "I said I'd let you—"

"Yeah, I remember." She looks at the woman technician. "This isn't Quanta's bioweapon, is it? It's yours."

The two technicians look at one another, then back at her. Then the woman looks at the floor.

"Look, I don't care who's at fault, I just want to figure out how to fix it. Why doesn't your Kinetitox work?"

"It doesn't match this version of the weapon." The woman looks like she's close to tears. "Its specific data set was destroyed and the master data set was what was stolen. And this version's designed to be almost impossible to reverse engineer. It would take months."

"That's the improvement Keces made to the weapon, isn't it? Making it harder to defend against." She takes a deep breath. "So what do we do?"

"We need the master data set," the man says. "With that we can rekey the Kinetitox we have on hand in a few hours of work. And we can start making new production runs in three or four weeks. Without it..." He trails off.

Gail runs a hand through her hair. "You need the set on the databox."

The woman nods mutely.

"How long can you keep Sky alive until we get it back?"

Allen takes that one. "We can't say that with any certainty, but the longer she's in this state, the more likely there is to be irreversible damage."

Gail swallows. "So how much time do we have for there to be a good chance of full recovery?"

"A week, at the outside."

Bunten's plan is to wait for Purity to make a run at Port Panorica and stop them there. Even if that works it's going to take a week or two. Or more. They might not try to go through the port at all; maybe they'll find a way to get it onto a cargo ship. Those runs are less frequent, using slow, vast ships that take the better part of a year to make it to Earth orbit. They don't leave from Panorica, and they might be fiendishly difficult to track. Who knows what connections they've made through Lantern? And Bunten can't control how seriously the PFS will take this, given both the pissing match going on between the agencies and the probable leak on the PFS side.

Sky can't wait that long. And the prospect of Purity getting their hands on the unlocked databox is terrifying. Victims will die—or at least be past the point of saving—before they can reverse engineer an effective countermeasure.

Gail turns to walk out, then pauses. "How much Q200 did they steal? More than this one canister?"

The man shakes his head. "I don't know if we can—"

"Just fucking tell me."

"Fifty kilograms," he says after a second.

"And how much does it take to do this?" She points at Sky.

"About twenty milligrams, give or take."

She walks back to the cafeteria, where they're all in animated discussion again, this time about her. Sidgemore's upset that she "walked in and bulldozed over" his "good faith effort to cooperate with Ring authorities." He falls abruptly silent when he sees her again.

"Ansel, check my math. What's twenty milligrams into fifty kilograms?"

"Two and a half million," Ansel answers. "What are you calculating?"

"The lethal dose of this weapon divided by how much of it they stole." His eyes widen.

Gail turns to Bunten. "I know you think we'll be able to get this databox back just by putting the right people in the right place and waiting. But Sky can't wait, and I don't think we can, either. We need to find them, on our own, fast."

The raccoon asks the obvious question in a simple, plaintive tone. "How?"

Chapter 22

GAIL WOULDN'T HAVE LEFT the hospital if Jack, Ansel and Doctor Allen hadn't all insisted. Kis tells her she hasn't missed a call from the bank, so she assumes they lied again, because that's what banks do. Nobody's going to be at Kingsolver at this hour; she goes back to Sky's.

It seems far too big for one person. She feels small, out of place. This isn't her home. But it's familiar from the last few days. It's familiar from decades ago.

It smells like her sister.

That's not new, but tonight it hits her like ice water. Any totemic would notice it, a light background scent of ownership that no circulation system, no chemical air cleaner can ever remove. They might even comment on it; among them, it's not a social faux pas to do so. She learned at a very early age that wasn't true for cisform friends, and you didn't comment on scents unless they were from a narrow range of Socially Acceptable Smells, like a good dinner or a scented candle or clean laundry.

Is it ever acceptable for prims to comment on someone's scent? She should never even *think* that word let alone say it out loud, but right now, tonight, after all of today, they look primitive in ways that have nothing to do with aesthetics. But all right: totemics can be just as brutal to one another, just as cruel, just as hateful. After all, they're only human.

If that stops being strictly true in the future—perhaps the near future—will they find new ways to screw each other over? As they learn which species have dominant genetic traits, they could invent hundreds of petty reasons not to trust one another.

Sometime past midnight Gail stretches out on the couch she's been sleeping on, resting her head on the pillow and staring at the ceiling. On *Kismet* she can extend the cockpit projection back to the cabin, making the ceiling look like glass so you can sleep under the light of a million stars, thousands of constellations. When this is all over, she'll take Sky out on the ship to do that, if she wants. It seems like something she'd like. It seems like something Gail should have offered to do years ago.

She doesn't expect to be able to fall asleep, but at some point exhaustion trumps worry. She can only be sure she slept because the clock suddenly reads 5:38.

Years ago someone told her that if you fall asleep thinking about a problem you'll wake up with a solution, because your dreaming mind will have solved it for you. She's tried it before and concluded it was just a charming lie. If it was true, she'd have woken up with an answer to Bunten's question: how. Right? That's what she fell asleep thinking about it, wasn't it?

Shaking her head, she heads into the bathroom, stripping out of the clothes she didn't bother to take off when she collapsed last night and stepping into the shower stall. A deep clean will take longer, but she feels grungy. She taps it in and stands back, closing her eyes. After a soft, inappropriately cheerful musical chime, the blowers roar on, dusting a cloud of powder over her. It quickly settles into her fur and disperses, spreading down to the roots, to the skin, and working its way around her body ticklishly. When she squirms too much the shower chimes more discordantly: *hold still.*

The seventy-five seconds for the cleaning seems interminable, but by the time the next chime sounds the powder has fallen off her in oily grey-brown clumps. It takes the last bits of now-unneeded bandage with it, save for some remaining goo on her tail. The fans switch on again, blowing harder, vents moving up and down to knock any inert cleaning agents off. A third pass at a light air volume spritzes lightly scented dry conditioner. She can feel the dispersing nanobots in it, too, running across her fur and down off her body. Another air-only pass and she's finished.

Okay, that's a better shower than what *Kismet* has on board. She thinks it's better than the inn's shower was—unless she missed it, that one didn't have the conditioning pass. She heads into the kitchen and punches what she hopes are the right buttons to get a cup of coffee.

So. Get the databox.

Problem: they don't know where it is.

Problem: even if they did know where it was, the RJC isn't set up to do paramilitary strike teams. The PFS might be, but they're still the most likely source of the leak that tipped off the pirates, so they can't be trusted. And she can't afford to hire an outside group.

The coffee cup's printed and full. She picks it up, takes a sip, starts pacing.

Solution: something that doesn't involve brute force.

So are you still running cons?

A con job. Clever, sure. But she doesn't have anything more valuable to trade than the databox, and she doesn't have a way to get in touch—

Wait. She still has Nelson's contact information. It could be, probably is, a throwaway drop, maybe not even in service anymore. And he'd have no reason to answer if she called, anyway.

But he might if someone else called, someone who wouldn't immediately be suspect. Someone who could convince them…convince them of what? Back to the nothing-more-valuable problem. From what she can see, Lantern wants absolutely nothing more than getting that databox to Earth.

They have to have a plan for that already, right? But if she'd gotten it for them, the plan would have been shipping it out on today's cruise to Earth, she bets, and that's a no-go now. If their plan avoids going through Port Panorica, it's convoluted and probably achingly slow. It's not what they wanted.

So maybe she can offer them fast, safe passage. Who could convincingly give them that? Obviously, only someone cisform. Jack? No, they know he's in bed with the mongrels. Who's that leave? Taylor's out.

Mara's Blood, how many other cisform people does she even know? She's *friendly* with dozens, but she doesn't *know* one she could drag into something this dangerous. Not that it's good form to be dragging friends into danger anyway.

She takes another sip of coffee, and bites her lip hard enough to hurt. Actually, what does Lantern really know about Jack? Nelson saw him arrest her, knows he's been working with the PFS. But he also knows Jack came here with her and Ansel. He *might* know Jack kept investigating this even after Interpol tried him off the case, although he might think Jack was here as part of that investigation. He definitely knows Interpol suspended him for it after he got to New Coyoacán.

Is that last one a point against using Jack, or for?

Nelson specifically asked about him, didn't he? He asked where he'd gone off to, and she'd snapped "how should I know?" She hadn't made it sound friendly. Jack hadn't sat with her and Ansel at the tribunal. These are factoids she could spin, aren't they? Jack has a standing order to fly back on the next cruiser to Earth, and he may be suspended but he's still a law enforcement agent. He's the perfect cover.

Perfect if he can sell Nelson on the notion that he's not going to just come back here and hand the databox over. Since that's exactly what he *is* going to do, and Nelson has no reason to believe Jack's secretly been sympathetic to Purity all along, that could be one hell of a hard sell. All this assuming they can even get in touch with him in the first place.

It seems like a very far-fetched—no, just call it stupid—plan, but it's the best plan she can come up with.

"Kis, call Jack."

"Yes, Gail." A few chimes sound, and she waits.

When Jack speaks he sounds sleepy. "Gail?"

"Hey. Did I wake you up?" She looks over at the clock. 6:14.

"I was having trouble sleeping." She can hear the yawn. "What's happening? How's Sky?"

"I haven't heard anything, so I'm guessing her condition hasn't changed. Uh, I'm sorry for yelling at you last night."

"No need to apologize. We're all under a lot of stress, you more than most."

"Thanks." She takes a deep breath. "I have a sort of weird idea I want to run by you."

"Okay." She's surprised he doesn't sound more dubious.

"I want you to join Purity."

"You—you what?"

She heads back into the kitchen and punches in a refill on the coffee, then starts explaining. When she's finished, she says, "What do you think?"

"I think it's a horrible idea."

"I know it's a horrible idea. Have any less horrible ones?"

"Waiting and letting the RJC do their job."

"That just gives the bad guys time to figure out their own plan for getting the box back to Earth. And—"

"Gail—"

"And lets Sky die."

His sigh makes the audio crackle. "Gail, you remember I'm not on this case anymore, don't you? You're asking me to risk my life for a mission that *isn't* part of my job and that I'd have no backup for. If I survived, I'd be rewarded by being fired."

"Because you didn't go along to get along?"

"Yes, because I didn't—" He cuts himself off, and there's a long silence. Then: "I don't know if I could sound anti-totemic enough to make this work. I haven't done undercover work in a long time."

"That means you've done it sometime, right?"

"I…" He sighs. "Yes."

"So you know how to convincingly act like a criminal. That's great. The worst that happens is he doesn't get back to you. That's the most likely thing, too, right?"

"It is." He's quiet another few seconds. "Who else have you told this plan to?"

"Nobody."

"So it's going to just be us, isn't it?"

She swallows. "I haven't really worked through all the fine details yet." Or coarse details. Or any details.

Another long silence. "All right. If we're catching them at just the right time—if they're in hiding and if they don't have a better plan already— they might at least try and get back to me. Send me Nelson's contact information."

The RJC building already looks like a construction zone rather than a crime scene, the debris removed, high opaque fences around the building's front. Bunten told her they're still assessing damage and wouldn't be able to actually begin reconstruction until tomorrow at the earliest.

She's sitting at a café across the street, one of the ones that's entirely automatic. The food's not nearly as interesting as Blue Coyote's, either, but Bunten chose it based on location rather than quality. None of them are there for the food, anyway. Bunten's here with a cisform woman who's been introduced to her as Ms. Zandstra. And they're sitting with Sidgemore, at Gail's insistence. He's even stiffer than he was yesterday.

"This simply doesn't sound like anything the Judicial Cooperative can support," Zandstra's saying. It's a variant of what she and Bunten have both said at least twice before.

"Look, I'm not asking for any kind of support. I'm asking you to officially not know about this, and to make sure the PFS doesn't know anything about this, period."

"You're asking us to edit records of Agent Thomas's cooperation."

"And I'm not entirely sure what you're asking *me* to do." Sidgemore's giving her a raised-brow skeptical look Jack would be proud of. Is that just a cisform thing she's somehow never noticed before?

"When Jack sent a contact message to Nelson, he got back to him with 'we'll be in touch.' That means he's trying to check out the story. Based on the message metadata, Nelson isn't on the Ring anymore. They might still have people on the ground here, but he's probably doing most or all of the checking remotely. What I want to know from you, Alfie, is whether or not Junior's associates at Quanta still trust you."

He looks taken aback. "I . . . as far as I know, yes. They do."

"Enough to, say, get in touch with you and ask you about Agent Thomas?"

"Oh." He furrows his brow, then nods slowly. "You'd like me to corroborate the claim that he's left the investigation entirely."

"Yeah. I mean, that's not much of a lie. He's not officially involved."

Sidgemore smiles faintly. She's surprised his face doesn't crack from the strain. "I don't believe you're officially involved either, Ms. Simmons, yet somehow you seem to be in charge."

"You know what I mean. Last night you saw Thomas and me yelling at one another in the cafeteria, right? He picked up his coffee cup and stormed out."

"I wouldn't say stormed out, and as I recall you only yelled at me."

"The video feeds from the hospital's public areas are publicly accessible," Zandstra objects. "He could check that story himself."

"I'm counting on it. They'll show me slamming my fists down on a table in the cafeteria in front of Mr. Bunten and Mr. Sidgemore here, and Jack looking upset, picking up his coffee mug and leaving." She spreads her hands. "All we're doing is presenting a slightly different spin on why. They know Jack knows about Shakti now, and that we all know what it can do for totemics. As far as Lantern's concerned my mother was a crazy anti-cisform radical and I'm interchangeable with her, so he stormed out because he's realized we're bound and determined to supplant the pure human race."

"I trust you aren't."

She looks sharply at Sidgemore, but he has that faint smile again. Did he just come as close to making a joke as he's capable of? She shakes her head. "Honestly, at this point I don't give a damn about Shakti one way or another."

He frowns again, taking a long sip of his iced tea, then looks to Gail. "If I receive such a call, I shall back up your story."

She sighs with relief, but Bunten frowns more deeply. "This plan strikes me as exceedingly unwise, Ms. Simmons."

"I know. But it's bad enough that this group has as much of this weapon as they do in the first place. We need to take every shot we have at keeping them from going into the weapons production business."

Zandstra folds her arms, fixing her gaze on the rat. "What now?"

"I…" Gail runs a hand through her hair, up along the back of one ear, bending it against her head a moment. "I go back to the hospital and sit with Sky, and wait for Jack to let me know if Nelson's going to take the bait. If he doesn't, we come up with Plan B."

And if he *does,* she comes up with the rest of Plan A.

Instead of just crossing the street and going right back to the hospital, Gail stops at a flower shop next door. The hospital must be a huge chunk of their business—they have small bouquets ready, mostly lilies and geraniums and other flowers which, the signs assure her, have low pollen counts. She picks up a little plastic vase of mixed Asiatic lilies. Does Sky like lilies? She can't think of a single time they've ever talked about flowers, but they're very pretty.

The cisform nurse she met yesterday is on duty, but she's not sure where everyone else has gone. Doctor Allen isn't around, the Keces lab techs aren't around, not even Ansel is around. Well. She can't expect him to be keeping vigil over someone he doesn't actually know. He'd gone back to his hotel before she went back to Sky's place last night, and he's probably out and about somewhere. He wouldn't go back to Panorica without telling her—she doesn't think—but there's not much he can do other than sit around and be worried at her. She checks in at the nursing desk and gets a go-ahead for the visit.

Yesterday Sky's room had seemed busy, frantic, but right now it's empty except for Sky herself. The wolf doesn't look any different than she did thirteen hours ago. Gail tries to find some place she can put the flowers, and settles on the countertop not too far from her sister's head.

Then she pulls up a chair, one with a surprisingly bad design for tote-mics, and sits. She manages to twist her tail into a position that isn't too uncomfortable.

She's silent for a minute or two, then finally says, "I'm sorry, Sky." She closes her eyes. "If I'd told anyone about Nelson threatening me, you might not be here. If I hadn't tried to smart talk my way out of this in the first place, or if I'd just given up when Jack got the databox. Who knows. Shakti would still come out eventually, right? Maybe it'd be set back five years, or a decade, but it'd have happened. Eventually."

She opens her eyes and swallows. "Yesterday I asked Ansel why I wasn't lying there with *my* organs failing, and he thought I meant it in that kind of 'it should have been me, not you' way. I told him I didn't. I know you hate that sort of self-pity." She furrows her brow, looking down toward the floor but not at anything. "But I lied to him. I kind of... I kind of did mean it that way. It shouldn't be either of us there. It shouldn't be anyone. But it especially shouldn't be you."

God, listen to yourself. She sniffles, wiping away a tear, looking back up.

Sky's eyes are open.

Gail bolts to her feet. "Sky?"

The wolf doesn't look over at her, but her ears flick.

Biting her lip, she leans over, taking Sky's hand in hers.

She hears quick footsteps behind her, and a moment later Doctor Allen walks around the bed to the other side, checking readouts, leaning over her patient. "Can you hear me?"

For a couple heart-stopping seconds Sky doesn't react at all. Then she whimpers. Does that count as a reaction? Is that an answer? Is it a yes?

Allen treats it like one. She strokes Sky's shoulder lightly. "You're at Mercy Point hospital. I'm Doctor Allen. Your sister Gail is here with you."

Sky makes another noise, hard to interpret, and nods her head fractionally.

Gail looks up at the tigress. "This is good, right?" she whispers.

Allen looks down at Sky, hand back on the wolf's shoulder. "Can you speak?"

After a moment the wolf shakes her head, just as fractionally as the nod.

Gail bites her lip, but the doctor just nods in response. "That's all right. You've been through a lot in the last twenty-four hours." She glances around at the machines, as if thinking *and you're still going through a lot,* but keeps a reassuring smile on her muzzle. "We've tapered off your sedative level. You should be stabilized enough to stay comfortable, but if you're in any pain just press the call button and someone will be here."

Another little nod.

"Um." Gail clears her throat and looks at Allen. "Is there anything I can do? I mean, I guess there isn't, but ... I just feel ..."

"Helpless. I understand. Just keep being supportive."

"Will she be, uh, able to talk soon?"

"I don't know." She pats Gail's shoulder. "Let me or one of the nurses know if you need anything." The tigress heads back out of the room.

Gail sighs, looking down at Sky, and takes the wolf's limp hand. "I guess I should go. I have some ..." Some what? Some crazy plans you wouldn't approve of? Some calls to make before I find out whether people I loathe have fallen into a trap I'm setting? Some prayers to say to some deity somewhere that the trap won't take off my head—or Jack's—when it's sprung?

For the first time since she woke up in the hospital bed, Sky looks directly at her, not just in her direction, and shakes her head, squeezing Gail's hand just a little.

"Okay," Gail whispers, not trusting her voice to stay steady if she raises it. She pulls the chair up close to the bedside and sits, hand still in Sky's.

She doesn't try to keep track of how long they stay together like that. Five minutes, thirty minutes, an hour. She just sits with her sister until Sky falls asleep, eyes closing again. This time the wolf looks less troubled.

Beedle boop "Call from Jack Thomas."

Gail squeezes Sky's hand gently, then gets up and walks out of the room.

"Jack." She keeps her voice low. "Did he get back to you?"

"He did. Someone did, at least." His tone makes the fur on the back of her neck prickle. Thoughtful, wry, deadpan, even angry—she's heard a lot of his voice over the last week and no matter the emotion he's always had energy. Now he doesn't. His voice is tired. Flat. Frail. "It's ... there are conditions."

"Conditions." Wait, that means— "He accepted? He took the bait?"

"They're open to it. They don't trust me, and they want a good faith measure. Something that proves I'm sufficiently alienated."

"Yeah, I guess that's predictable." She catches herself from saying *reasonable*. Nothing about this is reasonable. "What do they want?"

He falls ominously silent.

"Jack."

"I'd rather talk about this face to face."

She furrows her brow. "They might still be checking public video feeds. It's safer to be talking to one another this way."

"I don't think it'll matter even if they are."

Her ears lower and her voice comes out in more of a hiss. "What. Do. They. Want."

"You, Gail. They want you."

She knows that strangled noise she just heard was hers, but she doesn't feel herself making it.

"They didn't say why. They didn't give any details. All I got back was a brief text-only message about ten minutes ago. 'Bring Simmons using whatever means you see fit. Message this address with confirmation you have complied and are underway within four hours.'"

Whatever means he sees fit? Do they expect him to kidnap her? And Mara's Blood, what's the point? Nelson wants to get revenge on her for slugging him? Do the Burkes think martyring her will help them somehow? No. This is Corbett, isn't it? He's there. She has to hand it to him. It's a great test of Jack's supposed new loyalty.

"Okay." She runs a hand through her hair. "That's… unexpected, but we can work with it. We can come up with a story to tell them about a story you told *me*, maybe, some way you duped me into thinking this was a rescue mission when it's actually a trade."

"That was my thought, too." As he keeps speaking his words flow faster, but his tone doesn't lift at all. "But when we get to wherever we're going, before we dock I'll need to make it look like you're my prisoner. I'll have to bind your wrists."

She winces reflexively. She's been tied up and helpless in front of Purity nuts before and she's not interested in reliving the experience. But he's right; if she's free, it'll look suspicious.

"Yeah." She's made it outside the hospital now. It's not quite dusk, but it's colder out than she'd expected it to get. She still isn't used to being in a place that has this much weather. "Although before we get there I'd kind of like to figure out what I do to not stay behind and be tortured to death by Randall."

"Jesus, Gail."

"So, yeah. The plan should be to *not* leave me with the crazy people."

"How do I not do that?"

She hates the tough questions. What she needs is a secret weapon, like…crap. Like what?

Like a spaceship that can pilot herself and that the crazies might not know Gail's in constant communication with. She's not sure how that'll help, but she's pretty sure it's an advantage. "We'll have a few hours to figure that out. Meet me at Kingsolver Repair so we can pick up *Kismet*."

"What?" That finally gets Jack sounding more animated. "They won't let us take your ship."

"Sure they will. You've got me going along because I think this is a rescue mission, right? So of course I'm going to want to take my own ship."

"Then the plan is to let them know you gave me Nelson's contact information so I could try to fool them into thinking I was on their side just to get their location, but really I'm double-crossing you and *am* on their side."

"Exactly! Except you're really not."

His voice falls back to a tired mutter. "There are so many ways this can go so very wrong. All right, I'll meet you there. You've cleared up things with your bank?"

"Uh, well, no. But I have almost fifteen minutes to figure that out, right?"

Jack sighs deeply and disconnects.

Chapter 23

As GAIL TURNS TO HEAD to Kingsolver, she nearly smacks headlong into Ansel. "Gah! How long have you been standing there?"

"Just long enough to get worried about what you're plotting."

"I'm not plotting anything, I'm just on an errand." She starts walking. "I'll be back shortly."

Ansel isn't buying what she's selling. He starts walking with her. "Errand? You're going to Kingsolver to pick up your ship."

"That's an errand, isn't it?"

"You said 'rescue mission.'"

Her ears lower. "You shouldn't eavesdrop on your friends."

"My friends shouldn't fly off to do something suicidal."

She groans. "Please don't make this complicated." She starts walking faster.

Ansel starts jogging to keep up with her. "I don't think I could make it any more complicated than it already is, and do *not* leap into super rat mode to avoid this conversation."

She sighs and slows down, so she can look at him. "Ansel. You've gone *way* beyond the call of duty for me already. I've kind of destroyed your life over the last two weeks. People have tried to break into your computers and your apartment, you've been dragged to your least favorite place on the River, missed God knows how much consulting revenue, and it's just dumb luck that you're not dying in that hospital, too. And frankly, I'm not a good enough friend to be worth the risk."

He smiles crookedly. "That's not your call to make."

"Letting you in on this is, though."

The fox's smile disappears. "And you were just planning to disappear without saying anything, even though I think *you* think you might not be coming back from this."

She starts walking a little faster again. "I didn't say that."

"It's in your eyes."

"I assure you I'm going to do everything I can think of to come back from this."

"That doesn't change the 'disappear without saying anything' part."

"I've never been good with goodbyes."

His ears go back. "That is such a bullshit line."

"Yeah. Sorry. I don't know what else to tell you."

"What about Nevada? Travis? What about Sky?"

She clenches her jaw. She pictures turning around and stopping at her bedside for a moment, whispering the plan, knowing that if Sky so much as shook her head that her heart would crumple like foil. "I think I've said goodbye to her a little too often."

Ansel falls silent, but keeps walking beside her.

Gail increases her pace. He increases his pace. They keep walking together for another minute, until she finally turns and gives him a glare. "Okay, look, stop. Don't even think about telling me you're coming with me."

"Come with you? Hell, no. I'm trying to think of a way to stop you that doesn't involve knocking you out. Please don't make me try and knock you out, because you're a lot stronger than I am and that makes that plan just awful."

"Ansel, I appreciate what you're trying to do. I do. But I don't have any more time. I gotta try to get in touch with my bank to make sure I can even pick up *Kismet* without stealing her."

"And you're determined enough to steal her if you have to, aren't you?"

"Yeah. I am." She stops and abruptly pulls him into a hug. "I'll see you soon. I promise."

He hugs her back, tight. She feels his tail droop. "You'd better."

"I will."

"No goodbye, then." He pulls back just a muzzle length, the fur under his eyes moist.

She kisses his cheek. "No goodbye."

Gail waits for a good ten seconds to make sure Ansel's heading the other direction, like he's supposed to be, then hurries across the street. She sees a scooter rack there, so she won't have to waste time summoning one, and it'll be easier to talk and move at the same time—without being followed—on wheels.

She hops on a single-person standing model, identical to the one she took from Panorica's port to Acceleration, and sets it for Kingsolver Repair. Then she has Kis call her bank. "See if you can route it to Kimberly in the dispute resolution department."

"Yes, Gail."

It takes a full minute before someone gets on the line, someone who is, of course, not Kimberly. "This is Royce. How may I help you?" She can tell by the burr in his voice that Royce is a canine totemic of some kind.

"Hi. Uh, I was speaking with Kimberly about my case a couple days ago and everything with my account was supposed to be cleared up by close of business yesterday. I just need to make sure that it's all good now."

"All right, Ms. Simmons. Let me check." Silence for a few seconds. "There's still a hold on your account. I'm not sure why it hasn't cleared, but I can—"

"Lift it."

"I can't do that, but I'm sure by close of—"

"No. Listen, Royce. This has been going on for a week and every time I talk to someone at the bank they tell me it's going to be cleared up in a day or two. I can't wait another day or two. I am going to be at the repair shop my spacecraft is in two minutes and I need to fly that spacecraft tonight. Not after close of business tomorrow, or after close of business the next day or whenever someone finally presses the damn button that says 'yes, it's okay for Ms. Simmons to spend her own money again.' Tonight."

Royce's voice gets strained. "I understand how frustrating this can be. I can check on extending a line of credit to you in the meantime, if you'd like."

She's reached the port entrance building; the scooter wheels past it and down the more utilitarian ramp leading "underground" to the repair shops, which sit at the outer edge of the ring. Time's just about out. "Royce. You're a totemic, right? Fox? Wolf?"

"Ah." He's clearly caught off guard. "Wolf."

"Like my sister. Well, adopted sister. Uh, do you know who I am besides just your bank customer?"

He sounds even more uncertain. "Should I?"

"Ever heard of the RTEA?"

"Of course. I—uh…" His voice lowers. "There was a news story yesterday about an attack on a judiciary in New Coyoacán that sent Judith Simmons's adopted daughter to the hospital. She's, uh, your sister? I mean, you're *that* Gail Simmons?"

"Yeah." The scooter pulls up in front of Kingsolver, letting her hop off, then drives itself away to wherever its nearest rental rack is. "And I know it's horrible to lean on you like this, but I'm trying to save her life here. I may be trying to save a lot of lives."

His voice gets even lower in volume, almost a whisper, but higher in pitch. "You think there's going to be more attacks?"

"I—yeah, Royce, I think there could be. And I think I might be able to stop them, but only if I get my ship back." It's easy to sound sincere when you're not lying. "I'm not asking you to steal money for me or go around your own investigation. I'm not asking you to do anything shady. I'm just asking you to be the one who finally fixes this. Please."

She sees another scooter approaching. Jack.

When Royce speaks again he sounds more subdued, even though he's back to using happy customer service words. "The restriction on your account has been lifted, Ms. Simmons. This change will be reflected immediately across the TransactPanorica system, but it may take several hours to propagate across partner networks. That's not under our control."

She nods, not that he can see it. "Got it."

"Is there anything else I can help you with tonight?"

"No, but you've been the first genuinely helpful person I've spoken to at your entire fucking bank."

"Thank you. And…good luck."

"Thanks." She disconnects.

Jack's gone back to his formal agent look, the neatly creased dark pants and smooth white shirt under a jacket that match the slacks. His holster's back on, too; she hasn't seen him carrying since they all left Panorica. She gives him a faint grin. "You know, up until yesterday I'd have guessed these are the only kinds of clothes you own."

"I'm still not comfortable dressing down." He looks up at the repair shop's sign, then heads toward the door. "Although it's taken me about forty-eight hours of being out of this suit for me to wonder how much I still want to wear it."

"No matter what, they can't stop you from looking dashing."

That earns her a small smile, but he still looks haunted. "So." He steps past the threshold.

"So." She follows, stepping into the office. From here it's hard to get a view of just how big the hangar behind—and over—this building is, even if you look out the dirty panoramic window by the door into the repair bay.

They've arrived less than a half-hour before closing; nobody's at the reception desk, but an acknowledgement chime sounds when she steps up to the counter. "Thank you for choosing Kingsolver Repair." The voice of the automated receptionist is tinny, male, flatter than *Kismet*'s beautiful alto. "What can we help you with today?"

"I'm here to pick up my ship."

"Let me look up your records, Ms. Simmons." Pause. "Your craft, the *Kismet*, is ready for immediate pickup. You have an outstanding balance of three hundred twenty-five thousand five hundred dollars, payable in four installments of eighty-one thousand four hundred twenty-five dollars inclusive of service fees. We could not execute an automatic transfer from your bank as of close of business yesterday. Would you like to try again?"

"Yes."

The voice pauses for a few seconds. "We could not execute that transfer. Do you have another account?"

Jack lifts a brow. She grits her teeth. "Is Dani working now?"

"Yes. Would you like to speak with Dani?"

"Please."

"Just a moment."

As they wait, Jack clears his throat. "I don't know if I have enough to cover this."

"I have the money, I just can't get to it. No, *they* just can't get to it. If they were on Panorica's financial network this would have gone through." Assuming Royce wasn't yanking her tail.

"Gail!" Dani steps in from the repair bay. "It's such a relief to see you." The coyote looks like they've had a long day, but their smile is bright. They smell like machine oil. "I heard about the attack on the Judicial Cooperative, on your sister—it's awful. Is she going to be all right?" Their gaze hits Jack, and the expression shifts to slight wariness. "Hi."

He holds out his hand. "Jack Thomas. Interpol."

Dani takes his hand as gingerly as if it were an explosive. "There's not a problem I should know about, is there?"

Gail shakes her head. "No. I mean—not with you. I'm helping Agent Thomas with an investigation."

"That's the official line. Really I'm helping her."

"It's about the attack, isn't it?"

Gail nods. "Yes. And about saving Sky, and maybe saving a lot of other people. I need your help."

Dani's head tilts, tan fur rippling over the red undercoat.

"I've got everything straightened out with my bank now, but the release on the hold hasn't made its way from Panorica's network to here yet. Normally I'd just grit my teeth and wait until morning when you open again, but we can't wait. We have a really short launch window. We need to leave in the next hour or two."

"You make it sound like you're on some kind of dangerous secret mission."

Jack folds his arms. "That's not inaccurate."

Dani glances over at him, eyes widening, then looks back at Gail. "So…you want me to let you take your ship without paying."

"The money's there. I can show you—hell, it's probably already in your system. I just want you to let me pay with a delayed transfer order. Instead of starting the transaction on your side, we'll start it on mine, and it'll go through as soon as the network clears."

Dani bites their lip. The fangs come across as extraordinarily cute. "Let me check on a few things, okay?" The coyote heads behind the counter, pulling up an information window, and pokes at various spots on it with a claw tip. "Can you send that order?" They slide a pad of smartpaper across the counter, and a form fades in on it with Gail's bank routing information.

"Sure." Gail checks off the right boxes, signs the form and hands it back.

Dani keeps watching the display for about ten seconds, then nods, putting the pad away. "All right, it's all in place." The coyote looks across the counter at Gail. "We're not supposed to do this for customers we don't have an established relationship with. I could get in a lot of trouble if this payment doesn't complete."

"I wouldn't ask you to go out on a limb for me like this if I had a choice. But I don't. Everything should go through within the hour."

"I'm going to show up at your door if it doesn't."

Her door is *Kismet*'s hatch, which makes that threat pretty difficult to carry out, but Gail smiles.

The three of them walk together to the ramp leading to Kingsolver's docks, stopping at the doors. "Your ship should be as good as new. She's in marvelous shape."

"Thanks." She takes Dani's hands in hers. "For everything."

"You're welcome." The coyote's tail wags, then stills. "I hope to see you soon. After this mission." The voice remains casual but the expression gets serious. Is Dani flirting with her, or just picking up on *we may not be coming back* vibes? "Be careful."

"I'll try. And I'd like that." That sounds like *she's* flirting. Gail smiles awkwardly, and steps through the door, Jack following.

The hallway's long, but *Kismet* is moored at the closest of the three docks; it's less than a ten-second walk. "You got in touch with Nelson—or whoever—yet to let them know it's cleared?"

"I'm still trying to think of how to say 'I'm letting my prisoner fly me there in her own spacecraft' in a way that won't result in them either calling it off or shooting us on approach."

The dock's first door takes a moment to recognize her, then slides open. After they step through, the next door is her ship's. The air temperature drops about a degree with a rush of air from *Kismet*'s cabin. "Hello, Gail."

"Kis!" Gail runs inside. If she could hug a bulkhead, she would. "It's so good to be back."

Jack sounds amused. "It's been less than a week since the last time we were on her."

The ship, though, shows no cynicism. "It is good to have you back."

Gail sticks out her tongue at Jack. "Look, it's always good to get home, right? Especially if home can tell you that she misses you, too. Kis, start the preflight check."

"Yes, Gail."

He takes a seat in the cabin rather than heading to the cockpit. "In the past year I've lived in two hotels on the River, three hotels on Earth and a long-haul passenger cruiser between the two. My notion of 'home' is in flux." He pulls out his viewcard and looks around. "You have a terminal I can call up, don't you?"

"The slot's by your left hand."

"Oh. One of those." He slips the card into it and calls up a keyboard setup of the sort Ansel inexplicably loves.

After another look around the cabin, she gets herself a ginger apple drink—not carbonated—from the dispenser and heads to the cockpit.

As she straps in, Kis fades the star view in around her without prompting, and chimes. "We are ready for departure."

"Okay, we're just waiting on Jack's, uh, new friends to get us a course."

"It might be a while," Jack calls.

She unstraps enough to twist to the side and peer back at him around the seat. "What do you mean 'a while?' I thought they gave you a tight deadline."

"They did. And I've sent my message. That doesn't mean they're on the same deadline to respond."

She groans, throwing herself back in the seat and staring up at the ceiling. No, staring up at the underside of the Ring from a half-meter away, trying to guess whether that little discoloration came from a leaking ship or something else. A micro-meteor strike. A tiny repair on the ring's surface. Gremlin spit.

Something in the ship's different, too. She looks around. No, it's not visual. She sniffs. "Kis, did they give you a different air freshener?"

"Yes. This scent pack is lavender-rosemary."

"Oh. It's nice." She sniffs again. That's what Dani smelled like under the machine oil, wasn't it? Lavender and an herb she couldn't identify then. Changing the ship's air circulation system to remind her of the coyote whenever she breathes in deeply—okay, that's pretty bold. It's a shame she's too stressed to appreciate it.

She turns around. "When we get to wherever we're going, what's the plan going to be?"

"I'm going to bind your wrists, and we're going to walk out—or float out, depending on the docking situation—with me holding you at gunpoint. If Nelson is with them, they may know you've got strength biomods, so it has to be convincing."

"How do we keep them from just shooting me right then?"

"We can't. But I'm assuming they want you for something."

"Yeah." She sighs. "Chuck Emerson tried to put me on mock trial for— calling him out on his bullshit, basically. Maybe they want a repeat. How many of them are there?"

"I have no idea."

Of course not. Okay, she hasn't given herself time to think about what happens in the end game here. Jack hands her to the crazies, hopefully they hand him the databox, and...

And then what? Then he flies off, leaving her and *Kismet* behind. So she just has to get back to her ship.

Unless they make him take *Kismet*. But she won't fly without Gail, so that's out. They could force her to authorize Jack as a pilot, but maybe she can get around that. Maybe they won't think of it.

Either way, they're not going to trust Jack enough to send him out alone. Someone's going to be traveling with him. Jack'll have to take care of them on his own, and he can do that, right? But if she escapes before he can get control, they'll radio their watcher, and Jack will be in deep shit.

So the best thing to do will be to stay put even if she gets a chance to escape, to keep them focused on her, until Jack's completed his end of the run and sent a rescue team back. They probably won't get there in time to save her. But saving her isn't the important part.

"You holding up all right?"

"Yeah."

"You just made a … whimper. It wasn't happy."

She forces a casual shrug. "Oh. I'm, uh, running through a few options. Trying to figure out what gets you out alive and the databox back."

"And gets *you* out alive?"

"Still working that part out."

"I don't want to think I'm just leaving you there helpless."

"You know I'm not helpless."

He doesn't say anything in response. After a few seconds pass she closes her eyes.

A beep sounds from Jack's virtual console and he twists around. "They've sent a set of coordinates," he says after a second.

"I guess that's an implied 'we accept.' No other message?"

"An eight-hour time limit."

"Okay. Send the coordinates to Kis, and we'll get underway."

Jack taps out a few more commands.

After a few seconds, the ship speaks. "The flight will be approximately seven hours twenty-three minutes." The cockpit instrumentation fades in around Gail's seat like a greeting, and the engine drone kicks in.

Jack clears his throat. "So where are we going?"

She touches a control, bringing up the course overlay, studies it. It's not very far—in space navigation terms—from where the SC71 wreck had been. "I have no idea. There's no platform in the standard set of…" She trails off. Shit, but there *was,* wasn't there?

"What?"

"I think we're going to Alexandria."

"I've never heard of it, outside the historical context on Earth."

The ship chimes. "Signaling departure from New Coyoacán." The docking connections audibly release, making soft rings throughout the newly repaired hull.

"It's a historical context here, too. The only platform on the River that ever had a complete catastrophic failure. It was small, more a tourist and research station than a habitat, but they still lost close to four thousand people."

"Casting off." The ship begins to move, and the disorienting falling-up vertigo kicks in until the feel of *Kismet's* own acceleration overtakes it.

"What happened?"

She shakes her head. "Depends on who you ask. There's three official stories I can think of, and they all blamed a mix of bad luck, spotty maintenance and cutting one corner too many during construction. That hasn't stopped the conspiracy theories, but it never does, right? The most popular one is that Earth wanted to 'prove' River life was dangerous and engineered a catastrophe to scare us into coming home. But there's at least one story for every group somebody still hates. Which is pretty much every group."

"And of course any investigation that doesn't find evidence to support a conspiracy is just proof of how wide-reaching the conspiracy is."

"I see you've met a few conspiracy theorists."

"Interpol *is* funded directly by the Illuminati."

She laughs.

After the acceleration eases, she unbuckles, grabs her drink and pushes off back into the cabin, catching herself and swinging into the seat opposite Jack, clipping herself in. "God. I know I should try to get some sleep—we both should—but I'm not sure I can."

"I don't think I can, either." He glances ahead at the star-filled cockpit, then down at the floor. "You have any ideas yet? On what you can do to…"

"No, but I should still have *Kismet* there after you leave."

He looks up at her. "Are you sure of that?"

"No. But what I'm hoping is that they're going to force me to fly it for them—which works in our favor—or, more likely, they're going to send you off in one of their ships. So that leaves me with them, but also with Kis. That just means I need to get somewhere I can get to her."

"You make that sound like it's going to be easy."

She shrugs. "It's easier than *not* having her to get to. I'm a good improviser."

He sighs, leaning to the side and looking at the beverage station. "Can this thing do beer?"

"Yes, but don't let it. Get one from the refrigerator."

"Okay." He unbuckles and floats a couple meters toward the aft, opening the fridge and pulling a bottle out of the rack. He looks at it critically, then back in the box. "No lager?"

"I don't like lager. And all those beers are low carbonation, which lager usually isn't. Get a zero-g lid from right there." She points.

He shuts the refrigerator and grabs a lid. "Yes, captain." It only takes him two tries to get the lid on, and he manages not to lose any beer in the process. She's impressed.

After he's been sitting in silence for a few minutes, Jack stares into the plastic bottle. "I don't know why I agreed to this."

"Because we're not just saving Sky and three others, we might be saving thousands of lives." She stops herself from saying millions, because it sounds too far-fetched, too nutty. But it might be true.

"I know."

She sips her drink. "Now, if you're wondering how I roped you into it, frankly I have no idea. I didn't think I was that good at sales."

Jack smiles, but doesn't say anything.

"You're pretty good at sales, too. Better than I am, maybe. You sold Nelson on you turning."

His face darkens and he stares at the bottle. "Let's just think about what we're going to do when we get to Alexandria. And maybe try to get some rest."

Gail frowns. "I was just making a joke."

"I know." He shakes his head once. "Sorry. I just…" He trails off and takes a drink of the beer.

There's something about his tone that's off. She isn't sure just what, but she's been picking it up intermittently. When he first said Purity accepted the deal, when he made the Illuminati joke, and especially just now when he reacted to her comment about selling the plan to Nelson. "Okay. I get it. So let's think about that some more. You've heard my ideas about what to do when we get there, so let's hear yours. This is more your forte than mine, right?" As she speaks, she ramps up her visual system, studying his face carefully while trying to make it look casual. She hates to do this, but she has to know.

"I think you have it right. I'll hand you over to them. They'll more than likely interrogate me, too. If I pass, they'll send someone to fly back with me—hopefully on one of their ships—to Panorica." He's looking a fraction of a degree away from her eyes rather than directly at them.

"And then?"

"Whoever they send with me isn't likely to have biomodifications, given Purity ideology. So I'm going to have a significant advantage fighting them. After they're neutralized, I'll fly the ship back to the Ceres Ring." There's a slight twitch, a flinch, something she wouldn't have caught if she wasn't cheating. But then he notices her stare. "Why are you looking at me like that?"

She blinks, resyncing her eyes to normal. "To see if you're lying."

"What?" He draws back with a flinch anyone could pick up, bouncing against the seat back. "What do you think I'm lying about?"

"I don't know, Jack, but I'd damn well like to find out before we get there, because I don't think you believe what you just told me."

"You're just mistaking stress for lying. You think this is any easier for me?"

No, not appreciably, and sure, they're both stressed. But she can tell the difference. She meets the challenging glare he's giving her. "Kis, plot a course for the Rothbard Republic."

"Yes, Gail."

"What?" Jack tries to bolt upright, jerking against the zero-g restraints. "No! Have you lost your mind? We have a time limit. Kis, don't change course!"

"You are not authorized for piloting controls." *Kismet* sounds faintly reproachful.

"I guess this isn't the best time for a vacation, and pretty much the entire solar system will want us dead, but Rothbard doesn't have extradition treaties with anyone. Of course, eventually they'll start sending assassins. I don't know which 'they,' since I think we've got about a half-dozen candidates by now, but if we pay off the right—"

"They have Laurie!"

She stares at him.

Jack holds the side of his head with both hands. "They have my daughter. They sent me…pictures. Pictures of her at home. Her in the yard. Her with Claudia. Her alone. They're not pictures we shared. They're ones they took. And they're dated today." He closes his eyes. "I didn't 'sell' them on anything. I just gave them an opening."

Christ. How could they have pulled that off so quickly? They wouldn't need an ansible, though, would they? One-way messages to the inner system only have a half-hour delay right now. They'd have needed to get people in place damn fast, but Burke Junior has the resources for that.

But they haven't kidnapped his daughter, yet. They're just surveilling her. So she and Jack can do…something. "Then they don't *have* her, they just—"

That gets him to look at her. "They're *at the house*, Gail. That's as good as having her." She's never seen that kind of look on his face before. She isn't sure she's seen it on anyone's face before. Maybe Sky's, after their mother died. Not just sadness: sadness with anger. And a lot of that anger? It's aimed at her. Dragging him in was her crazy idea, not his.

She unhooks, kicking off toward the ceiling and "sitting" on it, staring down at him. "So were you planning to tie me up for real, and to really fly the databox back to Panorica?"

"I don't know."

"Are you still planning that?"

It takes him a longer time to repeat himself. "I don't know."

"The RJC knows we're coming out here. That means if you show up at Port Panorica without me, you're going to be stopped. Lantern doesn't know that, but you do."

"It's up to the PFS there, not the RJC. If Lantern has someone inside, they'd be tipped off to let me through."

She rubs her temples. He's right. "Jack, you can't let them bring the databox back to Earth. You know what's going to happen."

"No, Gail, I don't. I have a hypothesis about what happens. But what happens to Laurie if I don't *isn't* a hypothesis."

What happens to her when Corbett gets his hands on her, what happens to Sky without the countermeasure—those aren't hypotheses, either. But she isn't his daughter. Sky isn't his daughter. In the abstract, no one should trade a million people they don't know for one they love. But this isn't abstract.

"All right." She curls into a ball in midair. "I guess we have to find a way to save everyone."

Chapter 24

Kismet chimes. "We are approaching our destination. Please secure any loose items."

Gail unzips the duvet holding her in place and pushes herself free of the bunk she's been in the last two and a half hours. She may have drifted to sleep intermittently, but it wasn't restful; hearing Jack muttering to himself once or twice snapped her to full, paranoid wakefulness. Even so, being in her bed, surrounded by her sheets, her pillows—she's missed that. It's not as comfortable as the hotel bed was, not even as comfortable as Sky's couch. Especially in zero-g. But it's hers. She needed this time. It'd have been nicer if she hadn't been so terrified, but she still needed it.

Jack hasn't fallen asleep, either, but at least he's not sitting there holding a gun on her. Yet. He's going to have to, unless the plan changes radically. But that part of the plan isn't broken—it's the part he has to play after they separate, when she can't see him, that needs fixing.

"We need to take their leverage away." She floats past Jack toward the cockpit. Kis has drawn a red circle around the platform they're heading toward, a few degrees up and starboard from the ship's current facing. It's not big enough to make out any details yet. Just like the SC71, the circle has no markings around it; the platform isn't transmitting anything. Not surprising.

"How?"

"I don't know. Maybe we can grab a hostage, too."

"At best we get a staring match out of that, a battle to see who blinks first. That's not an answer."

She buckles in. "Then I'll come up with something else after you leave."

"So the plan is to leave you behind and hope you come up with something."

"For right now, yeah." She zooms the display in and leans forward.

Alexandria reminds her of nothing so much as the salvage yard she'd met Nevada at. It's bigger, but it's still a basic cylinder, docks at the bow off a stationary center spindle—and, like Emerson Salvage, it's orange. Not the same ridiculous bright shade, though: darker, more somber, more bronze. A hue appropriate for the physical library-slash-storehouse-slash-museum the platform aspired to be. The color's only visible on the bow of the station, though: that's the only part of the structure with operating lights. The rest remains in darkness.

Two smaller ships, one not even *Kismet*'s size, have hooked to the spindle, but it's a third ship that commands attention: a cargo liner, easily four times her ship's size, of a design older than most of the settlements across the River. The liner's bow forms a simple square, the cockpit, cabin and quarters taking up different levels. The rest of the ship is a grid of girders for containers to lock into, open to space, with fuel tanks and engines at the rear. It's ponderously slow, but hellaciously cost-efficient if they're at a full or nearly full load. When platforms were spreading like mushrooms across this sliver of the asteroid belt they could hit that easily, but now these ships are mostly relegated to non-perishable items you're willing to wait weeks on.

She frowns at its identification circle. It's got one, but it's not right. It's displaying metadata from a passenger liner. Tapping controls, she arcs *Kismet* in the hauler's direction, turning on her ship's strongest lights to help fill in what the beacons on the docking arm don't illuminate. The cargo liner's cab is connected to Alexandria with a long, flexible boarding tube like an umbilical cord. There aren't any containers locked in; instead there's a mesh grid along the bottom she knows isn't standard kit. Nodes cling to the mesh, hanging like dew clinging to a spider's web, tiny metallic egg sacs. "What are those?"

Jack pushes forward and looks at it, too, then shakes his head.

Kismet chimes again, and a message window fades in over Gail's control board. "We have been given docking clearance."

No vocal contact, and the message is, in its entirety, the docking port number. "Okay. Go slow and do a full circle around the platform. We want to do as much of a visual scan as possible."

"All right, Gail."

"What are you looking for?"

"Anything out of place."

What makes something out of place? One answer comes into view almost immediately: a gaping hole in the station's side toward the aft. It's large enough that *Kismet* could fly into it. The hull around the hole has been stripped away for meters in each direction, skin and meat carved from Alexandria's magnificent, ruined carcass.

"That's what destroyed the station?"

"Yes and no." She studies it as they slowly glide past. "I mean, yes, it was an asteroid hit. The station had drifted from its proper orbit and its defenses didn't break the rock up. It punctured the outer hull and took a slantwise tumble on the inside. The repair systems couldn't work fast enough, fires started, failures started cascading." She points at the hole as it rotates out of view. "I'm sure that started as the original breach, but a lot of plating's been scavenged. Some recently."

As they proceed along Alexandria's side and curve around the back, the breach seems less out of place—the station shows the effects of floating in space with no maintenance for four decades, a myriad of dents and pockmarks and scrapes left untended. The remains of a second docking spindle hang off the aft. The bodies and everything else recoverable of note had been removed within a year of the accident; then the pirates and salvors moved in to start stripping junked parts. It's a wonder there's enough left for Lantern to have cobbled together a base.

It's not until *Kismet* completes her orbit that signs of life reveal themselves. Parts of the hull near the bow, around the working lights, have been repaired and repainted. They didn't get the right amber color to match the original, but they came awfully close. It seems strangely image-conscious for crazy bioterrorists. The docking spindle looks like it's had sections entirely rebuilt. And to someone who's been doing salvage work for as long as she has, the high-gain antenna mounted about halfway down the arm sticks out like a flag on an asteroid. She points at that, too. "They had to bring a lot of new equipment with them."

"So that's that something out of place."

"Yes. And now that we're close, you can see the cargo ship's salvage, too."

"I can?"

"The lower engine isn't in operating shape." She starts to point, then waves a hand. "Trust me. And I don't think the crew quarters have power, just the cabin."

Kismet slows further, moving toward her assigned docking port, maneuvering herself into place.

"I thought Lantern had the backing of an insane trillionaire."

"One who's trying not to have this operation attract a lot of attention, right? There's only a few of those haulers still in service, so they refurbed a junker. I just want to know what they're planning to do with it." She zooms in on the silver nodes.

A series of bangs and hydraulic hisses cuts off his response. *Kismet* chimes. "Docking is complete."

What *are* those? She's seen them before. Recently.

"Gail. If I get the databox back to New Coyoacán, there's a good chance they'll get word of it here before we can get back to you."

"I know." She runs a hand through her hair. Think. Everything here's old except for what they brought with them, right? The infrastructure they're using has been thrown together ad hoc. So it's full of single points of failure.

Also, even though it's just two of them, they both have biomods, and Jack's right: there's a good chance nobody they're going to face will have any. At least some of them will know she has biomods, and the smart ones will figure Jack does, too—but they've still got an advantage.

Assuming he's going to be on her side.

"Look, you still have to convince them you'd have joined them without being blackmailed, and that's going to be hard enough without worrying about what's going to happen to me. Maybe there'll be some chance after their guard is down to—to do something. But if you have to leave me behind, do it."

"Gail—"

"You know I'm right." She stops, and looks back toward the cargo ship, toward the nodes clinging to the mesh. Dull metal tanks mounted on triangular frames.

Drones.

"Mara's Blood." She grips the closest bulkhead. "Those are fertilizer sprayers."

"What?" He squints at them. "You're sure?"

"Yes." She wraps her hands behind her head. "They're going to attack the Ring."

"Wait. That's too big a leap. Drones need atmosphere to fly. It can't be that immediate. They have to get them into place—"

"They just have to get the cargo ship through the Ring's top. Fly close to Ceres, then come up into the atmosphere."

"They've got to have defenses against that."

"They do, but…" She runs a hand through her hair. "That's why it's broadcasting the wrong metadata. Traffic control won't know until—"

Someone bangs on the outside hatch.

This was never just about Jack's daughter, never just about Sky, not in the long run. But dammit, couldn't she be handed only one impossible problem at a time? Figure out how to save Laurie, *then* figure out how to save Sky, *then* figure out how to stop them from deploying the bioweapon? No, it has to be all or nothing.

She lowers her voice. "Opening gambit time. Get out your gun, go to the hatch, and I'll open it."

He sighs, pulling his pistol out of its holster. "Hands behind your back."

When she moves her hands, she expects a cord to be wrapped around her wrists. Instead she feels the cold steel of handcuffs clicking into place. "Jack!" she hisses.

"She has the key," he whispers, then raises his voice. "Open the door."

What? She tugs on the handcuffs. She can probably break them at her full strength, but she might snap her wrists in the process. If she has to fight people by beating them with her broken hands, so be it. When she speaks, she's growling. "Kis, open the door."

"Yes, Gail."

Two unsmiling pale cisform faces, one man and one woman, look down from the other side. They have guns, too, each pointed at Gail's face. Why doesn't she carry a gun herself again? She knows how to handle one and with her biomods she's a pretty damn good shot. Of course, having one right *now* wouldn't do her much good, would it?

"Easy." Jack shoves her forward until the man can grab her left arm, the woman grabbing her right. They're wearing positively retro clothes: subdued pastel colors, squared-off shoulders on both his shirt and her blouse, cinched waists, a definite frilly look to hers. A third man floats nearby, middle-aged, handsome, trimmed black hair and tailored grey suit.

The docking spindle doesn't look like it's in much better shape inside than out, but she gets an image of what it might have once been like: sections of a long mural still remain, predominantly the same golden hue as the outside. The style shifts from section to section. What's it all trying to depict? Libraries through the ages? Museums? A quick history lesson as you head from your ship into gravity?

"Ms. Simmons," the man in the suit says, nodding once. "And Mr. Thomas. Put away your gun."

Jack looks between them all, then holsters his gun.

"After you."

Gail's "escorts" pull her along; the man in the suit takes up the rear.

"I'd rather not drag this out," Jack says. "I can take the databox, leave Simmons and be on my way."

She clenches her teeth. Stalling for time would be a lot better for her.

Suit laughs. "It's nearly a week until the next flight to Earth. Do you think we're just going to leave it in your care until then?"

Crap. That's a giant gaping hole in her master plan she maybe should have seen before the villain pointed it out to her. Sure, the master plan didn't cover anything after she got here, so it was always terrible, but—

"Isn't the entire point of using me that I *won't* attract attention heading back to Earth? If I disappear for nearly a week then suddenly show up back on Panorica, do you think there's the slightest chance I'll get on that ship without questioning?"

"So I should just trust you to hold the databox unsupervised for a week? You'll understand my skepticism. I'll have some associates discuss your unexpected offer with you in a few minutes."

They reach the elevator to the rim. It's as straightforward as the one in the Panorica Deck, just with handholds along the interior walls; riders have to be smart enough to be in a position where they won't get hurt as gravity increases. Gail gets held in place by her captors.

Suit reaches for a physical button, pressing it in with an audible click. She doesn't think she's even seen one of those outside videos. "I'd like to claim that's just for the old-fashioned aesthetic, but this base is a bit slapdash. Minimally viable, as they say."

"'Discuss.'" Jack lifts his brows. "Is that a polite way to say interrogate?"

"It is." He gives Gail a measured look, a small smile. "And you, Ms. Simmons. Several people here want words with you. Your childhood friend Mr. Corbett wants considerably more than words."

Her ears lower.

For the next ten seconds there's no sound but the hum and grind of the elevator, pitch deepening as gravity increases. The platform stops with a clank and the doors slide open, moving with a shuddering hitch rather than a smooth glide. Now the two holding her drag her forward, not just push.

She'd seen pictures of Alexandria before the accident, but it's shocking how grand the entrance plaza still remains. Copper walls—from the scent, it's not paint, but a true high-copper alloy—soar behind her up into darkness overhead. High, long windows provide multi-story panoramas of space and the ships docked outside. The plaza itself forms a wide, tiled avenue running between buildings, and the buildings, full of unnecessary steps and too-high rooflines supported by grand columns, drip with the opulence of wasted resources. The closest ones, she's sure, had been museums, the tourist destinations the platform's owners had expected to be the primary draw. If she remembers right it never came close to breaking even. One conspiracy theory suggests the owners sabotaged it themselves for insurance money.

Now, though, the plaza must be the only inhabited section, a half-dozen canvas tents scattered around the cracked tiles. No light reaches whatever walls lie between here and the hull breach; they've got most of the street lamps functioning in the immediate area, but that's it. With so much reflection from the plated walls, soft amber radiance enfolds everyone and everything.

Eight more people wait for them, lined up. All cisform, of course, but otherwise there's a range of colors and gender. How nice for Purity to be so inclusive. Nelson stands to the far end, arms crossed, looking bored. He's not even facing their direction. Corbett, though: he's there, and he's way too excited. He takes a step forward from the middle of the line, eyes fixed on Gail.

Suit walks forward, reaching into his jacket pocket, and addresses the man at the closest end of the line. "I believe you and Ms. Ziff wanted to have a conversation with Mr. Thomas." The man nods, and he and a dark-skinned woman step out of the line. Then Suit holds up a slim card: the databox. "What they tell me, Mr. Thomas, will determine both whether you leave with this and, if you do, under what conditions. And do remember our men are still watching your lovely daughter."

"Fair enough." Jack doesn't betray the least bit of concern as he steps into a walk beside them, projecting every confidence they're going to find him sufficiently reprehensible to send him on his way with the databox in short order. Two tents down, on the left.

"Now, Ms. Simmons. Gail." Suit moves to stand in front of her and folds his hands behind his back, head tilted. "Do you know why we asked Mr. Thomas to bring you along?"

"Randall's unrequited love for me."

Corbett stalks forward. "You goddamn little—"

"Patience, Mr. Corbett." Suit holds up a hand. "Care to try a serious answer?"

"Because you hate totemics, and you especially hate my mother. And you really hate that martyring her did more to turn the tide against Purity than anything else that could have happened."

"Hate totemics? No." Suit shakes his head. "In many ways, your Mara's vision was correct. Prophetic. You're all admirable. Every totemic is, by some measure, objectively better than a cisform, don't you think?"

Randall spits on the tile.

"I think we're all just people."

Suit chuckles. "As much the diplomat as your mother. We knew very early on that wasn't true. By now you've learned all about Shakti, no doubt. And Kali, of course." He waves up toward the docking spindle. "When my father sold off Quanta's transformation genetics group to Keces, the technology for Shakti was only theoretical. But we had internal reports— reports we've kept quite secret—about what happens if genes such as yours became inheritable."

"You're Thomas Burke, Junior, then. Sort of ironic for a company with 'biotech' in the name to be so against biotech, isn't it?"

"The company has never been against biotechnology. We made a decision not to support the ideology of radical transformation, however. Improving the human race is laudable. Fostering its replacement is suicidal."

"Just because totemic parents could give birth to totemic kids—"

"And mixed couples?" He tilts his head, waiting for her to give him the answer he already knows.

"How often do you think that's going to happen? Or are you saying those internal reports of yours concluded most cisform humans want to fuck fox people?"

"Shut up!" The woman holding her arm smacks the side of her head, right on her ear.

"I'm sure the majority don't. But by the time that majority fully understands the threat, it'll be far too late."

She can feel the incredulity spreading across her face. "This isn't some kind of war."

Randall growls, almost as well as a cat totemic would. A skinny, mangy cat. "It *is* a war." He thrusts a finger at her accusingly. "My mother was a casualty already."

"Jesus, Randall," she snaps. "You do not want to go there."

Burke looks pained momentarily, as if barely tolerant of Corbett's outburst. "It doesn't seem like a war to you because you're judging by intent. You don't *mean* to replace us. You simply *will*. It won't be in my lifetime, or my grandchildren's, or even their grandchildren's. But by then we'll already be the evolutionary backwater."

"So what the hell do you think you're going to do? Kill us all? Millions here, millions in the inner system?"

"All? No. Eighty percent, possibly even ninety, though. That should be enough to give those who come after us another generation or two to come up with a more permanent, stable solution." He sighs, looking up toward the cargo ship.

Eighty or ninety percent. Between the inner system and the River, from all the full totemics through the far greater number of partial transforms, the true believers and the artists and the aesthetes and the ones who just grew up as animal-people because their parents made the choice for them, that's at least five million. Maybe closer to ten. "How can you—even—"

"Again, you *are* at war with us, even if you don't see it." His voice is sharp for a moment, then relaxes again. "In countries on Earth we've tried pushing for legislation to restrict your breeding in simple, non-lethal ways, but there's no traction there. It's seen as far too regressive for today's enlightened age. Eventually they'll understand, although I suspect out here, they'll be far more brutal." The bastard sounds genuinely apologetic.

"So. To answer your original question." Burke clasps his hands. "You're here because symbols are important. You don't mean very much to me, I confess. But to Purity, you do. And to Mr. Corbett. Mr. Corbett's service means a lot to me. He wants to break you. The rest want a video record of your confession."

She stares at him. "My confession of what?"

He furrows his brow, then shrugs. "Honestly, I don't think it matters." He turns and walks away.

Randall steps forward and grabs her muzzle, clenching it hard enough to hurt. "Your confession," he hisses, "that it was your mother's bomb.

That it was *you* who started this. That we wouldn't have to do any of this if it wasn't for you." He yanks her head down before releasing it, and she bites back a yelp of pain.

"Christ, Randall. All of you! Don't you see what's going on? Burke just said point blank that you're all only useful idiots. And you know full well my mother never did anything more violent to anyone than scream in their face."

One of the other women, one of the ones who hasn't spoken yet, glares at Gail. "That's a lie. Everyone knows—"

"Everyone knows what they want to believe. But Randall knows the truth is his mother followed mine from New Coyoacán to Solera to be part of that demonstration. The truth is she believed everything my mother did. What do you think she'd think of you now, Randall? Think she'd be proud?"

Randall clenches his fists, then punches her in the stomach. The two holding her have the courtesy to let her double over. As her vision blacks out for a moment, she hears jeers, scattered applause.

She's been here before—not to Alexandria, not with these people, but surrounded by zealots who want to do her serious harm. Back then it was a smaller number of zealots, though, and one of them turned out to not be a zealot at all, taking her side. Here, she has either one friend—off being interrogated—or no friends. Even if this is the whole group except for Burke and the two with Jack, if she tries to take them all on at once, she's going to be creamed. That's assuming she can break out of the handcuffs. If she can't, or if she waits too long, she's going to be tortured.

What she needs is a serious distraction. And a way to keep Burke from telling his operatives on Earth to go after Laurie, so Jack won't be condemning his daughter to death by doing the right thing here. She needs to find—

—a single point of failure.

She keeps facing the floor. "Kis," she whispers voicelessly.

"Yes, Gail," the ship responds.

"Can you undock on your own?"

"Yes. There is no interlock that would prevent me from doing so."

"Are you speaking to someone?" Randall says.

"Undock and knock out the high gain antenna on the docking spindle. Knock it right off."

Kismet sounds mildly disapproving, in the fashion she always does when giving warnings. "That may damage the docking facility." She doesn't mention that it might damage her, too, but it might.

"That's fine. Do it."

"Yes, Gail."

Randall yanks her head up by her hair. "Are you speaking to someone?" he repeats.

She meets his eyes steadily, ignoring the pain from the way he's gripping her, and smiles. "I'm praying to the rat god."

A few people hiss derisively. "You think you're funny?" the woman spits. Randall glares, shoving her hard. She sprawls on her back. Nelson snorts. Is he a true believer, too, or just being paid?

If Kis gets her job done, how long will it take them to notice? What else will she need to do? The ships have radios—she's not sure about the cargo ship, given its state, but the other two have to be working. If things get chaotic enough in here, hopefully nobody's going to think the most important thing to do is to race up there and give the order to kill Laurie.

Randall moves forward, keeping her within kicking distance. "We kept back just one vial of the anti-totemic poison."

"Planning to force-feed it to me and watch me die?" She keeps her voice deadpan enough to dam the flood of fear, and surreptitiously glances to the side, seeing where Nelson's gone to. Still in the crowd, still not paying attention. He knows she's enhanced, he's the one she's going to have to take out first—

If she can bring herself to kill anyone. God. But if she doesn't, she's dead. Sky's dead. So somehow she will.

"Not until you watch every other mongrel in New Coyoacán—"

A screeching sound comes from high overhead. Metal scraping metal, tremors racing through the entire outside wall, a low hiss of escaping atmosphere. Everyone looks up.

Everyone but Gail. She kicks in all of her biomods and strains against the handcuffs. They don't budge.

Jack said she has the key. But she doesn't.

Oh.

"Kis, can you unlock these handcuffs?"

"Yes, Gail." The handcuffs chime and release with a mechanical snap.

She stands up, bringing her arms around to her front. "The rat god," she says, "has answered."

Chapter 25

THE WORLD SLOWS to a tenth normal speed.

Before anyone's even turned to look at her, Gail grabs the two people who'd been holding her, brings their heads together hard, refuses to think about what the cracking noise means. She charges toward Nelson before either of them hit the tiles, and just as he fully turns in her direction she's on top of him, both of them skidding from the force. He meets her eyes with a look of surprise spreading comically slowly across his face. Does he have a gun? Yes, of course. He's reaching for it. She takes it from him, scrambles to her feet, then brings her sandal down on his leg with the force of a war hammer. She knows exactly what that cracking noise is. By the time his scream starts she's already meters away and moving fast.

Jack, Ms. Ziff and Other Guy have come out of their tent, staring in slow motion confusion. Get it together, Jack. Maybe Other Guy isn't armed, maybe he's just slow, but Ziff already has her own pistol out. She's seen Gail, she's turning. Gail brings up her pistol—she doesn't see any signs of a biometric lock on it, so with any luck it'll fire for her—lines up the shot, and pulls the trigger. It fires. Ziff staggers, distracted enough by the sudden hole in her chest that she doesn't return fire.

The remaining crew—down by four already—start to react. One man's charging toward her like a bull. Another woman's got a gun out. Yet another woman's just screaming. Confusion, anger, terror. She might have a few more seconds in real time to keep taking advantage of it.

She runs hard toward Jack. Someone she didn't keep track of gets off a shot and she feels it go right past her ear.

Jack pulls out his gun, moving at what she sees as nearly normal speed, maybe eight or nine times faster than real normal. And—

—points it at her.

Okay, he's putting on a good show for Purity, but no time for her to figure out how to play it. Randall is moving, three others are moving, two other guns are out. She dives into a roll.

Jack fires. Misses. Deliberately? By the time she decides yes, deliberately, she's already barreled into him. They go rolling together.

"Kis took out their radio." She doesn't slow down her speech, letting it stay as ridiculously accelerated as the rest of her, hoping his own biomods are still engaged and he'll understand. "We need to get to Burke, get the databox and disable that cargo ship."

He stops the rolling, with him on top, and points the gun at her head. "Power down." He speaks loudly, at normal pace, so everyone else can hear. He has a swollen eye, a cut on one cheek. How much of the rest of him's been worked over?

"Jack—" she hisses low.

"Power down!" His eyes flick to the group, then back to her.

Ears lowering, she does what he says. Is this part of his plan? It wouldn't have been part of hers, if she'd had one.

For a split-second after she shuts off the biomods it's a relief, as muscles stop straining, nerve endings stop being overloaded. Then abruptly she aches everywhere. Ow. Christ, don't get a leg cramp. She'll have a couple bursts of reserve for later this way, right? If she gets a later.

Kis chimes in her ear. "The starboard fuel container has been damaged by the impact. The leak is slow, but we will not be able to return to the Ceres Ring. If we depart within two hours we will have enough fuel to dock at Kingston for repairs."

Great.

Jack sits up, gun still pointed at her. He winces, then gets to his feet, yanking her up with him. When they're both standing he braces an arm around her neck. It's not tight enough to hurt, but it's uncomfortable.

How many are left? Six. She did okay. Okay, if shooting a woman in the chest is okay, if cracking two people's heads together like eggshells is okay, if breaking someone's leg with a stomp is okay. None of it is okay.

Four of them have guns out, but they're all lowering them. She's been subdued.

She didn't see Burke run out of his tent, but he's here now, breathing hard, perfect hair finally looking out of place. He's joined by three new people she hasn't seen before. They don't have guns out, but she has to assume they're armed, too.

"What in God's name—" He looks around at the damage she did in the few seconds she had free reign. "You and you and you." He stabs his finger at people, including Bull and Screaming Woman. "Get up there," he points at the spindle, "and see what the hell the damage is. Bring pressure suits." They nod and scramble away, the woman flashing Gail a fearful look as she passes by.

Burke glares at his surviving crew before his gaze settles on Jack and Gail. "You brought her here, Mr. Thomas, yet didn't think to mention she had biomodifications above and beyond mongrel nature. Why is that?"

Jack gestures with his gun toward Nelson. Nelson doesn't respond; he's hugging himself, trying to look stoic and failing. He might be going into shock. "I assumed he would have told you."

"Did you." Burke walks toward Nelson. "And did you know?"

Nelson's teeth are clenched so tightly it takes him a second to get an answer out. "Y…yeah. Figured you'd…keep gun on her…"

"Perhaps if we'd known she was superhuman, we would have."

Gail makes a mockingly sad face. "Guess none of you are, huh? That wouldn't be pure enough."

"No." He smiles patronizingly. "But guns are a marvelous leveler, and I don't think it's fair for you to have one. Especially since I believe you've stolen it from Mr. Nelson here. Mr. Thomas, would you disarm Gail?"

Jack presses his own gun against Gail's head. "Hand me the gun, very slowly."

She swallows and hands him the pistol. Now that she has a moment to look at it, it's a nice one, one of the few kinds she recognizes: an eighteen-round magazine, three-round bursts, only two shots fired.

"Thank you." Burke approaches Jack. "And now give me the gun."

Jack holds out Gail's pistol, reholstering his own. "You're lucky you hadn't let me leave yet."

"And Ms. Simmons was lucky her handcuffs were so curiously easy to break." Burke slams the pistol's grip into the side of Jack's head, then turns to the surviving henchman who'd taken Jack into the tent. "Mr. Reeves. What was your impression of Mr. Thomas's sincerity?"

Reeves shuffles his feet, glancing back at Ziff's body, then at his boss. "He doesn't seem like he likes totemics much, and especially doesn't like her." He gestures at Gail. "And I think he's right that trying to keep him out of sight would just raise questions."

"Mmm." Burke steps away again. "It remains hard for me to trust this last-minute change of heart of yours. The databox would already be on its way to Earth if you hadn't taken it to, of all places, New Coyoacán."

Jack is holding one hand to his now-bleeding head. "I didn't understand the stakes…'til I learned what was on the box." He shakes his head once, then moves closer to Gail again. "Shakti…can't happen."

Burke steps back and crosses his arms. "If we're in agreement, I can tell you to shoot Ms. Simmons in the head—"

"She's mine!" Randall bursts out.

Burke turns. "Mr. Corbett, I'm aware of your feelings, but do not give me orders."

Jack leans toward her. "Power on," he mouths silently.

Her eyes widen fractionally. If it wouldn't get both of them shot she'd kiss him. Hard.

She turns on all her biomods.

"The whole reason she's here is me!" Corbett isn't paying attention to Gail and Jack now. "The whole reason we're *all* here—that's me. Me!" Randall gestures toward the rat, but his eyes remain fixed on Burke. "I'm the one who knew her, who knew who to call for the dark courier, who set—"

"Mr. Corbett." Burke's voice rises like a drill sergeant. "We are here to save humanity from itself for at least a few more decades. Fulfilling your pathetic vendetta against a do-nothing drifter is not our priority."

Reeves turns in their direction and he starts to exclaim—something. His hand makes it to the hilt of his gun before Jack shoots him.

Gail goes for Burke. They slide the same way she and Nelson did a few minutes ago, but this time she rolls, making sure he's on top of her when people start firing at her. She doesn't see who wings him, but she feels him jerk.

She lifts him up enough to frantically search through his jacket until she gets a hand around the databox and shoves it into her pocket. To her, it's long seconds; to him it's just fractions of them.

She grabs his gun—Nelson's gun—her gun now, goddammit—and lines up a shot, using Burke as cover. An Asian woman's taking aim at Jack. Gail shoots her in the head. A middle-aged guy, maybe a decade older than Gail, is raising a gun toward her, but Burke's body blocks his shot. It blocks hers, too.

She throws Burke to the side and shoots in the same motion, hitting her target in the arm, not anywhere vital. That's enough to get him to drop his weapon—he's no more a trained fighter than she is. Then she throws herself into motion, picking up speed, and slams herself into him. They both go down. She feels his ribs crack.

When she raises her arm she intends to slam it down on his chest with enough force to kill, but she makes the mistake of looking into his eyes. He's not just in pain, he's absolutely terrified.

For that moment she sees what he does: not a woman, not another human. He sees fur and claws and fangs. He sees a monster, as smart as he is but much stronger, much faster, smashing down him and his compatriots as if they were insects. Maybe he knows her superpowers are biomechanical, not genetic, that they can't be passed from generation to generation. But when he looks at her, he sees people who will always be a little stronger, a little faster, always have better ears, better eyes than *his* people ever will. He sees the future he has to stop.

Something punches her right shoulder and pain blossoms across it, nerves all at once aflame. Dammit to hell, she's been shot.

She spins around, raising her gun, but her biomods and her body have desynced. When she fires at the man who shot at her, the shot flies wide, high, and this time the recoil turns the flame in her shoulder into an inferno. She topples over onto the man she'd shot a couple seconds ago, and he screams again.

As she switches the gun to her left hand—not as good, but if she can get her damn circuits under control they'll compensate—the man she's trying to get a bead on crumples, blood and bone spraying from the back of his head. She rolls over and fires at a woman standing near Randall. Her target jerks backward, but she can't tell where she hit yet. Seeing it all at ten-times acceleration makes it surreal. It's felt like minutes since Jack "switched sides," yet in real, objective time, it's not even ten seconds. Randall's gun is out but not pointed at her or Jack. He's staring at the man Jack just shot to save Gail.

No. He's staring at the man *he* just shot to save Gail. Mara's Wounds.

The only people left standing are her and Corbett. Jack's sitting, at least, not sprawled somewhere, but he's clutching his thigh. Shit. They've both gotten off a lot easier than they could have, though.

Burke's pushed himself up into a sitting position. The side of his suit's soaked with blood. "What have you done?"

Randall looks back at him, but points the gun at her. "I said she's mine!" His voice shakes with hysteria.

Gail winces at her throbbing shoulder. Shouldn't the biomods be helping with that? Maybe they are, and it's going to hurt much worse when she shuts them off. Great thought. She swings her gun around. "Randall, you *know* I can shoot you before you squeeze the trigger."

Burke pushes himself to his feet and staggers toward the elevator.

"Take another step, and I'll shoot Randall and then you."

With a pained sigh, Burke turns around, raising his hands in the air.

She keeps her eyes locked onto Corbett, watching his face for any slight tic, any indication he's about to fire. "Jack, are you okay?"

His voice is strained, wheezing. "Been better."

Back to Randall. "I swear to God if you don't drop that gun right now I'll drop you."

He trembles, eyes filled with a hatred too deep to have a name, and lets the gun drop to the tile with a clatter.

When she shuts her biomods off again her shoulder explodes anew. Ow. Jesus ow. She takes in a sharper, more gasping breath than she intended. "Kis."

"Yes, Gail?"

"Send a message to Bunten and the RJC with our location, that cargo ship's faked registry information, and the image of Thomas Burke Junior here I'm sending now. Wave to the mongrels, Tom." He gives her a sour, affronted glare. "Good enough. Tell them to send help, right now, and to get Jack's family back on Earth to a safe house."

"Yes, Gail. I'll connect them directly to you if they have questions."

"Okay, but tell them to hurry. And bring medics."

Burke sighs thinly. "And you have a transceiver in your head, talking to...you'd have already called anyone hiding on your ship, I would think. Your ship's control system."

"Good guess. Now we have to—"

"Gail!" Jack's yelling, lurching toward her. She turns just as something smacks her back and abruptly her vision goes to static. Crap, not again.

When she comes to, she's moving. She's being dragged. When she tries to switch her biomods back on, part of the HUD lights up, but nothing else. How long was she out? Only a few seconds, she thinks, but that's too long.

The middle-aged guy, the one she shot but didn't kill, had the stunner. He's dead now. She hears shots from high above. Jack's running. Burke's running.

She manages to flop one arm against her vest, feeling the pocket. The databox is still there. Her stolen gun's gone, dropped on the tiles. Where's Randall? He's the one dragging her. Now he's lifting her up.

"Y…" Her voice isn't working quite yet.

Burke lurches into the elevator. The hell—he's going for the one part of the plan she hasn't screwed up for him, isn't he? The cargo ship.

Jack jumps back as a round of fire from above ricochets off the ground in front of him, and catches sight of Gail. He freezes for just a moment.

She forces her jaws to work, screaming hoarsely. "Go after him! Go—"

Randall slams her back against one of the panoramic windows. At least this side is real glass. He may be scrawny but right now he's looming over her, and he's mad as hell.

She raises her voice. "Jack! Go!"

He goes, climbing up the service ladder. That has to hurt, but he doesn't show—

Randall punches her right in the muzzle. She feels something crack somewhere, and her mouth fills with blood.

"Guh." She shields her face, now that it's too late to help. He slugs her in the chest instead, and she slides down the glass.

"A ship has been dispatched from New Coyoacán," *Kismet* announces. "The estimated arrival time is six hours thirty-nine minutes." Good. Whatever it is, it's fast.

While he's still seething, he doesn't kick her. Yet. But he doesn't need to. He still has a gun, and it's out, pointed at her. "It'll only take a couple minutes to launch the ship. Even if I'm the only one left, I'm going to make you watch."

Heaving gasp. She needs air, to inflate her lungs again. "You…" Another gasp. "Burke's…not gonna…suicide mission."

"Of course he will." He laughs. "You don't see it? We're just like you. We're just like your mother. We'll die for our cause."

Her wind's almost back. She looks up at him steadily, even though that puts her almost nose to barrel with his pistol. "My mother didn't…want to die for her cause…any more than yours."

"My mother didn't believe in blowing up innocent people!"

"Neither did mine." When he continues not shooting her, she risks sliding back up the wall, slowly, warily, hands still in front of her. There's no one else left moving in the plaza, and she can't tell if any are even still alive. "But we're both here right here, right now, because Purity does."

For a second, it's on his face. He knows she's right. Of course he knows. How couldn't he? He knows the people he's working with are the people who killed her mother, that to them *his* mother was just collateral damage.

Gail straightens up without leaning on the wall, trying not to wobble. She's beat to hell, somehow Randall's remained almost untouched, and she's going to have to fight him, without a gun and without biomods. At least there's a slight waver as he holds his gun on her.

When he speaks, the waver's in his voice, too. "I told my mother not to go with yours. But she said it was important. She said it was a mission. Can you believe that?" He looks into her eyes, and for a moment she sees the twelve-year-old kid there, a child who's just been told his mother's been killed in an attack on someone else. How could that happen? She sees someone who still doesn't have an answer twenty years later.

"Yeah, Randall, I can." She wipes her mouth; the fur on the back of her hand comes away bloody, but at least the taste's fading. Did he break one of her front teeth? Is she feeling that with her tongue?

The anger comes back to his eyes. "Turn around. Look out the window."

"Jack will stop him. Even if he doesn't, I've warned them. It's over."

"Turn around!"

She does so. She tries to trigger her biomods one more time and gets a painful electric shock running through her arms. At least they're responding. Is that better or worse?

"The warning won't help." The tremble in his voice has grown. "We worked out just the right flight path, just the right transmissions."

Her ears fold down. God, she can see the flight paths in her head. They could really do it. Then Randall's going to shoot her and take the databox. "You think making me suffer before you kill me is going to make you happy?" She turns around again, partway, looking at him.

He watches her with an expression as uncertain as it is hateful. He's very close to her. Too close. There's never going to be a better moment.

She leaps for him, driving her head into his chest. He fires, and she feels the bullet punch her good shoulder. While she desperately hopes the force will make him fall over, it doesn't. Gail's not heavy enough, doesn't have enough momentum.

Steeling herself, she digs her claws into his sides. They're blunter than a real rat's, and without biomods she's little stronger than any other one-point-six meter high, thirty-something woman in good but not terrific shape—right now, not even good shape. As dark blood wells around her fingers, Randall screams. But the wounds she's causing are superficial, even when she yanks her claws out and the blood runs more freely.

It's enough to make him drop the gun.

She brings up her knee, slamming it into his stomach, grabbing at his head. But it still doesn't throw him off balance. With a guttural roar, he runs straight forward, slamming her between him and the window. The back of her head cracks against the glass, hard.

Before she can recover Randall kicks her in the leg, stomps down on top of her sandaled foot and grinds. The scream she's been holding in gets out. She can't stop it. He grabs her by her shoulders, leans down, Jesus, he's trying to goddamn *bite* her.

Come *on*, biomods, turn on turn on turn on—

They turn on.

Instead of helping block the pain, they just add their own layer. They've been stressed too much, run too hard, scrambled. But she only needs them for a moment. She grabs Randall by the sides, lifts him up into the air, and whirls around, slamming him into the glass hard enough to send a web of cracks through the inner surface. He impacts a good meter and a half over the floor, face-first, then slides down into a crushed pile, leaving a bloody streak.

She powers off, letting herself drop back to just the expected pain level, and limps over to grab his gun. When she kneels by him it's more of a stumble. He tries to draw away. She wonder how much of her he can even see through his ruined face.

"The crazy thing, Randall." She takes a shuddering breath. "The crazy thing is, I'm sorry. After all you've put me through, I'm genuinely sorry you're dying for a lie you've been telling yourself for twenty years. I never wanted to kill you."

She takes his chin and tilts his head toward hers. His eyes manage to focus. "But I can't just sit here and watch you suffer, like you wanted to do with me. Do you know why?"

Randall whines.

"Because," she says softly, "I'm not an animal." She brings the gun up, presses the muzzle to his temple and fires.

After his body topples to the side, she drops the weapon and tries to drag herself back to her feet. Okay, that's not working. Great. She looks at the elevator. She hasn't heard any gunfire from up there, but she's been distracted. Maybe Jack got Burke.

Something in the outside view changes, and she presses herself against the fractured glass. The cargo ship's good engine is lit, and the umbilical cord is detached. Oh, God. She can see *Kismet*, too, floating stationary relative to the docking arm, wheeling through Gail's field of vision as the platform rotates.

"Kis," she gasps. "Do you have any location for Jack?"

"There are no location sensors in the area."

She slides her hands up the glass to pull herself back to her feet. "You sent the cargo ship's transponder metadata to the RJC?"

"Yes. However, the ship is transmitting a different signature now."

She stares at it as it slowly starts to move away from Alexandria. That shouldn't be possible. But if it can transmit the signature of a ship that's supposed to be there—one Burke might well know about, given his connections—it could easily get close enough to get its drones into the atmosphere before it gets torpedoed. "We can't let it go."

"There are no ships in the area that can be signaled to intercept it."

Jesus, she should be on *Kismet* right now. She's faster than the hauler; she could get ahead of it and—no, not with the fuel leak. Dammit. Think. "Fire the tow cables at it. Hook... something."

"We did not replace the tow cables."

She swallows. The pirate ship. Right. "Goddammit." She pounds her fist against the glass, ignoring the new burst of pain. "I haven't gone through all of this just to have them get to the Ring. Think." She rubs her head. "Think."

"I can weigh probabilities," Kis offers.

Gail bites back a bitter laugh. "What's the probability that ship will reach New Coyoacán if we don't stop it?"

The answer comes almost immediately. "Point nine eight three."

"And the probability that it can release its drones within the Ring's atmosphere before being stopped?"

That takes the ship several seconds to chew on. "There are too many factors for me to evaluate beyond a simple answer of high, medium or low. But the probability is high."

"So how do I stop it?" Even as she asks, an answer comes to mind. *No.* There's another option, there has to be.

"That is not something I can compute." Again, Kis sounds slightly apologetic.

Dammit, a high probability isn't a certainty. They might be going somewhere else. The Ring might be able to stop it.

But she can't take another chance that things will turn out all right if she does nothing, if she stays silent, if she just lets things go. Especially not on this.

The cargo ship's already enough of a speck that she has to zoom in her vision to make it large again. "I—Kis…can you still intercept that ship?"

"Yes."

"You…" Gail rubs her face, feeling tears welling up, and looks out the glass. "I can't do this. It's too hard."

"You are trying to make a choice."

"Yes." She half-smiles, even though her vision blurs.

"You told me that sometimes a choice is between the easy thing and the right thing. Is that the case here?"

"Yes. It is." It comes out in a hoarse whisper and she closes her eyes.

Her ship waits expectantly.

"Kis, I want—no—you…" Then she takes a deep breath, clenching her fists. "You need to ram that cargo ship. As fast a speed as you can build up. Hit it in its good engine."

Kismet's beautiful alto remains achingly calm. "You must confirm that you understand that will result in my destruction."

Her throat closes up, but she chokes the words out. "I understand."

"All right, Gail. There will be approximately twenty seconds in which I will be able to abort." Her ship—her home, her expert system, her best friend—cruises slowly past the window, picking up speed, until she passes out of sight.

The seconds crawl past. The cargo ship gets smaller, even with her vision cranked to full magnification. She can't see where *Kismet* is.

Fifteen seconds pass. Sixteen. Seventeen. Eighteen.

A metallic streak barrels toward the cargo ship from the right side of her field of vision.

Twenty seconds.

"Goodbye, Gail," *Kismet* says. "I love you."

What—that can't—she—

The two ships meet, blinding her momentarily with a flash of perfect brilliant light.

A few seconds pass, or a few minutes, or a few lifetimes. The remains of the cargo ship drift apart. Gail remains motionless, standing by the fractured window, until she hears the elevator descending. She wills herself to turn, face it, train the gun on the door.

It opens on Jack. He nearly falls out of the cab, his shirt soaked in blood, his left hand mangled. "I tried. But Burke and...one other...got to the cargo ship." He drops into a sitting position, staring at Randall's corpse. "Maybe the RJC can...intercept."

"We stopped it," she says hoarsely.

He focuses unsteadily on her. "We did? How?"

Gail tries to answer, but it undoes her. She sinks to the tiled floor, eyes squeezed shut, and begins to sob.

Chapter 26

SHE'S ON BOARD *KISMET*, in the cockpit, flying toward the cargo ship, accelerating. Kis, stop, we're going to hit it.

That's what you want, Gail.

No, it isn't. I don't want it. I don't want it.

It's your order, Gail. Do you love me?

She sits bolt up, awake.

Now she's in a bed, a hospital bed, full gravity. Another dream? No, she must be back on New Coyoacán. She is. Yes. The room resolves into focus. So do all the little aches. Thousands of them. But they're all little. She feels her tooth with her tongue. Still broken. Okay, that happened. It feels like she has physical bandages clamped around the top of her muzzle and wrapped around one of her feet.

"Yes, what?"

She blinks muzzily and looks toward whoever just spoke. Doctor Allen. "Mmm?"

"You jerked awake and said 'yes.'" The tigress tilts her head, giving her a curious smile.

"Sorry. A dream." Speaking hurts, and the bandage makes her sound mushy. She takes a weak breath. "You have the databox? Nakimura ... key." In her head that's a complete sentence: *Nakimura has the key, or should be able to get it.* Is that true? What if he doesn't? What if he can't get it? What if they're too late?

Allen puts her hand on Gail's shoulder. "The technicians from Keces are working with it. Let's keep our attention on you for right now, though. You and Agent Thomas were both shot and beaten. He's worse off than you are, but we're keeping you here at least two more nights. We've already done mending work along the bridge of your muzzle and your toes, but some of your biomods need to be replaced. And we should take care of that tooth. You're going to have to take it easy for at least another month. Use a crutch, keep your weight off that foot, and don't strain your shoulders, either, since they *both* took bullets. We'll give you some exercises to help build strength back up."

"Jack?"

"I'll let you know how the surgery went once I know myself."

"Did … anyone else survive?"

"Nakimura's assistant, Mr. Nelson, is being treated for shock and a crushed leg."

Nelson. He should be thankful she left him alive; he certainly wouldn't have returned the favor. But she had questions about him, didn't she? Things she thought of while sleeping. Yes.

"Are you feeling up for any visitors?"

"Who?"

"From the way the receptionist described it, half of New Coyoacán. I'll see if I can run triage." She steps out of the room.

Oh, come on, there can't be that many. Ansel, she supposes. Nevada, maybe. Travis? She rubs her muzzle. Speaking doesn't hurt much now, at least. If she's going to have to be a chatterbox for the night that's important.

Bunten, Captain Taylor, Wolfe, and another RJC official all file into the room. They call this a debriefing, right? Taylor's using a cane, but she guesses he's recovering well.

"Gail." Bunten smiles warmly, sympathetically. "How are you feeling?"

"Horrible, thanks."

"No, thank you. You've done incredible work. We'll do all we can to help you and your sister with recovery. Could you tell us more about what happened? Without records from your ship…" He trails off, smiling more apologetically.

What can he do to help? Well, she doesn't have enough money in her bank account to pay off the repair bill for the ship she no longer has, and oh yes, she has no job, because she has no ship. And no home. No anything other than what's in her bag at Sky's place, and a promise of a settlement from Keces she might not see for years. She closes her eyes, then nods. "Yeah."

It doesn't take long to recap the highlights. She even manages not to choke up when she talks about *Kismet*, although she doesn't mention the ship's impossible final words. She'll just sound crazy.

"Agent Thomas's wife and daughter were both moved to a safe location," Wolfe says. "There's no sign that they're in danger."

Taylor stiffens. "This is the first I've heard of that."

Bunten clears his throat. "As we've already outlined, Ms. Simmons made a good case that the PFS has a leak."

"That's not a valid reason to keep me out of the loop." His eyes narrow at Gail. "Are you accusing me of being the leak?"

She gingerly rubs the back of her ear, flicks it experimentally. Ow. "Look, someone came after us on the trip from Panorica to here, and nobody but PFS staff knew about that. Someone at the PFS decided to let Corbett out on bail and, after that, countermanded the warrant to bring him back in. There has to be a leak at the PFS, and if it's not you, it's someone you report to." She looks back to the raccoon. "Nelson probably knows who it is, and I bet he'll roll on them."

Bunten clears his throat. "We'll keep Mr. Nelson well-guarded, then, and see if he can be persuaded to give us any names." He swipes his finger across his wristband and taps its face twice. "Captain Taylor, I'd like you to take a walk with Ms. Keating and I."

Taylor swallows, nodding stiffly, and heads out between the others.

When the room clears, she looks around, tapping her fingers on the mattress. The technicians from Keces are "working" with the key. That's a good sign, but she should be in Sky's room. She should be with them, helping them, by—by—asking stupid questions and generally being in the way. Okay, scratch that.

She turns to her right. Wasn't there a control panel for the entertainment system here? She pulls it up, flipping through the guide. A lot of shows she doesn't recognize. Figures. The Ring always has to be idiosyncratic—

"Hey."

Ansel's standing in the doorway. She tries to smile. "See, I told you I'd be back."

He comes in, sits down by her bedside. "It looks like most of you kept the promise." He looks across at the video guide. "Have you seen yourself on the news yet?"

"I'm…on the news? Why?"

He folds his arms. "The daughter of the RTEA's most famous activist shows up on New Coyoacán for the first time in a decade, gets caught in the first terrorist attack here in *four* decades, goes on a secret mission to an infamous ghost platform, and single-handedly stops a shadowy organization of fanatics planning genocide."

She groans, looking at the ceiling. "That's way too melodramatic. And it wasn't single-handed."

"Sorry. I forgot your sidekick, the dashing Interpol agent gone rogue."

"Stop it." She laughs. Ow, *that* hurts. "How long are you here for?"

"I have an evening flight back to Panorica tomorrow. I won't be around when you get out of the hospital, but Nevada's promised to keep me informed." He leans forward and lowers his voice. "You didn't tell me her husband was that—that he was so—"

"Godlike?"

"I'd have accepted 'handsome,' but I like yours better. Anyway, they've both visited, but your doctor doesn't want to crowd you."

"She made it sound like half the Ring was out there."

"No, it's not that bad. A few people have asked about you, though. Other teachers who work with Nevada, I think. Even a couple students. A rabbit girl named, um..."

"Josie?"

"Yes, that's it. She was too shy to talk to me much, but I think she really wants to see you."

"Oh." She swallows. Does Josie hate her for not letting the RJC know about the attack before it happened, for not stopping her mother from being killed? Or does she think Gail has some consoling insight about losing your mom to a terrorist attack?

Ansel fidgets. "I'm sorry about *Kismet*. I don't know what else to say."

"I don't think there is anything else to say."

"No." He sighs softly. "Once you're healed, are you planning to move back to Panorica? I'm sure I can help get you set up somewhere, and maybe I can find you some contract work."

"Thanks. But I don't know. I don't feel like I know anything. If Sky... maybe I'll stay with her for a while, make sure she's fully recovered. I don't know what I can do around here, but I've still got my citizenship."

He clucks his tongue, although his disapproval is belied by his smile. "I see. You'd rather take a handout from the state than your friend."

"My friends have been through more than enough for me."

"And I'd say the state owes you as much as the rest of us do." Ansel pats her hand. "Do what you need to. Maybe you'll get another ship again in a few years."

"I could only get *Kismet* because of my inheritance."

"Yes, but you could make a lot of money by being famous if you want to, you know."

Even though she'd never considered it, she sees what he means: speaking engagements, videos. Maybe she could do a lot of good. And maybe she could drastically shorten her life expectancy by making herself an even bigger target. She sighs. "I don't care about making a lot of money and I don't want to be in the limelight. But maybe I want to do more good in the world than I can by floating around picking at space wrecks."

He gets up and gives her a careful kiss between her ears. "I'll check back in on you in person before I leave. And we *are* going to keep in touch, no matter where you are, all right? Not just when you want something."

"All right. And you can get in touch when you want something, too."

As he reaches the door, she can't hold back what she's been thinking about ever since she woke up. "Ansel?"

He looks back inquisitively.

"She's not...backed up, is she. Ships are like databoxes."

"All of the data that's yours should be recoverable. Contacts, navigation history."

"But *her*. I mean..." She swallows. "She said 'I love you.'"

He takes a few steps back into the room. "What?"

"Before...before *Kismet* rammed the cargo ship, she told me, 'Goodbye. I love you.'" She spreads her hands. "I know—I know an expert system could be programmed to have that as a response. I know there's all sorts of tricks for personalization."

Ansel nods slowly. "Yes."

She takes a deep breath. "But I hadn't said anything to her. Not right then." She looks up at him. "Have you ever heard of ships programmed to tell their owners they love them just before they're destroyed?"

"No."

"You'd tell me it wasn't possible, wouldn't you?"

"Oh, it's possible, it's just...not..." He rubs the back of his head. "Are you *sure* that's what you heard?"

"Yeah," she whispers. "Positive."

He heads over and squeezes her hand, holding it for a few seconds, then heads out silently, looking troubled.

No one else pops their head into the room over the next few minutes. It's late. She turns back to the entertainment system, settling on a comedy serial she watches occasionally. Which was the last episode of this she saw? Twenty-five? Twenty-seven? "Kis, what was the..."

She stops herself, then lets out a long, thin sigh. Stabbing the choice for episode twenty-six, she leans back on the pillow, making herself focus only on the screen. She falls asleep halfway through episode twenty-seven.

"How does that feel?"

Gail taps the tooth with her tongue, lightly. "Like a tooth. Everything still aches, though." She studies herself in the mirror; without the bandages she looks nearly normal. Except for the hospital gown.

"Like I said, you're going to be sore for at least a week. Don't put weight on that foot or that shoulder." Dr. Allen points helpfully at each body part as she speaks.

"I know. Yes." Gail starts to push herself up into a standing position. Both shoulders twinge angrily. She gasps in pain.

"What did I just say? No weight!" The tigress glares. "Sit back down and wait for the wheelchair." She turns to a control surface and taps on it a few times. The wheelchair in the corner beeps and navigates toward them.

"I thought I could use a crutch."

"Tomorrow." The wheelchair stops and waits for Gail to pull herself into it. Allen barely waits before leaving the room; the chair jerks into motion, following her and carrying its passenger along.

"Look, I feel fine."

"You just told me you didn't a minute ago, and even if you hadn't, I'd know better. The reconstruction needs time to set."

"But—"

"No saving the world for a few more weeks, and that's final."

"Yes, ma'am."

They walk/wheel past her room's door. She starts to say something, then realizes they're heading to Sky's room. "Mara's Blood. Did they finish?"

"They did."

"And you didn't tell me?" Gail almost leaps out of the chair despite it still moving.

Allen puts a hand on her shoulder, without pressing. "You had your own healing to do." She lets the chair roll ahead of her through the doorway.

"Yes, but…" She trails off. The room's the same as it was two days ago. The Keces scientists are almost in the same positions. Sky's in the same position. Everyone seems very somber.

Oh, God, it didn't work, did it? They've brought her here to say goodbye.

"Ms. Simmons." The man, still in the same lab coat, nods to her. "From what I've heard you had one hell of an adventure recovering the program for us."

"Yeah. Did you … is it…"

The woman, standing by Sky's bedside, looks between the wolf and a monitor. "Yes, and yes."

Gail's heart leaps. She fumbles for the manual controls to the wheelchair, guiding it over to Sky's bedside.

"She's going to have to stay on hemodialysis for the rest of the day, and we're assessing the extent of the damage past her kidneys. But over the last five hours her prognosis has shifted from poor to excellent."

"Thank you." She takes Sky's hand in both of hers. "How long can I stay with her here?"

Doctor Allen smiles. "As long as you want."

The tigress leaves. One of the technicians leaves a few minutes after that, off to give a status update to Mr. Nakimura; the woman technician stays behind, still monitoring.

An hour past that, Sky's eyes open. Gail's own eyes widen, and she leans forward. "Sky?"

The wolf turns her head, slowly, and looks at Gail. She takes a long, shallow breath. "What happened to you?" she whispers.

Gail laughs, tears starting to run down her muzzle. "That's kind of a long story."

Sky smiles. "I'm not going anywhere."

Coda

"Mmm?" She's sure somebody just said something, and that's rude. She's clearly lying here sound asleep.

Confirmation comes in the form of a pillow thwack to her head. "I said wake up!"

Gail covers her face. "We don't have to rush. The kid's a day old. She's not going anywhere."

"We're supposed to be meeting Jack and his daughter in less than two hours. Barely an hour and a half."

"Stop counting down. It's only a half-hour walk."

"And we have to stop to get Josie." The coyote pushes the pillow out of the way, leaning over and blowing on Gail's closest ear. "Don't make me bite you."

Gail rolls over to look up at Dani's mock-threatening growl. "Promise to bite later."

Dani's growl becomes a groan. The coyote pulls Gail up to a sitting position, then climbs out of bed, heading toward the bathroom. "Up, rat, up."

After watching the dark grey tail disappear, Gail slips out from the sheets, heading to the closet and pulling on a bathrobe. Some of Dani's clothes are hanging there now, too. She's sure she's left a couple things at Dani's place, though. At least she hopes she has. If she's staring at all her worldly possessions, they still fit on two shelves and ten hangers.

Naturally, Sky's already up and starting coffee. "Good morning. I hope you finally got to sleep."

"Hmm? Yeah, I didn't have any problem sleeping." She flicks her ears. "We didn't, uh, keep you up, did we?"

"Oh, no." Sky says that with the measured pace of someone who actually means yes.

Smiling sheepishly, Gail takes a seat. "I was doing some apartment hunting over the last week. There's a one-bedroom place that's opening up a block from here."

Sky's brows lift as she sets three coffee mugs down. "Oh?"

"Well, you've let me take over your den for nearly a year now."

"Yes, and the whole time you've been telling me it was because you weren't sure if you were going to stay in New Coyoacán." Sky takes her own seat, crossing her legs.

"I wasn't. I'm…" Still not? She got busy here much faster than she'd expected, than she'd intended. She still misses Kis, and still misses the stars, but she honestly doesn't miss her old job. There's much more she'd miss here. "My contract with the school is going to be extended."

Sky sips her coffee and smiles slightly, then flips through the smartpaper she's left on the table, scanning headlines and grunting. "The crowd we're going to be navigating through at the hospital might be reason enough for *me* to leave New Coyoacán. They've got reporters from the inner system there."

Gail looks into her coffee mug. "Is it too early in the morning to add rum to this?"

"Oh, come on." Dani steps out of the back room. "You're excellent at handling reporters." The coyote's gone very femme today, a calf-length dark blue batik skirt, sleeveless, modest neckline but backline plunging almost to the tail. It looks loose and casual until you try to figure out the mechanics of how it stays on, and begin to suspect the only options are nanotech or black magic. The overall effect is a little drool-inducing, but Dani can create the same effect in a tux. As far as Gail's concerned, Dani can create the same effect in a burlap sack.

"Not by choice. Besides, out of sight, out of mind. They were all over us for a month, then left."

"Other than the reporters with the long-form articles," Sky corrects. "And ones regularly asking you what you think of the news of the day, or just fishing for what you're doing with your time now."

Gail clears her throat, but doesn't contradict her sister. That's another reason she's considering moving out—Sky enjoys public attention even less than she does.

Dani picks up the remaining coffee cup, spooning sugar into it. "And the documentary crew."

Gail nearly drops her cup. "Documentary crew?"

The coyote grins. "Just predicting, sweetie. Give it another year."

"Mara's Blood." She sighs, taking another sip of her coffee before standing up. "I'll go get ready."

When they get to Blue Coyote they're a few minutes early, but Jack's already there. Gail spoke with him two days ago when he and Laurie arrived on Panorica and he looked good. In person he looks—relaxed. She's seen him in denim and a casual polytee before, but now he looks like he *wants* to be wearing that, like jeans are no longer an uncomfortable, alien place.

Laurie's cute. She has her father's eyes, but the straight black hair has to come from mom. Those eyes look wide even before they catch sight of Gail, Sky, Dani and Josie approaching.

Gail gives Jack a hug as he introduces them all to his daughter—the three he knows, at least. He hesitates at the rabbit girl.

"I'm Josie Dupree. One of Gail's students."

Laurie looks at the rat appraisingly. She's already a few centimeters taller than Gail. "You're a teacher?"

She shakes her head. "I'm a substitute teacher sometimes, and I help with tutoring and counseling." That inverts the order of how she spends her time when she's working with students, but *counselor* sounds … well, like something she's not qualified to do. She and Josie connected because they understand each other.

"So you're not going to be teaching one of my classes." Laurie's tone has a touch of challenge to it.

Gail laughs. "No, you're safe."

Jack clears his throat, flashing his daughter a warning frown. Laurie rolls her eyes.

They talk over breakfast, filling in gaps on each other's recent pasts. Interpol "released" him back to the FBI; the FBI kept him on the payroll another four months doing nothing, then pushed him into early retirement. His separation has become a divorce with alternating custody. Claudia isn't thrilled by her daughter spending a year halfway around the solar system, but Laurie is.

At least, she's thrilled by Jack's telling. Laurie stays conspicuously silent.

"Okay." Gail waves a sopaipilla in the air, a tiny cloud of powdered sugar raining over her fingers. "But I want to hear *you* tell me why you decided to move here."

Laurie answers before her dad does. "He says there's more wilderness on the Ring than there is on Earth."

"More accessible wilderness," Jack corrects. "We live—"

"Lived."

"—a thousand kilometers from any unmanaged land."

"Dad, this is a giant artificial ring in space! It's all managed."

Josie perks up. "There's a lot of this section of the Ring we leave as open space. I don't know if that's what you call unmanaged, but it's real wilderness."

"Isn't it just… I mean, land, space, whatever you call it here, it's got to be so expensive. Isn't building it just to leave it undeveloped a huge waste?"

"No." Josie shakes her head, looking earnest. "Our green space naturally does a lot of what other places on the River need to do mechanically. And mixing nature and technology is, well." She laughs, and gestures at herself. "It's us."

Laurie looks puzzled. The rabbit scoots her chair closer to the other teen. "How much do you know about totemics?"

"A little." They lower their voices, creating their own separate conversation.

Jack's finished one of his sopaipillas, and addresses the other adults as the two girls keep speaking. "I took a break for a while, and it's been relaxing, but I need to get back to work. Sky put me in touch with the right people to ask about consulting with the RJC."

Gail grins. "Not that it won't be nice to see you occasionally, but there's got to be places a lot closer you could be consulting with."

"I could have gone into private security work. But…" He shakes his head. "The big contractors in the United States combine everything Ansel would argue against with everything I would argue against. I'd rather work for a private judiciary out here than there. Maybe that's where I'll end up. But this is where I have contacts. Now, you haven't told me just how you got into education."

"I started working with some teachers after hours to learn more about artificial intelligence design and programming. I'd already met Josie here and she's deeply into AI, like much smarter than I'm ever going to be, and … well, she and I had a lot to talk about beyond that." She clears her throat. "Anyway, that led to working with other students."

They keep talking for another few minutes until Sky announces, "We need to head to the hospital now."

Jack looks at Laurie. "You can come with us if you want, or head back to the hotel."

"Could I go out with Josie? She wants to show me around."

"We might go to the history museum," the rabbit adds. Laurie nods.

"The history museum? Sure. That sounds good. Call if you need anything, and be back at the hotel at … sixteen o'clock?"

The two head off, Josie in the lead, talking animatedly.

Jack stares after her. "She's going to a museum. Voluntarily."

Gail grins. "You look incredulous."

"Museums are not the natural habitat of most teenagers."

"Josie's unusual."

As they approach the hospital, it becomes clear Sky'd been right about the crowd. But it's not just reporters—it's protestors, too. Seriously? Here? She reads the smartpaper signs with scrolling slogans. *Species is a choice. No tyranny of biology. Xenos matter.*

Someone spots them and a cry goes up, mixed cheers and boos, an attempt at a chant that thankfully doesn't get far enough for her to figure out what it would have been. It alerts the reporters, though, and they dart toward the group like a school of carnivorous fish. "Ms. Simmons!"

"Single file," Jack advises. "Head down, move fast."

Sky takes the lead, arms out to the side, baring her teeth a few millimeters, parting the sea through sheer force of will.

"Gail, if you have—"

"—think of this momentous—"

"—concern about this shift—"

"—could some totemic species go extinct?"

What? She turns to look at that reporter, but Dani steers her past the RJC guards at the hospital's entrance and on inside. She knows why Nevada chose to have her birth here instead of at home—there were too many unknowns for anyone to be comfortable without a full medical staff—but getting her back out through this gauntlet is going to be a nightmare.

"Gail." Bunten's waiting there, of course, standing by a totemic doctor she doesn't recognize. What is he? Feline, yes. Serval? Bunten clasps her hand in both of his for a moment. He's checked in on her a few times over the last year. It's the person standing next to him she didn't expect: Jason Nakimura.

"Ms. Simmons." He nods slightly to her. "I trust you've been well."

"All things considered. It'd be nice if your settlement came through, finally."

"That's not under my control, I fear."

After more greetings the group moves together down the hallway toward the obstetrics wing, the doctor in the lead. She falls into step beside Nakimura again. "So are you here for the good PR?"

"I've been here since before Ms. Duarte went into labor, along with Keces technicians. Her daughter is the first totemic live birth delivered outside our laboratories, and the first with the potential to naturally pass totemic genes to her children. She's of great interest to us."

"So that's a yes."

"It is." Keces won't be collecting license fees on Nevada's grandchildren, but they'll have an immense first mover advantage in providing the *in utero* transformation as long as it remains necessary. It'll be years before anyone else gets the expertise to offer the service, and no one else will be able to claim they invented it. They didn't fight the compulsory licensing order as hard as they've been fighting her settlement payout.

It takes another minute of walking to reach Nevada's room, with another set of anti-reporter guards. It's a big room, but already has a crowd: two nurses, Travis and his full transform cervine parents, and an older cisform woman Gail doesn't recognize. When she looks at Gail it's clear she recognizes her, though, her smile stiffening.

And, in the center of it all, Nevada, sitting up in bed, looking tired and disheveled and radiant. She's looking down at her arms, at the blanket she's cradling, at a being unlike any that had existed in the universe before yesterday. Her baby. Her daughter.

A vixen.

Gail walks slowly toward the bed. Travis touches his wife's shoulder and she looks at him, then over to the rat, her eyes lighting up. She smiles back, gets close enough to the bed to stand by Travis. His parents almost push her closer.

She looks tiny, almost lost in the blanket, and at first like an optical illusion: is she a fox, or a human? Proportionately, human, but she has a muzzle, ears flat against her head, fuzz all over—far more orange than Nevada's silver look. Squint and she changes. Fox. Human. Fox. Human. No antlers.

"She's beautiful," Gail breathes. And she is. Gail's never wanted children, but watching this impossible little infant makes her heart flutter in an unexpected way. "What's her name?" She knows they'd picked one out, but they'd refused to share.

"Carmen," Nevada says softly. She touches a finger to the little vixen's nose. "Carmen Gail Duarte."

Gail makes a choking noise and flicks her gaze rapidly between Nevada and Travis. "Oh, you didn't."

"Too late." Travis pulls her into a one-armed hug. "Come here, godmother."

Fortunately, that's not another surprise he's springing on her. They'd already talked about it, although she got the distinct impression she wasn't allowed to demur to that, either. She hugs him back, feeling tears start to well up.

Everyone claps, except for the woman with the stiff smile. As she looks at Carmen, though, her smile softens. Of course: she's Nevada's mother. From Solera. When was the last time she and her daughter have spoken? Does she still insist on calling her Linda? What does she think when she looks at her granddaughter?

But—she's here. She's made the trip. That's something. Gail doesn't know how much, but it's surely something.

Nevada leans to the side, and gently holds Gail's goddaughter out to her.

The bartender has glasses set down in front of them before they take their seats.

Dani laughs. "Are we really that predictable?"

He grins. At first glance he's cisform, but then you catch the transforms: bioluminescent tattoos and slit-pupil cat eyes. It makes him look unsettling, but he clearly enjoys that. "You want a different sweet gin or vodka drink every time, Gail wants a rum drink every time. A good bartender learns patterns."

Gail taps the miniature snifter he's set in front of her. "This is just a shot of rum."

"Rum is definitionally a rum drink."

She picks it up and takes a sip. "Well played."

They'd left the hospital through a back entrance, parting ways with Sky and Jack, and circled back toward Dani's neighborhood. The coyote had introduced Gail to the Four Rivers Pub a few months ago, and Gail had introduced Dani to spirits rather than beers, a shift made with great enthusiasm.

Gail looks over at Dani as she sips. "One of the reporters tried to ask how I'd feel about species disappearing entirely."

"Why would that happen? Non-inherited transformation won't go away. And just because Carmen's born a fox doesn't mean she has to stay that way. She could grow up and decide she wanted to be something else."

"Could she, though? We have generations of experience saying that remaking yourself more than once or reversing a transformation carries a lot of risk."

"But she's starting with *no* transformations. You and I are transform humans. She's a cisform totemic."

"A cisform totemic." She feels her viewcard ping in her pocket, and reaches in to pull it out. "That's a hard phrase to wrap your head around."

"What is it?" Dani leans over.

"A call from Ansel. Excuse me a second." She gets up and heads outside the bar, then connects the audio. "Hey."

"Well, hello. Speaking to me from your head again, so you must be out."

She laughs. "Yeah, out at Four Rivers with Dani."

"Oooh." As if that's shocking. They've been dating over eight months. "So did you get to see Nevada's child?"

"Yeah. She's ... I mean, she's exactly what you'd expect, and that's completely unexpected. Does that make any sense?"

"For you, absolutely."

"Ha ha. They named her after me. Carmen Gail." As proud as she is, she knows she sounds incredulous. She's that, too. "And I'm the kid's godmother. I agreed to that and I don't even know what it means."

"You're every natural-born totemic's godmother, dear. Listen." He takes a deep breath. "You asked me to do a deep search for reports on emergent behavior in expert systems when I had free cycles. I finally did."

Her ears lift. "And?"

"And I've found at least a hundred reports. About three-quarters of them are, ah, let's say pretty fringey, but there's at least two dozen from expert system labs."

She's pretty sure a report of her life with *Kismet* would sound pretty fringey, and not just the ship's last words. "Wow. Josie and I have only found a half-dozen."

"Nearly all of these reports—and all of the ones from actual research-ers—came after a point about twenty years ago, when a new generation of systems hit the market and were deployed in more sophisticated envi-ronments. Like spaceships."

She runs a hand through her hair. "So why are these reports so hidden?"

"They're not hidden, they're just…anecdotal. No one can reliably reproduce the results. The only two peer-reviewed papers I could find are inconclusive."

"And if they were reproducible, they'd raise a lot of questions people don't want to ask."

He sighs. "Maybe." Abruptly he changes both his tone and the subject. "I'm expecting to see you and Dani—and Sky, if she'll deign to have fun— at Acceleration for my birthday next month."

"What about Jack?"

"Jack?" Ansel sounds delighted. "He's back out here?"

"Yeah, and not just visiting, either."

"Oh, my God. You *have* to get him to come along."

"You just want to get drunk and argue politics."

"You bet your naked rat tail I do."

"We'll be there, I promise."

When she takes her seat by Dani again, the coyote's looking contem-plative. "This morning I heard you mention the idea of renting a one-bedroom place near Sky's flat."

Gail nods. "Yeah."

"You didn't like it when I brought that idea up a few months ago."

"I wasn't…" She wasn't ready for the possible future she sees now, of staying here, with the school, with Dani—God, sitting here, it makes her stomach twist. But it's not the old feeling of dread, not in the same way. Now she dreads not having that future. Is home where are you are, or who you're with? With Kis, it was always both. Maybe it still is. "You know, I still don't think I know how to settle down."

"But?"

She takes the coyote's hand, entwining their fingers together. "But everyone has a home port."

Acknowledgements

The novel that became *Kismet* has been through multiple iterations over a dismaying number of years, shifting focus, protagonists and, at least once, verb tense. What finally led to its current form—indeed, to it being finished at all—was taking an early partial draft to a novel writing workshop held at the Gunn Center for the Study of Science Fiction at the University of Kansas. So I owe a huge debt of gratitude to the workshop's instructors, Kij Johnson and Barbara Webb, as well as my fellow attendees: Marcy Arlin, Elizabeth Bourne, Jennifer Campbell-Hicks, Dominick D'Aunno, Kevin O'Neill, Dayna Smith, and Tim Susman. Their suggestions, critiques and "what ifs" didn't just make it a stronger work, they made it *work*, period.

My local writing group, the Unreliable Narrators, dealt with the first completed draft: Ryan Campbell, David Cowan, and Tim Susman again. Barbara also provided critique on this draft; I followed a lot, but not all, of their advice, so we'll just assume that anything you didn't like was my fault and not theirs. Christina Bass also gave me both comments and copy edits.

Lastly, I'd like to thank Argyll's editor/publisher, Mark Harrison, both for his work and for agreeing to all this.